The Resurrection of Nat Turner,
Part 1: The Witnesses

The Resurrection of Nat Turner, Part 1

THE WITNESSES

Sharon Ewell Foster

HOWARD BOOKS
A Division of Simon & Schuster, Inc.
New York   Nashville   London   Toronto   Sydney

Howard Books
A Division of Simon & Schuster, Inc.
1230 Avenue of the Americas
New York, NY 10020

First Howard Books trade paperback edition August 2011

HOWARD and colophon are trademarks of Simon & Schuster, Inc.

For information about special discounts for bulk purchases, please contact Simon & Schuster Special Sales at 1-866-506-1949 or business@simonandschuster.com.

The Simon & Schuster Speakers Bureau can bring authors to your live event. For more information or to book an event, contact the Simon & Schuster Speakers Bureau at 1-866-248-3049 or visit our website at www.simonspeakers.com.

Designed by Davina Mock-Maniscalco

Manufactured in the United States of America

10 9 8 7 6 5 4 3 2 1

Library of Congress Cataloging-in-Publication Data

Foster, Sharon Ewell.
    The resurrection of Nat Turner, part 1 : the witnesses / Sharon Ewell Foster.
        p.   cm.
    I. Title.
    PS3556.O7724R47 2011
    813'.54—dc22   2011016825

ISBN 978-1-4165-7803-1
ISBN 978-1-4516-0621-8 (ebook)

For my people—for strong women and men, especially for fathers like mine, who guard and protect their families. For my mother, who nurtured my precocious reading habit and on whose nightstand I first saw *The Confessions of Nat Turner*. For my grandmother, who bequeathed to their children their own love of reading. Thank you to my maternal grandmother, church secretary and lover of true crime stories. Thank you to my paternal grandmother, who was principal at a small segregated East Texas school and who also risked her life teaching illiterate adults to read.

For my *Gashe* Getatchew Haile—theologian, professor, curator of the Ethiopian Study Center, Regents Professor of Medieval Studies, and cataloger of Oriental Manuscripts, Emeritus at the Hill Museum of Manuscripts Library, Saint John's University, Collegeville, Minnesota—who shared with me the ancient wisdom of Ethiopia. For my children, who inspire me and see me as greater than I see myself. I thank God for you and for His precious gift of love.

Finally, for the weary, heartbroken, and those who are held captive. There is hope! Awaken!

Fellow-citizens, we cannot escape history. . . . No personal significance, or insignificance, can spare one or another of us. . . . We—even we here—hold the power, and bear the responsibility.

—President Abraham Lincoln, State of the Union, December 1, 1862

And it shall come to pass in that day, saith the Lord GOD, that I will cause the sun to go down at noon, and I will darken the earth in the clear day: And I will turn your feasts into mourning, and all your songs into lamentation. . . .

—Amos 8:9–10a (KJV)

contents

prologue

Many, many, many years ago in the month of Yekatit, Jonah, a young *shimaghilles*, a young wise man from Palestine, heard the word of the Lord. "Arise, go to Nineveh, that great city, and cry out against it; for their wickedness has come up before Me."

Jonah ran from the Lord's command. Nineveh was too large a city and he was too small a man. There was great wickedness and great arrogance in Nineveh; how could one man stand against it? The king and his people would scoff at a backwoods holy man, especially a young one. They might kill him.

Even worse, because he knew Him to be a merciful God, Jonah feared that God might forgive Nineveh. In the capital of the immense and blustering nation of Assyria, Nineveh's king, Xerxes, had taken many of Jonah's people, even his relatives, and made them slaves. Son of Nimrod, son of Cush, son of Ham, King Xerxes had used his captives as free labor to build his kingdom and to build his wealth.

So, Jonah ran from the Lord. He boarded a ship for Tarshish, that great city of trade, which some say was once in India.

But God, whose great eye follows even the smallest of those He loves, saw the place where Jonah hid away. God loved Jonah as a good father loves his sons, but was displeased with him, as good fathers have been known to be displeased with disobedient sons. And so God stirred the seas, because the God of the whole universe has everything in His hands, including the earth, the waves, the weather, and the stars in the sky.

While Jonah slept in the belly of the ship, the waves battered the vessel. The *ferengi* above were terrified! The captain, the ship-mates, and the other passengers were afraid for their lives. Fearing the ship would sink, they threw overboard their furniture, their clothes, and the goods the merchants had planned to sell in the rich markets of Tarshish.

The *ferengi* prayed, yet nothing would calm the storm. Thrown side to side, clothes drenched, choking on water, one of them said, "This is not a natural storm. God is angry because someone on this ship has offended Him."

The captain went below and found Jonah, the young *shimaghilles*, still unaware and fast asleep. "What do you mean, sleeper? Arise, call on your God; perhaps your God will consider us, so that we may not perish."

On deck now, Jonah joined the others in prayer. Lots were cast and fell upon Jonah. "What have you done? Why have you involved us? Why is God angry?"

Jonah confessed that he was running from the omnipresent Lord. "I am a Hebrew; I fear the LORD, the God of heaven, who made the sea and the dry land."

"What can we do to save ourselves?" the *ferengi* moaned.

"Pick me up and throw me into the sea; then the sea will become calm for you. For I know that this great tempest *is* because of me."

The *ferengi*, knowing that God protects his people, did not want Jonah's blood on their hands, so they tried to row to shore, to pray, anything to avoid taking the life of God's servant, even one so disobedient.

"I am a Jew, a follower of the One God, and I have offended Him," Jonah lamented, reasoning with the captain. "My fate is my fate. Throw me overboard and I will trust my life to God. In Him I have a hiding place."

So, the captain and the crew, praying for forgiveness, threw Jonah into the sea, and God, whose name is Love, caught the young *shimaghilles* alive in the belly of a whale.

For three days, without food, inside the whale, like a bug in the ear, Jonah stayed alive. He prayed, repented, and he sang a song to the Lord.

> . . . I cried out to the LORD because of my affliction,
> And He answered me.
> Out of the belly of Sheol I cried,
> And You heard my voice.
> For You cast me into the deep,
> Into the heart of the seas,
> And the floods surrounded me;
> All Your billows and Your waves passed over me.
> Then I said, "I have been cast out of Your sight;
> Yet I will look again toward Your holy temple."
>
> The waters surrounded me, even to my soul;
> The deep closed around me;
> Weeds were wrapped around my head.
> I went down to the moorings of the mountains;
> The earth with its bars closed behind me forever;
> Yet You have brought up my life from the pit,
> O LORD, my God.
>
> When my soul fainted within me,
> I remembered the LORD;
> And my prayer went up to You,
> Into Your holy temple.
> Those who regard worthless idols
> Forsake their own mercy.
> But I will sacrifice to You
> With the voice of thanksgiving;
> I will pay what I have vowed.
> Salvation is of the LORD.

God, merciful and mighty, God, whose name is Love Everlasting, heard Jonah, forgave him, and the great fish that held Jonah spat him upon dry land.

So, God spoke to Jonah a second time. "Arise, go to Nineveh, that great city, and preach to it the message that I tell you." Jonah, the young *shimaghilles*, began the journey to speak to the king. Nineveh was a great metropolis and the journey to the heart of the city would take three days. On the first day, Jonah passed slave markets in the midst of wealthy places. He saw women used as concubines. Jonah wept as he walked past the unburied dead of his people. He heard the wet bite of whips and moaning people crying out for mercy. Jonah proclaimed the Lord's word: "Forty more days and Nineveh will be overturned."

The people of Nineveh believed God. Immediately, around Jonah, the people of Nineveh began to repent. "Forgive us, Lord." They did not think themselves too great to believe Jonah. Instead, from the greatest to the smallest, they called a fast, took off their finery, and put on sackcloth. The word spread across Nineveh, like a great winged bird, and reached the ears of the king.

Great King Xerxes, whose name terrified nations, whose hands squeezed the life from people from shore to shore, stood and reached his mighty black arms toward God and then bowed his head. He stepped down from his throne, removed his royal robes, and put on slave's clothes—because as great as he was, King Xerxes knew he was not as great as God. He sat in the dust and submitted to the one true God and then issued a proclamation to his city, God's city, the great city of Nineveh.

> . . . By the decree of the king and his nobles: Do not let any man or beast, herd or flock, taste anything; do not let them eat or drink.
>
> But let man and beast be covered with sackcloth. Let everyone call urgently on God. Let them give up their evil ways and their violence.

Who knows? God may yet relent and with compassion turn
from his fierce anger so that we will not perish.

God, merciful, gracious, and compassionate; God, slow to
anger and abounding in love, Who loves the just as well as the unjust, heard the repentance of King Xerxes and of the people of
Nineveh. As He had been with Jonah, God was moved with compassion and spared them.

And so it is that the Great Church, including many believers
in the great nation of Ethiopia and those in exile, even to this day
remembers God's grace and mercy. In gratitude and memorial, for
three days each year they keep the fast of Nineveh, which falls between the months of Ter and Yekatit.

Will hunkered down, a muslin shirt and pants his only protection against the cold, the slushy snow, and the ice-chipped mud that sucked at his feet. He stared inside the church. Cold pulled the long vertical scar on his face taut. Over his shoulder, he heard Nat Turner's voice and the voices of the other slaves—ripened carob pods covered with snow, bare feet like ice blocks—outside with him on the gray cold Sunday morning.

"God hears our prayers and our groans. God hears the cries and the moans of suffering people!"

It was too cold to be outside; people had only come to stand with God. Will heard them, but his attention was on the ones inside, the ones with coats, the ones sitting on the pews. He didn't want anyone inside to die before his time.

In the great state of Virginia, just west of the Tidewater, beyond the Nottoway River, and just above the North Carolina border, lay the county of Southampton—a county known for apple and peach orchards, enterprise, and brave men, lovers and defenders of freedom—truculent men.

Cabin Pond, which lay northwest of Cross Keys and just off the Giles Reese farm, was covered with thick, white ice. There was dark water underneath. Fish still swam there, as did turtles and snakes. The water moved beneath the ice, though it had no beginning or end, like a hand stirred it from below.

Brittle snow, with soft powder underneath, ringed the mouth of the pond, and beyond it were stark trees with no leaves, littered with abandoned birds' nests, and everywhere was cold, flat, hard, dead ground.

In the heart of Southampton, beyond the hamlets of Jerusalem and Bethlehem, just beyond Barrow Road in an area called Cross Keys, sat a small church, Turner's Meeting Place.

In the pulpit of Turner's Meeting Place, Reverend Richard

Whitehead looked out at the congregation before him. "'And the children of Israel sighed by reason of the bondage, and they cried, and their cry came up unto God by reason of the bondage.'" He smoothed his starched white collar, slicked back his shiny black hair, and, for dramatic effect, lifted his hands into the air. "'And God heard their groaning, and God remembered His covenant with Abraham, with Isaac, and with Jacob.'"

It was February and cold, but the iron stove behind the preacher belched out heat that warmed the small church's congregation. They had cast their coats and cloaks aside. A few women fanned. Will saw fire in the stove, red and angry. The reverend sweated. He wiped his brow. "'And God looked upon the children of Israel.'"

Young Nathaniel Francis, Will's master and son of one of the original trustees of Turner's Meeting Place, and his young wife, Lavinia, sat on the first pew. Nathaniel's unsmiling face was fringed with a brown beard. Lavinia's heart-shaped face framed innocent blue eyes. The Newsoms, the Turners, the Whiteheads—all descendants of the original trustees, sat near them.

It gave Will pleasure to watch, knowing they did not know he watched. Reverend Whitehead leaned forward on the wooden podium, an image of Christ on the cross engraved into it. "God hears our prayers and the moans of our suffering. He hears our lamentations, the groans of people whose property and lives have been stolen!" The indoor preacher wiped his face again. "When the king of England denied us our rights as men, God heard us and struck down those who were against us!"

Will listened to the comfortable calm of the indoor preacher while behind him he heard the plaintive wails of those outside in the cold—the outside preacher's words pounding cadence, a drum, demanding.

Inside, Reverend Whitehead nodded. "God even hears us when our own countrymen, our own statesmen, stand against us to deny us our rights as free men of property." He smoothed the pages of his Bible, then raised his fist into the air. "Have no doubt. God will smite His enemies!"

Will was careful not to be seen. He was not there to cry like the others who stood outside in the snow. He was there because he wanted to be near his master. Wanted to be certain no white person stumbled, to be sure no one was attacked by desperate hungry wolves, to be sure no white person froze. No one should die, not before time.

Unlike Nat Turner, he didn't want to warn them. There was going to be a Judgment Day, and that right soon, a day when the light would leave their eyes. No one should die before that day.

Will raked the soaked, frozen sleeve of his shirt across his nose. He would be kind. He would give the whites one final mercy—quick death. No slow torture, no starvation. No rape, no beatings. His only pleasure would be in their bloody, bloody end. He prayed for his arm to be strong.

Will turned again to look inside the church at Reverend Whitehead. The time would come. *The sun and the moon shall be darkened.* He would be ready. All of them would die.

Harriet

chapter 1

There was a bounty on her head.

What more did they want from her? Hadn't she done enough?

Harriet retied the ribbon under her chin, tucked her graying hair underneath, and straightened her black bonnet. She wrapped her black woolen shawl more tightly around her and settled back into the carriage. It was early spring in New England; chill in the air and the morning's fog had not yet burned away. The click of horses' hooves on the pavement reminded her of a metronome. She scooted farther back in the seat so that her feet dangled over the edge like a child's.

A lie was an evil thing. It did not seem so. Sometimes, in fact, it seemed like a kindness. A simple, small thing.

Harriet watched a small fawn-colored spider scurry determinedly along the window of the coach in which she sat. She looked past the spider out to the gray morning and sighed. She still ached for her baby son, Samuel. She still saw the cherry blush of fever on his cheeks. She still saw him suffering and fitful as cholera tore his insides apart. The worst was that she could do nothing to stop it, nothing to comfort him. The worst of it was the powerlessness and letting him go. How could she let him go? How could she live through seeing the light leave him, of hearing his last exhale? Could any mother survive losing her son?

Harriet still ached, though she had learned to manage. She had found a way to let God use the grief that tore at her heart so that now she saw the suffering of other mothers. How could Mary have borne it—her son's hands and feet driven through with spikes, his side pierced?

The spider left the horizontal and began to vertically climb along the window opening.

Harriet had watched her son die, had held him—touched the clothes and the blanket that swaddled him. But how could Mary bear to see?

She sighed again, focusing on the spider. A lie seemed so innocent. But told over and over again, it created a delusion. And two lies or three lies told over and over again were a web.

The spider climbed and then retreated, finally reaching its web in the window corner. Lies and webs. They seemed impossible to untangle. But, perhaps, that was the work.

She felt her bag, reassuring herself that her paper was inside. She would need to take notes this morning. She had written books about travel and homemaking, but this seemed to be the work— finding daylight in darkness, unwinding the web. Unraveling the truth. Finding, digging, seeking.

Perhaps even harder was separating the different truths. The more she studied, the more she realized there was the truth of history, the truth of culture, and then there was God's truth—and sometimes it was difficult to know which was which. It was hard, most times, to separate the truth of the way things had been done, the way people were used to believing and behaving, from the truth of who God was.

Every day she was more convinced that she could not read and understand the Old Testament without looking at it through the lens of love and truth. The Old Testament said to stone a woman caught in adultery—that was true. But God's truth, God's love said to forgive the woman and to use her sin as an occasion to judge one's own heart and behavior: . . . *forget not my law; but let thine heart keep my commandments.* . . .

It frightened her, sometimes, to think these things. Her father, whom she loved, took the law just as it was written. But she was coming to believe that the law was nothing without love. Her father would disapprove. Others would disapprove.

At forty-five, she sometimes wanted to turn back and write only about canning and homemaking, to only write sweet romances, or about travel. That was her plan before *Uncle Tom*. Others would approve.

The industrious spider was still at work.

But truth was insolent and did not care that she was frightened. Truth did not care that she trembled when she uncovered lies that had been told. Truth did not care that the web was sticky or that she was frightened of the spider. Truth woke her at night and sent her on unplanned journeys. She glimpsed it under stairwells and hidden among leaves on tree boughs. It sang to her. It brandished its fist at her.

Her mind had planned an easier way, a way where she would not be criticized or threatened for talking about things women shouldn't. She had planned to be a wife and mother—maybe a teacher at her sister's proper girls' school. She would pray with other women and talk to them about Jesus—that had been her plan. She was just a woman, a tiny woman at that; who was she to stir in the affairs of men?

Where were the men who should tell this story, find this truth? But that was one of the lies, too, wasn't it? That God did not love women, that God considered women less, that He only spoke truth to men? It was Esther who spoke to the king and saved the Jews from India to Ethiopia. It was Deborah who judged the nation and led Israelite general Barak in the victory at Kedesh. Jesus was born from Mary's womb, and it was at Mary's side that He learned the suffering of poor women, of mothers, of rejected women. Mary of Bethany studied with men, and it was the Lord who said it was good. It was the women to whom the Lord first revealed himself when He had risen.

Let not mercy and truth forsake thee: bind them about thy neck; write them upon the table of thine heart:
So shalt thou find favour and good understanding in the sight of God and man.
Trust in the LORD with all thine heart; and lean not unto thine own understanding.

Her understanding told her to stay at home and embroider, but truth insisted and now Harriet was on her way to Boston. Wasn't *Uncle Tom* enough? Hadn't she paid enough?

Twenty-five years ago, she was a girl of nineteen living in Boston, her brother Henry seventeen and home from school in Amherst, when the sun turned blue. The two of them, the closest of the eleven Beecher siblings, had stood together outside their Massachusetts home gazing up at the sky. Harriet had wondered out loud if it was the end of the world.

But the world didn't end and the blue sun, except for a newspaper mention here and there, was quickly forgotten. Days later, her family and all of those she knew learned a new name: Nat Turner, a mysterious Negro from Southampton County in Virginia who had seen the same indigo sun.

He was a patriot and a preacher. Turner was both vindication and consolation since young abolitionist William Lloyd Garrison was constantly chiding her preacher father about the church's failure—particularly her father's own failure as the man held by many to be the voice of the Protestant church—to do anything about the slavery issue. Garrison argued that Nat Turner's uprising was proof that the church was a stumbling block instead of the place of refuge it should be.

People gathered at the Beecher home to debate the matter—

Lyman Beecher, sons, and daughters arguing robustly with the most respected minds of Northern clergy and the abolitionist movement—while her stepmother, Harriet Porter Beecher, served refreshments. Harriet and Henry were wide-eyed and thrilled to be part of the debate.

Nat Turner was proof that Negro slaves were not content with their lot, bondage was not natural for them, thereby refuting one of the most common arguments put forth to justify slavery. Nat Turner was a symbol of justice—a Negro freedom fighter who would not bow down to the ravages and chains of forced bondage. William Lloyd Garrison published an editorial about Nat Turner in the *Liberator*, thumbing his nose at the South, applauding Nat Turner, nudging the church, and prophesying that there was more violence to come if America did not mend her ways.

Garrison and others demanded action. "What kind of God, what kind of gospel, what kind of church can sit idly by while people are allowed to malinger and die simply because of the color of their skin?" There had to be others like Nat Turner and it was the duty of men of conscience to assist them. How could religion, white religion, be real if millions of souls were forbidden to hear the gospel simply because they were black? "Where is America's William Wilberforce?" Garrison had looked at the people seated at Lyman Beecher's table. "I cannot help but believe that if such a man does exist he is in this room." He had stared at Harriet's father.

Turner's uprising was electricity, inspiration in the air. Conversation about him rattled the dinner table and shook the Beecher debates. Maybe it was time to confront the South. Maybe it was time, in the name of the Lord, to take up arms.

Then, almost as suddenly as his name was raised, the horrible truth came out in the form of Nat Turner's own confession. Nat Turner was a fiend with no remorse, a baby killer, a religious fanatic, a megalomaniac, and a common thief.

Who could argue with Turner's own confession? The horrible

news deflated everyone and confirmed her father's belief that churchmen ought not put their hands in the muck. Don't incite the slaves to insurrection; preachers' hands should be filled with Bibles as their weapons, he said. He preached against it, but said let those involved in the slavery mess clean it up. It would all be resolved in time, her father, Lyman, said. Stick to saving souls. (Garrison needled him, asking weren't black souls worth saving.)

"Let us mind our own. I have gotten word that Virginia's governor Floyd will speak to his legislature and demand that Virginia adopt a plan of gradual emancipation. You'll see: slavery men will take care of the matter. Leave their sins to them; we have enough on our hands getting men to turn away from the spirit in bottles and toward the Spirit of God," her father said.

But her father was wrong, slavery did not go away. Governor Floyd, on the eve of his planned address to the Virginia legislature, had received a visit from United States vice president, ardent slavery man, and war hawk, John Calhoun. Floyd had a sudden change of heart. Instead of advocating gradual emancipation, Floyd took a granite stance directing most of his vitriol at arousers and agitators—freemen and Negro preachers, like Nat Turner.

Because of Nat Turner's revolt the Virginia legislature argued openly, in 1831, for the first time, the merits of emancipation. Then their hearts hardened. Instead, Virginia would lead the other states in creating black codes, tough laws with fangs to govern their slaves. Negroes were forbidden to preach in Virginia, no Negroes could attend church services without the approval of their masters and only then under the teaching of white preachers, white preachers who taught them that they were the descendants of Ham doomed by God to serve white masters.

Those who broke the law risked death.

Free Negroes were ordered out of the state. Virginia's Negroes were happy being slaves, Floyd said, and the government of Virginia was going to do all it could to keep them docile and content, even if Virginia had to hang every Negro who believed in Christ to do it.

Virginia would take the straw away, their religion—the only thing that gave them comfort and hope—and tell them to keep making bricks. Harriet could not help noticing the biblical parallel: every time the poor wretches pleaded for freedom, their masters hardened their hearts and the slaves' conditions worsened. Despite Harriet's attempts to mind her own business, the slavery matter kept insinuating itself, as difficult to overlook as a blue sun.

Harriet had seen the change. She had heard stories. Some of the Negroes, out of fear—hoping to distance themselves and to appease vocal and violent slavery supporters—had taken to mocking their own Negro preachers and churches. *Ignorant chicken thieves!* Some had begun, it seemed, to believe the white masters who told them that the Negroes were the children of Ham and they, the white masters, were the sons of Japheth. The Negroes had begun to believe that it was God's decree that the slaves could only please God if they pleased their white masters in every way. Black holy men had become objects of ridicule at best and at worst, dead men tortured and hanged for their faith.

But her father, Lyman, had remained ambivalent. He had preached antislavery messages against the Missouri Compromise, but embraced neutrality. Harriet and her brother Henry had whispered to each other about it for years.

Then came railroad expansion. The Beecher clan moved west to Cincinnati to spread the gospel on the new frontier. The slavery matter raised its head again; students at Lyman's Lane Theological Seminary argued aggressive abolition while Lyman held to neutrality. Soon many of the students, frustrated, left to join Oberlin College.

Since their move to Cincinnati, more than two decades had passed. During that time, Harriet married Calvin Stowe, biblical scholar and professor, and bore him seven children—she had buried one of them, her sweet Samuel. Most of her brothers and sisters, like Henry, had also started families. Samuel Morse invented the telegraph so that news now traveled more quickly. And in her living room was a newly invented sewing machine so that stitching no longer had to be done by hand. The world had gone on turning.

But, contrary to her father's prediction, life only worsened for the slaves. In Cincinnati, at the edge of the Ohio River that separated free Ohio from the slave state of Kentucky, Harriet and Henry were able to see firsthand how cruel slavery was. They saw at close quarters that slavery was not satisfied to own Kentucky. It slithered down the banks and slid across the river into Ohio, recapturing fugitive slaves, refugees who had made it to freedom. It even wrapped itself around the necks of free Negroes who had never been slaves and, demanding them as its own, dragged them back across the river.

The Negroes in Cincinnati were always on guard, always angry, and wary of any white face, no matter how it smiled or prayed. They never knew which white person, or black person seeking lucre, might betray them. They never knew which white face would help slavery snatch them away. Harriet imagined it must be the same in other slavery border states and towns. By federal law, there was nothing anyone could do. Any white person could claim to own any Negro and other whites were bound by federal law to turn the poor Negro over or risk being prosecuted.

Now each person, no matter his conviction, no matter how far geographically removed he was from slavery, was forced to support it. The federal government had passed the Fugitive Slave Act of 1850 and by doing so made every American a slaver.

Any slave who escaped had to be returned. Knowledge of his escape or assisting the refugee might lead to beatings, fines, and prosecution. No one would be exempt; a gray-hair in Maine or a Pennsylvania Quaker, the person was bound to take hold of the suspected fugitives and send them, man, woman, or child, back into captivity. Worse, whites in need of money might be seduced to aid slave merchants, receiving a few dollars' reward in return for innocent lives and spirits—turning themselves into slave merchants, manstealers.

It had been easier, somewhat easier, before the Fugitive Slave Act to be blind. It had been easier to obey her father when the matter was someone else's problem. Her family didn't call Negroes filthy names. They weren't slave owners. They collected money for charity. Wasn't that enough?

Harriet looked across the carriage at her brother Henry, into the eyes of her lifelong friend. Middle age had crept up on them.

Now, her poor brother felt caught in the middle. His sentiments were antislavery, but his heart was with honoring their father.

At his church and all over the country, his large blue eyes brimming with tears, Henry preached impassioned antislavery messages. It was known by quite a few that his Brooklyn church, Plymouth Congregational, was a stop on the Underground Railroad, defiantly offering shelter and assistance to refugees making their way from slavery to Canada. He had even gone so far as to stage mock slave auctions and collect money to purchase freedom for slaves.

Then, suddenly, when Harriet knew he was thinking of their father, Henry's words would distort, saying the slaves must be patient and that the slavery men must be given more time.

Harriet loved her father, adored the father who had taught all his children, sons and daughters, to be great thinkers and debaters. Some of the greatest minds—lawyers, conservative and liberal clergy, students, abolitionists—met around her father's table. She loved him, but it seemed that the past few years had put her to the test.

It was difficult to find a path that would allow her to honor her earthly father and her heavenly father. Was she willing to give up father, mother, and home for the sake of the gospel, for the sake of the truth in the Bible—truth that her husband, Calvin Stowe, said came from the minds of Eastern men?

Harriet had seen slavery's growing muscle. It was the mid-1800s and there were sewing machines, but women still did not vote and most did not even speak publicly about politics or slavery. Her father's voice continued to insist this was a matter for slavery men. It was hard to find middle ground. It was hard to find a way to avoid the fight she saw coming.

Harriet had supported the American Colonization Society, had prayed it was the middle ground she hoped for. Perhaps the right thing was to collect money and send the poor kidnapped Africans back to their homeland.

But it was not enough. Truth still called to her, still roused her at night.

She could write, the thought came to her. She could tell the truth about slavery through a story, an allegory. Writing was her part; God would do His. So, Harriet had begun to write *Uncle Tom's Cabin*. It would be a serial, published in the *National Era*.

But it was not as easy as she had thought it would be. Each word she wrote frightened her. A voice in her head chided her. *Who appointed you the world's savior?* Each word was a struggle, a gnarled battle between good and evil, so that the first words, sentences, chapters were almost unintelligible. Her husband and family supported her, prayed for her, but she needed more. She begged her husband, her dear brother, and even her children to keep her bathed in prayers so that evil would not overcome her. To honor her father, her homage to middle ground, she added an ending to Uncle Tom sending the refugees back to Africa as missionaries.

Harriet wrote. God reciprocated. The words of *Uncle Tom's Cabin* canvassed the globe. The book took her on journeys and introduced her to friends she never would have imagined, like the Duchess of Argyle. Harriet blushed. She still owed the duchess a letter of thanks for the money that the duchess and other women of England had given to her to help with American abolition efforts.

She listened to the clop of the horses' hooves on the cobblestones. Outside the carriage window green trees rushed by interspersed with new buildings that shot up from the ground like cornstalks among patches of blue sky. Boston's population had grown to more than 150,000—people crammed together in colleges, department stores, federal buildings, churches, row houses, boardinghouses, and tenements. Hardworking, God-fearing, mind-your-business folk—without the luxury of nosiness. Fishermen, seamstresses, garment workers, and meatpackers. Protestants, Catholics, English royal bloods, immigrants, Irish, Italians, Chinese, Jews, abolitionists, and runaway slaves. All tied together by trolleys, shipyards, railroads, turnpikes, harbors, hills made low, and newspapers. Boston opened her arms to Emerson, Hawthorne, Longfellow, and William Lloyd Garrison's *Liberator*.

Harriet looked across the dark interior of the carriage at her brother. Henry was beginning to gray now, and had a great kettle for a belly. He was still as charming, and she saw the passion of the younger brother she knew still in his eyes. He had come to her defense when slavery men had attacked her in the newspapers, even calling for a bounty on her head after publication of *Uncle Tom's Cabin*. "Our niggers are happy in their rightful place except for the agitation of nigger preachers and troublemaking trolls like you," one man had written to her.

Since *Uncle Tom*, she had made associations with fugitive slaves who had escaped slavery to become great orators and abolitionists—Sojourner Truth, Henry Bibb, and Frederick Douglass. Douglass had also defended her when she was attacked in the press, but in private he was adamant that she must tell the whole truth. He and the other black abolitionists took her to account for suggesting that blacks should return to Africa. "How can we return? Our blood and sweat is here. We have toiled to build this nation. We have paid a price here, are we not entitled to reap the rewards? Why should we leave behind what we have planted? Our African forefathers' bones are here and, though they would deny us, the blood of our European fathers runs through our veins. Would you force us, like the Cherokee and the Choctaw, onto someone else's land?"

Harriet had thought *Uncle Tom* would be the end of it. But now they wanted more. Now they wanted her to write a book refuting the notion of contented slaves. She must tell the story of Negroes who hated slavery, who would not bow down like Uncle Tom, patriots who had the courage to fight and even die.

Douglass had tried his hand at novel writing, penning *The Heroic Slave*. But he was not satisfied with it. "The colonization societies use your book to defend their plans to force us to Africa. Your brother and I preach against it. You must use your pen and set things right," Douglass said.

Harriet sighed and watched the spider at work on his web. Twenty-five years after his hanging, Henry and Frederick insisted she must retell the story of Nat Turner.

chapter 2

She had begun to have dreams about dead men, of resurrecting them. In her dreams, Harriet resisted trying to bring the men back to life. It seemed unholy, sacrilegious. Then, one Sunday in church, a passage of Scripture stood out to her: *Now faith is the substance of things hoped for, the evidence of things not seen.* Harriet couldn't count the number of times she had read the eleventh chapter of Hebrews. She had memorized most of it as a child. Her eyes skimmed over the words.

Whenever she felt afraid, whenever she felt powerless to do something, verse six always undergirded her. Alone she might not have been able to write *Uncle Tom's Cabin*—the blank pages had stretched out in front of her impossible to fill—but by faith she had done it. If God could part the Red Sea, if He really existed, then He could help the wife of a poor Bible teacher write a book that might save lives and souls.

Her mind had drifted from the preacher's voice as she focused on the words in front of her. *By faith Moses, when he was come to years, refused to be called the son of Pharaoh's daughter; choosing rather to suffer affliction with the people of God, than to enjoy the pleasures of sin for a season. . . .* She had neither title nor throne to give; she was only the wife of a poor professor. She wrote *Uncle Tom*, and despite what she thought at first, she had survived the threats and the taunts that followed. She was still a wife, a mother, she still had friends.

But Nat Turner was troubling—maybe it was the thought of bringing something so unpleasant, something perhaps better forgotten, back to life. A confessed baby killer. How could she, who had lost her own infant son, write a story about such a monster? Maybe it was the dreams, dreams of resurrecting a man that frightened her: . . . *By faith the walls of Jericho fell down, after they were compassed about seven days. . . . By faith . . . Women received their dead raised to life again. . . . Women received their dead raised to life again. . . .*

Months later, in idle conversation with a new acquaintance, she posed the idea. "I am thinking of writing a book about Nat Turner and the Southampton slave revolt." The acquaintance had looked shocked. "I will change the names and the setting, of course." By faith she might be able to write and awaken Nat Turner's memory. *Women received their dead raised to life again. . . .* But hadn't she already done enough?

The carriage stopped. The spider scrambled to the corner.

There was not a person in America who would not have recognized the man who climbed aboard.

chapter 3

His woolly gray mane and beard were famous through-out the world. *His head and his hairs were white like wool, as white as snow; and his eyes were as a flame of fire; and his feet like unto fine brass, as if they burned in a furnace; and his voice as the sound of many waters.* Harriet wondered if God were a man if this is what he would look like.

"Good morning, Mrs. Stowe," he said in his booming voice.

"Good morning, Mr. Douglass."

Her brother Henry laughed as he shook Frederick's hand. "You are forewarned to be careful what you say; my dear sister will immortalize it and your life in one of her novels."

Frederick Douglass nodded. "You are ready to meet the fellow, then?"

Harriet looked across the carriage at the two men; the vehicle seemed too small to contain two of the most well-known abolitionists in the world, men whose courage and words changed the course of nations. "Indeed, Mr. Douglass." She would meet the fellow, but offered no promises.

"He is a business owner now, but still a fugitive. You will have to be careful not to disclose his identity, residence, or the names and locations of those who might have helped him."

Harriet tried to keep the pressure she felt from coloring her face. "I understand."

Henry knocked on the roof of the carriage and the vehicle rolled again.

chapter 4

Boston was bustling, full of new buildings and businesses sprouting up from the earth. But there was at once something historical and revolutionary in the Boston air. Everywhere Harriet looked she thought she saw a minuteman or a son of Paul Revere.

"I will introduce you to a man who will share a great story," Douglass told her.

They soon arrived at a small shop on Phillips Street, on the North Slope of Beacon Hill. Upon entering, Harriet looked around the room, forcing herself not to stare at the man who greeted them at the door. But it was hard to keep her eyes from him.

The Confessions of Nat Turner had made him out a monster, but the word that came to her mind was *calm*. He was very dark. Something about him reminded her of a cloud before a silent rain. His hair was silver and it was hard to believe he had been a violent man, a baby killer, except for the scar that zagged across his face like a bolt of lightning. Harriet cleared her throat. "Thank you for meeting with me."

"I promised one day I would tell the story. So many lies have been told and I won't live forever." He smiled. "It seems today is someday."

Harriet nodded at the man. If the truth were told, if the truth were resurrected, they might stave off the coming war, the corn might not be spattered with blood. She shook his hand, reminding herself that she had not given consent to write; she had only agreed to listen.

"You may call me William," he said.

chapter 5

While they sipped tea, and Henry and Frederick waited in an adjoining room, William told Harriet a story she had not expected to hear, the story of an intelligent and earnest young man. The young man's identity was common knowledge, in a Southern way—hidden from his sisters, but his brothers, who knew they shared paternity, hated him because their father favored him though he was born a slave—his skin black and theirs white. It was a story of brotherly love and betrayal, vengeance and mercy, of heartbreak and hope.

As William spoke, it was the first time Harriet had thought of Nat Turner's mother. Another grieving mother.

It did not seem that they spent hours talking. Harriet was surprised to see the light outside the window dimming. The story he shared was intriguing. She looked around the shop. Like his clothes, it was threadbare. "I have money from the women of England. I could purchase your freedom from your master so that you no longer have to hide." It was a small thing to offer. Perhaps she could help him with his business also.

William's eyebrows raised and his nostrils flared. It was the first sign of anger that she had seen and a chill passed through Harriet. Maybe he was the monster *The Confessions* described.

"Pay the one who called himself my master? Nathaniel Francis has already received enough blood money! No man is owed money for stealing what God gave me freely. Nathaniel Francis owes me a lifetime of wages; payment for each scar on my back and on my heart. Let him pay me!"

So much anger, it startled her. "I understand how you feel. I only thought—"

"No, you don't! How could you? Let him pay me for every stripe, for the years when I was dead and separated from God, for when he deceived me and stole my birthright. Let him pay me the price he owes for stealing my wife and child!" He pounded the table. "They are gone now! My sweet little daughter . . . let him pay me!"

She tried not to show her fear. "You believe he owes you a debt?"

William sat back from the table that separated them. He breathed deeply as though trying to calm himself. "I leave that decision to God. Let the ones who refuse to repent, who smile with their mouths while their hearts are full of anger and lies—let them stand before God and His Word and let the Great Judge decide." William sighed, lines of weariness deepening on his face. "I have forgiven Nathaniel Francis . . . I think . . . sometimes. I have presented him no bill. Let him face what he has done and render what is due to God."

Harriet thought of her sweet Samuel. "I lost a child, too, though through different circumstances. How do you forgive?"

An ironic smile turned up the corners of his mouth. Harriet thought she saw tears in William's eyes. She turned her line of questioning back to Nat Turner. "You must have had great respect for him, for Nat Turner?"

He seemed amused. "I hated him. I only knew him from a distance." A genuine smile came to William's face. "You are surprised?" He nodded. "From a distance, it seemed that life was easy for him. It seemed that he had everything I had lost." He nodded. "There are many stories about Nat Turner—his mother's, the one who owned him, his friends' and enemies'. Mine is only one. I will share with you what I know and what I have heard."

Sallie Francis Moore Travis

chapter 6

Cross Keys, Southampton County, Virginia
February 1831

Sallie was convinced they would never be satisfied. They didn't approve of her, or her husband, and there was always talk about Nat Turner. If she wasn't careful, they would kill him.

Her brothers—Wiley, Salathiel, and Nathaniel—didn't think her husband, Joseph Travis, was good enough. They thought he was too soft. They thought he was a dreamer. He was not what they considered a man's man: he was gentle, he didn't call her names when no one was around to hear, he came home every night, he did not drink, and he sat through church most Sundays without yawning.

Sallie had lost one husband to death and then God had sent another. She promised herself she would always sing satisfied. She looked out the window. It was cold and gray outside. Night was coming.

Sallie Francis Moore Travis grabbed a rag, ripped from an old croker sack, and reached for the baking pan of corn bread. The cast-iron oven glowed red on the inside, the pieces of wood radiating heat. The heat flushed her face and lifted her hair. She pierced the center of the bread with a broom straw. When the stick came out clean, she withdrew the pan and gingerly set it on top another piece of croker sack that covered the wooden table that her husband had built. Sallie used her arm to brush the sweat-dampened hair out of her face.

Last week her husband and some of the boys had set about hog butchering; this year her family had only one hog, so there would be many meals without meat. She didn't have a girl to do it, so she had had to render the fat to make lard all by herself.

Heaven knew Marie, her husband's spinster cousin who was living with them, was too good to help out—she would devour the ham—but was too good to let the fat touch her.

The heavy grease was still on Sallie's face and she knew the smell was still in her hair. She appreciated the meat, knew her family needed it; men worked hard butchering, but she hated that women always had to render the fat.

The grease was like a thin sheath, a second skin; she wished for fresh water. Hair washed with clean water, maybe just a splash of apple cider vinegar added to the rinse, or maybe dried rose petals in a bath, would do her good. Being clean wasn't a new dress to show off to the other women, but, still, it would do her good. The heat in the kitchen and the oven, along with the pig fat, were ruining her hair.

She hoped for rain enough to fill the barrel outside, or even snow that she could melt in the pot on the stove. Not much, just fresh water so she could wash her hair before going to Mrs. Caty Whitehead's next Saturday.

She stooped again, reached inside the oven, and, using the rag, grabbed the second large pan of corn bread. As she withdrew it, her arm brushed the edge of the oven. The hot metal seared her flesh and angry pink rose up around the black shriveled line, stark against her white skin. Sallie yelped, sighed, and then spit on the burn. She touched the spot gently with the rag.

It was just one more thing to hide. She looked at the scabs of older, not-yet-healed burns on her arms. She could hide them under the sleeves of her dress. But she couldn't hide the ones on her hands. They were healed over, but the telltale scars were there, the signs. All the women knew she cooked for herself, that she didn't have a girl to do it, and if they didn't know, Cousin Marie would be happy to tell them. The other women were too genteel, too Christian, to talk about it to her face, but she knew what they thought. It was the same thing her brothers thought.

Sallie looked down at her hands. Nigger hands. Hands that had been forced to do too much work; hands that said her husband wasn't wealthy enough to do any better. The other women would never say it—they were Southern ladies and would never say such things—and they didn't have much more themselves. But Southern ladies weren't known for poker faces and Sallie read disdain in their eyes.

What would they say if they knew she was also cooking for her darkies, for the few slaves she had? It was good that the farms in Southampton County, especially in Cross Keys, were far apart and that no one came around much to see.

What the women wouldn't say, her brothers, the Francis brothers, seemed to take pleasure saying, especially in front of their mother. They never failed to bring up that she cooked for Nat Turner; they accused her of pampering him. Her brothers and their drunken friends, particularly John Clarke Turner, hated the slave, seemed obsessed with him. It made no sense to Sallie since all of them had grown up together—John Clarke and Nat Turner were practically brothers. Some uncouth people even whispered that they were.

But her brothers were right—whether he had grown up with them or not, Nat Turner was a slave, and no decent white woman should cook for a slave. The custom in the area was to give the slaves their rations for the week or month—a measure of cornmeal, maybe corn on the cob, and some salt pork for Christmas if there was pork to spare. Cooking their rations was left for slaves to do when they came in from the fields. No mistress would serve slaves. But here she was with burned hands. Sallie grabbed a knife from the unpainted cupboard with her free hand and began to slice through the bread, cutting large squares.

She turned to stir the cabbage. The stink of it told her it was ready. The salty fat meat and the heat made the leaves soft, translucent, and shiny. Sweet onions and pepper rounded the smell. She grabbed the wire handle of the kettle pot and moved it from the flame so it wouldn't burn. There was not much worse than the bitter taste of scorched cabbage.

It had not been a good year for crops, not that her husband was any kind of farmer. But because of the poor harvest, no one had extra money. The other farmers only called on her husband for repairs to wheels and wagons when they could no longer patch them themselves. With the scant harvest, no one dropped by, rolling up the dirt lane that led to their house, knocking at their front door. No one asked her husband to build them a new set of chairs or an ornate mirror frame. This was not a time for artistry; it was a time for making do.

She opened the door to the room where she stored her few canned goods and grabbed a jar of spicy pear preserves. It wasn't Sunday, but something sweet helped a tough day go down better. Sallie looked at her arm as she reached for a jar of precious coffee. Too bad sugar wouldn't do anything for all the burns or she would spare a little. But the cool room—it was cool enough for the butter and cheese to be kept on a high shelf—felt good and cooled the sweat on her face.

She smiled. Mrs. Mary Barrow wouldn't be caught dead perspiring this way . . . or in a cupboard . . . or in a kitchen. Not even Lavinia would allow herself to sweat so. They all had cooks and personal servants. None of them were like the Grays or the Jeffersons, who had slaves and money to spare. But the other whites did what they had to do to have the basics. They didn't have the stench of pork grease hanging in their hair.

Sallie walked out of the pantry and closed the door behind her. She carefully set the jars of preserves and coffee on the table. She dipped some grounds of coffee, just a small amount—it had to stretch—and made very weak coffee. Her husband would not allow whiskey—not even brandy or wine—on the table. When it was finished boiling, she set the cooling liquid on the unvarnished table. Then she set plates and glasses for them all.

The bread was cooler now. She lifted half of the corn bread squares from one pan and put them on top of the other pan. She grabbed the pot of cabbage and ladled heaping spoonfuls into the empty half of the first pan. When she was finished, she removed her everyday shawl from the nail in the corner, threw it over her shoulders, and stepped outside the door onto her back porch with the pan of half cabbage/half corn bread in hand. The wind blew on her face and into her mouth when she opened it to yell. "Nat and Hark, you boys come get your food now! Come on, while it's still hot!"

Two figures emerged from the dark shape of the small barn behind the house, taking more form as they got nearer the kitchen window's light.

One was tall and muscular, like some statue carved of onyx. "Hark, I hope you two appreciate all this hard work I'm doing. You can bet no other mistress is cooking for darkies."

Hark reached with his large hand for the pan. "Thank you, ma'am."

The second man stepped into the light. He was much smaller, much fairer—in the dark, at a distance, those who didn't know him might have thought he was white. "You must not be very hungry, Nat Turner." Like most other people, black and white, she usually called him by both names.

There was something gentle about his presence. His hands were scarred and calloused like the other man's, and he had his share of knots and scars like the others, but there was something peaceful about him, not wild like her brother Nathaniel's boy, Will. "Yes, ma'am, I'm hungry." He nodded. "Thank you."

"You be sure that you bring my pan back when you're finished. I don't want to have to send little Moses down there hunting for it." Nat Turner smiled at her in that way of his. It reminded her of the way some dogs looked, like they were smarter or knew something you didn't know, but were content to let you think you were superior. "We'll be sure to bring it back, Miss Sallie. Clean."

She watched them walking away. "And don't you scamps go roaming around out here at night. You have got to be up before the sun. There's work to do." It hadn't been a year yet and already the boys' clothes were too ripped to try to mend. She would have to hunt around for more croker sacks and stitch them up something. Maybe it was spoiling them—one pair of pants and one shirt should have lasted them the whole year—but she would do it anyway. It was all right for the little ones to run around half naked, but it wouldn't do for grown men.

Darkness had crept up on her. The stars in the black sky were like diamonds, like the ones Mrs. Mary Barrow wore around her neck, like the ones that glittered on Mrs. Caty Whitehead's fingers. These stars were probably the only diamonds she would ever have. She was not the belle of the ball.

There were days when she was ashamed of the graying, rough-cut wood of the house and the fence, but she and her son had roof enough to take in relatives, like lazy Marie Potts. Her brothers didn't think Joseph Travis was good enough. He was not hard enough on the slaves, they said. But Travis had welcomed her and her son, Putnam, into his home, his two-story home.

None of her brothers could claim more. Salathiel's one-room shack—not much bigger than a privy, made of rough planks that looked like they had been thrown together—was so small that when the corn was high you almost couldn't find it. Nathaniel's home was not much bigger—one room with a loft and kitchen.

Travis had made a place for her and allowed her to feel at home.

Her brothers were men and they didn't know how it felt to be a woman alone responsible for a child, especially a male child. How would she teach him to hunt, to sit with other men? They didn't know how it felt to lie awake at night worrying about how you would feed your son, how you would eat the next day—trying to smile so your son wouldn't know how poor you were, how close to death. Her brothers didn't know how it felt staying with people after you've worn out your welcome because you had nowhere else to go.

They didn't know how she scurried to swallow the subtle snipes and slights so her son wouldn't be poisoned by them. She sat, unmarried, among married women, women who considered themselves superior because of their attachment, because fate hadn't taken their men. Remarks, looks, and hints—dropped by people so comfortable they didn't have to care or think how others felt—had left bruises. They didn't know the weight and hopelessness of the word *widow*.

She hadn't had anything much—just her son, Putnam, and the slave who had been willed to him, Nat Turner. She had hired Nat Turner out, letting him take day jobs—to plow, to help with harvest, a little millwrighting, whatever Nat Turner could do. She took the money the slave earned so that she and her son would have a few pennies. When she and her son were still alone in the Moore house, before it had become someone else's property, Nat had chopped the firewood, fetched the water, and hunted for squirrels or coons, something to put in their pot. When wolves threatened them, or there was a crawling snake, Nat Turner was the only one she could trust.

No one came around, especially not the brothers full of complaints; no one wanted to come too close to grief. It had been a lonely time, a quiet time. The silence had added to the sorrow. She had even thought of inviting Nat Turner inside to eat with her and her son. Instead, she had taken to handing him his food out the back door. That was how she had started cooking for Nat Turner, and it made sense to her since she still had to cook her own food to cook for the slaves as well.

Her brothers always nagged her to sell him, saying he was "too smart" and smart niggers were trouble. But how could she sell him? Nat Turner had kept her and Putnam alive. That didn't matter to her brothers. She had a feeling that they would as soon see him dead as alive, not that they cared too much more for Joseph Travis.

After the corners of her mouth had drooped from worry, Joseph came along with a flower in his hand. It was just a daisy, a field flower; but soon after, they were married and she was in a house with mirrors and pictures on the wall, and curtains made of material she chose herself. It was not a fancy house, had only one coat of worn white paint, but it was a house she and her husband could call their own.

Sallie pulled off her shawl and apron and rehung them on the nail by the door. She looked in the mirror and smoothed her hair, and then called her family downstairs. They gathered at the table—Joseph, Putnam, and young Joel Westbrook, Putnam's age, who lived with them. They said grace and ate dinner by candlelight. The slave, young Moses, who still lived indoors, sat in a corner eating his dinner—corn bread and cabbage like the other slaves—from a tin pan. His being in the kitchen eating while they ate was just another thing for the women to gossip about if they knew. But he was still young and it was too cold for him to fend for himself alone outside—she could not afford an old auntie grandmother like some of the others to care for him.

Sallie smiled at the crumbs around her son's mouth, crumbs easier to see than the beard he thought was growing there. The yellow glow of the candle in the darkening room warmed her family's faces. She thought again as she looked that her husband's eyes were the purest blue.

"I think snow might be coming," he said as he took a big swallow of weak coffee.

Sallie promised herself that no matter what she didn't have, she would never allow herself to fall asleep dissatisfied. She had a family, a house, food, and a man. She smiled and offered her husband more corn bread.

chapter 7

It wouldn't do for the other women to see her sitting next to him. Nat Turner stopped the wagon, turned, and held out his hand to help Sallie from the seat where she sat next to him to a seat in back of the unpainted wooden wagon. They already thought she pampered him too much.

When she was reseated, he clucked at the horse, shook the reins, and they started again down New Jerusalem Road on their way to Mrs. Caty Whitehead's. Sallie pulled the rough green blanket around her shoulders, legs, and feet to keep warm. "You be careful there, now, Nat Turner, and don't kick up too much dust. I just washed my hair and I don't want it to be dirty before I get there." Around the edges of her day cap, she touched her curls. Snow had come—not much, but enough to melt and wash her hair. It was clean and smelled of rosewater, from the tiny vial she kept in her closet.

Sallie breathed deeply. The sun was bright today—but still cold enough that pork in the shed would not spoil before it was finished curing—beautiful and clear. "You hear me, Nat Turner?" He said nothing, like she was his little sister tagging along and getting on his nerves. He was peculiar.

He belonged to her son, Putnam. But until Putnam came to the age of majority, Nat Turner was her responsibility. Besides, Putnam didn't see to his care. Putnam never took food out to him.

It was amusing owning him. He wasn't strong or tall like Hark, or like her brother Nathaniel's boy, Will. Will could knock a stubborn mule to its knees with his bare fist, but that same mule would probably drag Nat Turner all around the farm. Nat Turner wasn't much suited to farmwork.

His mother, people said, was Ethiopian or Egyptian. Maybe that accounted for his peculiar ways. But it was amusing to watch him strutting around like a rooster, thinking it was running things, but without sense enough to know that it was just property. And like a rooster, at any moment its life could be ended, floating in a hot water pot.

Her brothers had something to say about everything he did— counting their peck of corn in her bushel. Sometimes he talked about being free and what had been stolen from him, but he was harmless, just a dreamer too smart for his own good. She had learned to ignore him, like a temperamental cat.

Her brothers said Nat Turner was always trouble, always thought he was as good as them, or better. Even so, she wasn't going to sell away Putnam's inheritance, his property. Nat Turner was just odd, that was all. Sometimes she wondered if her brothers were jealous.

It sounded ridiculous to think of white men being jealous of a slave, but it was possible to be jealous of most anything, she supposed—a flower, a sunset, a river that could go where it pleased. Maybe they were jealous that Nat Turner could read, not just read well enough to write his name, but read so that people would stop him and get him to read their mail for them, or to show off for visitors. From time to time she had done it herself. Most of the white people couldn't read, though they were ashamed to admit it, and it seemed peculiar that he, a slave, could. He said no one had taught him—there would have been trouble for whoever had—he had been able to just pick up a book as a child and read. Now he was a novelty.

Sallie pulled the blanket tighter and up to her chin. She watched the slave's neck bobbing as the horse pulled the wagon along the hard road. There was something beautiful about him. Not like a man, but still, something beautiful, like a bird you notice because it doesn't seem to belong. He even fancied himself a preacher. People, mostly darkies—though he had baptized one white man—actually came to listen to him. When he preached— his hair curling on his head, around his top lip and on the tip of his chin, his fawn, almost cream-colored skin—there was something wild, something exotic and true, about the way he talked that made her almost believe what he had to say.

But only almost. She wasn't to be duped or bewitched by him like some Ethelred Brantley. Nat Turner was only a slave.

His eyes on the road, he jiggled the reins and whistled to the horse. Her family didn't have much, but she had been thinking. Not many people needed her husband's services, but she owned the smartest slave in the county. The woman Nat Turner called his wife, Cherry, had been bought by Giles Reese. Every child Cherry turned out increased Giles's wealth. The children would be prime—intelligent, fair, good-looking stock—and worth a lot of money, pickaninnies that would make Reese wealthy.

And Sallie had been thinking that maybe her husband could find someone willing to exchange a child, to give them one of the children, for Nat Turner's studding for a year or two. Sallie's husband didn't have money to buy her a girl, but maybe they could trade Nat Turner's stud service for one. It would be a baby worth little or nothing until it came of some age, but once able to work and breed it would be worth hundreds of dollars, worth even more than their land. Maybe it would be a girl who could tend to Sallie, who could grow to do the baking. A girl who could grow and then breed, maybe with Hark, and bear others—more slave children who could work the fields, or be sold to bring in some money for Sallie's family.

Her husband would have to ask other men about studding Nat Turner—after she talked him into it—because people would be shocked at the thought of a woman thinking of such things. But she had had to take care of herself and her son when she was a widow, so she had learned to be enterprising. Sallie wasn't educated, she wasn't cultured like Caty Whitehead, or beautiful like Mary Barrow, but she was smart. She could think of things.

When they reached the Whitehead place, Sallie shrugged off the blanket, stood, straightened her cloak, and smoothed her gown. She looked down at her dress; it was plain. Nat helped her down from the wagon. Some of the other women, a few in fancy carriages, had already arrived. "Don't you go wandering, now, Nat Turner. You stay right here." He nodded, his expression still indulgent.

Sallie walked past Mary Barrow's black carriage adorned with brass wheel trim. It was lovely and it turned heads, but it was nothing compared to Caty Whitehead's. Sallie reached out her hand, tempted to touch the dearborn. Mrs. Whitehead had ordered her carriage special, modeled after one of President Jefferson's coaches. Caty's green coach with golden wheels was the talk of everyone around.

Sallie touched her hair, brushed dust from her dress, and headed for the door. Her dress was an old checkered cotton gown, but perhaps with the new adornment the women wouldn't notice. She touched the new bow she had added at the collar. She wore her only pair of ruffled cuffs on her sleeves, cuffs she had made herself. She could not afford to buy lace ones like some of the other women, and she could not afford to have someone make them. They would have to do.

All the women looked forward to this winter event. It was too cold to travel, but it was a party, held annually on the Saturday just before Valentine's Day, none of the women would miss. Caty's party would be special. There would be tea and cakes and bits of honey-glazed ham—almost like a Jerusalem, Virginia, party.

Sallie walked closer to the front door. She could already hear women giggling inside. There might be roast pheasant; apple tansy covered with warm cream, nutmeg, and sugar; and there might even be syrup-covered popcorn—a feast that Sallie's family could never afford. Caty and her daughters had fine penmanship, and though all the ladies could not read, there might be a painted handwritten card for each one. There would be stories, surprises, and gifts.

Of course, there would be a brief explosion. With Mrs. Whitehead there always was. Something would light the fuse and the cannon would blow. But such things must be expected at Mrs. Whitehead's since they had so many slaves—not as many as the Parkers or the Edwardses, but a respectable number nonetheless. The trouble, whatever it was, would be a temporary and trifling thing.

Sallie stopped and turned, looking toward the fields where she could hear the Whitehead slaves singing. It was cold and there was little to do, but Caty's son, the Reverend Richard Whitehead, would invent something rather than see them loafing about. He did not believe in letting them rest. It was not good for a slave's hands or mind to be idle, the preacher often said. Slaves were beasts of burden. They needed to be kept working at all times if they were to be kept content.

The Whitehead slaves certainly sounded content. The singing was melodious, slow and deep. First there was a single voice, a man's voice.

> I love the Lord, who heard my cry,
> And pitied every groan.

The other voices followed, singing mournful words she could not understand. It was beautiful the way the creatures sang. No matter how hard the work, they were always singing—always content, always singing. And they were lovely to see; brown skin draped in cream against the stony brown of the fields. Their backs bowed, their arms moved in rhythm with the song, a living painting. Sallie envied them, sometimes, and wished she could find joy in simple things as they did, contented with nothing.

The leader's voice rang out again.

Long as I live and troubles rise,
I'll hasten to God's throne.

She had never heard Nat Turner or Hark singing. Perhaps one needed more slaves, a certain number before they would sing. It was exquisite, like the singing of grieving angels or the lowing of cattle. Sallie sighed watching them. Slaves were so simple and their temperaments so gentle. Too much work made her tired. It made her back ache. It made her want to cry. She looked down at her scarred hands. Who could doubt that the Lord made the creatures for hard work; they always smiled and sang. She had never heard one complain.

A cold wind blew then and Sallie gathered her cloak around her. She turned from the fields and back toward the house. If she didn't pay attention, she was going to miss the entire event. Before she could knock on Caty Whitehead's front door, it swung open. Greeting Sallie was one of the Whiteheads' old aunties. "Welcome, Mrs. Travis."

"Thank you, Venus." Sallie stepped inside the door. She smelled an apple pie baking and sweet cider. This was going to be a Saturday afternoon worth the cold ride it took to get here.

THERE WERE DELICATE lace curtains at the windows, shining hardwood floors like glass. The furniture was polished, the silver picture frames gleamed. Mrs. Whitehead was an extraordinary hostess, a fine housekeeper. Sallie nodded as she entered the room.

Some of the most noted women of the community sat in the room where Mrs. Caty Whitehead was holding court, not that any of the women were wealthy like the Jerusalem women. Sallie's sister-in-law Lavinia, her brother Nathaniel's wife, was there, with her personal slave, auntie Easter; Mary Barrow was also there with her personal slave; and, of course, in the kitchen were slaves, all at the Whitehead women's beck and call.

Sallie smiled brightly as she sat, hoping her cheeks were especially pink and that her eyes glowed especially bright. She hoped that the other women would notice her freshly washed hair and not how ashamed she was that she did not have a darkie gal to attend her. When she was home, with her family, what she lacked was not so keen. But here with women, even younger women, who had more than she had, she felt the prick of need.

Here in front of the other women, she felt ashamed, as though she had come to the gathering with dirt under her nails, the smell of hog grease in her hair . . . or burns on her hands. She tucked her hands away and hoped the other women wouldn't see. She would speak to her husband when she returned home about her studding idea.

Mrs. Mary Barrow, her corded petticoat holding her splendid gown like a cloud around her, was whispering, "He left her so many times." Her lace and taffeta fan, colored like jewels, created a breeze that lifted her hair. "They say she said the Lord told her to do it!" Her dress was adorned with double rows of ruffles.

Mrs. Caty sat on a chair in the center of the other younger women. Her white hair was neatly coifed and her gown lay around her just so, a touch of expensive lace peeking from her collar and cuffs. "Well!"

Lavinia, Sallie's sister-in-law, was pale, the color drained from her face. "She always looked heartbroken."

Sallie knew who the *she* was whom they were talking about. All of them knew who the *she* was, but they were too genteel to openly speak her name. Mrs. Lila Richardson had taken her husband's life.

He took her far away from her friends and family after he changed her name. No one spoke of how many times he had beaten her, or of how she defended him to others after the beatings, or of how many times she had taken him back. How many prayers had Lila prayed? The servants had found her sitting in a pool of her husband's blood.

As matron and expert, Caty Whitehead, having successfully navigated a marriage that lasted thirty years until her husband died, knew how to steer a conversation away from unladylike things. She had many stories to tell them and a lifetime of good advice to share. "You must always look your best for him, no matter how tired you might be."

Sallie, with practiced surreptitiousness, looked around at the other women as Caty spoke. "No matter how disappointed you are, keep a smile on your face and a girlish blush on your cheeks."

Sallie looked at the other women's dresses. They were all Cross Keys women, but Mary Barrow's dress was made of the most exquisite fabric and in a violet color that complemented her eyes. Her gigot sleeves were perfectly puffed, and the pleats in front of her dress were perfectly pressed in place. Mrs. Caty and her daughters were all in varying shades of blue. Lavinia, her brown hair piled atop her head in curls and braids, wore peach that favored her complexion. It was obvious that none of them had spent the night before in the kitchen; none of them had to rend lard from their own pigs.

Sallie looked down. She slid her feet, in brown lace-up shoes, back to hide them under her skirt. Her shoes had no decorative buttons along the side; they were not soft leather like the pretty ones her sister-in-law Lavinia wore. They were not tiny, pinchtoed, satin slippers like Mary Barrow's.

A silent sigh lifted her chest. She should not covet. She should not expect too much. It was the order of things.

It was left to Mrs. Sallie Francis Moore Travis and to the other women in the room to teach the prevailing rules, just as Mary had taught them to her son, Jesus, so many centuries before, Mrs. Whitehead told them. It was their role to teach order and manners to their sons and daughters, to guide them to their rightful places. It was their role to teach the order to the slaves, who, not being very intelligent, were often confused. She smiled. "Sometimes they will get beside themselves and you will have to get behind them!" She shrugged, the lace from her collar brushing her earlobes, and the other women giggled.

It was the order. Someone had to be better and someone else worse. Someone had to be prettier than the others. It was what helped Sallie to make peace with the limited hand life had given her.

She wiggled her fingers beneath her skirt. Food and drinks would be served soon; she wouldn't be able to hide her scars much longer.

Someone had to be smarter. Lavinia had been educated to read in North Carolina and so there was talk of her someday, like Mrs. Waller, opening a school—maybe only a mile or two from their farm so that Putnam could learn to read. Someone had to be the tidiest, or, like Mrs. Caty Whitehead, the hostess above all others. This hierarchy of gentlewomen all rested on order and on civil agreement—someone must be best and someone must agree to be the least. The order was a dance played out among friends, among mothers and daughters, among women everywhere.

Women signaled to other women the roles they were willing to play: "I am a horrible housekeeper." "I am so blessed that my husband keeps the books, I would be a pauper if it were left to me." "I never know what to do with my hair." "Oh, I could never read a book that thick."

If each person did not willingly play her part, if no one was willing to be less, or if one tried to carry the title of Best in too many of the coveted categories, then things fell apart.

Nothing made gentlewomen angrier than someone who did not play her part. She ruined it for everyone, the one who stepped out of her place. The women were confused by the fat woman who persisted in thinking she was beautiful and adored, and they were dumbfounded by the woman who did not covet blond hair. Worst of all was someone who wanted to have it all.

Mary Barrow sat near Mrs. Whitehead, fanning herself. "What a lovely fan," someone said to her. Mary responded, "It's imported from France, you know." Mary had long been known as the loveliest woman in Southampton County. When she married the older Mr. Barrow, who in return for her beauty gave her wealth and fine clothes, she became a contender for Wealthiest and Best Dressed. It was not rumors about her improper behavior that angered other women; it was too much wealth and too much beauty, too much "best" concentrated in one woman.

Someone also had to be least. It was sad but true. The assignment of "least" in each of the categories was a most unladylike thing, and challenged the ladies' notions of themselves as good women, gentlewomen. This assignment often involved pouting, broken friendships and alliances, and even, sometimes—in the most difficult cases—swooning.

Like politics, it was a messy, dirty business. In fact, it was so cruel, the competition so vicious, that some women abdicated their positions rather than play. Some gave up combing their hair, stopped courting, and stopped keeping their figures. But, as in politics, to keep things going the messy business needed to be done.

Mrs. Caty Whitehead was now pouring tea. "Always be sure to serve your husband's dinner first. They work hard for us." She smiled.

Mary Barrow dramatically waved her fan. "They say we are weaker. Why shouldn't they serve us first?" She pretended to be joking, but they all knew she meant it, the vain, vain thing.

Mrs. Whitehead smiled graciously. "It is what great ladies, real ladies, do. Not to mention that our men are fragile and will take the tiniest oversight—like receiving their food second—as a slight. So easily wounded." She laughed and the other women giggled with her.

For the women of Southampton County, the distasteful business of deciding who was least had been socialized, codified, and ratified. She might not be prettiest or wealthiest, but Sallie knew she would never be least.

The women who were least were in the kitchen, on the other side of the wall. God had kinked their hair, given them thick lips, and dark skin as signs to others.

Sallie pulled her hands from beneath her skirt. She would never be the least. She might not be prettiest, but she was not ugliest. She might not be best married, but she did have a faithful husband. She might not be wealthiest or have the most slaves, but she had the smartest slave in all Southampton County.

Two of the women from the kitchen—dressed in drawstring skirts and shapeless blouses of bleached white muslin—entered with silver platters piled with warm, sweet tea cakes. Mrs. Caty Whitehead clapped her hands. "I thought these would never come," she scolded the two dark-skinned women with the lift of her eyebrow, and then turned back to the gentlewomen. "You will love these treats. They are such a delight!" She spoke to her two servants again. "Please hurry with the tea!" When the women from the kitchen—their heads wrapped in white muslin, too—had served the gentlewomen, they disappeared again back behind the wall.

Sallie nibbled at the tea cake she held in her hand. It was sugary and golden brown, with crisp edges. She watched the others, following their lead, to be certain she didn't take too big a bite.

The dark women in white returned from the kitchen carrying a teapot and cups with painted roses on a tray. Mrs. Whitehead sighed with disappointment. "I told you the pink ones, not the yellow. How many times must I repeat myself? Do you enjoy humiliating me?" She waved them farther into the room to serve her guests. "You try my patience," she said.

The women from the kitchen poured tea, bowing to each woman they served, offering them lemon for tartness and honey for sweetness. Sallie looked at their skin, so smooth, and at their hands that were burned like hers. When they finished, like ghosts they left the room.

Mrs. Caty Whitehead cleared her throat. "We are the fairer sex, but difficult things often fall to us. We must manage things. We must keep our houses tidy and our house darkies from being unruly so that our men do not have to intervene. We should never add to our husbands' burdens."

Sallie looked down, staring at her hands.

"I know we have tender hearts and we want to give them extra and teach them to read, but it will only stir trouble." Mrs. Whitehead was too gracious to look at her directly. Sallie knew that Caty was speaking about her own servants, but Caty was also speaking to her.

It stirred trouble, Nat Turner being able to read when so many white men couldn't. It was a problem, his thoughts and the way he spoke, his not staying in his place. She sighed listening to Mrs. Whitehead. He was so gentle; sometimes it was easy to forget. He spoke so well it was easy to be tempted by what he said. But she would never allow herself or her family to be made fools, not like Ethelred Brantley.

Brantley had been a man respected and feared for his control of the slaves, a Southampton overseer willing to whip or flay any slave, to make them so afraid when they were around him that they would not speak or lift their heads. No slave had taken liberties with him; none dared.

Then Brantley himself said he had heard Nat Turner speak and had been persuaded—persuaded that all of slavery, and his part in it, was sin. He had come to the Negro meeting to cast the fear of God into them, but instead the fear of God had fallen on him. Brantley said Nat Turner knew more than any man he had ever met about God and that what he spoke was true religion. Brantley had fallen at Nat Turner's feet asking for forgiveness, and asked Nat Turner, a mere slave, for baptism. Nat Turner had come with Brantley to visit Mrs. Caty's son, Richard Whitehead, the preacher at Turner's Meeting Place, and asked that both of them be granted baptism.

Brantley had been fooled, but Richard had kept his head and sent them both hightailing. So Nat Turner had baptized Brantley in Pierson Mill Pond, right in front of all the people, and then Brantley had broken the water's surface and baptized Nat Turner. It was a scandal!

It got worse when Brantley, covered with some skin ailment, consulted Turner, who prayed and sent him, again, for a cure in the waters of Pierson's Pond. She didn't see it for herself, but people said Brantley came away clean.

Brantley was a source of shame among white people. He was an embarrassment and eventually they ran Brantley, who had been one of them, out of town. How could a white man, even one of low estate, allow himself to be manipulated by a slave, by the very ones he'd overseen? How could he allow himself to sit among them and listen to the words they said? He'd been brought low.

Sallie was careful. She knew people, including her brothers, worried that Nat Turner had some power over her, that he might turn her as he had Brantley. But she was the master. She was no Ethelred Brantley and she would never let the slave dupe her. She would never be fooled and ruined by him.

Nat Turner was a problem, but he was her property; he was Putnam's inheritance. If she sold him, all her plans would dissolve. If she sold him, she would be just another poor woman, not the woman who owned the fancy slave. He was a problem, but she would keep control of him.

The kitchen girls returned with trays of meat, more cakes, and other treats. One of the younger ones stumbled and a small cake slipped to the floor. Mrs. Whitehead didn't speak; she simply rose slightly, cuffed the girl, and then slapped the girl again. The girl bowed her head, stooped to pick up the dropped cake, and didn't say a word. When the kitchen girls left, Mrs. Whitehead spoke. "Ladies, we must be firm."

Sallie picked at the food on her plate. She would have to do something about Nat Turner. She sighed resignedly when Mrs. Caty Whitehead spoke again. "They are given to us by God as our children and it does not do to spare the rod."

Mrs. Whitehead was right. Abolitionist men, interfering cads who didn't know Virginians, said they were heartless and cruel, devoid of true religion. Those men didn't know that despite what they might have to do to hold fast to the rules, the gentlewomen were overflowing with love. The abolitionists didn't know about the love between master and slave, particularly between mistresses and slaves.

Someone not genteel might have pointed to an occasional whipping, pinching, or pinpricking committed by the gentlewomen and called it cruelty. But it was the mistress who suffered. It was a horror even to be brought to the point where she had to do such things. But sometimes it had to be done. It was a love the abolitionists could never understand.

Mrs. Caty Whitehead clapped for the trays to be taken away. The darker-skinned women breezed into the room, grabbed the trays, and took them out again. There was order about the way they moved. Contentment. When they were gone, Mrs. Whitehead smiled and spoke gently. "That is what we are able to achieve, ladies, if we will have the courage to take a firm hand. It is what they need, what they desire."

The explosion was over.

Mrs. Whitehead was right about the servants and right about Nat Turner. It wasn't right the way he sometimes didn't answer her. It wasn't right, even after she told him not to, the way he roamed around preaching. He should know his place. It would be good for him; he would be more content, if she took a firmer hand. Like all the other darkies, he was easily confused and sometimes didn't know what was for his own good. For his own sake, something would have to be done.

Confused. She lifted her head.
Something was wrong.
The room was suddenly dark.

chapter 8

Some of the women ran to the windows and then pointed to the sky. Sallie stood to join them.

Outside, she saw Nat Turner standing next to one of the Williamses' slaves, Yellow Nelson, whom she had heard also thought himself to be a preacher. Both of them were pointing at the sky. She drew back from the window—something about the two men and the darkness frightened her. Sallie forced herself to breathe. "What do you think it means?" she whispered.

Next to her, Mary Barrow laughed. "You are almost as superstitious as the darkies!"

Behind her, Mrs. Whitehead laid a hand on Sallie's shoulder. "It's nothing to be frightened of, dear. God is giving us an early Valentine's Day gift, ladies. It's an eclipse!" She called to her servants. "Light the candles!" Sallie turned to see Mrs. Whitehead smile. "Step away from the windows, ladies, and back into the sitting room. We will have our party by candlelight!" Mrs. Caty clapped her hands, the candles ignited, and Sallie's fear vanished.

THE SUN CAME out again. Sallie made her way to the wagon where Nat Turner waited for her. The others were watching. "Move quickly, now, boy." She had to handle him firmly in front of the other women. "We have to get home before nightfall." He didn't say a word, simply extended a hand.

Before she reached Nat Turner's hand, she heard a syrupy

voice behind her. "Oh, Sallie." It was Mary Barrow. She had added an exquisite pelerine, a cape, and a stylish ruffled lace day cap to what she wore. The beautiful woman extended her flawless hand. "So good to see you, Sallie."

The woman grabbed Sallie's hand so she could not easily pull away. Mary smiled and looked down at Sallie's hand, at the scars, turning her hand each way. All the shame Sallie had been fighting came and rested on her shoulders.

"Such a pity about your hands. If you should ever like to borrow one of my girls, I have a few extra I can spare."

Sallie could not speak. She only shook her head.

Mary was still smiling. She curtsied, dropped Sallie's hand, then turned her back.

Sallie looked down. There was no place to hide. Nat Turner, again, extended his hand and helped her into the wagon.

Mary Barrow grabbed her voluminous skirt and was helped into her carriage. It began to pull away. Then Mary hit on the roof for it to stop and leaned her head out the door. She called to Sallie in a singsong voice, "By the way, dear, I meant to compliment you on your dress. I don't think I've ever seen you look lovelier. Have you worn that dress before?"

When Mary's carriage was gone, Nat Turner turned the wagon away from the house and onto the road. Once out of eyeshot and earshot, Sallie pulled the rough green blanket back around her shoulders. She looked at her hands, touched the bow at her neck, and then began to weep.

They drove on that way, neither of them saying a word. Past barren trees, the smell of smoke from distant chimneys drifting through the air. Brittle, abandoned nests rested in timber arms. "She is no lady."

Sallie raised her head at the sound of Nat Turner's voice. His back was still to her. Sallie wiped her eyes. She should not have been crying in front of him. She should not allow him to say such things. Mary Barrow was a white woman, a distinguished woman of Southampton County.

He turned to look at her. "She has everything but she is poor—poverty makes her mean." He stared into her eyes and Sallie began to weep again. He turned and did not speak again until they were home.

chapter 9

It was the same every year. Spring finally came. Every farm was busy preparing the ground. The smells of fresh earth, manure, and awakening apple trees were the perfume of good things to come. Sallie's husband, Joseph, needed every hand in the field, but he had agreed to let Nat Turner drive her into town. She sat in the wagon behind him.

Every year winter came and the cold froze the creek over and ice tried to hold the water in place. To stay warm, they chopped down trees for firewood while the night overtook the daylight and shortened the days. Cold hypnotized the trees and ground and put them fast asleep. Night settled in like winter, thinking it had won. In February, it looked like spring would never come.

It looked, in winter, like things were dead; but the water was always fighting underneath the ice. In winter, spring and summer lost the battle, but they never completely died away. Just when cold relaxed, having convinced them all it would never leave, warmth crept back on whispering feet. The dark water beneath the ice kept bubbling, fighting to break free. Then it happened: The pond water broke through, grass poked up, and crocus punched up through the ground. Daylight kept fighting darkness until it brought the longer sun. Spring came.

Sallie was convinced it didn't happen all at once. She watched every year; she wanted to see it happen, to see the firsts. There had to be a first blade of grass, a first leaf, a first bird, a first egg. There had to be a first bubble to break through the ice, brave enough to fail.

Nat Turner steered the wagon down the road with no name.

Barrow had a road, Person and Drewry had mills, and even the Indians had Indian Town Road. Someday. Maybe someday the road
with no name would be Francis Road, named for her family.

Nat Turner drove quietly. He slowed when they passed the
Giles Reese farm. "Don't poke there, now, Nat Turner. We don't
have all day." They were making their way to Barrow Road on their
way to Jerusalem to do some shopping and to check the mail.

Nat Turner was silent. He clucked his tongue and picked up
the pace.

Joseph and the boys, and Hark, were in the fields, so she was
alone. In the quiet, she could hear the birds. She could almost hear
the light wind. The trees were green again. Not many weeks ago, it
had been easier to see into the woods along the road. Now the
trees were awake and used the leaves to draw the shades on the life
that was stirring within. She caught a glimpse of a leaping fawn.

Spring gave her hope, but it was also a wild thing. Every winter
they cut down trees for firewood, to set aside to build things, and
to clear out the land and the road. But every spring it all seemed to
rush back again. There was always a seed, an acorn, that blew to
some unexpected place and took root. For every tree they cut
down, five little oaks poked their heads up in the fields. The trees
crowded in around them—the roots from some stump they had
thought dead reaching out in the road to grab a wheel. Spring
pressed in on them, trying to reclaim the fields and the house. It
crept under the doors and into the pantry trying to steal what little
food, the meal and the flour, they owned. Spring made their live-
stock want to wander and their slaves roam. It was the growing
season, but you could not trust it. It was a good thing but it had to
be controlled. Spring was wild; it would turn on you. You could
not turn your back.

ON THE STREETS of Jerusalem, sheep wandered, bleating,
getting in the way. Pigs rooted around doorways for anything that
might fall, squealing and bolting when dogs barked at them. She

did not come to town often, but it always amazed Sallie how many people she might see—maybe even thirty or so in the course of one day. Nat Turner helped her to the ground. She hadn't come to town for much—some flour, to check on croker sacks for replacement clothes for the slaves, and to see if there was some mail. She pointed to her two baskets still in the wagon and Nat Turner grabbed them and hung them across her arms. "Don't you go wandering, now, Nat Turner. You stay near the wagon. You be here if I need you."

She had no free hand to lift her skirt; the mud made the bottom of it brown. Sallie dodged the animals, shooing them, and made her way around the horses tied to posts. There were more men in town today, most likely voting on the new Virginia constitution. She pushed at the swinging door.

"She killed him dead! He was living and then he was gone."

"Why would she do it? It was insane."

When she stepped through the door of Samuel Trezvant's store the men quieted. There were more of them than usual milling around. All winter the women had been talking about Lila Richardson, who killed the man she loved. Now the men were dragging Lila into spring.

Everyone knew he loved her, though she frequently wore his blue tattoos on her eyes or on her arms. No one talked about it. They all turned their heads. How many times had Lila prayed? What did they expect poor Lila to do?

The postmaster and shopkeeper, Samuel Trezvant, brother of Congressman James Trezvant, rose to his feet and nodded to her. Someone had told her that the Trezvants had long ago lived in Cross Keys, outside the city of Jerusalem. They said that the Trezvants and Francises were distant relatives, but Sallie could see no resemblance. "Good morning, Mrs. Travis, good to see your smiling face in town."

"Good morning," she responded.

"How's the family? I saw your husband, last Tuesday, I believe, in town to cast his vote."

"All well. I cannot complain," she said.

"I just saw your brothers at Mahone's Tavern voting, doing their civic duty. I imagine they are still in town." The postmaster and his brother were politicians, opportunists some said, and they could always be found in the thick of things.

"I hope I see them, then." Sallie smiled and nodded. If they were visiting Mahone's, they were sure to be drinking and she hoped not to see them. Whiskey sometimes made them into men she didn't want to know—especially her younger brother, Nathaniel.

"That son of yours will be voting soon. It seems just yesterday that he was born."

"Shooting up like a blade of grass," she said. "I won't interrupt you. I have a few things to purchase." She turned to explore a new pile of fabric.

She rubbed her fingers over a piece of crimson silk and imagined it as a gown for a grand lady. Her fingers tapped their way to a blush-colored piece of cotton that would make a lovely gown for Sunday wear. A piece of golden taffeta caught her eye. There was lace for a fancy day cap she could wear to cover her hair.

Postmaster Trezvant turned back to the group of men lounging around him. He rejoined the conversation midstream. "Oh, this new constitution's a good thing, all right. President Jackson's right, every free man ought to vote. This is America, not a nation run by royalty or a wealthy few. Every free white man with an adequate amount of property, not just the wealthy, needs to have a vote." He sat back down on his wooden stool. "We have to protect ourselves. Property value in the county has gone down, even the price for the slaves, and if we don't change the constitution we might lose the vote ourselves. But we have to be careful with this vote—there is the threat from our brothers in the west, mountain men like our governor. They would like to see us as poor as they are with no slaves to tend our fields. We can't give the vote to just anybody."

Sallie's husband, Joseph, had voted already. He was a dreamer, but never one to wait around, though the men had several months to vote. She had overheard him talking to her brothers. The new Virginia constitution would open the door for more free white men in the east to vote and keep the door closed on Virginians from the western part of the state, who were poorer and, for the most part, against owning slaves.

One of the gentlemen shook his head. "We don't have anything to worry about from the west. We are not so poor."

Trezvant sighed, like he had too much to carry, but Sallie could see the melodrama was part of his effort to keep all eyes on him. It was always that way with him and his brother. "You don't see what comes through here, the things that come through the mail." He lowered his voice. "The governor is pushing for investors, for railroads to cut through our land, to carry our goods to market, even to the western territories. But he's having a hard time convincing the moneymen, investors that have never lived here. Once we were the fifth wealthiest county in the state, now we are at forty-three. And they are nervous about us having slaves."

"Nervous? What is what we do with our property to them?"

Trezvant leaned forward. "They are afraid of an uprising."

"An uprising? Ridiculous!"

Samuel leaned in closer, lowering his voice more dramatically. "Our brothers in the mountains talk against slavery, and the moneymen aren't ignorant—they've heard of slave uprisings in Haiti and Santo Domingo. They worry that should there be an uprising, our own white men in the west of Virginia might side with the darkies."

Another man spit tobacco juice on the floor. "If what we do in our state as free men offends them, let them take their money elsewhere, these investors, or whoever they are. I won't allow any man to take my freedom or tell me how to live."

"Abolitionist cuckolds! If they think they can rob me of my property, they are mistaken," the first man said. "If they think I will be driven to poverty without a fight, let them come and see!" His face flushed and he slapped his knee.

Trezvant nodded his agreement. "Oh, the moneymen don't

care one way or another about slavery. They are not filthy, unpatriotic abolitionists. What they care about is green. They care that their money will be safe and give them a return. They want stability. Order. They want to count on money in the pocket." He turned to the first man. "The abolitionists, you are correct, are beating at our doors. Almost every week, there is some kind of pamphlet that has made its way through the mail trying to turn our darkies' heads. They don't know the favor we do them keeping these darkies from going wild."

Trezvant was incredulous. "Some of these pamphlets are written to the darkies by darkies themselves! By so-called Negro preachers, like David Walker and Richard Allen. Chicken-eating buffoons and baboons is what they are! Writing to darkies as though they could read." Trezvant frowned. "They hope to fill our slaves' heads with all kinds of foolishness, telling them they can learn, be free, and be property-owning men. That someday they might vote!"

One of the men laughed. "A nigger voting?"

Another flushed. "I will kill them all before I see a nigger owning property like a white man."

Trezvant waved his hand at the man. "Be careful, there, sir. A lady is present."

Sallie kept her eyes on the fabric as though she didn't hear.

Trezvant lowered his voice again, pointing at his fireplace. "You don't see what's coming in the mail. The U.S. Postmaster General is supposed to block it, but some of it slips through. Now there's a new one from some rascal named William Lloyd Garrison and he's a troublemaker if there ever was one! I have to keep the order." Trezvant whispered, "If some darkie who could read, someone like Nat Turner, got ahold of writings by Garrison or David Walker, no telling how it would stir him up! Put all kinds of crazy ideas in his head! Then he'd pass on the foolishness to the other darkies. This land wouldn't be worth nothing and we couldn't give our slaves away!"

Postmaster Trezvant chuckled. "You don't have to worry, though," he stage-whispered. "I make short work of the trash! I do my job." He chuckled again. "If they want to send paper, I have a place for it to burn." He pointed at the fireplace. "That's Garrison and Walker keeping us warm, right now." He and the other men snickered. "But abolition is not the worry of the investors. Order is the concern."

The first man sat back and crossed his legs. "If they are worried about malcontents, then they have only to visit. They worry for nothing. They don't know our slaves. Our darkies are happy. They are at peace here."

The second man agreed. "If they are counting on an uprising here, they are sadly misinformed. There are no more contented, gentle, and loyal creatures—I would even say masters' friends—than the ones we have here."

Postmaster Trezvant nodded. "True, but these New York moneymen are long in the tooth; they know our history and they say Virginia breeds rebellion. They've heard the story of Bacon's Rebellion, the Great Revolution, and most of them know of Gabriel's rebellion in Henrico County. They say we're rebellious and we breed rebellious slaves."

"Henrico County is a lifetime from here."

Sallie felt the silk one last time and then walked away. Feeling the silk was wasting time, only dreaming. She got the few things she needed. Silk was for the wealthy women, Jerusalem women.

Postmaster Trezvant, speaking to the men, looked in her direction. "A lifetime away for most of us, but to these moneymen and politicians who travel all the time, it is just a stone's throw away. Santo Domingo, Haiti—and if Cuba falls we have trouble. Why, all the Negroes could practically swim over here from there. Cuba's just a big boiling pot of trouble. All we need is a bunch of angry insurgents—blacks and mulattoes—to come spilling out here. The moneymen feel the same thing—with all the blacks allied—could happen here."

When Sallie had finished her shopping, she nodded at Mr. Trezvant. He came and took the baskets from her. "Anything else you are needing, Mrs. Travis?"

"Would you have any flour bags, old croker sacks?"

"You're in luck, Mrs. Travis. I do."

After he had bundled everything and placed it in her baskets, Sallie watched Trezvant figuring the total in his head. "Is there any mail for us?" she asked him.

"No, sorry, Mrs. Travis." There never was.

She paid what she owed. When she heard men in the street, shouting as though they would fight, she looked out the window to see.

Sallie Travis gasped. She clutched her baskets to her.

chapter 10

"Nat? Nat Turner?" Sallie ran from the store. "Nat Turner, come over here right now!" Nat Turner stood, legs astride and fists clenched, in the street. Her brothers Salathiel and Nathaniel had grabbed him by his ragged clothes.

"I need you to carry these things!" She tried to sound calm, but she heard her voice cracking as she yelled.

His eyes still on her brothers, he turned his body toward her.

"Nat? Nat Turner?" Her lungs contracted, she could not breathe. She fought to keep herself from shaking. Her brothers would kill Nat Turner if she didn't step in. They were looking for any excuse.

Blood dripped from Nat Turner's nose. Nat was far shorter than both her brothers, but she knew he would not back down. It would only get worse. He was a bantam rooster and if he ever began fighting, he would fight to his very death.

The men inside stepped out of the dry goods store. She heard them mumbling behind her, their voices getting louder.

She had told Nat Turner to stay by the wagon, to stay out of the way. "Nat Turner, come over here! I need you to carry these things!" She tried not to look like a mother hen flapping her wings. Sallie didn't need trouble. There had been spring flowers and fawns and fabric; she wanted it to end a pleasant day.

Near her brothers and Nat Turner was a straggler. Benjamin Phipps, poor as a church mouse, was meddling in the way. She would have to calm things down. "Nat Turner, come over here," she repeated. "I need you to carry these things." She smiled, speaking as though she didn't know what was going on.

Nathaniel grabbed for Nat Turner's shirt, but Phipps again stepped in the way. Nat Turner stood his ground. Sallie fought not to wring her hands, to give her anxiety away. She turned and smiled at the men behind her. "They are like children, these creatures God has given us for a burden. We can never take our eyes off them." She turned to the street again. "Nat Turner. I said come over here, right now!"

Nat Turner unballed his fists and turned. "Yes, ma'am." He crossed the muddy street, avoiding a man riding a mule and a mangy dog. He took the baskets from Sallie Francis Moore's arms. There was nothing in the way he nodded to her that said he had been fighting, except for his reddened face . . . and the blood.

Her breathing was even more ragged. "What have you been up to, Nat? Just like a little boy." She felt faint. But she would not faint. She could not faint. Sallie cuffed him gently, a show for the sake of the men watching her, a show to tell them that she had him in hand. She pulled his ear. "I have to keep you by my side to keep you out of mischief."

Her brother Nathaniel called to Nat Turner from across the street. "She won't always be here to protect you, you can count on that. I'll see you sold down the river, or I'll see you dead, Nat Turner!"

Sallie watched Nat Turner walking to the wagon, mud on his feet, more tears in his shirt. Benjamin Phipps was shuffling the other way. She turned to calm the men behind her. "This is all nothing, just spring in the air. They have known each other since they were boys. I'm afraid spring has my brothers' natures high." She smiled again, satisfied when the men went back inside.

She crossed the road to her brothers. "Nathaniel, Salathiel, I see that you two are voting." She wanted to pretend that nothing had happened, to distract her brothers.

Nathaniel's eyes were red, his face flushed. "I have told you, Sallie, that you must get rid of him. He is impudent. Do you see him standing there looking at me"—he pointed at Nat Turner—

"looking at us like he's a man?" Nathaniel raked his hand through his hair. "Look at Salathiel's Red Nelson, there. You never see him out of place."

She looked at Red Nelson grinning. Kinky sandy-colored hair and blue eyes, he was Salathiel's only slave, his grinning constant companion, a pip. Red Nelson bowed. "It is a servant's honor to serve his master." Sallie did not like Red Nelson's toady grin.

"Nat Turner is my property. I will handle him," she told her brothers.

Nathaniel put one hand on his hip, and bent down to look into her eyes. He was a man now—his posture said so—no longer little brother to her older sister. "I believe Nat Turner is actually your Putnam's property. At least last time I observed."

"You are correct, Nathaniel." She fought the fluttering inside of her, the threat she'd felt when she was alone, after her husband died. "Nat Turner is Putnam's property, brother, but he is my responsibility until Putnam comes of age."

Nathaniel smiled at her. "Well, if you mean for your son to have him, then I suggest you keep your yard dog on a shorter rope." He stood upright. "If he tramples in my garden, I promise I will shoot him down."

Sallie nodded at her brothers. The fluttering would not go away. She tried to reassure herself: she was not alone now, she had a husband, she didn't have to allow anyone to bully her. She bowed and quickly turned to walk away.

"I will tell Mother you asked after her," her younger brother taunted as she walked away. Nathaniel would tell their mother every detail, probably add a few, of what had happened today. He would be the hero, she the failure. Sallie nodded and hurried to her wagon.

"NAT TURNER, MY brothers are white men and you must stay in your place. You knew each other as boys, but that is past; they are men now." Sallie settled the baskets around her. "I told you to stay out of trouble. I told you not to cause trouble. I was in the store getting sacking to make you new clothes, and this is how you repay me? You embarrass me in front of the whole town?"

Nat Turner said nothing.

The chirping of the birds irritated her now. "I have not lifted a hand to you. But maybe I have been wrong—spare the rod and spoil the child." She shifted on the hard wagon seat and patted her foot. "You have no right to look at white men that way, balling your fists!" She took a deep breath. "Don't think I am weak because I am a woman. If need be, I will take the lash to you myself!"

The slave didn't respond. Maybe he *was* impudent, as her brother said. She had never seen him as insolent, just a little peculiar. She had to teach him properly. She could not pass him on to Putnam, when her son came of age, wild and out of hand.

It was like Postmaster Trezvant had said; there were too many influences telling the darkies they were human and as good as any white man. The abolitionists and darkie preachers were confusing them, especially smart ones like Nat Turner, the postmaster had said. For years everyone said Nat Turner was too smart for his own good. She had always admired his reading, but who knew what foolishness was being put in his head? He had been so quiet lately.

Red Nelson disgusted her with his fawning, grinning ways. But Red Nelson had learned his lesson and knew his place. He had run away from a wealthy master—actually, several masters—and had been living his life passing as a white man. But Red Nelson had been found out, his darkie blood discovered, and been carried away in irons and chains with people staring after him. *My, he looks to be white. He is one they will have to brand in the face so that we all will know.*

Red Nelson did not seem to mind telling the story of his capture. He grinned whenever he repeated it. And he repeated the story many times.

His owner determined to sell him farther south. *They will teach you a lesson, teach you who you are. And I will get back the money I have invested.* But Red Nelson had convinced his owner—who was no whiter than he except for some dark drop he claimed he could trace to Red Nelson from long ago—to give him a chance to find his own situation.

No other wealthy man would purchase him. They had heard of wily white niggers. *You will run away, disappear; money thrown away.* There was nothing Red Nelson could offer a rich man who had plenty of slaves. But, he reasoned, he could offer a poor master something that he lacked. He found Nathaniel, who purchased him for a pittance and brought him to Salathiel. Salathiel said he could not tolerate black skin and blue gums around him, could not stand the wild smell—could smell a nigger miles away. But Red Nelson was light enough for Salathiel, he was funny, and he knew his place. So, Red Nelson became the property of Salathiel, a bachelor with no one to care for him. And because of Red Nelson, Salathiel became a white man with enough property to vote.

Salathiel and Red Nelson shared a tiny cabin in the midst of cornfields, a shack of rough logs daubed with mud. Red Nelson didn't run anymore. He said the right things; Salathiel was always right. He became who and what Salathiel wanted him to be. Red Nelson was always at Salathiel's side, fawning over him. Sallie thought Red Nelson was a toad that had chosen survival over being a man.

All the other slaves looked at him from the corners of their eyes. She had seen them. They gave Red Nelson wide berth. They told him nothing, so he had no secrets to tell. But he knew which direction the wind blew; he knew how to make things work for himself.

In time, most white people came to adore Red Nelson. They were entertained by his aristocratic manners and his funny stories. They allowed him to drink with them, and laughed especially hard when he told darkie jokes. They slapped him on the back when he answered Salathiel's door like the butler at some grand mansion. They relaxed with him, but they did not forget about the dark drop. They laughed with him as long as he also remembered. Red Nelson stayed in his place.

But Nat Turner was another matter. Nat Turner had embarrassed her in front of her brothers, in front of the whole town. And this was not some place like Richmond or Washington. Everyone knew everyone else here, and soon the word would spread. They would talk of her as they did Mrs. Lila Richardson, in whispers that would quiet when she walked through the door.

Nathaniel would run home and tell their mother. Another addition to her mother's growing list of disappointments: daydreaming husband, poor farm, widow, and now this. Sallie would have to teach Nat Turner better. For his own sake, she would have to teach him better.

Who was going to want to breed a girl with a buck that was out of hand? Selling him was not an option. The men in the store had said the prices were low. If her brothers killed him, everything she would have done for the darkie, every meal she had given him, would have been for nothing. Putnam would have no property, no vote.

She had been good to Nat Turner. She had not beaten him for reading, for pretending to be a preacher. Sallie fed him food she had cooked with her own hands. She overlooked his roaming around; people told her they had seen him different places preaching to other darkies. But she would not be misused or made a fool of by a darkie, not even Nat Turner—especially Nat Turner. No creature she fed was going to send her to bed at night upset. She would whip him and chain him if she had to. She had to show her son how to stand up and be a man, to be boss.

"You get hold of yourself, Nat Turner. If you don't, I promise I will get hold of you!"

chapter 11

Sallie stood outside in the warm May sun. She brushed cornmeal from the front of the apron pinned to her dress, and then breathed deeply. The sky was blue, all the trees were green, and the clouds were fluffy and white. The sweet smell of apple blossoms filled the air.

She looked toward the sun, closed her eyes, and prayed for a good harvest, apples enough to keep them all through the year. She prayed that Hark's and Nat's hands would be busy, that Putnam's and Joel's hands would overflow with apples. She chuckled, imagining apples raining down on them, apples enough to make pies and hundreds of bottles of cider and brandy that they could sell. She smelled them and tasted them, sweet and tart. Crisp ones, cooked ones, apples everywhere.

She opened her eyes when she heard the thunder of horse's hooves. It was her brother Nathaniel galloping toward her house. Sallie wiped her hands on her pinner. "Is it Mother?" she yelled to him. "Is something wrong with Mother?"

Her brother charged into the yard, his face red, his horse plowing down her garden. "Nathaniel, what is the matter?"

He slid from the horse and in one move was in her face, jabbing his finger at her. "That boy of yours is crazy!"

"Who do you mean? Putnam? What has he done?" Her son had not been far from home and he—

"I mean the one you and everyone else around here pampers!" He whispered, as though someone else were listening. "Your slave, the preaching nigger!"

"Oh, Nathaniel. Nat is harmless. You know the darkies and

their religion." Things had been quiet, but quiet was not her brother's way. Every event, to him, was worthy of a commotion, especially if it concerned Nat Turner. She tried to calm him, to speak calmly to him. "He talks, sometimes, about what should have been. But he is harmless. He fancies himself some traveling preacher . . . but he is just a dreamer, nothing more."

"Crazy as a loon is what he is. I saw him out at the pond yesterday."

"At the pond? What were you doing at the pond?"

"Don't you question me! I am a man! I go where I please! But, then again, it seems Nat Turner is the free man."

"Oh, Nathaniel. The way you go on, I would think you were jealous of a slave!" She laughed and touched his cheek. Maybe shaming him or teasing him would quiet her younger brother.

His face flushed. "Laugh if you want to, Sallie, but I saw him—down at the pond, crazy drunk and talking out of his head."

"I have known Nat longer than you've been alive. He has never taken a drink in his life, everyone knows that." If there was someone she'd expect to be drinking, it would be her brother Nathaniel and his friends. "He doesn't curse. He doesn't steal. He doesn't carry or think about money. You know that. He is as tame and as peaceful as an old auntie." Tame and calm in a way that she would only wish that her younger brother was. "You know that, Nathaniel. He might be a little zealous, but his religion has made him tame." Sallie pointed toward the apple trees, hoping to distract her baby brother. "How's your planting? I was just praying for a rich harvest."

Her brother would not be sidetracked. "He is a maniac, raving about what's been stolen from him." Her brother, his eyes angry and red, stepped closer to her. "I got closer so I could hear him. I heard him for myself pretending to talk some mumbo jumbo, like some foreigner, like some witch doctor, bowed down with his face to the ground." Nathaniel pounded his fist into his other hand. "You'll listen to me one day. You with Nat, and Salathiel with Red

Nelson, taking them on like pets." He pointed at the boy Moses, who cowered near the house. "And that one is the same. You'll have trouble if you don't treat them like the animals they are."

Sallie thought she saw young Moses tremble, eyes darting, as he always appeared whenever her brother Nathaniel was near. The slave boy lowered his head and quickly ducked around to the back side of the house. Nathaniel jabbed his finger in the boy's direction. "Shouldn't take them inside any more than you'd take in a wolf!"

His voice had been rising steadily. "I'm telling you, I saw that boy yesterday and heard him for myself. On his knees, reaching his hands in the air, like some fanatic. I tell you he's crazy, and you're better to kill him and be done with it."

"Yesterday? Well, why didn't you tell me yesterday? Why do you come rushing over here now?"

He sputtered. Nathaniel's face flushed brighter. "I'm here now! I have my own life, my own things to worry about. I'm here now, but for what? You're not going to do anything. Why should I even bother?"

Her brother always let it be known that even though he was youngest, he carried the weight of the world on his shoulders. The baby of the family, he'd even had to take in their aging mother.

"He's harmless." She smiled at her brother, trying to tell him he was foolish without saying it. It wasn't Nat Turner who kept her stomach churning.

Nathaniel nodded his head. "You think I don't see you, Sallie? I know you. I'm your brother. I know you." He grabbed her scarred hands. "Look at them."

She felt naked then in front of her brother. She tried to jerk her hands back from him. He would not let them go. She fought not to cry. "I don't know what you mean."

"You know. We all know. I see you. I see right through you. Cooking for him, fawning over him. It's always Nat Turner this and Nat Turner that. If you're going to fawn over a nigger, let Hark be the one. Give Hark an extra share; that bull will plow any heifer you put in front of him and make you rich!

"But no, it is always Nat Turner! Weak and good for nothing. Always bragging over him, but that smart nigger will only breed trouble." Her brother pounded one hand into the other. "I tell you this, Sallie, you will not shame our family. I don't care whose property he is, I'll kill him before you shame us." He threw her hands back at her and then leapt on his horse. "You do something about him, or I will!" Nathaniel stormed away as fast as he had come.

Sallie staggered. A hard, cold wind blew through her. Her knees weakened. Nathaniel would go straight to their mother. He was better, the favorite son. Sallie stared after him. She bit her lip and tears blinded her. She wilted onto her front steps, wiped the tears from her face, and then hid her hands underneath. Ashamed and accused. What were the others thinking of her and Nat Turner?

They were going to kill him. She felt it. If she didn't do something soon, her son's property would be gone.

She found him underneath an apple tree, a shovel in his hand, shirtless. His arms and face and neck—always in the sun—were light brown, yellow, like a wildflower or a rose. But his chest and stomach—usually covered by his rough tunic—were almost as white as hers. She would never have imagined.

When he saw her, he smiled that same patronizing smile, as though he were looking at a younger sister.

Sallie pulled at her sleeves and then at her apron. "My brother . . ." She stopped herself from wringing her hands. It didn't matter what her brother had said. She didn't owe Nat Turner, a slave, any explanation. She steadied herself. She had to declare herself. She had to get him in line.

Sweat rivulets on the sides of his face wet the curls in his hair. Her hand itched to reach for them and feel how soft they were. Instead, she yelled. "This is the end of all this foolishness!" She had to protect her son's property rights. "You have been . . . There will be no more trouble, Nat Turner! Do you hear me?"

Nat Turner looked confused. He turned to face her.

She stepped closer to him. She would not be intimidated by chattel, by someone, something she owned. She breathed harder . . . closer . . . they were almost face-to-face. "You are the cause of all my troubles!" She slapped him. Her hand stung. A red place appeared on his cheek in the shape of her palm. "I have told you that I am not having it." She slapped him again. The second slap was easier.

At least now the superior look was gone from his face. His eyes searched hers.

She was close enough to smell apple blossoms on his breath. "You are who you are. You are no better than the rest of them."

He spoke softly. "I am no better than anyone."

"You are a nigger!" she said. She spit the word at him, waited for him to react. He said nothing. He leaned on the shovel in his hand. "All your preaching and your praying, and telling people you talk to God. You stop it now!" She grabbed at his arm, leaving a scratch. "What god would listen to you? What god would care what you said?"

There was silence between them, only the sound of the wind lifting the leaves of the tree. Then apple blossoms, like snow, drifted down on his head. His sigh was heavy.

"You are a slave, a creature, Nat Turner. What god would listen to you?"

Nat Turner cleared his throat. "One born in a manger. One born in Bethlehem near Jerusalem. One born of generations of slaves."

Sallie was dizzy and she could not breathe. What was she doing out here with him? Why was she trying to reason with him? Then she remembered Putnam. She steadied herself. She was Putnam's mother; it was up to her to set the example for her son. She remembered what Mrs. Whitehead had taught her. Sallie planted her feet. "You let me hear of you praying again and I will beat you myself. You let me hear of you preaching and I will peel the skin off your back! No more talk about you and your freedom. All of that is behind you. All of that is over!"

Nat Turner was quiet; he did not yell as her brother would have. He looked at her as though he did not recognize her, or as though he was recognizing her for the first time.

"I am finished pampering you, Nat Turner. This life of ease is over. If I have to, I will be the one to bring you to your knees!"

chapter 12

Spring melted into summer like sugar into water. Now, everything was sticky. Blazing. July. Bees humming, green grass carpets. Morning butterflies danced from blade to blade. Sallie lifted her hand above her eyes to shield them, blond sunshine on her hair and face. The day was hot already; her dress clung to her arms, wrapped around her legs. Even the ground beneath her feet felt hot. She looked for shade.

At Parker's Field most of the folks were already settled into comfortable conversations, having claimed whatever cool there was to find, catching up on news of distant relatives or talking about Fourth of Julys past. Apple brandy had already convinced some of the men to remove their ties and coats, had even convinced some of the women to take off their bonnets and let down their hair.

Others, like Sallie and her family, were just arriving, though judging by the aroma, the pigs had been cooking since late last night. The pork's aroma, mingled with the smell of the sweet, smoky, smoldering applewood that covered the meat, was drifting through the air while smoke puffed up, doing snake dances, above the four pits.

Thomas Pettigrew, the traveling butcher, was there all the way from Petersburg. As in years past, he had been paid to dress the hogs; he only came this distance for a price. Even in front of husbands, he looked the women up and down as they passed by in pastel gowns.

The Grays, the Trezvants, the Parkers, and the Barrows—the wealthy families of the community—had each supplied a pig. The Whiteheads, who aspired to wealth and were known for great hospitality, provided fried chicken, sweet cakes, and the tea cakes for which they were well known. The Drewrys provided lemonade "from fresh squeezed lemons brought from Washington City." Those families, along with the Cobbs and Blounts, had cloistered themselves under a large oak tree not far from the makeshift stand from which the orators would speak.

Sallie found a passable place under an apple tree. Her family would be able to see the games in the middle of the field and hear all the speakers, if they spoke loudly enough. She grabbed quilts to lay down for her family while Joseph grabbed the large kettle of beans that was her family's contribution to the Fourth of July feast. She looked at the budding apples above her. It was too soon, but still she looked for the first one, the first brave apple to show its color.

Over half of Cross Keys and Jerusalem must be here. There had to be almost a hundred people. Women, wearing yellow, blue, and pink dresses, looked like bouquets sprouting from the ground. There were faces she hadn't seen in months; she waved and nodded. She looked about to see which families had newborns. The farms were so far apart, they might not see one another for seasons, or even a year, at a time; a sort of friendly nosiness was necessary to hold the community together. Putnam and Joel Westbrook, their boarder, ran to join the other boys who were beginning a sack race.

Elizabeth Turner waved from across the way, sitting on a quilt with her best friend, Sarah Newsom. Salathiel was there, the fawning Red Nelson by his side. Levi Waller was already stumbling, thrown off balance by the brandy in his hand. Sallie waved to Waller's wife, sitting across the field with her own children and some of the students she taught. Poor dear had to make up with her school what her intemperate husband drank away. She managed so well, Mrs. Waller, despite all the time Levi spent at his still, and now people said he was trying his hand at corn whiskey. Sallie nodded to the Williamses and the Vaughans. The widow Thomas, with her son George and her other children, sat on the other side of the field with the Mahones.

Men under a nearby tree made bets on the sack races. When

one man's choice lost, he swore and kicked the earth. "You have my word," he said to another man. "Tomorrow, I will deliver you my slave." Another drink. "Here, let's bet one more."

Before noon, the program began with a tribute to womanhood by Samuel Hines. "How lovely are the women of Southampton County! Their beauty is known throughout our fair state. Our women are as pure in thought as angels. To know her is to love her!" The people clapped and celebrated their agreement with an apple brandy toast. Hines's tribute was followed by a song sung by Margaret Whitehead, the daughter her family called Peggy. One of the Waller boys played a banjo to accompany her as she sang,

> Come, haste to the wedding, ye friends and ye neighbors,
> The lovers their bliss can no longer delay;
> Forget all your sorrows, your cares and your labors,
> And let every heart beat with rapture to-day . . .

Sallie, fanning herself with a white cloth, leaned to whisper to Joseph, "She's a beauty. Caty's going to have her hands full fending off the suitors."

Joseph laughed. "A beauty she may be, but thank goodness for droning bees that drown out what she sings." He chuckled as he leaned back to rest his head on Sallie's lap. She laughed as some men nearby began to sing the "Zip Coon" song.

There were plates heaped with food. There was coffee, pickles, fried chicken, pork, beans, apple pie, strawberries, and fresh cream. Dancing and smiles, salutes to Washington and Jefferson.

Men mounted the stage, papers in hand and hands on hearts. Parkers, Edwardses, Newsoms, and Grays. Trezvants, Turners, and maybe someday a Francis would speak. The Declaration of Independence and "The Star-Spangled Banner."

Sallie stood with the others as people shouted their approval and lifted their cups. Even her Joseph's face was flushed with pleasure. She looked around the field at her family, her friends, at all the faces that were so familiar. She took Joseph's hand and squeezed. There was no place, no nation where she would rather be. She thought of all the young men in uniform and the veterans around her who had lost limbs, and of those who had died to protect their liberty. She looked at her son and wondered if someday he would be called to serve.

O! say can you see by the dawn's early light,
What so proudly we hailed at the twilight's last gleaming . . .

It was difficult to fight the land, to try to raise a family on not enough. But listening to the words, listening to the voices—even the ones singing off tune—looking at the people, at the beauty of the land, Sallie was overwhelmed with gratitude.

As she sang, as she danced, Sallie felt her hair and her heart loosening. She skipped and her dress brushed the grass. Joseph stomped his feet, clapped his hands, and hooted with joy as he watched her with the other women. They were brazen enough, joyous enough not to care about flashing their ankles. "Yankee Doodle." How was it that she ever felt separate or unwanted by these women? They were her sisters. They shared a heritage as sure as the blood she shared with her own brothers and sisters.

"Let us remember South Carolina!" Some of the people stood again to cheer. It was Richard Whitehead speaking now. "Let us stand with them as they defend a state's rights! When one of us is not free, then none of us is free!" The people applauded.

"God is with us. He is always with the oppressed." Reverend Whitehead lifted a Bible that he carried in his hand. Some of the men shouted their agreement. Sallie looked at Joseph as he nodded his head. Putnam had come to join them. He smiled at her then looked at his stepfather with adoring eyes.

"Pray that God will confound those who would try to steal our wealth and our property," Richard Whitehead's voice thundered. "Lord, break the arm of the wicked man!" Men and boys whistled and stamped—Joseph, Putnam, and Joel jumped in the air throwing their fists toward the sky.

The sun rose, crested, and slowly began its descent, as though it did not want to fade, to the rhythm of more speeches and songs. Apply brandy then corn liquor, straight to the head, a flag and a banjo, a peach-colored baby dripping ice cream and curls.

By dusk, the adults were too stuffed to move, but the children played racing games and chase the hoop until James Trezvant called the crowd to order. He lit a pine knot torch. Others lit theirs and they began the march to Cabin Pond. Stark moonlight waving on black water, and white flashes against the midnight sky. Sallie was breathless; she pressed her hands to her chest. She sang softly, white fireworks splashing overhead, with those around her.

> Now it catches the gleam of the morning's first beam,
> In full glory reflected now shines on the stream . . .

Sallie looked on and imagined gold stars, blue stars, green stars, red stars falling out over the water. Why did she ever worry about what she didn't have when she had so much? She breathed in the freedom, the joy, the hope.

> 'Tis the star-spangled banner, O! long may it wave
> O'er the land of the free and the home of the brave.

STUFFED AND SUNBAKED, her family reached their farm by moonlight. It was late, but Sallie imagined Nat and Hark, already in from the fields, were hungry. She had left nothing for them to eat. When her family was settled, Sallie lingered in the kitchen. The romance of the fireworks and speeches was still in her heart and her face was still warm from the joy and apple brandy. She swayed from side to side as she dipped leftover beans from the kettle. She added two small bits of pork as a treat. When she called for the slaves, only Hark came. "Where is Nat Turner?"

Hark waved his hand toward the barn. "Not feeling well," he said, taking the pan.

Not feeling well? Still breathless, Sallie brushed the hair away from her forehead. Concern for Nat Turner mixed with the afterglow of the Independence Day celebration and it was hard to tell which was which. "Do I need to tend to him? Do you think he's going to be all right?"

Hark nodded. "Yes, ma'am." He turned and walked back toward the dark barn.

"Do I need to check on him?" she called after him.

Hark shook his head.

"Don't you boys forget to bring back my pan." She heard Hark respond from near the barn.

Nat Turner's trips to the house with Hark to get food had been infrequent since their disagreement in the apple orchard; since she made it clear to him that she was the mistress. He might not be sick at all. He might simply be pouting. Sallie turned back toward the house and stepped inside the kitchen.

What difference did it make if Nat Turner was angry with her? What difference did it make if a slave was displeased? She was the mistress and he was her property, Putnam's property. They were entitled to life, liberty, and to maintain their property. She wasn't Nat Turner's slave; she was the mistress and Putnam would be master. It wouldn't have come to all this if she had established that fact long ago, and if old Benjamin Turner had set things right with the boy from the beginning. But she hadn't done it, neither had Old Ben, and now Nat Turner was beside himself, bucking and sulking.

She was not his friend, she was his mistress. If relations between them had to be unpleasant, then for Putnam's sake, that's the way it would be. Sallie blew out the lamp, grabbed a candle, and made her way upstairs. She had to break Nat Turner for Putnam's sake and for Nat Turner's own good. She was determined; she would do whatever was required.

chapter 13

July 17, 1831

Her fan only stirred hot air. On Sunday, Sallie sat next to her husband on their usual pew in Turner's Meeting Place. Outside, the darkies sang. Most likely Yellow Nelson was preaching—Nat had been forbidden. She tried to focus on Richard Whitehead, but the music outside called her, reminding her of the Whiteheads' cotton fields, the fireworks on Cabin Pond. She had not stopped dreaming about the Fourth of July and the sisterhood she'd felt.

> Am I a soldier of the cross,
> A follower of the Lamb?

Sallie strained to listen. She did not recognize the leader's voice. Instead of singing, he rendered the words like a great orator.

> Must I be carried to the skies
> On flowery beds of ease . . .

The other voices followed, elaborating as they sang, repeating the leader's words.

> Are there no foes for me to face?
> Must I not stem the flood?

Sallie turned her head toward the open window. She still did not recognize the leader's voice.

Sure I must fight if I would reign;
Increase my courage, Lord. . . .

Joseph, Putnam, and Joel turned to look. She noticed other people's heads turning toward the window.

Darkies outside were shouting now. She imagined them jerking their bodies and whirling about. She liked the singing, but the frenzy troubled her, frightened her, like they were lunatics or tortured by some unseen hand. The leader's voice calling loud, the others responding.

The rabble outside was so great, all eyes turned toward the window. Richard Whitehead slammed his Bible shut and stepped down from the pulpit. Red-faced, he strode to the window. His mouth dropped open. He shook his fist and yelled, "It is the scoundrel, Nat Turner!"

chapter 14

Sallie's brother Nathaniel led the group of men as they stormed from the church, pushing through the darkies. They rested on the church steps, crowding the church house door, facing away from the church and toward Nat Turner, enthralled by him. The other slaves scattered, but Nat Turner would not move. "'They have cast lots for my people; and have given a boy for an harlot, and sold a girl for wine, that they might drink.' Can't you see that we are your brothers?"

Her brothers and the other men moved toward him. Nat Turner continued as he stood his ground. "'. . . Love your neighbor'"—he swept his arm toward the black people behind him—"'as yourself.'" He pointed toward the sky. "God is watching. He sees what you have done. You have stolen freedom, you have stolen property, and you have stolen and sold God's people!" Nat Turner glared at the group coming toward him.

How could Nat Turner embarrass her this way? After all she had done for him! He had no respect. What was he trying to prove? Her knees weakened, heart pounded.

"You know the law and you have been warned. 'If a man be found stealing any of his brethren of the children of Israel, and maketh merchandise of him, or selleth him; then that thief shall die; and thou shalt put evil away from among you.'" Nat Turner pointed at the group. He looked at Sallie, at Joseph, and at those standing behind the group that approached him. "You have not put evil away from among you. You have held them to your bosom. They preach to you. You choose them as leaders even knowing they are wrong. You count their blood and their friendship more important than God's word. How can you call the evil that you do good? How can you pretend this evil is God's will?" Sweat poured from his forehead.

Her brother Nathaniel had been right. He told her that she would have to get Nat Turner in hand! What were Caty Whitehead and the other women thinking of this? Sallie looked around to see who was watching her.

Nathaniel Francis shook his fist at Nat Turner. "Who are you, a nigger, a lunatic, to preach to us? You think you can speak to me this way? You are forbidden to be here! My sister gave you an order. You forget we are your masters."

Nat Turner stared at them; still preaching, still railing, he did not flinch. "How can you see the suffering of your brothers and sisters and turn away? Your sacrifices, your sacraments are an abomination to the Lord!"

"You are a fanatic!" shouted Salathiel, beet-red and spitting.

Nat Turner continued to preach. "'Behold, I will raise them out of the place whither ye have sold them, and will return your recompense upon your own head: And I will sell your sons and your daughters . . . to a people far off: for the LORD hath spoken it.'

"You heap trouble on yourselves! Your proud hearts are an abomination to the Lord! You stink of arrogance, the pride that goeth before destruction! You choose the best for yourselves and force the least on others—a false balance is an abomination to the Lord!"

The blood rushed in her ears, to her head. Sallie was sure she would faint. She should have listened to her brother.

Nathaniel Francis stepped closer, Salathiel behind him, until he and Nat Turner were face-to-face. Though much shorter, Nat Turner would not budge. "I told you this day would come," Nathaniel told him. "I told you the day would come when you would die!"

Nat Turner stared him in the eye. "We are brothers! God is tired of your wickedness. Wake up, time is running out!"

"You crazy loon!" Salathiel hooted.

Sallie looked to her husband, Joseph, but he stood shaking, frozen in his tracks. Perhaps if she could say something . . . maybe there was still a way around it. A way to make it all stop.

Salathiel nodded his head and clapped his hands. "This is your day of reckoning, Nat Turner!" He motioned to Putnam. "Come over here, boy, and pay attention."

Nathaniel looked at Sallie. He had warned her. He looked back at Nat Turner. "You are out of your place. You are a slave like all the rest." Sallie heard her mother behind her. *A shame, a family disgrace, a public spectacle like this.*

Nat Turner continued ranting. "An army is assembling! The terrible day is at hand! I've come to warn you. My brothers and sisters, repent! The Day of Judgment is at hand! 'Put ye in the sickle, for the harvest is ripe: come, get you down; for the press is full, the fats overflow; for their wickedness is great.'"

Why wouldn't he shut up? Did he want to die? Reverend Whitehead joined Salathiel and Nathaniel. He had a coiled whip dangling in his hand. "You know all about wickedness, don't you, boy? You dare desecrate this house, you heathen?" Sallie looked at Joseph, who grimaced, staring silently at the three men before him, still frozen.

Nat Turner looked at Reverend Whitehead calmly. "This is my Father's house. It was my Father Who built it." Sallie looked at the other darkies who had backed away, fear and panic on their faces. Some of them, like auntie Easter, were crying. Nat was still talking. "All you do here is built on lies! Repent, before it is too late!" Nat quoted: "'Multitudes, multitudes in the valley of decision: for the day of the LORD is near in the valley of decision. The sun and the moon shall be darkened, and the stars shall withdraw their shining.'"

Richard Whitehead uncoiled the whip. "You dare to preach to me? To teach me? Remember your place, nigger!" The whip was a fancy one with an etched grip and a tip that divided into three tails.

"No, you have never known your place. Pampered." He spat on the ground. "You don't know who you are."

"What does 'pampered' mean? That I was free, that I was treated as human?" Nat Turner looked at Richard Whitehead as though he were his equal. He was crazy! "You are no priest, and no clerical collar, no title, and no diploma will make you one. You know all the rules, the law, but it is all whitewash. You hold others to account, but not yourself. Your faith is useless because you have no love."

"Shut up! You shut up!" her brother Nathaniel raged. Spit flew from his mouth. His eyes bulged. Joseph took a step forward, then stopped, frozen, again.

Why couldn't Nat Turner stop? Perhaps her brothers were right, maybe he was insane. "I know who I am," Nat Turner said. "I am a child of God and this is my Father's house."

Nathaniel was leering at him. "You think because you can read that you are the equal of a white man. You will know this day who is your master."

She wanted him to run, she prayed for him to back down, but Nat Turner kept talking.

"You have grown up not to be a man, Richard, but a whore of the world. You and yours, to get the best steal from the least. You turn corn into whiskey while all around you men, women, and children starve for the corn they've grown."

Sallie stepped toward them. There had to be some way she could calm all of this! Nathaniel and Salathiel grabbed Nat Turner's arms and dragged him to the church. They pinned his hands against the walls.

There must be words she could speak!

Nathaniel pushed his face close to Nat Turner's. "When you ran away before, boy, you should have kept running! You'll wish you'd never come back!" Richard Whitehead flicked the whip in his hand.

She did not want him to die. Sallie looked at the people

around her. They wanted him to behave and think like a man. But Nat Turner was like a child, he was smart but he was a slave, and he did not understand. And they would not understand if she intervened. Putnam looked to Joseph, both of them staring, their eyes wide like they were viewing a nightmare.

She shook her head. It was as Caty Whitehead said, Nat Turner was property. He was wrong and he had to be broken, he had to learn.

When her first husband died, Nat Turner had been all she and Putnam had. But she could not think about that now. He was a slave. He was property and he had forgotten his place. For Putnam's sake, he had to learn.

They ripped off his shirt. She looked at him, at the old scars on his back from where Samuel Turner had beaten him before. His arms stretched out, he looked so very small.

Richard Whitehead removed his coat and Jacob Williams held it for him. Her brother Nathaniel nodded to the minister. "Teach the black devil the will of God! Whip the skin off of him!" He nodded to the crowd of whites. "When you tire, I'll take hold."

Nat Turner shouted from where they held him. "I warn you! The sun and the moon shall be darkened, the stars shall withdraw their shining!"

"You, my friend, are a superstitious fool." Richard Whitehead flicked the whip again, testing it. "It's a new one, but you'll help me break it in." The reverend judged the distance it would take to cut just so and made his stance. "'And that servant, which knew his lord's will, and prepared not himself, neither did according to his will, shall be beaten with many stripes.'" He flicked the whip, testing it. "Luke 12:47."

Nat Turner spoke through gritting teeth, preparing for the first blow. "I call no man 'lord.' I only have one master!"

Whitehead drew back the whip. It cracked in the air and when it returned left a bright red stripe across Nat Turner's back. "Be prideful if you want. This is only the beginning." He popped the whip again; this time the barbed tip of the whip tore away flesh. The reverend repeated the Scripture he had quoted. "'And that servant, which knew his lord's will, and prepared not himself, neither did according to his will, shall be beaten with many stripes.' Luke 12:47."

"...I call no man 'lord,'" Nat Turner repeated as the whip made another stripe on his back. "...only one master."

Salathiel snickered. "Maybe he's thinking of my sister."

Sallie felt ashamed. All of this was her fault. All of this was because she had failed to keep Nat Turner in line.

Richard Whitehead laughed. "All right then. 'And that servant, which knew his lord's will, and prepared not himself, neither did according to *her* will, shall be beaten with many stripes.'" He struck Nat Turner again. "Luke 12:47."

Nat Turner gasped for air now. His lungs moved in and out like bellows. His small frame shook. "...no man 'lord.'"

"You are a rebellious, disobedient devil!"

A voice shouted from the crowd of slaves. "Rebellion to tyrants is obedience to God!"

"Yell again, and you'll bleed with him!" Richard Whitehead yelled to the slaves, and then called Putnam to him. Putnam stood stiffly, his knees shaking, his eyes still questioning Joseph. "Stand beside me, young man, and pay close attention. We are helping him, ridding him of confusion." He shook the whip and spoke to Nat Turner. "Are you bold enough to say this boy is not your master?"

"He is not!"

Richard Whitehead lashed out with the snake in his hand. Blood soaked Nat Turner's pants. Richard Whitehead nodded at Sallie. "Are you ungrateful enough to say this woman is not your master?"

He was panting. "...no master but God."

Sallie took a step closer. If she didn't step in he would die.

His chest heaved. "...no woman 'lord.'" He shook his head. "...one master."

Sallie froze in place. Her brothers had been right; Nat Turner was stubborn and disobedient. Maybe he deserved to die! Nathaniel and Salathiel looked at her, nodding. She felt her mother watching her. He was a slave . . . and a fool, and if she did not bring him in line he would drag all of them down.

Richard Whitehead gave him three more lashes, the whip running red.

". . . my Father's house," Nat Turner gasped.

Richard Whitehead slid his hand down the whip, from hilt to tip, to squeeze away blood and flesh that had collected in the leather braid. He taunted Nat Turner. "Come on, now, Nat. Is it worth all this?" He raised the whip. He hit again. Again. Again.

Warm blood splattered on Sallie's face, on the bodice of her dress. Putnam looked bewildered. Nat Turner had held him, fed him, and bounced him on his knee. She would have to show Putnam the way. Nat Turner was not a man. She would have to correct things, even if it meant Nat had to be killed. Nat Turner was not his equal. Putnam was master. She wiped her face, then stepped toward Richard Whitehead and held out her hand.

She was not Nat Turner's friend, she was his mistress. Sallie lifted the whip. It was heavier than she had imagined and felt alive in her hand, coiling and uncoiling. Her stomach knotted. She fought panic. It was man's work, but it needed to be done. Sometimes men's work was left to women.

Sallie stepped closer so that she would not have to cast far. She repeated the phrase Richard Whitehead quoted. "'And that servant, which knew his lord's will, and prepared not himself, neither did according to his will, shall be beaten with many stripes.'" The muscles pulled in her back when she cast her arm overhead. Once the whip struck, it bit and sliced his flesh with a will of its own. "Luke 12:47." She willed herself not to stumble and faint. Stars and stripes. She thought she heard Nat Turner weeping. ". . . my Father's house," he shouted. "No master. No right! Free man . . . my house!"

Sallie willed herself not to feel. He was a fanatic just as her brother had said. He was the slave. She was the mistress. She lost track of how many times she hit him.

Finally, Nat Turner slumped against the wall. ". . . my Father's house!" Then his head drooped and his body sagged to the ground.

chapter 15

On the third Sunday in August, a blinding hot day, when she and her family had returned from church, she waved them on ahead. "Go on inside. Dinner's in the oven." Sallie headed first to the barn.

She had been sick in her heart since that Sunday in July. It didn't matter what people—including her brothers—said. She had not been able to sleep since it happened. Her heart was knotted, food lodged in her throat. When Sallie stepped into the barn it was quiet, except for the cooing of pigeons. It was cool inside. "Nat Turner." She called his name several times but there was no answer.

Sallie headed toward the orchard and walked among the trees. Hark had looked after Nat Turner, nursed the wounds on his back. She had sent out bandages and received the speckled pan back, water pink with blood. It had been almost two weeks before he was able to hobble around, and that was a miracle.

Brothers and sisters! The terrible day is at hand! Nat Turner's words from that Sunday still troubled her. She had known him all her life. When there was no one else to help her and Putnam, when the women made her cry, made her feel unwanted, it was Nat Turner who comforted her.

Sallie walked under a Jonathan apple tree, the smell sweet and tart. She could taste it in her mouth. She closed her eyes, opened them, and then there it was before her. It was too soon, but there it was, the first red apple. She reached and plucked it, then rubbed it on her skirt. She bit into it, crisp and juicy, and then she swallowed. She smiled, satisfied, and made her way back to the house. She would find Nat Turner later.

* * *

SHE HADN'T LOOKED for him again. Sallie put on her night-gown and she snuggled in next to her husband. She had not told Joseph about the first apple. She had not told anyone. Sallie kissed her husband on the cheek, then, turning over, she sighed. Through the window, she saw the moon and stars hanging in the sky like jewels.

She should have found Nat Turner. She should have kept looking until she found him. She was sick thinking of what had happened that Sunday in July. Sick, even if he was disobedient, about what happened. She had been thinking she should make it right. How could God be happy about any of this? So many tears. So much heartbreak.

Keeping Nat Turner was never going to make them rich, never going to make them more than they were. Maybe Nat Turner was right. Maybe in the end Putnam would give him what he wanted: his freedom. She would talk to her son about it. Maybe they should free the darkies, all of them.

People like her were never going to catch up with the wealthy ones—owning slaves they couldn't afford wouldn't change things. She and the others like her were dirt farmers; poor, honest people living off what the land could give. "Peasants"—that's what the wealthy people called them behind their backs, sometimes "white trash." They, and their children, would probably never have much more than the jewels in the sky, than the earth they planted, and the waters of Cabin Pond. Wasn't that enough?

She would tell Nat Turner, when she found him, about the apple. It would be their secret; something he would understand. She would tell him the thought she'd had, about there always being a first.

She would tell him that she was his friend. She would tell him she was sorry.

Maybe when no one was around, she would have Nat Turner teach her son to read. If Nat Turner could teach him, maybe

Putnam could become a lawyer and make a new life, a better life.

She should have searched for Nat Turner, Sallie thought. Then she laid her head upon her pillow.

SALLIE OPENED HER eyes in the darkness.

A flash of silver in the moonlight.

Will

chapter 16

Prophet?

WILL HEARD THE bell that called him and the other slaves to rise. As he readied himself, a wolf howled in the darkness. Will looked in its direction, and then in the direction of the farm where the slave called Nat Turner lived near Cabin Pond. He had seen Turner many times, sometimes on Sundays, most times a long way off. But Will's eyesight was keen. Even from a distance he knew Nat Turner. He recognized the knock-kneed gait. Nat was small and thin; the plow looked like more than he could handle. But Nat never gave up. It was obvious who he was; he was just like his father.

Prophet? More likely a coward. Church boy. Circus monkey reading for white folks too trifling to learn.

Nat Turner. Will spat and then reached for the pine knot torch in front of him. He secured it in the ground so that he could see without its tipping over. He knelt behind the waiting horse and then set to filing the hoof he gripped between his knees.

They let Nat Turner have two names. Not two full names, like white men—not Nathaniel Turner, but Nat Turner, like a compromise. *You don't tell who your daddy is and we'll give you two names.*

He was Turner's boy. That's who he would always be. No matter who he belonged to, no matter the name of the family that owned him, he was Turner's boy.

When Old Ben Turner died, his boy Nat became the property

of his brother, Turner's oldest son, Samuel. When Turner's knock-kneed son, Samuel, died, his wife, Elizabeth, sold Old Turner's boy to Benjamin Moore, but he was still Turner's boy. When Benjamin Moore died, Old Turner's boy became the property of Moore's schoolboy son, Putnam (though he really fell into the hands of Putnam's mother, Sallie Francis Moore). Nat Turner had fallen into a lot of hands, but he would always be Old Turner's boy.

Two names, but he would never be Old Turner's son.

Will had one name, just like the horse whose hoof he filed. The horse was Jetty. He was Will. He looked across the field in the direction of Travis's farm. Nat Turner was probably eating now—cornmeal mush and a biscuit, maybe a piece of fatback—preparing to work the fields. He was not strong enough to do it, but Turner's boy would do it anyway. Two names, preacher, field hand, prophet—whatever he was, he was still a slave.

Owned. Just like the horse. High yellow. Neither one or the other.

Will pressed the weight of his shoulders onto the file and ground it back and forth on the horse's hoof. He closed his eyes and tried to forget. Back and forth with his eyes closed. He could feel the specks, gritty like sand, flying off, landing on his sweaty wrists and forearms.

He felt the cut before he saw it. He smiled. It was too early for the blood that welled up at the slit in his arm to be red. It was more like melted chocolate he had seen one time. He dipped a finger in and tasted the salt and grit.

Will looked at the sky. The sun hadn't shone yet. There was still time, still early enough, that he could hope. Early enough to hope for a cloudy day, a rainy day, a snowy day—a dark day that would leave the trees and bushes, the fields, and even his blood the color of death. Will turned his head to look in the other direction to see the house of his master, Nathaniel Francis.

One day there was going to be blood. One day he was going to put in the sickle and reap the harvest. One day, the sun wouldn't rise and he would kill the boy, Nathaniel Francis, and his wife. Only twenty-three years old and he was running people's lives, ruining people's lives.

He would kill them—Nathaniel Francis and his wife—before they had babies, and when he killed them in the day without sun, he would rub their lifeless blood over his face, over his shoulders and arms, and across his chest. Then, he would be alive again. When they couldn't feel anymore, then he would feel again. He would draw their last breaths into his lungs and breathe again and see again as he stared into their lifeless eyes.

He would not use darkness to run away. Freedom would deny him what only slavery could offer. They were fools enough to believe that black men shouldn't be free and fools enough to believe that black people didn't know better. Horses knew better. Dogs knew better. Slaves knew they were meant to be free. But he didn't want freedom now.

He had seen enough of white freedom, convenient freedom, freedom at the expense of others. He had found his father-in-law's freedom deep in the woods. When they were finished with the old man, after he had built their houses and sired their next generation of slaves, after he had tended their farms, after his body was broken and aching, after his eyes were blind, they gave him his freedom. They carried him into the woods to sit in his own filth. They put a wood covering over him that they called a shed, to assuage their guilt, and left him there to starve. He sat there, overwhelmed with their generosity, crying because of their kindness, until finally, covered with sores, crawling with lice and maggots, he gasped and died alone.

Will had seen the freedom up close, dead and putrid. It was a freedom that made slaves afraid to run, afraid to be disobedient for fear that they would be abandoned to the woods to become meat for wolves and vermin.

When he had found his father-in-law's freedom, he had hidden it away so his wife would not find it. Her own dreams of her father's freedom, of him walking on free land, had kept her strong. Only he knew where the white man's promise of freedom was buried.

Will didn't want freedom. How could there ever be freedom when all he had loved was gone? How could he be free without them?

He wanted death and blood. He would be close enough, because of slavery, on that dark day, to watch life leave their eyes. Will was sure the day would come. White men were too greedy, too proud, and too arrogant to repent, especially at the word of a black man, no matter how white Nat Turner was.

Will would not rest until he killed the young thief. Then he would find the ones that Nathaniel Francis had stolen from him.

Will pressed the blade harder. Harder. Harder, until the horse sidestepped to pull away, but Will held its hoof fast between his knees.

When she was still with him, he had held his little daughter up so that she could rub her small hands across the horse's muzzle. He had no money, no clothes, no food to give her. But he had shown her that she could take pleasure in small things, like the smoothness of a horse's coat, or the gentle patience in a horse's stare. There were even stars and wildflowers—orange ones and white ones—that not even slavery could keep from them. His daughter and his wife had been like white man's brandy, they had pacified him. Her tiny nose against the horse's neck. He had loved the horse once, but now that his daughter was gone, its pain suited him better.

He wanted pain. He wanted vengeance. More than freedom, he wanted blood. That was why he still went to church, why he sat outside in the sun or stood in the rain. He didn't go to hear the words of the fools, fools who hadn't lost anyone, telling him to turn the other cheek or forgive his enemies. Those words left him cold.

He endured the service so that he could flush alive when he heard the true words, like *vengeance*. He would kill *everything that pisseth against the wall.*

Nathaniel Francis, all of them, had taken the last thing from him that mattered. They had murdered his family, his heart, when they stole them away. He could not be free without them. No one came to pay condolences. But that was not enough. Now they expected him to pretend that he did not feel, that he did not care. He was not supposed to weep.

So, he did not. He died and he would kill them before he could live again. He memorized the words about vengeance and murder and blood. He dreamed the words. *Beat your plowshares into swords and your pruninghooks into spears . . .* He would use the words, he would speak the holy, bloody words over their dead bodies. One day. Where his little daughter had once been, he now kept his axe.

The horse turned and looked over its haunches at him in a slow, knowing way, as though the beast read his thoughts but did not judge them. Jetty blinked and slowly whipped her tail. Will patted her rump, released her hoof, and then bent to gently rest her other rear hoof between his knees. He looked across the fields toward the place where Nat Turner lived. They could call him what they liked—prophet, preacher, Turner's boy—he was still just a slave. Currying favor, not man enough to fight.

Will looked at the sky, still early—the overseer Henry Doyle had not come yet—and prayed that daylight would not come. He prayed for the dark day that would set him free.

chapter 17

Daybreak had come and he had worked another day. He had suffered being kicked and bruised. He had silently endured being cursed. Another night had come. He was biding his time.

Will burrowed into the straw, covering himself to keep away the cold. Earlier he had sat around the fire, watching the other slaves.

The Southampton night was black and cold around them. Not the kind of night that hides lovers, but the kind that makes strangers gather—even if they are afraid of one another—around the fire. They gathered as lambs and lions are forced to draw together at the same water. They huddled against the frost and the darkness, against the things that watched with hungry eyes.

Dred was there and Sam—both friends of Prophet Nat. The women were there and two boys, Nathan and Tom. Closest to the fire was a boy, maybe of nine years, who leaned on a stick propped under his arm. He had no coat or shoes, just like the others. His shirt and pants, the only ones he had, were ragged. Every move and sound caused him to jump. He looked at the shadows beyond the campfire as though he might be safer there, but he didn't leave.

Will knew most men would do anything to find a way to avoid the darkness. They made candles and lamps. They cut down trees. They would dig for coal and oil at the risk of their own lives. But still they could not keep the darkness away. They huddled together, waiting for daylight; but he was disappointed each day the light came.

He stared across the fire at the crippled boy. He had been born headfirst attached by his ankle to the one that followed. Will remembered the moaning and screaming. When the midwife shrieked, the baby had screamed, still attached to the one inside. They shared a foot in common. The midwife sent for the boys' master, who came and settled the matter with his axe; and so Two Feet, whose real name was Davy, came into the world with the extra stump of his brother's leg on his right one. His brother, Foot, followed, his left leg just a bloody stump. Davy's right pants leg was always pulled tight; it was his misfortune to enter the world with too much. Foot did not live; he had come into the world with too little.

Davy lost his mother and his brother the night he was born and wore his loss on his face, especially in his eyes. Nathaniel Francis took pleasure in reminding the boy, Two Feet, that it was his axe that had saved him, that he had lost property saving his life.

Sparks drifted from the fire. Will watched the haunted boy. Most likely, he would never leave. If he ran into the darkness, the wolves or the bears would eat him, he had been told—if the patrollers didn't get him first. If he or others ran to the water they would drown; Nathaniel Francis told them darkies could not swim. Better to stay put and slowly die—die by the inches—from too much work, too little food, too little sleep, and no shelter. Who else would be as good to them as Nathaniel Francis?

But the truth was, like them, Nathaniel Francis had never seen the ocean. It washed up on the banks of the Eastern Shore, he had heard men say. But Francis had not been there. He had no time and no money to get to Norfolk. Like the crippled boy, Nathaniel was probably afraid to journey much beyond Jerusalem.

Will had not been a cruel boy. His father had been a freeman of Northampton County, a third-generation landowner who remembered when his own grandfather could vote, could stand before a court, testify, and make suit. He remembered when a free black man could call the sheriff—when a black man could have indentured servants. But gradually, then more swiftly, things had changed. White planters and traders felt pressure from other whites to no longer buy and sell to him. "We must think of our own families," those that had once been his friends had told his father. In time his father had fallen into debt.

First the creditors took the land, and then his father signed away his own freedom in return for a promise that his family would be spared. But slavery encroached, devoured them one by one like a fungus. His mother was next. She had left his sister in his care. But he was just a boy and soon the fungus was on both of them until they were all forced into slavery.

Their past lives as a family in their little house, sitting by the fire, father and son hunting together, a mother who scrubbed his clothes, cooked his meals, and told him to comb his hair were all erased as though they had never existed. All he had ever been was what he was now.

The cold air froze his lips and burned the inside of his nose. He heard and smelled the horses in the stalls next to him. He heard rats scurrying in the rafters overhead. Will dug his feet, cracked and bleeding from the cold, farther into the straw.

It was dark now and he was alone. No daughter. There were times when he saw her face so clearly and almost heard her sweet voice, almost felt the touch of her small hands. Night was hardest. At night he missed his wife. He would not allow himself to think of her during the day, to think of her on some farm or some plantation, forced to breed like a cow, with some other man, some stranger who did not love her. At night, he could not keep the thoughts away.

Pretty women were like pearls; he had thought he would never have one. His mother had been pretty, he thought, but he could not remember for sure. It was too painful losing her and he had put memories of her away.

Will knew that his gloom and contrariness, after the loss of his father, mother, and sister, were not attractive to women. But his wife had loved him anyway. She was the one good thing in his life, until she gave him a little daughter. Then there were two of them, like birds, like stars, two pearls, and he could not believe they loved him. They adored him, even his scars, and thought he was beautiful. Will was only beautiful when he was with them.

When he had been tired, when he had had his shirt ripped from his back and his pants removed so that he could be whipped, his pearls were his consolation. His pearls were his hope.

When they were alone, his wife would gently kiss his head, his shoulder, someplace that the whip had not found. "It won't be this way always, Will," she would whisper to him through his pain. "They got my freedom locked away," she would say as she touched his back tenderly with a torn wet rag. "But they sure don't have my man. It ain't a man like you in all Virginia, and that includes Mr. Jefferson himself!" In the dark, she would wrap herself around him to keep him warm. "They can beat you, tie you up, or even hang you from a tree, but they can't take away your manhood." He heard her gentle weeping. "Cowards!" She whispered the word hot enough to set the barn on fire. "Nothing they can do to take who you are away."

There was hardly a day that went by when someone wasn't whipped, hit, or beaten, or even burned. Every day everyone spent the day jumping, praying it wasn't them. Praying an impossible prayer, that it would never be anyone they loved.

But then, he learned, having a loved one beaten was better than having her taken away. Her love kept him alive. When they took his two pearls when he was out in the fields, fever had gripped him. He had prayed to die.

God had betrayed him. The church had betrayed him with all the songs about heaven. The church had sacrificed him for money, given him up so she could be popular and not have to take a stand. The church sacrificed his family to keep white people in the pews. Where was the One Who was supposed to fight for the poor? Where was the One Who was supposed to keep him, his wife, and child from evil? Where was God the Protector in all of this? Where was God the Avenger?

Will believed in God, but that only made his anger worse. He believed in God but Will no longer trusted Him. Will had belief but had lost his faith. There was no preacher he could look to for comfort—the white preacher mocked him and wielded a whip, and black preachers like Nat Turner were weak, no power. There was no God looking out for Will and other black men.

Now it was hate and dreams of vengeance that kept him alive. Nathaniel Francis, a cruel, nasty boy, had stolen his freedom, then he had stolen Will's pearls, the joy, from his life. Francis had stolen what was Will's and sold them away. Had sold his heart.

A day of darkness would come. Let it be tomorrow, Will prayed out of habit. He would kill them all.

chapter 18

Soft, quiet snow was dusted around him. Will sliced through the bark of the tree as if it were skin and kept his face blank, his eyes dead, and his ears low so Nathaniel Francis and the other white men would continue to ignore him even though he was no farther from them than the height of two men.

Still waiting. Still cold.

It was February and the sun had darkened two days ago, an eclipse. He had grabbed his axe thinking it was the time. Will had gone to the barn to prepare himself, sharpened his axe. He had walked toward the rear door of the Francis house, placed his foot on the back step, and then, just as suddenly as it had darkened, the sun had returned.

His time had not come yet.

He drew back the blade, feeling the weight of his axe in his arms and shoulders, feeling the pull of the muscles in his stomach, and then he let the axe drop, hacking into the flesh of the tree. He was cutting wood to warm Nathaniel Francis's house. Will watched them—Nathaniel Francis and his friends—watching the girl, Charlotte. Still just a girl. A pearl.

Nathaniel Francis and his friends—Reverend Whitehead, Levi Waller, Jacob Williams—swigged from a jug of corn liquor and ogled the girl, leering, drooling. She was fruit sweetened by taboo. Any child born to her they would deny, except for the coins it brought. She was pleasure for them, born of desire whispered in dark places; desire they denied, for they knew the rules. It meant the loss of everything—power and possessions. Banishment. But in the shadow of the trees, Nathaniel Francis and his friends whispered.

Have you tasted that dark plum? It is yours for the plucking.

If I could only have one slave, I would choose a girl, a young one—one who could increase my purse and warm my feet.

Will raised the axe higher and hacked again, cutting and tearing the old oak.

Maybe a dainty like our President Jefferson had—may he rest in peace—a yellow one with just a hint of spice.

One with woolly hair, an exotic thing. A safari through Africa. Then see black give birth to yellow or pink.

It soothes me as well as it fills my purse.

Will saw them, felt them, leering at the girl. They were not afraid to do it in front of him—he meant nothing to them, no more than an ox, even less. Charlotte was pretty like his little daughter. It galled him, men like these standing around, lazy men who had others do their work, leering at his little pearl.

It was a curse for a slave woman to be beautiful. Not that the woman had to be beautiful for white men—or for the black men who lowered themselves to become dogs in their masters' images—to sniff after the women, to savage them. They didn't have to be women or even girls. He knew. He had seen. And there was no shame. There was no law, no punishment, so there was no shame. They swaggered, they rutted and belched like suited boars.

They were thieves. Nothing had value or pleasure unless it was stolen.

He felt the axe calling to him, first softly, then louder, begging him to swing her now. *That one there*, she begged him. *Or the one next to him.* She could take all of them and rid the world of their foul, rabid smell. Stop them from infecting others.

Will hacked again at the tree and fought against the axe that begged him to avenge his wife, his little daughter, the girl Charlotte, the boy Davy, and all the others who had no names, all the ones stolen by beasts masquerading as men.

But now was not the time. Now was too soon: if he did it now he would leave others alive, too many others. He willed himself to wait. He fought against the axe. He fought, his muscles straining, to force the blade to the tree. Will raised his axe again. He would wait for the darkness he had been promised would come.

chapter 19

Will swatted at the mosquitoes that circled his head. Winter had passed; spring had come and gone without a sign. It was summer now. He listened to the cows lowing, moaning in the midnight heat. Summer, and still the sun continued to rise. The third of July had come and he had prayed that on the fourth the sun would not rise. But it had come anyway.

He and the others had worked in the fields, but he smelled the pigs roasting and at night he saw the white folks' fireworks in the skies—fireworks that mocked all the people they abused, all the people whom they kept in chains.

He heard them singing their songs. He had heard the songs for years.

> Hail Columbia, happy land!
> Hail, ye heroes, heav'n-born band,
> Who fought and bled in freedom's cause . . .

What made them heroes? Were they heroes because they stole and sold people? Because they raped women? Because they forced others to do their work, chained, and by them became wealthy?

WILL HAD HEARD the words so many times that he knew them by heart. He had heard the words and seen them waving their flags—red, white, and blue—dipped in the blood of all those they had slaughtered and abused. He was ready, when darkness came, to pay freedom's cost. He was ready to pay the cost to live again.

Firm, united let us be,
As a band of brothers joined . . .

There was no band of brothers to join. He looked at his axe. There was just the two of them. He knew after killing them he would die. But when they died, even if only for a moment, he would live again.

The hay stuck to the salty sweat of his body. The smell of the cow and horse dung was overwhelming. He could not sleep.

No, it was not the smell or the heat. Will looked at the axe lying beside him. It whispered to him now all the time. When it caught him sleeping, when she caught him sleeping—it had a woman's voice—she woke him. *Kill them, now! Kill them all!* His axe had lost patience; she no longer wanted to wait on a signal from heaven, she no longer wanted to wait on the sun.

He could not put her away; she could no longer stand to be apart from him. She was insistent like a nagging, clinging wife. She shrieked at him to go to work, to get to the job. She was thirsty. She was cold. Her edge could only be whetted by warm blood.

He wanted to kill them, but she wanted it even more. So, Will had prayed that the Fourth would be the day that he would get some relief. He saw the fireworks exploding. He began to hum their song softly to himself so that no one else in the barn would wake and hear.

The Fourth had come and the slaves worked, sweating, starving in the fields. They worked, worried that some drunken bet might tear a loved one away.

Immortal patriots, rise once more,
Defend your rights, defend your shore!

But the Fourth had come and gone and still there was no relief. A week passed and she would not be silent. More days, and she grew louder. She was obsessed. When nagging would not work, she tried to seduce him, promising him pleasure. She told him how strong it would make him, how powerful, how full of life. When seduction would not rouse him, she turned to guilt, reminding him of his kin and of his little girl.

> *In Heaven's we place a manly trust,*
> *That truth and justice will prevail,*
> *And every scheme of bondage fail.*

Independence Day. Will rose from the hay and, with his axe in hand, left the barn to look at the house. Almost two weeks had passed, then today at church they had beaten him, Two Names. Will had stood far off but he had seen it all—Auntie Easter crying, Nat Turner's mother crying. They had beaten Nat Turner today, beaten him and celebrated.

The moon was full tonight, veiled only by drifting clouds and the lacy shroud of blackened leaves. Silk covered him. Residue from the first corn harvest, it glistened in the moonlight.

Will stared at the dark empty windows of the Francis house. She begged him for blood. He tried to soothe her. It was Sunday night and most likely Nathaniel Francis was not home; most likely at Waller's helping him tend his still. But Sunday would pass and on another night Francis would be in his bed.

Will would do to Nathaniel Francis what had been done to him. He would first quietly kill the little boys that Nathaniel kept in exchange for board—his mind was always on money—and then Nathaniel Francis's mother. He would climb down from the loft where the mother slept and then, in silence, kill the wife. He would not wake Nathaniel Francis; he would let the warm blood from his wife's body rouse him.

Will looked at his insistent axe. He would call her Liberty. Together, the Immortal Patriots, they would finally kill Nathaniel Francis. The boy, his face torn with horror, would see with his eyes and feel in his heart and body what it felt like to be alone, to have your loved ones taken. Will would wait until he saw insanity slip into the boy's eyes and then he, then they, would loose Nathaniel Francis's head from his body.

> *Firm, united let us be,*
> *Rallying round our liberty . . .*

Will felt his hand trembling and then his arm shaking. Not yet, he whispered to Liberty. The movement traveled to his shoulder. He was losing control of her. He was losing control.

chapter 20

Will held his breath and raised the blade above his head.

He drove it with all his might into the earth and cut away the strong roots of the dandelions. Hot, the August sun overhead burned his neck and made him feel dizzy. There was no breeze. All the shiny green leaves around him were still. The hoe in one hand, he wiped his other arm across his forehead, leaving a trail of corn silk fibers on his face.

Liberty lay near his feet, still talking. *Now!* Liberty called to him.

The green cornstalks around him reached over his head and hid him from the sight of those around him, though he could still hear their voices. He liked the feeling of being lost in the corn. He stretched his arm and wrapped his hand around one of the ears. He held it gently but firmly, and felt the individual bumps of the kernels. Tomorrow, or the next day, they would be harvesting again.

He let go the ear and turned his hand back to the hoe, fighting back the weeds. It would be a good crop and he had overheard Nathaniel Francis telling his overseer, Henry Doyle, that he was going to invest some forty bushels in Waller's copper whiskey still. He expected Waller was an expert in stilling . . . and in drinking; he spent all his time there. "Waller can get four gallons of whiskey from each bushel." Money for Nathaniel's pocket, whiskey for the head, empty bellies all around.

Will knocked a worm off his hand. He turned to look behind him at Liberty and thought about his wife and about his little girl.

Heat sucked the air from his lungs. Not a leaf moved. Will looked up at the sun, at his feet. Liberty began to hum.

Immortal patriots, rise once more,
Defend your rights, defend your shore!

He looked down at her. She shouted to him, *The time is now!*

And then ...
... the sun ...
... darkened.

BEFORE HIS EYES, the sun turned from yellow to silver to blue. It darkened. Indigo. He had prayed for it but did not believe it would happen, not like this. The air around him glowed blue, blue corn, blue skin. Will dropped his spade and watched as black furuncles erupted and danced across the face of the sun.

Now! Liberty called to him. Will lifted her from the ground and then he heard them, heard their feet running up the rows.

Dred and Sam ran, spades still in their hands. *Follow them,* Liberty shouted. *Now!* She sang, not caring who heard. He followed them. Dred and Sam were younger and faster; Will slowed his pace but kept them in sight. Soon enough, he knew where they were going. They were running to meet Nat Turner.

They were heading for Cabin Pond.

chapter 21

His arm swept back green branches glowing blue. Will heard Nat Turner's voice before he stepped into the small clearing where the preacher and the others were gathered, black men, blue men. "This is not a war of revenge. We serve as soldiers of the Lord."

He was part of the Lord's army if what the Lord wanted was revenge, if He wanted death. He didn't want to hear any more preacher talk about mercy.

Almost as though he heard Will's thoughts, Nat Turner responded. "We will give no mercy to those who have shown none. Kill all those whose feet walk upon the ground, who say they are His children but mock the truth of God, those who tell lies in the name of God, those who use His name in vain."

It was what he wanted to hear. A band of brothers, a group of patriots to join.

He heard the song in his head as he used Liberty to push the tree limbs aside so that he could step into the clearing. The prophet turned toward him. "Why are you here?" But there was no surprise in his eyes.

"I am as willing to die for this cause as anyone else."

Nat Turner nodded and continued speaking. "I have a dream. A dream of freedom for our wives, our sons and daughters, for ourselves. But our dream must have a first step. No freedom without courage to strike the first blow." His voice was calm as though he were speaking peace instead of war. So small. The church boy?

Will looked around the circle at the others. Hark, Sam and

Dred, Yellow Nelson, and even some freemen—the Artis brothers and Hathcock. Even Berry Newsom, the white boy, was with them—freedom fighters. What Will wanted was death.

Some had met before. They knew each other and already had some plans in place. They talked about the previous date that had been planned: July 4. They had made a pact that if they survived, and if any man was tried, each would plead not guilty—the Bible and the Declaration of Independence demanded that they set themselves, the captives, free. Now, Will joined them.

Nat Turner looked at the men and boys gathered around him. "We are not trained soldiers, but that is nothing to God. We have no guns, but we have a promise of freedom to come. Men without guns, men without swords, we must have the courage to attempt more than we can imagine. We must find the courage, even in chains—though they call us slaves, niggers—to rise up as kings, as warriors, to rise up as men.

"We have been called lazy for so long, animals for so long, but today we rise up as men! Men of Bethlehem and Jerusalem, God knows each one of us—this is the time, it is the place, and He is calling our names."

Will was not so certain that it was God calling. He looked down at the axe in his hand. Liberty was calling, calling him to revenge.

He hadn't expected these words from Nat Turner, from Two Names, from the preacher, the prophet, who always prayed for mercy. He had never seen Nat Turner fight back; he hid behind the church, behind his prayers, behind Jesus's skirts. Reading for them, praying for them, running errands for them, he thought they owned him. Will looked around the circle again, and there, silent and almost hidden in the brush, was the girl Charlotte. He frowned. Charlotte?

Nat Turner spoke to the men, as though he didn't see her. "They count on our fear. And when we go into battle, no doubt, some of us—maybe all of us—will be afraid. Animals run when they are afraid. But we are men. Only men, against all odds, despite their fears, summon the courage to stand.

"Take courage, men! Be strong, brothers! Look to Africa; look to Ethiopia; look to God!"

Charlotte was frozen, her gaze riveted on Nat Turner.

"Bend our plowshares to the task, use what we have in hand." Blue light framed his head and figure—Will reminded himself that Nat Turner was a mere man, not a saint.

"We will not do what has been done to us; we will not rape or steal. We will not destroy property. We are called to render God's judgment and judgment shall begin at the house of God."

At the house of God? Kill the church people? It was the last thing Will would have expected of Nat Turner, the preacher, Nat Turner, who quoted Scripture, Nat Turner, who had baptized Ethelred Brantley.

"Judgment will begin with the members of Turner's Meeting Place. No matter what anyone else has done, judgment will begin there."

It was the church Nat Turner preached outside of Sunday after Sunday, the Methodist church that Old Benjamin Turner had built. It was the church where Reverend Whitehead and the others had pinned Nat Turner's hands to the wall, beaten him.

A tree branch shook near Will. He turned, his axe raised. He didn't care who it was or what church they went to; if they were white he was ready to kill.

Nat Turner raised his hand and then turned. It was the boy Davy, Two Feet; Nat Turner welcomed him into the circle. "I want to join with you," the boy stammered. "I want to go with you and the other men." The boy had hobbled to the clearing on his stick, falling behind all the others.

Turner stared at the boy and then motioned around the circle. "We all will most likely die."

"I want to join you," the boy said again. The same fear was on the boy, the fear that Will saw at the winter campfire; it bowed

Davy's head and lowered his eyes. "I want to go with you, to try."

Nat Turner knelt, lifted the boy's chin, and nodded. He placed his hands on either side of the boy's face and then, whispering, he prayed. Will was not certain, though others said it later, that he saw the disfigurement leave the boy's leg. But he did see a greater miracle, that afternoon of the blue sun; he saw fear leave the boy's eyes. He saw hope in the boy's eyes, hope that he would become a man.

Nat Turner shook Davy's hand and welcomed him. Then he turned back to the group. "It takes no courage to fight a weak enemy and not much more to fight one you hate or one who has no name or face you know.

"It takes a strong man to go to war knowing that he will most likely die. It takes a man, a God-believer"—he touched his heart— "a God-bearer, to fight and hope when there is none. If we have any success at all, we will owe it all to God.

"God is commanding you to fight a strong enemy, an armed enemy, and an enemy that you know. Some of us will stand against an enemy we love. Judgment will begin at the house of God, with names and families, our blood."

Love? How could any of them be fool enough to love someone who had stolen so much? How could they use the word *love* in the same breath with the likes of Nathaniel Francis? With the likes of Richard Whitehead and Levi Waller?

"It is hard to make war against enemies you love. It is hard to take up arms when for a lifetime you have turned the other cheek."

Will was ready. Ready to die, and he did not care who he took with him. He wanted them all to die.

"We are men of valor. That is what God calls each of us. We may not see freedom on this earth ourselves, but it will come. If we lose this battle, we will not lose the war. If we fall, another will take our place."

Will looked at Liberty. The others might be afraid, but he was ready. He had been waiting to see the blood, to feel his heavy blade slice through.

"Generations from now people will remember what we do here in Virginia, in Cross Keys, in Jerusalem. Generations from now—Hark, Sam, Will"—Nat Turner nodded in Will's direction—"Dred, Nelson, Jack, Davy—our names will be on their lips, mere slaves, but they will remember. God has called us, the least, to render judgment.

"Raped and tortured and starved. Our freedom, our wives, our children, our dreams—all stolen from us. They have even tried to steal God.

"But God's law says, '. . . He that stealeth a man, and selleth him, or if he be found in his hand, he shall surely be put to death.' That is the witness of Moses."

He that stealeth a man, and selleth him . . . put to death. The one who stole his daughter and wife would die!

"They have refused to obey. And it is the witness of the apostle Paul that manstealers are numbered with the ungodly, the unholy, with murderers, and the lawless. We were stolen from our homelands and the penalty for stealing men is death."

Liberty trembled in Will's hand. He needed no convincing. He looked around the circle at the others. It seemed strange to him, but his stomach fluttered and he wanted to laugh. It seemed stranger, though, that Nat Turner did not seem angry—after all they had stolen from him, after the way they had beaten him? He was calm, a slave carrying out his master's orders.

"God is long-suffering, full of mercy, but He has said the time is now. Tell only those you know who will not faint. Ten days from now war begins." They were not a mob, Nat Turner said. "We must plan, we must make ready, we must pray." Nat Turner began to point at them one by one. "'Behold, I will raise them out of the place whither you have sold them, and return your recompense upon your own head.'" He nodded as he pointed, his voice rising.

"'Beat your plowshares into swords and your pruninghooks into spears: let the weak say, I am strong!'"

One by one, the men around the circle, emaciated and threadbare, began to raise their fists. Scarred hands and arms. Burns. Amputated fingers. Torn clothes hanging from them like scarecrows, they began to stand. Will had come only seeking death. But with the spirit of the men around him, something grew inside him, something rising . . . pulling his fist to lift with theirs.

Will looked at Charlotte, to see if her fist was raised. She was gone.

"'Put ye in the sickle . . .'" Nat Turner motioned—a swipe and jerk, as though he were hacking down cornstalks. Will thought of his axe and all the trees on which he had practiced. "'. . . for the harvest is ripe: come, get you down; for the press is full, the fats overflow; for their wickedness is great.'"

The air hummed. Blue light connected them. Will felt the blood on him already, the warm blood. Saw the terror in his victims' eyes.

Nat Turner's gaze was fixed, his manner somber. "This is the beginning. There will come a greater war. 'And brother shall deliver up brother to death, and the father his child . . .'" Calm until now, Nat Turner's voice rose higher.

"War will grip this whole nation! The blood of martyrs cries from the ground!

"Today, I call you men! At this place, on this day, before the God of our fathers, rise up! Stand up! Warriors, your time is now!"

chapter 22

Planning was not easy. Men and boys spoke of things suffered. "Killed her," men said. "Sold him away." "Too shameful to say what they did to me." They showed scars that criss-crossed their backs. "She threw my little girl to the ground, beat her over a piece of bread, killed her. She gone, no flowers for her grave." "Beat my brother before my eyes and killed him. No sheriff came. Like he never existed. That man that killed him, why should he and his family live?" They showed ears that lacked lobes, hands missing fingers, and feet without toes. "Why shouldn't we take their guns? We know how to use the weapons; we've hunted food for them." But Prophet Nat was insistent. This was not a war against all white people, or even all white slave owners, at least not now. God was clear. Judgment only at the house of God—only farming instruments. "If we are to have success, we must not be like them; we must obey God's commands."

Nat Turner, Hark, and Nelson planned most of the strategy. They discussed who would be home and who would most likely be at Waller's still. "We have no place and no one to guard prisoners, and our work must not be discovered." Nat Turner looked at each one of them. "If you are with us, then you commit to doing what must be done." Will knew what it meant; anyone who discovered them, even women and children, could not be spared.

They would begin in small groups and finally gather at an agreed-upon place. "Be prudent with your tongues. Quiet is our friend in this matter," Nat Turner said. "When it is dark, just before daybreak, we will meet at the Travis barn. If someone stops you, tell them their British enemy is afoot and taking over the land."

War would not come as the oppressors expected. It would not come from overseas in red uniforms, it would not fire cannons. It would come quietly while they lay sleeping. It would creep upon them like a hand over the mouth from behind, like a plague, unexpected. *For he shall have judgment without mercy, that hath shewed no mercy. . . .*

TEN DAYS LATER, Sunday night underneath the sickle moon—with the three boys Davy, Tom, and Andrew—Will met with Sam, Dred, Yellow Nelson, Hark, and Nat Turner. Darkness enfolded them, clouds drifted in front of the moon. Will looked for signs of fear in the others. He was surprised that they were all there.

Liberty in his hand, Will followed Nat Turner as they made their way to the upper floor of the Travis house, climbing like leopards up the ladder and through a window. Nat Turner, who knew the house better than the others, led the way.

Silence. The sound of Will's breathing magnified in his ears. Every floorboard creaked. It was a dream.

Nat Turner signaled for Will to wait, then made his way quickly downstairs to ease open the front door to the others. Silence.

Nat Turner crept back upstairs, and in the darkness Will could barely see him. They edged, step by step, down the hall toward the master bedroom door.

On edge. It surprised Will; he had been waiting so long. His mind screamed at him, *Turn back, you cannot win! You will die!* But Liberty exhorted him. *Steady! Take courage!* Inch by inch. Then he was through the bedroom door.

Tell no one who is faint.

God has chosen the least likely.

Will had hoped for, but not believed, he would actually live this moment. War. Vengeance. His heart swelled, his lungs expanded against his rib cage, his heart pounding. Liberty sang her war song. Nothing must stay his hand.

A floorboard creaked as he stepped inside the bedroom. Joseph Travis and his wife, Sallie, slept peacefully in their bed.

Planted next to the bed, Will lifted Liberty. She dropped and warm, wet life showered his face.

auntie Easter

chapter 23

G round glass. Chokeberries.
It was going to kill her. Easter tried to find a spot to lie on, a spot on her body that did not hurt. She was too old, it was too cold, and her bones ached sleeping on the floor.

The two of them, Nathaniel Francis and his wife, Lavinia, and his mother—even the two little boys they kept, the master's nephews that hardheaded Charlotte looked after—slept on beds, mattresses she had stuffed with dried corn husks and stalks, warm underneath quilts that she had made.

With knotted fingers, she stuffed mattresses she would never lie on. She fashioned beautiful dresses she would never be allowed to wear. She had scarred her hands cooking food for them—sizzling chicken; warm, soft scrambled eggs; and hot biscuits made with white flour—that they would not share with her; she was good enough to cook but not good enough to dine.

She shifted again. Hoping to get enough sleep before she had to rise, before it was time to make the fire and make the bread. All this—the pain of it, the shame of it, the sadness of loving people who did not love her back—was going to kill her.

Not that death was bad. She was ready to see the Lord whenever He saw fit. She was going to put on her long white robe and wear a starry crown. Easter shifted again.

Death, she thought, sometimes was better than love. They used her love against her. Her father had owned her, had been her white slave master, though she could never call his name or claim him. She longed for him, for him to love her—to confess her. He did not, though he knew she loved him. He allowed her to serve him tea, to take care of his daughter, her sister, because he knew Easter loved him. He did not return her love. With it, he yoked her.

There had been men, none of her choosing, who could take her and use her. She had never had the gift or the luxury of choice. She had no right to chastity or to honor. It was exciting for them; it was shame for her. Easter had dreamed once, during the spring of her life, that some man would rescue her, some man would claim her and steal her away. Back then she noticed men, their eyes, their shoulders, their thighs. But that was all over now. Winter had chilled her and she didn't expect any fire to come. Men no longer burned when they looked at her.

In the fall, cold eased around the windows into her joints and down her spine. Now it was winter, cold marched right through the door and lived inside of her, making her stiff. December's snow had been hard and heavy and the freeze was still in the air. Sometimes she was so cold she couldn't think, too cold, so cold she panicked and thought of running outside into a blanket of snow that would cover her. If she could have just had a quilt it would have made everything better. There was no comfortable place on the floor, and as long as it took her to find her way to shivering sleep, just that soon there would be a foot, a boot in the side of her.

Nathaniel Francis was just a hard-eyed young man. His mother, upstairs in the jump—he loved her. But even with her sometimes he didn't have patience; there was a sharp word here or there. So, she, auntie Easter, shouldn't expect any more. She took care of him and she had raised the girl, Lavinia, but they could slap her face and push her down and never blink. Like swatting a fly.

It was going to kill her, or she was going to kill somebody just like that white woman Miss Lila Richardson had killed her husband. Easter turned to her other side, careful not to make any noise. If she didn't get away, she was going to kill somebody.

What was the use? She was too old to stand up or to run away. Or maybe she didn't have the courage to go. What would she eat? Where would she sleep? Where would she go? Maybe she was too old or too afraid. Perhaps it was both. All she could do was pray. Pray for a better day; pray because Prophet Nat had told them a better day was coming. *If You are a God of mercy, there will be a better day.*

She hated her masters, her owners, for using her up. Time would come when they would throw her away, "Oh, auntie Easter, you're free now!" Free when she wasn't able to cook for them or make do for herself. Then they'd run her away.

She hated them.

But she loved them just the same. They told her they loved her and called her auntie. But it was not for her, it was for them. Their love didn't keep her old bones off the cold floor. She wasn't auntie enough to have a blanket or a quilt. And she didn't know how many more kicks she could take from the two little boys, how many slaps she had left in her, how many more times to have the child she had raised talk to her like she was nothing.

It grieved her that she loved them anyway, but she did. Especially the girl, Lavinia. How do you nurse a baby at your breast, feel her pull milk from your body, your bones, and not love her? How long? It was going to kill her.

Lord, have mercy. Easter put her hands between her legs to warm them. *All going to be the end of me.*

White folks said God was only for them, said His plan was that black life would be hard. Prophet Nat bellowed that it was all a lie. God was their shield, their glory, and the lifter up of black folks' heads.

Morning would be soon. She listened to Lavinia breathing. She had loved the girl all her life, but sometimes you killed the ones you loved. But to kill the ones you have held in your arms . . . Someone would have to leave, something would have to change, or someone would have to die.

chapter 24

It was February. Too cold and she was too old to be standing outside in rainy snow on the muddy frozen ground, no shoes, no coat. But what was she going to do? Easter wrapped her arms around herself, trying to find some small warmth. The girl Charlotte, the one who tended Nathaniel Francis's young children boarders, came up from behind and encircled Easter. "Come on, Mother Easter. Let me warm you up." How was Charlotte going to warm her up when the girl was cold herself?

Easter looked at Will with his eyes glued inside the white church. He crouched at the window like a hungry wolf. He was all the time wanting something he couldn't have—his wife and daughter back or to be inside out of the cold. He was never going to see his family again in this lifetime; and no matter how warm it was inside, it didn't do any good to look. White folks were never going to let him in. Better he should keep his eyes on Nat Turner. Sometimes she listened to the prophet and she was almost able to forget.

Moses and Hark, who belonged to Miss Sallie Francis, Miss Sallie Travis now, and her husband stood near the slave preacher. Yellow Nelson stood close by, too. Nat Turner stood in front of them, preaching and quoting Scripture, though there was no Bible in his hand—it was illegal for him to read, though everyone knew he did—as though his feet were not frozen and snow was not showering down on him.

"'For, behold, in those days, and in that time, when I shall bring again the captivity of Judah and Jerusalem, I will also gather all nations, and will bring them down into the valley of Jehoshaphat, and will plead with them there for my people and for my heritage Israel, whom they have scattered among the nations . . .'" Pleading the blood. Moaning the blood.

All of them outside Turner's Meeting Place, frozen in the white snow, black people listening to Prophet Nat. Easter looked up at the dark smoke curling from the church's chimney up to the sky.

Most white people believed that hard times just came in cycles and they looked for an earthly cause. When hard times came, most black people ignored the cycles and fastened their eyes on God. They listened to hear a word that could keep them alive. They stood in the snow because they felt God coming. They felt His growing fury.

They had been trying to tell the white folks—singing to them, preaching to them. Auntie Easter tried to stamp her feet, but her knees were too cold and too old to cooperate. Frozen right through.

Black folks wanted to be free. They prayed for the foot off the neck. They were willing to fight to be free, but mostly, like an abused wife, like Miss Lila, they prayed that the white people would come to their senses, say sorry, and that the nightmare would end. She hummed right along with them.

What was wrong with white people? Couldn't see? Couldn't hear? She guessed most white folks wouldn't listen because they believed the white God talked only to white people.

Prophet Nat had told them all about the lie. He had nodded at his mother. "Like my mother, your forefathers were stolen by other men, and God's penalty for manstealing, for slave trading, is death." Death? How could it be a sin to capture slaves, own slaves, sell slaves? White people did it all the time. It was their right. White people, slave-owning people, said they could do whatever they wanted to anyone who wasn't white, and they said the Good Lord said so.

Easter shook her head just thinking about it. The most heinous, most vain use of the Lord's name is to use it in a lie. And soon the lie swelled like a boil, saying that God said dark people couldn't be leaders, couldn't own property, couldn't vote, couldn't marry, couldn't go to church, and couldn't even read. But it was all a lie, a big old lie. Prophet Nat looked in Easter's direction and spoke to her just like he was reading her mind.

"Their eyes are blinded and they do not see.

"They quibble with the law, as though the God who said 'Thou shalt not steal' meant goats and corn, but not men. As though the God who said 'Thou shalt not covet' meant everything but our labor, our families, our wealth, and our dreams."

It was a lie that God wanted white folks inside the church warm with coats and shoes and fire while black folks stood outside freezing, bleeding. The girl Charlotte rubbed her hands up and down Easter's arms. She appreciated the girl, but hands, even young ones, weren't a coat and they weren't shoes.

Easter looked at Nat Turner's mother, Nancie, standing off to the side with some of the other women. Her soggy drawstring skirt was saturated at the bottom with mud, flecked with snow. Like the other slaves she had no coat, but her eyes were glued on her son. Cold as Nancie might be, she had a son, a son she could hold in her arms. Easter's arms were empty; her love had been sold away.

God is tired, black folks wailed. Most white folks heard it as a cry for vengeance and missed the warning. But some white folks heard and understood, like Ethelred Brantley. And then there was poor Berry Newsom. Berry Newsom, standing alongside the freemen, was so poor he might as well have been black. There weren't indentured white people anymore, except for Berry.

The freemen, the Artis brothers, Indians of the Cheroenhaka (Nottoway) tribe whose mother had married a black freeman, and Isham Turner and Thomas Haithcock, held the reins of their horses and shook snow from their coats and hats. All of them outside, unwanted inside, listening to Prophet Nat. The preacher shook his head. "God is pleading"—Nat Turner pointed toward the church—"begging them to hear before it's too late."

It was too cold to be outside, but there she was. There is nothing like God loving you when everyone and everything, including the law, says He should not. There is nothing like being loved by God when no one else does.

Easter saw war coming. She didn't know her name, but she saw her powdering her face, rouging her lips, and sticking her feet in her shoes. God was tired. Frozen feet, chattering teeth were all just signs. God patted His foot, ready to give war the nod.

But God had a sweet spot. He was, as she had once heard an old woman say, a mercy God—merciful enough to even forgive white folks. If they confessed, they could be forgiven; if they were sorry and sincere, God would repent. Anybody could choose mercy—to give it or receive it—at any time. Yes, even white folks. All they had to do was turn. Mercy and love trumped everything.

So, she stood outside in the snow with the others, outside Turner's Meeting Place, fussing and praying—not for vengeance, even though vengeance was due, but because she kept hoping white folks would turn. If war came, even the good would be hurt.

Feet bound with ice-coated rags, her eyes ran and water from her nose froze on her face. There was no point in trying to wipe it. It was too cold to be outside in the snow. Easter sighed and her teeth chattered. Charlotte held her tighter.

If something didn't change soon, people were going to die. Easter had a feeling it wasn't going to be a few.

chapter 25

It was so unnatural—all the pretending and lying. She'd gotten too old now to keep track. Easter's head bumped along in time with the ruts in the road. She hated coming to the Whiteheads'. Easter especially hated the Valentine's Day get-together. It was still too cold outside for so much falsifying.

When they stopped, her neck jerked. It took her awhile to get herself together, but then she crawled down from the carriage. Easter walked past Hubbard, the Whiteheads' head house slave, who snubbed her, too good to talk. He was big and strong and the white folks kept him off them by letting him bully other slaves, let him think he was special. She had heard he enjoyed beating other men raw, the coward. They gave him a whip and a title and told him he was in charge; let him do the beating so they wouldn't have too much blood on their hands. Mollycoddled.

"Will you be all right, auntie Easter?"

"Don't you worry about a thing, Miss Lavinia. You just concentrate on having a good time!" Auntie Easter smiled as brightly as she could at Lavinia and took her wrap.

Lavinia paused.

"Miss Lavinia, don't worry 'bout me." Easter kept the smile on her face as she watched the peach dress she had made walking up the steps. Lavinia, the child she raised, never looked back. Easter turned her head, wiped away the painted smile, and started around the back of the house toward the kitchen. Now that she was older, she couldn't carry as much weight as she used to and granite smiles were too much to bear.

In the kitchen, she hung Lavinia's cape. She hated being at

Miss Caty Whitehead's. Something about the old woman and about her good-for-nothing preacher son brought out the worst in everyone around them. Easter looked at the women gathered in the kitchen. Laughing out loud, but not loud enough to be heard, and always underneath was sorrow. Beyond them, she heard the other women, the white women, laughing gaily in the other room. She imagined her Lavinia with the others. There was a wall between them.

Easter looked out the window to see the men and the women outside working in the cold, barren fields. Inside, three women in the kitchen, dressed all in white—drawstrings and bleached flour bags—busied themselves preparing refreshments. Of course, only one woman was really necessary to cook the Valentine's Day meal, but just like all the extras on Miss Caty Whitehead's coach—too green, too golden, too ornamental for the muddy, rutted roads of Southampton County—more were needed to keep up the illusion. The Whiteheads wanted to be what they pretended to hate: highbrow people, Virginia royalty.

The three women waved to Easter to come in. "You sit yourself down, Mother Easter." As Easter sat, she noticed a girl, Beck, sitting on the floor in the corner.

"Hanky-panky," the baker, round and light brown, said as she grabbed a rag to take tea cakes from the oven. "Hanky-panky," the second one agreed, thin and honey-colored, as she carved the ham. "Um, hanky-panky," said the third one, young, short, and lemony, as she put slices of warm pie on china plates.

Easter sat quietly. Everyone knew all the stories, everyone knew about the reverend. No one recognized holiness like a prostitute, or hypocrisy like a sinner, and no one knew the master's sins like the dogs and the slaves he owned.

The women in the kitchen knew they were supposed to be the least. No one was supposed to want them. It wasn't true, but it was a secret the women in the kitchen were supposed to keep, especially from the women in the other room. No one was supposed to know that men like Reverend Whitehead came creeping by in the dark of the night.

The lie had been told to the women in the kitchen, the seed planted before they could remember; at least Easter could not pin-point a time before it. Published in newspapers, in the Constitution, and in books, the lie was sung in songs and acted out in plays. It was taught to children in nursery rhymes and bedtime stories, taught in schools and preached from pulpits.

The women in the kitchen did not believe the lie, at least they told themselves they did not. It was hard not to surrender to the lie; each one of them knew people who had. Each one of them had been seduced by it. It was hard not to give in to the temptation to be who and what others said they were.

The lie was simply and elegantly cruel: God, whose name is Love, did not love them. God, who created the universe, did not delight in them. God, the Father of all good things and all good plans, had no plan or place for them.

The proof was there for all to see, they had been told. *Look at your hair, your skin, your lips, and your nose—all inferior. Your thoughts are those of animals and your smell is even fouler, your blood tainted and impure.*

They worked hard to reassure themselves. But it was hard not to believe they were less when the lie was repeated to them night and day.

You cannot read, you cannot reason, you cannot speak properly—listen to your slurring—and you certainly cannot lead. For proof, look to the dark wild place from which you came. There are jungles, men with spears, and godless men who eat other men. There are no bridges, no buildings, no great churches, no paintings, no books, only savages and fires and blood.

It was hard not to believe the lie. There were no pictures, no books to reassure them, no people to remind them of their past.

God does not love you. He has no plan except that you are a slave; you were born to serve. There is no hope for you in God. But on Sunday Prophet Nat told them that God was the lifter of their heads.

Easter's head had been low for so long. It was hard some mornings to get up and try; it was part of the cold in her bones. To just live, trying to believe, took all the strength she had. She sang sometimes so she could feel God, so she could keep the lie at bay. She sang to remind herself that the lie was not true. But the lie was unrelenting; it was always there.

The three women continued preparing the holiday meal. "My, my," said the first one. "It is a mess and a shame. One day lightning is gon' strike him. Wearing that collar, ought to be ashamed." The second one shook the fork and the knife she held. "Black folks looking like white folks, and nobody knows how it happened." The third one held the rim of the pie pan and sliced with her knife. "Oh, they know how it happened. Just don't want to know."

The first one chuckled. "We know. The preacher out making late-night converts." The second one waved her hand in the air. "Seen that pine knot burning and bobbing along at night. He out fishing for anything he can find. What's done in the dark will be born looking white!" She laughed at her own joke. The third one cut another slice of warm pie. "But his momma don't know. It would kill Miss Caty if she knew." The first one snorted. "We all know." She looked at the other two women. "She knows, too."

Easter sat quietly. Richard Whitehead wasn't the only one. The evidence was all around them, cooking in kitchens, working in fields, and sold into fancy houses farther south, in New Orleans.

The first one sniffed. "She know, all right." The second snickered and arranged the ham on a platter. "It's a lot of hard work keeping up appearances and a lot of responsibility sitting on the first pew." The third one set cups on the counter and poured tea in the china teapot with yellow flowers. "Heavy is the head that holds up the hat." The first one picked up a large wooden rolling pin and baptized it with flour. "Um um, my, my, hanky-panky. Apple don't fall far from the tree, does it? How can the son help but do what the daddy did?" The second one giggled. "The lie is calling that man, that boy of his, Yellow Nelson. He ain't yellow. He shot past yellow, past light, bright, and is most nearly, just like that Nat Turner." She giggled again. The third one sighed and shook her head. "They might as well sign both of them up and let them vote. 'Specially that Red Nelson." That was sorrow's voice, mocking things that cause pain. Yellow Nelson, Nat Turner, Red Nelson, and so many others who couldn't call their fathers by name; their only inheritance a lighter shade.

The first one used a towel to reach in the oven and grab another sheet of tea cakes. "Why white folks so hardheaded? They don't believe fat meat is greasy. They don't believe that God gets tired."

Easter perked up inside, listening, but not wanting to appear particularly interested. It was what she had been thinking, thinking but afraid to say aloud—even among friends it was hard to know who the lie would cause to betray you.

The second one lifted a stack of saucers and on each one she placed a piece of cake. "Child, I don't understand. Who know, maybe they'll listen to the preacher and turn." The third one set the cups on a tray. "They ain't gon' listen to no black preachers like Yellow Nelson or Nat Turner, no matter how white they are."

When they had arranged the tea cakes on the silver trays, the three women held the sweets before them and floated down the hall to the room full of white women. They were quiet, bowed, unspeaking. Ghosts.

Easter picked up a tea cake while they were gone, without permission, and took a bite. The white people would beat her if they saw her, but she did it, this once, anyway. She couldn't fight them, couldn't run away, so Easter took a bite. She looked across the room at the girl, at Beck. The girl was coming of age—not that any age, boy or girl, was too young—and Easter knew what that meant. She could see it in the girl's eyes. Golden. Delicious. An apple ripe for picking, a gentle lamb—unaware that it was begging to be touched. Midnight visits, whiskey breath, things done to her that even a dog would not do. Pretty was the worst thing for a colored woman. It was hard not to believe the lie.

Never good enough, never pretty enough, and never loved, the song played behind their words. Too wild to be free, but tame enough to tend their children. Too filthy to eat at the table, but clean enough to cook and serve. Never best, always least. Unwanted but always demanded.

In the kitchen and in the field, the women tried to play the parlor game; they tried to be the best—someone's skin was lightest (maybe as light as that of the women sitting in the other room); someone had the straightest or waviest hair; someone had the most authority; and all the women in the kitchen had better jobs and better food than the women outside in the field.

Never good enough, never pretty enough, never loved. But no matter how pretty in the kitchen, no matter how white in the kitchen, no matter how smart in the kitchen, no matter how graceful, if you were in the kitchen you were never good enough.

They tried to play the game. But the women in the kitchen didn't have the power to play the game—to decide who would be beaten or sold, to decide which boys would push their carriage in the rain. They didn't have the power to force others to have babies for more money to buy more clothes. Couldn't even choose a man. They had no power to complain or refuse. The women in the kitchen and the fields could never say no.

The three women in white whisked back into the kitchen. They put the teapot and cups with yellow flowers on trays and then floated out the door, back toward the parlor.

Easter looked at Beck. The anger hadn't set in—her face was still soft, her voice still light. She hadn't learned the game. She would know soon; they all knew the rules. Everyone knew the taboos, and everyone knew the agreements. No white woman could openly love a black man or give birth to a dark child, to a slave. No white woman would dishonor herself, her family, or her community in such a way. A white woman who risked such behavior might be made a slave herself. In return for her propriety she was given a place of honor and a chance at wealth.

While white men might plant the seeds that gave birth to slave children, children with lighter-colored skin than that of the generation of slaves who came before them, no white man openly could love or marry a black woman. No white man could openly say a black woman was beautiful or that he preferred her; to do so was to betray his tribe. Such a one would be a turncoat. Such improper behavior would subject him to ridicule, exile, and maybe even death. In return for his propriety, great deference and power were given to him, and certain unseemly nocturnal behaviors were overlooked. He was entitled to black women, but in daylight white men denied the children and their attraction to the dark women who bore them.

The proof worked in the kitchen and labored in the fields. But the men did it in secret, while their women pretended not to know. The proof would soon be in Beck's eyes.

It seemed to Easter that the men even tried to hide their misdeeds from themselves. The men blamed their mannish desires on them. Black women were wild. Seducers. As punishment, the men beat them and sold their children away, like the son she had borne, a son pulled from her arms. Unfairness, shame, secrets, loss—those were the fruits of the lie.

They were all women (though the women in the parlor would have been insulted to be associated as equals with the women in the kitchen). Women in the kitchen and fields worried, just like the women in the sitting room, about their children—about coughs that would take them away, about fevers that might close their eyes. They could have held hands and wiped each others' tears.

The woman in the kitchen, who managed to make even her wrinkled drawstring skirts more stylish, might have sat with Mrs. Mary Barrow and traded notes on fashion. The women in the kitchen might have told Mrs. Caty Whitehead that her carriage was foolishness, everyone knew she was not Cinderella, and that for such a gentlewoman it was a cruel thing to make three barefoot boys risk their lives in the snow and mud to push it along. They might have told her that she was good enough and smart enough that she didn't need the carriage—a woman as wise as she was could have found a better use for her wealth. The women in the kitchen might have told Sallie Francis not to be ashamed of her kindness, that it was more beautiful than any lace.

But the women in the kitchen and in the field, unless they were willing to risk violence and death, didn't have the ability to tear down the walls or question the order.

The women in the sitting room valued the wall. Who would they be without it? They might lose everything with change.

The women in the parlor might have given a great gift to the women in the kitchen—telling them they were beautiful, assuring them they were loved. But what would happen if the women in the sitting room admitted that they secretly envied their slaves' lips, their hair, or their skin? The payoff for being best was wealth, power, and handsomer men. The whole economy and society might fail. Who would wait on them? Who would wash their things? Each ruffle cost a thousand tears, each petticoat a thousand beads of sweat, and a cloak or fancy shoes could be had for a thousand drops of blood. They weren't willing to pay the price themselves.

Gentle enemies, there was a wall between them.

The three women came back to the kitchen from the parlor in disarray. Mrs. Whitehead had wanted the pink flowers and not the yellow. They pointed at each other, arguing who had made the mistake. The baker took charge and quickly the others gathered the cups and plates with pink roses. The women from the kitchen piled the trays with more meat, more cakes, and other treats—making certain that they only used plates with pink roses. "Come with us this time," they told Beck. "You got to learn." They gave her a tray of tea cakes and she walked behind them when they swept out the door.

Easter looked after them as they left. It was hard not to believe the lie. It made her uncertain, so she had no confidence; she was always unsure. What if the One Who created them shuddered at their ugliness and repented of creating them, believing them His only mistake? Even in simple things—like using the pink cups instead of the yellow—the lie was there to remind them, to slither in and tell them they made the mistake because of God's plan, because they were not good enough. They made the mistake because they were cursed.

Easter had tried to learn to read, but each time she was uncertain about a word, there was the lie waiting for her and reminding her. *Stupid! Cursed!* When she was younger and had thought of running away, the lie appeared, sneering at her. *Leave and you will die! Run and the Lord will kill you!* Where could she run from God, who had intended her to be a slave, from the God who did not love her?

It was hard not to believe. All the lovely pictures she saw were of beautiful white women. When she was a child, white children had laughed at her hair. When she was grown, the child she nursed, Lavinia, had laughed at her. The lie laughed and pointed at her.

Easter had accepted that her hair was too wild, too bad. Her lips too full, her hips too wide, her backside too big, her feet too long. She had surrendered her body to the lie.

The lie nodded and smirked at her. She was not beautiful and no man wanted her, not in the daylight. No law protected her, no law needed to because no one desired her—despite hands up her skirt, blue eyes that followed her when she walked, things she could not mention. It was their birthright, their entitlement, and they took it—and anything else they pleased—with no apologies. Her body, her honor belonged to them. At least that had been how it was when she was young, before cold had set in her bones and gray had frosted her hair.

Easter had surrendered her body to the lie, but she still fought to hold on to what was left of her mind and her soul. But the lie would not surrender; it was always there, sneering at her. It was hard to believe that she was good enough, to believe that God loved her—she who wore sackcloth—as much as He loved the ones He gave fancy dresses, as much as the ones He gave carriages in which to ride. *Cursed!*

God had parted the Red Sea. Couldn't He change it all in the twinkling of an eye? Couldn't He lift her head? Couldn't He make her first? Couldn't He set her free, free of slavery, free of the lie? She prayed in the mornings. She prayed at night against the lie. But so far, nothing had changed.

It was hard not to believe the lie.

The three women and the girl, Beck, came back into the kitchen. Now, Beck was crying. "You gon' have to toughen up, girl," one of the women said. Beck's face, especially one cheek, was red.

"You stop crying, girl," another woman told Beck. "You want to live? Then you don't cry; you smile. And say, 'Yes, ma'am' and 'Thank you, ma'am,' no matter what." Beck, a third woman explained to Easter, had dropped a tea cake on the floor.

"You bet not make them mad. It won't be the last time you be hit. You keep crying and they will beat you for sure.

"You want to live? Be who they want you to be. Curtsy and tell them they are right. Tell them what they want to hear. Don't fight when they come to you at night. Say, 'Yes, sir.' Find some way to make them like you.

"You got to be two people. One you let them see and the other one you keep inside. The one on the outside, you keep her smiling and nodding. If you got to cry, you cry on the inside.

"They've never been beaten so they don't want to believe, they don't want to hear that it hurts—that they're the ones doing the hurting.

"They think patting you on the head later, handing out a cold, stale biscuit to an old black man they call uncle, or shedding a tear when one of us dies, is enough. They think that little thing makes it all right, makes them good. Well, you let 'em if you want to live."

Easter knew even her Lavinia, just like her daddy had, needed to feel good. They confused their own good feelings with how the ones they owned felt.

So, they forgot, when they were figuring, that husbands who beat their wives and children, who kick their dogs, also love them and bring them trinkets to make things better. They forgot about Mrs. Lila Richardson, the white woman who got fed up with her loving husband after he had brought her a bright pastel nosegay because it came after too many blackened blue eyes.

Her slaves had seen her crying and, many times, had wiped the blood from her mouth. She had loved her husband even the morning when she awakened thinking that his love was killing her. He loved her and he wouldn't have allowed her to go free. So, Miss Lila revolted and took her life, liberty, and her happiness in her own hands and left little of Mr. Richardson behind. The gentlewomen didn't add in Mrs. Richardson when they thought about their slave love.

Easter loved Lavinia. But having forgotten Mrs. Richardson, Lavinia and others confused that love for contentment, confused the fires Easter made and the biscuits she baked for her being satisfied, for everything being all right.

The gentlewomen didn't know that sometimes, like Miss Lila Richardson, people felt they had no choice but to kill the ones they loved. Miss Lavinia and the others didn't know that sometimes people grew weary; love spread too thin won't cover one beating too many, one more insult heaped on the pile, one more hunger pain. After so much hateful treatment, love and stingy kindness start to look just like one more insult. The masters and mistresses gave love that drooped like threadbare cloth stretched too far.

It was slave love—"I love my darkies." Such love wasn't patient and it wasn't kind—not real kindness that meant you sometimes did without so that others could be free. It wasn't love enough to say it was all just a lie; you really are smart and beautiful and loved

by God. It wasn't the kind of love that put others first and allowed
the darkies to wear the hoops while the gentlewomen took the
drawstring sacks for themselves. It didn't return the houses they
built or years of unpaid wages. It wasn't love that could admit your
lips are beautiful, your brown skin is fascinating, and your exotic
kinky hair is like the Virgin Mary's. It didn't celebrate the women
in the kitchen and in the field, let them get ahead or give them
their freedom. It wasn't love enough to give up the coach, to stop
playing princess, to not slap the cheek.

Slave love sold them down the river and turned its head when
they stretched out their arms crying. It was not beneficent or powerful love, but needy love that loved only if it could be first, if it
could steal and beat with no recompense. It wasn't love that gave,
or healed, or delivered; it was love that made the gentlewomen feel
better. It was only slave love, which wasn't true love at all.

The baker handed Beck, who was still sniffling, a tea cake. "A
better day is coming," she said. Easter wasn't sure she or any of the
other women believed it. The lie had been around so long.

The kitchen was quiet, except for Beck's hushed weeping.

And in the silence, they heard the people out in the field singing:

My God, I cried, Thy servant save,
Thou ever good and just;
Thy power can rescue from the grave,
Thy power is all my trust.

The baker nodded. "He is going to deliver us. He will with His
sure right hand."

Easter looked at Beck. She knew how the girl felt. Their bodies, their children had paid for Mrs. Whitehead's carriage. Their
minds and souls had paid for all Mrs. Barrow's dresses. Their
blood paid for the houses and land handed down from generation
to generation. Their blood was on all the white people owned.

Easter listened to the singing as she sat in her chair. She

thought about Lavinia's love for her and her love for Lavinia. It was love that shamed her, that made her angry and ashamed that she loved the one who abused but did not care for her. It was hard not to believe the lie.

And then
the sky
turned black.

chapter 26

July 21, 1831

Endless crying, endless heartbreak. It seemed to Easter that things had gotten worse and worse since the sky went black, since the eclipse. Oh, spring had come since that February with singing birds and dreamy clouds, but she smelled trouble coming like she smelled rain before a storm. Flowers bloomed and trees budded. Now summer had come and it seemed like hot weather just made white folks meaner. And she hadn't thought they could be crueler than she had already seen.

Easter hid behind the tree, out back of Master Nathaniel Francis's house, a towel stuffed in her mouth. The branches hid her, but she kept her eyes on the back door. She was far enough away that they could not hear her, but close enough to watch who came and went. It had rained early in the morning, but it was so hot, the water evaporated to steam. She didn't even bother with the gnats that swarmed around her. What more could they do to her? Still crying over yesterday.

Outside, in God's daylight, in front of God's people, they beat Nat Turner. She could see him on his knees with his arms stretched wide. They had beaten him because he would not lie, because he would not lie about who he was, because he would not be small like they wanted him to be. Pinned his hands to the church wall.

They beat him. Easter screamed, the rag smothered the sound. They beat him. She pounded the grass at the base of the tree. They beat him. She tore the grass up by the roots with her hands.

Easter cried.

And when they were finished, they laughed—even her Lavinia had laughed. On the way home, they mocked him, joking about how his body shook and how he bled. After sitting in God's house and walking on His earth, they laughed like it was their Fourth of July, another celebration.

Prophet Nat, the gentle one, blood on his face and in his eyes—his body lurched with each blow. Poor young man, poor boy, poor baby; he could have been her son.

Easter tore and jerked at the sackcloth she wore. Prophet Nat on his knees, blood spattering. Where was the Father? Where was the One who promised to protect them? Easter didn't wipe at the tears that ran down her face or the water from her nose.

They took turns beating him. "What now, prophet?" They laughed as they pulled the skin and raw meat from his back. Snickered at the blood running down. Easter's chest heaved and she stuffed the rag deeper in her mouth. She wanted to run. It frightened her to watch them, to think she lived with them—people who called themselves Christians and civilized. She lost her breath seeing the hate and the anger; it made her afraid that God, like their smiles and their love, was just a lie.

How could people who say they loved have so much hate, and take so much joy at the hate in their hearts? They were never happy, never at peace, never filled up—unless someone else bled. They were bullies in hoop skirts, top hats, and tails. White folks knew black folks were not animals; she had never seen them be so cruel to their animals.

Maybe some of them thought it was wrong, but no one stepped forward to stop the others or to reason. Too afraid, so afraid they let a man almost die. He was probably, right now, dying in Sallie Travis's barn.

Even the old grandmothers, their wise women, cackled as they beat him. It was horrible to watch their faces, laughing and jeering. Worse still was the face of her baby, her Lavinia, twisted so she almost did not recognize her—Lavinia, the one she had nursed, the one she had protected all of her life.

And where was God? Easter looked at the sky, at the sun. *The sun and the moon shall be darkened. . . .* They were still monsters. Oh, the sun had gone away for a moment, but it had come back— always there, just like the lie. She didn't have the words to plead with Him. All she could do was cry.

Her Lavinia laughed like she didn't know that when they were laughing and whipping Nat Turner, they were whipping her auntie Easter, too—the one Lavinia said she loved. But *auntie* was just a word, a word that never touched the heart. Slave love. It was love that didn't care about her tears.

Sometimes, times like this, Easter prayed that she would die. Death couldn't be worse. It was the cold wickedness, the hard-hearted wickedness that frightened her so. To see them doing wrong, evil, right in the sight of God, but going unpunished while they beat the life and spirit out of everyone around them. God had heard, but where was Jesus, where was mercy?

It chilled her soul, made her afraid to sleep. She wept to see them—to see wickedness laugh as it wiped blood from its hands, to see it come home, sit down, smoke a cigar, or eat a piece of cake, and tell itself it was good.

And the great army of the Lord was silent.

Easter took the rag from her mouth and wiped her face and eyes.

She had lived a long, long time and nursed children that were not hers. She had learned a thing or two. There was always a blood price for good. Men were hard-hearted and stiff-necked, and it was a rare one strong enough to accept God's will without bloodshed. Easter wiped her face again. She prayed that this blood, Prophet Nat's blood, streaming down the wall of the church, would some-how be enough to turn their hearts, enough to break the chains.

Easter righted her skirt and touched her hair. They would be looking for her soon. She forced her face to relax. She pressed her hand to the mossy side of the old oak, her confessor, and used it for leverage to stand.

A smile on her face, her joints aching and tears in her heart, Easter made her way back to the house.

All this was going to kill her.

chapter 27

Before she cleared the trees, Easter saw Charlotte stepping out of the house, a burlap sack in her hand. The girl smiled and looked back over her shoulder. Wickedness, in the shadow of the kitchen, smiled down at her.

Easter had been watching them, the two of them together. All spring and on into summer she had been watching Charlotte and wickedness, Nathaniel Francis. Young people were bold, but they didn't have common sense. After seeing Prophet Nat beaten, it seemed like the girl would have had enough. It seemed Charlotte would have enough sense to leave Nathaniel Francis alone.

Nathaniel Francis had been chasing after Charlotte, but he was the master. He had the right. He was taking everything from the girl, even more than the Lord allowed. That was his privilege. He was a white man.

He stalked the girl when his wife was not watching. Easter had seen Charlotte, the first few times, come back from the woods looking frightened and confused. Master Francis came back strutting and ignoring Charlotte. She was no more important than what she could give him.

But then something had changed. Now, when Miss Lavinia was not around, hardheaded Charlotte put her hands on her hips and batted her eyes when she talked to him. Charlotte flirted with Master Francis like it was a moonlit night and he was a man to jump the broom with, a man she could take back to her cabin. Easter had tried to warn her. "You better leave that man alone."

"What man?"

"You know what man. That man is married . . . and a white man at that."

"If it's the man I think you must be thinking about, I know he is married, but what is it to you? How can I bother him? He owns me. He has the papers that say I'm his."

Easter shook her head. She had lived. She had the scars to prove it. "There is a lot of storm caged up in that man, that boy. Don't let it blow out on you."

"I ain't doing nothing to him. I can't help it he likes what he see."

Charlotte toyed with Master Francis and he seemed confused about who he was. It was a dangerous thing to play with a master. It was better to be quiet, to let him do what he had to do and let him walk away. But Charlotte kept fooling around with him like she didn't know who she was, who he was, or who they both were.

The girl was still young. She hadn't seen as many people killed or beaten just because a white man was frustrated. Easter tried to warn the girl. "He don't like that he like what he see, Charlotte. Every time he like you, he hate himself. The more he like, the more he hate. You just be careful not to let that hate come back on you."

"So, you a prophet, too, now, auntie?"

"No, but I know some things. They already think we're wild; they think we're harlots and we want them. What you're doing just make it worse, worse for all of us. And don't think his wife, don't think Miss Lavinia don't see."

"What do I care what she see? She just a silly little girl playing house, buying dresses when they don't have food or enough oil for the lamps." Charlotte rubbed a hand over her arm and tilted her head. "If I'm so much trouble, he could set me free and I wouldn't be underfoot to either of them. I would pick up today and go to Ohio and they would never see me again. Their choice."

"You be careful, Charlotte. Take care."

"Take care? He do whatever he want to to me. Things he wouldn't do to his dog, you hear me?"

Easter had put her hands to her ears. She knew already. She had lived it already. "I don't want to hear!"

"Take care? Who am I going to cry to? Who is going to come and rescue me? Niggers can't rescue themselves, let alone me. Who? The law? The church? It ain't happening to them, so they turn away—it's not their responsibility.

"I know I'm here to be used. If I'm going to be used, let me get something for it. I'm just doing what I have to do, auntie. What other chance do I have? Maybe he'll buy me a dress instead of this old sack, some ribbon for my hair. He want me? He want a baby from me? What's wrong if it's a yellow baby like Mother Nancie's, like Nat Turner? Maybe if it's yellow or pink, I will be able to keep my baby around. What choice do I have? When could a nigger woman ever say no?"

When Easter came into sight, Nathaniel Francis pulled back and walked away. She whispered to the girl Charlotte, "Didn't you see Sunday? Didn't you see them folks beat Prophet Nat, even that woman?" Easter grabbed a side of the bag Charlotte was holding and they made their way to the garden for food.

The smile was gone. "I see. What I see is I got to find a way to live." Charlotte rubbed her belly.

Easter shook her head. "Oh, child, no."

"Don't talk about what you don't know about, auntie. Don't ask about what you don't want to know." Charlotte stooped to pick up a tomato that was lying on the ground. "We don't have many choices, auntie. But this, what I'm carrying, is mine. This child I'm carrying is going to have a different life. I'm going to make sure of it. Nathaniel Francis is not going to sell my baby."

"Oh, Charlotte, that man don't care about you. He will sell you and that child away."

"Wherever I go, my baby is going. I promise you this before God—my baby will not be a slave!"

Easter looked to the sky. How long?

chapter 28

She wiped sweat from her forehead with the back of her arm and then swatted at the flies that buzzed about her head. Since the sky went black in February, Easter had been waiting for something, for some sign that things were going to change. All she had seen and heard was more mean, like Prophet Nat's beating at the church in July.

With an old cup, she scooped dried beans from a barrel in the pantry. She scooped eight cups into a pan, covered them with water, added salt, and then began to look for mealworms. It was too hot to move.

Prophet Nat, Old Turner's boy, Nancie's boy, had been telling them to keep the faith. He had been telling them to have hope. Maybe it was just enough that he had lived. Maybe it was miracle enough that a month later he was back on his feet.

Spring, summer, and nothing had changed. It was hot now, and the frost was thawed from her bones, but winter would come again. Time was passing and nothing had changed.

Everything was changing. Miss Lavinia and that wild girl, Charlotte, both of them showing, both of them big with child. Those two babies would be born, probably looking alike, but one light and one darker. Those two babies would be born and everything would change—Charlotte and her baby sold away. No one would point at the father, except to slap him on the back for the white baby and the profit he made from the black one. Everyone would pretend it never happened. Nothing would change.

Since the beating in July, Easter had been waiting. *The sun and the moon shall be darkened. . . .* About two Sundays ago, the sun turned blue and she had rejoiced. Thinking it was the moment.

> *The sun shall be turned into darkness, and the moon into blood,*
> *before the great and terrible day of the LORD come.*

She had hoped, allowed herself to hope. Maybe this was the day the Lord would deliver His people.

> *And when I shall put thee out, I will cover the heaven, and*
> *make the stars thereof dark; I will cover the sun with a cloud, and*
> *the moon shall not give her light.*

Still nothing happened.

White folks were still saying it: *Cursed.* Prophet Nat was still telling black folks God was their shield and their glory. It might take some time, but things would change.

But it still looked the same. Fall was knocking and change still hadn't walked in the door. War still hadn't come to town.

Easter began to quietly hum a song they had sung at church that morning. She imagined a day when the great army of the Lord would come. There would be hundreds of warriors, thousands, and they would overwhelm the white people of Southampton, like the Egyptians of old, and set the black folks free.

She conjured a picture like the paintings she'd seen—flaxen-haired young men in brand-new formfitting uniforms with brass buttons and shiny boots. They would have cannons and guns, swords and sashes, feathers and flags. The Lord's army would march into Southampton wearing shining new boots and set her free! March around Nathaniel Francis's yard and into the kitchen, feet stomping so the whole house would shake!

Oh, she knew God could do it! He could have done it yesterday. He could do it in the twinkling of an eye.

She used her hand to scoop away the tiny dead worms that

floated to the top of the salted water. Sometimes she let herself get excited, let herself believe, but then she remembered that she was just a slave living outside of Jerusalem, just a slave in Southampton County. She knew who Nat Turner thought he was and what he thought he knew, but the white folks thought they knew better. And, so far, no matter how she prayed, when she awoke, the white folks still had the upper hand. Love and faith didn't seem to make anything better.

All she had seen was bad times. She had heard that Old Benjamin Turner called on Nat Turner to quote Scripture in church, even in front of all the white people. She had heard that Old Benjamin had even allowed the black and the white to sit inside Turner's Meeting Place, though the blacks were in back, together. But Old Benjamin was dead and what he allowed was all over by the time she came to Southampton County from Northampton County in North Carolina.

Nat Turner could believe what he wanted to believe, but Easter knew the white people. Easter had been around white people all her life, civilized white people, God-fearing white people. When they were with black people there were no tipped hats, no curtsies, and no fair deals. It seemed to her most took off their civilization and became violent, greedy, and folk with no conscience. When they were in the presence of white people, well, they put their civilization and religion back on again.

Still, she prayed and she sang. Just wasn't no telling when God would turn, when He would say, *Enough!* Easter hummed, then sang under her breath.

> *Come, we that love the Lord,*
> *And let our joys be known;*
> *Join in a song with sweet accord . . .*

Prophet Nat told them God loved them like a mother. Easter smiled to herself. It was funny to think of God that way, but Prophet

Nat had said the words to them over and over: *O Jerusalem, Jerusalem, which killest the prophets, and stonest them that are sent unto thee; how often would I have gathered thy children together, as a hen doth gather her brood under her wings.* . . . The Lord had been poor himself, and born in a manger, sleeping in a barn, Prophet Nat told them. He had been born to a poor girl, to a daughter of slaves.

Then Prophet Nat would chant to them. Sometimes he said the words in a language she didn't understand: *As Gabriel greeted you, Hail, Maryam, full of grace, the Lord is with you through virgin in conscience as well as body. Blessed are you among women and blessed is the fruit of your womb . . .*

He told them that the Lord, Jesus Christ, had given the people of Africa to His mother as a precious gift and that she prayed for them. A blessed mother's words to counteract the curse.

He told them about Africa and about the highlands, great mountains where black people prayed. He told them that the Ethiopians were great warriors and that even now, in Jerusalem, Ethiopians were guarding the holy tombs. Prophet Nat said that thousands of miles away, Ethiopians who did not know her were praying for her even as she stood in the kitchen on aching feet. Easter wanted to run away and find Ethiopia, to find the highlands he talked about, but she was so afraid.

Prophet Nat told them not to give up. "Don't turn around," he would say. "God fights for us, He cares for us, He is God Almighty, the Many-Breasted One." Then Prophet Nat would say in his singsong voice, *Our Father who art in heaven, hallowed be thy name. Thy kingdom come, thy will be done, on earth as it is in heaven. Give us this day our daily bread and forgive us our debts as we forgive our debtors, and lead us lest we wander into temptation, but deliver us from the evil one, for Thine is the kingdom and the power and glory unto ages of ages. Amen.*

Easter wanted to believe Prophet Nat, that there was a place far away, a place with pictures of Jesus and His mother that looked like her. She wanted to believe that there was a place where dark-skinned people built great churches, were there were plump brown-skinned saints with halos resting on their kinky hair. But it was hard to believe. White people laughed and called him crazy when they heard him say such things.

She poured the water from the beans, then added more water and salt to rinse them again. There were moments when she could summon the courage to believe there would be a perfect day—a day when she, and others like her, would be free.

The sun and the moon shall be darkened, and the stars shall withdraw their shining. The LORD also shall roar out of Zion, and utter his voice from Jerusalem; and the heavens and the earth shall shake: but the LORD will be the hope of his people, and the strength of the children of Israel.

Didn't she live just outside Jerusalem? Wasn't Bethlehem nearby? It had to be a sign of the Lord's coming. It couldn't just be coincidence. There were times when Easter believed the last would be first, a day when the skies would part and she would stand amid the crystal sea. People from all over the world would be there— all the tattered and the torn, the ones battered by life's storms, and there would be a jubilee! Even old Ethelred Brantley would be there, when the elders cast down their crowns, having asked for forgiveness and bowed his knee. Oh, it would be a great day, indeed! The rest in their finery and their firstness would be left behind in their willful blindness. Their hearts dead and hard until—too late—only too late would they acknowledge all the damage they'd done and all the hearts they'd broken. Easter was sure that they would be dragged downward on fiery pitchforks screaming, banished for eternity to the hell in which they'd forced others to live.

Sometimes. But most times it was hard to believe in jubilee when every day began and ended the same way. Maybe Prophet Nat was crazy, imagining things the way he wanted them to be. Maybe he was too young and he didn't know. But Easter could see it clearly;

every morning when she woke, white people still had the upper hand. Every morning the same thing rang in her ears. *Cursed.*

Easter loved the way the water bent her fingers, made them look like they didn't belong to her. The water seemed to make the knots on her hands go away. She picked out beans the worms had already eaten on.

Easter envied Prophet Nat his mother. Even more, she envied Nancie her son. Easter's son had been stolen away. Sold. The ones who took him didn't know how that could tear the heart, or what it could do to the mind.

She thought of Will, who'd begun mumbling to himself and cooing to his axe. Going mad. Some slave men's families kept them from running; Will's family had kept him sane and alive.

She knew. She remembered her own time—torn from her arms, tears on the ground, dust in the mouth and eyes. Afterward, the ones who sold him told her they loved her. Her baby sold for seed; it made her hate the fields. She would never see him again in this lifetime.

Easter trailed her hands through the water as she sang to herself.

We're marching to Zion,
Beautiful, beautiful Zion;
We're marching upward to Zion,
The beautiful city of God.

Sometimes Easter dreamed her son was grown, like Prophet Nat, and that he was beside her. She dreamed that she was a great woman in a hooped skirt, with ruffled lace cuffs, and a large feathered hat. She dreamed that her son was a preacher, a prophet, that they walked through apple orchards and that he held her arm. He smiled at her and patted her hand.

We're marching to Zion,
Beautiful, beautiful Zion;

We're marching upward to Zion,
The beautiful city of God.

In the dreams, her hands were not knotted, her hips did not ache. In the dreams, her son told her she was beautiful. She had no scars.

In the dreams, she still had all her teeth and she smiled. There was plenty for her to eat. There was fruit from the trees, there were cakes and cheese, and there were eggs—soft scrambled—and meat everywhere. She was never thirsty.

She dreamed that, like Maryam, the Lord's mother, she was highly favored; dressed in emerald-colored silk and the finest lace, pearls at her throat, she was beautiful and beloved, not cursed. In her dreams, her son was close, close like Prophet Nat was to his mother, Nancie, like Jesus to Mary.

But it was all dreams. Her son was gone and Prophet Nat had been beaten, pinned against the church wall. The blood was everywhere and he had almost died. Her son was gone, part of the curse. The two women—Lavinia and hardheaded Charlotte—would have the babies and one would be sold away. Charlotte's arms would be empty and cold, even in the summer, when she fell asleep at night. Miss Lavinia was the closest thing Easter had to a child. She was the last baby, good or bad, to nurse at her breast.

We're marching to Zion,
Beautiful, beautiful Zion;

When she was through picking through the beans, Easter lifted the pan to drain the water from the beans and then dumped them in a kettle. She covered the beans with water. Maybe, wherever her son was, he would be free one day. Maybe the young ones would be free, maybe Charlotte's baby. Easter was too old. She was too afraid.

We're marching upward to Zion,
The beautiful city of God.

chapter 29

August 22, 1831

Easter had worked all day and into the night. Her hands, her shoulders, her back ached. But she had fallen asleep as soon as she lay down. Even the hard floor couldn't keep sleep away. She dreamed of streets of gold and chariots of fire. She heard people shouting and cannons exploding.

Lavinia woke her, stumbling over her on the floor. "Light the candles," she demanded. "I don't care what Nathaniel says. He's not here now."

"Oh, Miss Lavinia." Easter rose and lit a candle. She saw Lavinia sitting on the floor now with her nightgown billowed about her, a nightcap askew on her head, and a cup of whiskey in her hand resting on her swollen belly.

"I am tired of them leaving me, leaving me behind." The girl began to cry.

"Yes, ma'am." Master Nathaniel Francis and his mother were probably at Waller's, at the still socializing with the others. Nothing changed.

The girl pushed Easter away when she tried to comfort her. Lavinia tried to stand, but stepped on her gown and tumbled to the floor, and began to laugh.

"Miss Lavinia, you be careful. You don't want to hurt yourself or your baby."

"Don't you tell me about this *baby*! This is my baby and I don't need you to tell me about my baby!" Lavinia touched the cup to her stomach again.

"No, ma'am."

"They didn't have to leave me behind, again, Easter. I'm not too far gone!" Lavinia lifted the cup, the liquid sloshing over the edge. "I can still hold my liquor."

"No, ma'am. Miss Lavinia, you shouldn't drink so much. At least drink the apple brandy instead of that old corn whiskey. It's not good for you or the baby. You should go back to bed."

"He ought to be here with me." Lavinia tapped her stomach with the cup. "Where are you, Nathaniel Francis?" the girl crowed. "This baby could come any minute, auntie Easter!"

"Yes, ma'am."

Then Lavinia started to cry again. "He doesn't care about me. He doesn't love me."

"Of course he loves you, Miss Lavinia. He thinks the sun rises and sets in you." Easter tried to take the cup from the girl, but she jerked it away.

Master Nathaniel hated it when his stuff was misused and there would be hell to pay. Lavinia had pulled at the jug before when she was left behind. The master hated it when anything was missing—stolen from him, he said—whether it was a stale biscuit or a dried apple, but especially a jug of whiskey. Like before, some-one was going to feel the lash over his missing whiskey. Someone had to pay for what was stolen from him and he would never charge the debt to his wife.

When Lavinia awakened from her drunken sleep, she would know she was the cause for the beating, but she would turn her head away.

"He loves you, Miss Lavinia."

Lavinia grabbed the jug beside her and poured more whiskey into her cup. She looked at Easter, the angry look from the church in her eyes and on her face. "No, he doesn't. No, he doesn't. Don't try to fool me, auntie Easter." She shook the cup and took another drink. "No, he doesn't. You know. You see." She gulped down what was in the glass. "You know. He doesn't love me." Then she began to weep. She let Easter sit down beside her and hold her in her arms. Summer heat and mosquitoes, flying imps, and moths drawn to the candle's flame stirred around them.

"Hush, baby. Hush, baby." Easter straightened Lavinia's night-cap and tucked the hair that had straggled loose back underneath. Lavinia was the only baby she had.

"He told my daddy he was going to take care of me." She looked at Easter. "He begged my daddy to marry me. You remember, auntie Easter. You remember; you were there."

"Hush, baby. Yes, I remember."

Lavinia pointed at the candle. "I don't care what he thinks. I don't care what he says. I'm going to burn these candles all night if I want to." She looked at Easter, her eyes wide and bright and believing, like when she was a little girl. "He told my daddy he was going to take care of me."

"Yes. Yes, he did say that."

"Now, look where I am. Sitting here in this old house—wind, rain, and snow blowing in from outside—can't even burn candles at night, can't buy the dresses I want because we're too poor." Lavinia gulped down what was in the glass and then filled it again. "I'm not trash. I can read! I could be a teacher! I'm not poor, auntie Easter. I'm pretty enough. I could have had any man." She gestured with the cup and spilled whiskey on her gown. "Now, here I am, all alone, poor, and left behind while they spend the night at Waller's still."

"It's going to be all right." Easter rubbed the girl's shoulder.

"He said he loved me. Look how he treats me." She frowned and looked as though she were searching Easter's eyes. "And do you know what he's been doing? He thinks I don't know. With that nigger girl! You know, too, don't you?"

"You should try to get some sleep, Miss Lavinia." There was no point in talking about Charlotte. There was nothing any of the women could do. Easter patted the girl's head and Lavinia let it droop, like a wilted flower, on Easter's breast. She held Lavinia and rocked her like she had when she was a child. When she heard the gentle snoring, she tried to take the cup and the whiskey bottle, but Lavinia startled awake and jerked them away.

"Don't you try to trick me, auntie Easter. Don't you try to mollify me. I'm the mistress, not you." Lavinia gulped what was in the cup. "If they won't let me go with them, I'm going to drink here anyway. And don't you try to stop me." She shook a finger at Easter. "I'm the mistress, you do what I say."

"Yes, ma'am."

Lavinia struggled to her feet, teetering, finally managing to stand. Her belly in front of her, her gown trailing behind her like a ghost, Lavinia plopped herself down in a corner. "You stay over there, auntie Easter, and I"—she looked down at the bottle and the glass she held—"and the three of us," she laughed, "will sit over here."

Easter stared at the girl, fretting. Morning, come soon. Everything was changing. Everything was the same.

chapter 30

C harlotte shook Easter awake. "We rising up!"

Easter sat up quickly. It was almost daylight and she had not made the fire or baked the bread! She looked around, quickly scanning the room. Thank goodness Nathaniel Francis was not home yet.

Charlotte, the crazy child, was smiling. "All that is over now!" Easter wiped at her eyes and, holding Charlotte's outstretched hand, hoisted herself from the floor. Nathaniel Francis was going to be mad about his wife's food not being ready. He was going to be mad about the whiskey and the candle. He would be there soon, shoving Easter around.

Charlotte placed one hand on Easter's arm and with her other took Easter's hand. "He's over at Waller's and all of them are gone. We are free, Miss Easter. We are never going to be slaves again!"

Miss Easter? Easter followed the babbling girl to the kitchen. The child had lost her mind! Charlotte seated Easter in a chair.

"All of them are dead, even the folks at Waller's still, and all of us are free! We rising up, like we been praying for, and all this crazy is over! Dark days over!"

chapter 31

Easter mumbled to herself and pulled at the edges of her hair. *Our Father who art in heaven, hallowed be thy name. . . .*

Charlotte was smiling, rubbing the baby that poked out her belly. "All that is over," she said. "We never going to be slaves again." She lifted her skirt up in the air. Crazy laughter bubbled and she danced, holding her baby like holding a partner. "Don't you lift a finger, Miss Easter. You sit right there." She smiled as she moved to the stove. "I'm serving you today." Charlotte let go her belly and grabbed a knife. "They gone."

Who was gone? Easter closed her eyes and bowed her head. When she opened them again, there was a plate set before her with stewed apples and, next to that, a hunk of cheese. Easter felt herself trembling. Lord, Master Nathaniel was going to be mad about his food.

Easter squeezed her legs together, pulled her drawstring skirt tight around her, and wiped her hands across her eyes. Charlotte said judgment had come with daybreak. "We ain't niggers no more. We free!"

Judgment? Free? What was she supposed to do now? Easter stood up. She looked around her. The floor was shaking, like the heavens had busted wide open. Free?

She clasped her hands together and then wrung them. She looked at her confused feet and wondered if she should run. "Lord, what is happening?" She grabbed the frayed collar of her tunic and pulled it close around her. Outside, she saw black men moving about and she heard voices. "Lord, who are all those men?" She ducked to see.

Charlotte was smiling. "Don't you worry, Miss Easter." The floor shifted and Easter looked for something to hold on to. Charlotte came to her and touched her on the shoulder. "They took the overseer and the children last night. All quiet." Charlotte spoke gently to Easter as if she were her mother. "It's all right, Miss Easter." There it was again. Why was the girl calling her Miss?

The smile left Charlotte's face when she looked toward the other room, at Lavinia in the corner. "We are going to have to take care of her, Miss Easter."

"What?" Easter felt her heart thumping.

"I said we are going to have to take care of her. She was supposed to be at Waller's, too."

"They left her behind. She's too far gone to let her go to Waller's."

"We are going to have to put her to sleep, too."

"To sleep?" The girl, the jug and cup still beside her, was passed out on the floor. "She's already sleeping." Easter looked around for any excuse she could pull out of the air.

"I mean asleep for good, Miss Easter. We can't leave her alive to run and tell the other white folks. If we leave her alive we risk everybody."

Risk everybody? What was Charlotte talking about? "Wait! Wait, now!" Easter stumbled like a strong man had hit her. Lavinia still had not moved; alcohol stupor had deafened her. "What, now?"

"The white folks are dead, the Turner's Meeting Place white folks. We can't let her live."

Dead? Easter felt like she was sliding off the side of the world. She looked back at Lavinia. "But she's my ... what about the baby? There has to be some other way."

"When did they ever care about a brown-skinned baby, Miss

Easter? When did they ever go out of their way to save one of us?"

Charlotte walked toward the other room, toward Lavinia, but Easter grabbed the girl's arm. "Don't do it, Charlotte. Look at her, she's passed out. We could shoot cannon off in here and she wouldn't hear."

"Miss Easter, everybody could die if we leave her alive."

Everybody die? White people dead? She didn't understand it all, but she knew she had to protect her child. She couldn't lose another child. Easter took Charlotte's hands in her own. "She won't wake up. I promise. If she does wake up . . . I promise, I'll take care of it."

"Miss Easter . . ."

"I promise. I will. By the time she wakes up out of this"—she looked at Lavinia lying on the floor—"it will all be over."

chapter 32

It hurt where Easter's heart was, her head was heavy, her stomach in knots.

"You calm yourself and sit down," Charlotte said, and she went back to patting her belly. "If I don't live to see another one, this been a good day!" She pointed at the plate. "You sit down now and go ahead, eat."

Easter picked up the spoon, her hand trembling, and dipped it in the apples. Her hand shook, but she managed to get them to her mouth. They were warm, juicy, and sweet. She was still afraid, but her mouth smiled.

"You eat what you want, Miss Easter. What you don't want, you leave behind."

Easter was surprised by the tears in her eyes. She dabbed at them with her fingers.

"Hold on a minute." Charlotte left the room and Easter heard her rumbling. She came back and handed Easter a handkerchief covered with lace. Easter recognized it. It belonged to Lavinia. Oh, Lord, when Master Nathaniel Francis got home there was going to be hell to pay. But for right now he was at Waller's. He was at the still.

Charlotte pressed the handkerchief into Easter's hand. "You keep this, Miss Easter. It's yours. Bought and paid for."

Easter looked at the handkerchief. She turned it over and over in her hands.

"What do you want me to fix you, Miss Easter?" Charlotte was back at the stove. "Tell me what you want to eat."

What she wanted to eat? All her life Easter had been cooking for other people, cooking the food they wanted to eat. *I feel like biscuits. I want ham today. I want chicken. I want soft scrambled eggs.* All her life, she had been eating whatever food they gave her—mostly corn—they gave a portion to the pigs, to the horses, and to the slaves. How was she supposed to know?

"I got hot biscuits for you in the oven, Miss Easter."

Easter smelled them now, hot butter. She looked at the handkerchief in her hands, then back at the room where Lavinia slept in the corner.

"How about some biscuits, some bacon, some soft scrambled eggs? You free now. Just say what you want."

That's what freedom was? Being able to tell people what you wanted for your own meal? Eating food you didn't have to fight pigs for?

"Yes, ma'am!" Charlotte bustled around the kitchen, flour on her hands. She pointed outside at the men. "They leaving now but they are coming back again."

"Who's leaving?" Easter looked toward the window.

"Yellow Nelson and some of the boys. Even Red Nelson is with them."

"Red Nelson?"

Charlotte was smiling. "Yes, ma'am. It's been an uprising. Been a revolution! The men have stood up to protect us. We are free! No more white hands on us no more!"

Protect us? Easter looked outside and saw men and boys she knew—the cowardly Red Nelson, scrawny Shad, and pigeon-toed Joe. There were others she knew by face but not by name. Was this the great and terrible army of the Lord?

They had no uniforms, they were in tatters. They were not shiny-faced white men, but dark-skinned with kinky hair. There was no huge number, just a few men. They were poor men, slave men, just ordinary. These were the Lord's men of courage and valor, the men God had chosen to rescue her? These were the heroes?

Charlotte's smile got bigger. "Set free! Killed them all dead!"

Killed who? *Even the ones at Waller's . . . ?* Easter rubbed her fingers over the lace and embroidery on the handkerchief in her hand.

Charlotte was like water in a spring. "We are going to wring up some chickens and fry them up for the men. But first, you eat, Miss Easter."

Easter clutched the handkerchief in her hand. "Killed? You sure?" She looked out the door at the black ragtag army.

"Yes, ma'am!" Charlotte looked toward the other room. "Some of the men said they killed a woman coming up the road. I thought it might be Miss Lavinia . . . Lavinia coming back from Waller's."

"And the boys?"

"Like I said, it was all in the quiet last night, them and the overseer. I baked them some sweet cakes laced with chokecherry leaves. They always liked those cakes." She shrugged. "What else could we do?"

Poisoned them? Easter pressed the handkerchief to her face. She looked at the apples and at the other food Charlotte was cooking.

The little boys? And Overseer Doyle? Gone? No more of Doyle beating and yelling and whipping? "You sure?"

"The men outside came to the door looking for her. I thought sure she was gone and told them she was at Waller's. We are going to have to do something, Miss Easter." Charlotte looked toward the room again. "What if she wakes up? She could run and tell everybody. We gon' have to do something."

Easter looked at Lavinia slumped in the corner. The baby she had nursed . . . the tiny girl she had held to her breast . . . kill her? It was impossible to imagine her gone. Charlotte came to her, held her hands, and spoke to her like a mother again. "It is the only way to get us free, Miss Lavinia." Charlotte stopped herself and shook her head. "Lavinia and Nathaniel Francis were never going to let you go. Not as long as they lived."

As Charlotte spoke, Easter saw Lavinia that day as she was at the church—not the baby she raised, but the monster she did not know. She saw the young woman with the angry mouth, the one that frightened her. Easter knew that the girl Charlotte was right, right like Miss Lila Richardson was about her husband.

Charlotte hugged her. "I know you love her, but your love didn't mean a thing to them. You spent all your time as a slave crying and they didn't even see." Charlotte rubbed her hands. "How many prayers did you pray, hoping things would change?"

Easter nodded. They could push her down, even the young ones; just like swatting a fly. She sighed. She had been praying for years there would be another way, praying for a change.

"Paid for this already." Charlotte pointed at the food and at the room around them. "You going to spend the rest of your life, use up all this freedom, crying? Wipe your face now, Miss Easter. Had to be done."

Easter used the handkerchief; she breathed in the perfume and wiped the tears away. Easter looked back at the room again and then at Charlotte. "Let her be. If she wakes, she'll be my responsibility."

Charlotte frowned and shook her head. "Miss Easter, I don't think this is such a good idea. This is war and we are fighting for our lives." Charlotte touched her stomach. "We are fighting for our seed."

"She drained that bottle last night, Charlotte. She won't wake up." Easter could hear the pleading in her voice.

"What if the men look in and see her?"

Easter knotted the handkerchief in her hands. There had to be a way. "You said Red Nelson is out there? Well, call him in here. He can help us. We can move her to the jump and try to hide her."

Charlotte looked doubtful. "Hide her? What if she wakes when we move her?"

Easter felt her heart calming. "Just call Red Nelson. We'll cross . . . I'll cross that bridge when I come to it."

Red Nelson came inside, an axe in his hand, the first time Easter had seen him with an axe, and they took him to the other room so he could see Lavinia. "We need you to help us get her up the ladder to the jump," Easter said.

Red Nelson looked at Lavinia like she was trouble. "No one can be left alive now. Maybe when we have more control of things some of them can be spared. But not now." He shook his head at Easter. "No, ma'am."

Easter tugged at his sleeve. "Look at her. Drunk and passed out. She's not going to wake. By the time she wakes it will be all over." She looked at the girl she loved. "And look at the baby in her belly."

Red Nelson stared at Lavinia. He looked around the room and then back at her. "All right." Red Nelson nodded. "But if something comes of this, I won't be held to it."

Easter took his axe and laid it on the bed. "It's all on me."

Red Nelson lifted the girl, her gown trailing and her head bobbing, and carried her up the ladder to the jump. He laid her in a corner of the ledge, wedged in beneath the ceiling. Then he covered her with a mattress and quilts that Easter and Charlotte handed up to him.

When Red Nelson made his way back down the ladder, Charlotte pointed at Nathaniel Francis's gun collection. "Take them."

Red Nelson shook his head. "No guns, no whips, only plowshares turned to weapons. Only farm tools readied for war." Easter watched him walk out the door.

Everything had changed.

chapter 33

She knew she shouldn't be happy about the death of someone she loved—she loved even the ones who mistreated her—that's what she had been taught. But still Easter felt something lifting off her shoulders. She felt a loosening around her heart.

She shouldn't be happy about the death of anyone, especially a little child. But she felt lighter than she could ever remember feeling. Easter felt it coming. Right or not, joy was coming on anyway.

There it was! Great day in the morning! She was happy, sad, and free all rolled up into one. She leaned her head on Charlotte's shoulder and threw her arms around the girl. That baby inside the girl would never know the hurt, never have to know the shame.

Lavinia was hidden away now. And the nightmare that had lasted all her life was finally over. Easter held on to Charlotte. She couldn't let go.

She and Charlotte listened to the men moving away from the house.

> . . . a great people and a strong; there hath not been ever the like, neither shall be any more after it, even to the years of many generations.
>
> A fire devoureth before them; and behind them a flame burneth: the land is as the garden of Eden before them, and behind them a desolate wilderness; yea, and nothing shall escape them.
>
> The appearance of them is as the appearance of horses; and as horsemen, so shall they run.
>
> Like the noise of chariots on the tops of mountains shall they

leap, like the noise of a flame of fire that devoureth the stubble, as a strong people set in battle array.

She hadn't had the courage to free herself. She didn't have the courage or the faith to do it, not even the faith to walk away. She hadn't had the courage to spit in the soup, to plunge the knife, or feed them ground glass. She had thought about it, when they stole her son, when they lifted her skirt, when they mocked her and knocked her against the wall. If they had been angry after she took her revenge, what else could they have done but kill her? What did it matter if she died? They were killing her anyway. But she had been too afraid.

The young people had done what she and the other old ones couldn't do. They were still brave enough, still young enough to believe. Easter rubbed her hands over her knees. Her aches reminded her of all the nights on the cold hard floor. No quilt, no coat—all over now.

When Charlotte put the biscuits, bacon, and hot eggs on her plate, Easter bowed her head. She said a prayer for the ones she had loved and for Lavinia still asleep in the jump. Then Easter lifted the spoon to her mouth and swallowed so that she could live.

chapter 34

She helped Charlotte catch and kill the chickens, feathers flying, squawking as though they knew they would be sacrificed. Master Nathaniel Francis would burst wide open if he knew. He would take her into the forest, shoot her, and leave her body for the birds. But he was at Waller's, with the others at the still, and he was gone now.

Easter went to the garden for fresh things—tomatoes, green onions, and peppers—they were feeding the army of the Lord, the strong army of the Lord!

She and Charlotte poured scalding water over the chickens and plucked away the feathers. She looked at Charlotte. "It's hard to believe this meal is for us."

When they had the chicken frying, chicken for them to eat, Charlotte disappeared through the door. She came back with an armful of clothes. Easter recognized them—Lavinia's dresses.

Charlotte dropped the pile at her feet. She held a peach-colored dress up against the rags she wore. "Won't I look good in this one?"

Easter tried not to touch the gowns, the ruffles, the caps. Then she grabbed at them like a starving woman. She stooped and reached for a blue gown. She and Charlotte, laughing, both reached for one trimmed in red. Giggling, they began to pull and tug. Easter, who had given up everything, would not let it go.

Freedom meant clothes enough, clothes enough so she could be warm. Clothes so she could be pretty. It meant food enough so she would be full for once in her life, food enough so her stomach wouldn't always growl. Food that tasted good on the tongue.

Freedom meant a life where she could choose what would be

on her plate. One thing she knew she didn't want was corn mush—she had had enough of it.

She would be called "Miss."

Easter stopped tugging. She froze. Charlotte was still young; she didn't know how bad things could be. How could the nightmare be over? Had they really killed everyone? "What about Nathaniel Francis? What about Master Francis?" The breakfast she had eaten churned in her stomach. She looked at the dish and the spoon she'd used to eat, at the pots on the stove. He would kill her!

Charlotte laughed. "You don't have to be afraid, Miss Easter. Remember, I told you? Nathaniel Francis gon'. Sallie's house was the first house they struck. All of them gon' right with her. He and his mother were at Waller's, at the still, and all of them are gon' now, too."

"You sure?"

"Miss Easter, it's all over!"

All over. Tomorrow they were going to have to think about the harvest, have to think of how they were going to take care of each other. But today? Easter snatched the dress with the red trim from Charlotte's hands. She had been cold and naked . . . and ugly . . . and cursed so long. "You want it?" She shook the dress at her. "Catch me if you can!" Easter ran into the bedroom, but instead of going to the spot where she usually slept, she flopped upon the master's bed.

She rolled on the sheets and on the cornhusk mattress. Being free meant having a bed of her own. Being free meant no more cold and no more aches! She flipped until the sheets bunched up around her. Then Easter smelled her, caught the scent of Lavinia. Easter sat up, her feet dangled from the bed. She pressed the sheets to her nose.

Charlotte stared at her from the doorway. She rubbed her stomach. "What choice we have, Miss Easter? How many prayers? They were never going to let us go."

Easter nodded at her. "Never." It was a mean choice to make

someone make, to have to choose life without you, to choose death so she could live. "Lord, have mercy on us for what we've done," she whispered.

Charlotte nodded. "The Lord knows. This was freedom war— our Revolutionary War. No more curse, Miss Easter."

Easter stood to her feet. "As Gabriel greeted you, Hail Mary, full of grace, the Lord is with you . . ."

Rubbing her belly, Charlotte joined with her. "Blessed are you among women and blessed is the fruit of your womb. Holy Mary, the God-bearer, pray that your beloved son, Jesus Christ, may forgive us our sin. Amen."

The two women joined hands. This was freedom—joy seasoned with a bit of sad. Arm in arm, they walked back to the kitchen.

THEY FILLED A platter, piled it high with hot, salty fried chicken—only the best parts. They had thrown the scraps—the feet, the necks, the gizzards, the wings—to the dogs. On the table were the pieces meant for people, for free people—breasts and thighs and legs. There were potatoes, not corn, boiling in salted water and tea cakes baking in the oven.

Easter wiped her brow. It was late fall, still too hot to cook, but it was different when you were cooking for yourself somehow. Charlotte grinned suddenly and grabbed the dress, the one with the red trim, from the chair where Easter had laid it. "Sure do like my new dress!" She grinned.

Dresses, hair caps, and no more chains. Easter had seen chains on her father, the price he paid, along with the whip and brine, for trying to run away. She had worn them once herself, she knew the weight of them. But that was over.

Easter laughed at Charlotte and began to tug again. "Not with your belly pulling at it, it won't!" Freedom meant having the liberty to argue. Freedom meant Charlotte keeping her baby. Easter yanked the gown and then she saw the ghost.

chapter 35

Easter stared at the ghost in the white gown. Lavinia! Lavinia stared back at Easter, then at Charlotte, frowning. The ghost walked toward the two of them. Easter wiped her eyes and then shut her mouth. She looked at Charlotte—the girl was frozen.

The ghost, Lavinia, shook her right fist. "You are going to die! You ungrateful . . ." the ghost sputtered. "These clothes are mine! You thieves!" The ghost pointed at Easter. "And you, you of all people! After all I've done for you! After all my family has done for you!" The ghost snatched the dress with red trim from their hands. "What do you think you are doing? When my husband gets home, he is going to skin you alive!"

Easter shook. It was all melting around her. Warm water ran down the inside of her thighs. She should have known better. She dropped her head as Lavinia railed.

Lavinia pushed her shoulder. "You look at me when I'm talking to you, do you understand?"

Easter nodded.

"Don't nod at me, you crazy old woman! You speak to me!" She pointed at the chicken on the plate. "What is all this? You lost your minds?"

"Yes, ma'am."

Charlotte spoke up. "No more! No more, Miss Easter! Slavery over!"

Lavinia's face was twisted, like that day at the church. "What did you say, gal?"

Charlotte took a step closer. "I said no!"

chapter 36

Don't you say no to me!"

"I'll say it again, La-vin-i-a. I . . . said . . . no!"

"You have lost your mind, you devil! How dare you call me by my first name?"

Charlotte shook her hips. "Lavinia! Lavinia!"

The ghost shook her finger at Charlotte. "You are crazy if you think I don't know what you been doing. You are going to die, but first they are going to skin you alive and cut that bastard out of your belly!" She turned to Easter. "I trusted you to work in my house! And you've been plotting all along?"

Charlotte spoke again. "Didn't you hear me? I said it's all over! I said no!"

Lavinia shoved Easter, then looked down at the puddle at Easter's feet. "You get some rags, you"—she paused and then she shoved Easter again—"you, nigger! And get up your stinking water!"

Easter felt herself dissolving. "Yes, ma'am."

"Don't you touch Miss Easter! There are no more niggers here!" Charlotte took a step toward Lavinia. "All your people are gone now. You the only one left. Your drunken husband died at Waller's." She moved to stand between Easter and Lavinia. "And now you going to join them!" Charlotte grabbed Lavinia then.

Easter watched the two younger women fighting. She backed toward the wall, pressing herself there. Let Charlotte be the one to do it, to do what had to be done. The girl, Charlotte, was brave, she was still young. Easter didn't want to be here. She closed her eyes. She didn't want to see.

"I'm going to kill you and your baby! That monster inside you will never grow up to be master over mine!"

Easter didn't have the courage to do it. She didn't have the heart. She pressed closer to the wall and squeezed her eyes tighter. How could you kill the one you loved? She heard them scuffling. Easter forced her eyes open. She wrung her hands as she watched them, wrestling with their bellies pressed together, still not moving from her spot. Charlotte grabbed a knife from the counter. In one swift movement she grabbed Lavinia's hair, pulled her neck back, and exposed her throat. Easter saw the fear in Lavinia's eyes. Easter whispered to herself, *Holy Mary, the God-bearer, pray . . .*

Lavinia's life probably meant the loss of Easter's freedom— probably her own life; but the girl was still her baby. Lavinia's life probably meant all the others' lives, but she was still the one Easter loved. "Don't kill her!" Easter grabbed Charlotte's arm that held the knife. "Don't do it, don't kill her! Don't kill my child!"

chapter 37

hat you doing, Miss Easter?"

Easter grabbed Charlotte and began to pull her away from Lavinia.

"Miss Easter, you promised! What about all the other people?"

Easter looked at the handkerchief lying stained in the puddle of water at her feet. She looked an apology at the girl. "I just can't." She shook her head. "I just can't stand by and see it."

Easter hugged Charlotte. "I'm sorry." She knew she should not stop Charlotte. She knew it was wrong. Easter shook her head again. "I'm sorry."

She had been free for a little while. "You pack up," she told Lavinia. "You get away from here." She looked back at Charlotte. "I'm sorry. I can't. I can't." She shook her head. "Let her go."

Easter went to the cupboard. She got a wheel of cheese; she had no milk to give her. "All your people are dead now."

"D-Dead?" Lavinia stuttered.

"Killed last night, Miss Lavinia."

"But, Nathaniel . . ." Tears Lavinia had cried because she hated him now flowed because he was dead. "You are lying!"

Easter tucked the wheel of cheese under the girl's arm. "You go on. Make your way to your daddy's house. Keep to the woods."

Charlotte tried to push past Easter, lunging for the other girl. "But she's going to get us killed, Miss Easter!" Lavinia was her baby and Easter was ferocious; Charlotte was restrained by honor, honor for her elders.

Easter wrapped her arms around Charlotte's waist to hold her, held her like she was her child. "I know. I know." Easter felt the weight that had left her pressing back down. She felt the aches returning. She felt the shame and the sadness coil back around her. "Let her go. Just let her go on her way."

Easter looked at Lavinia, her baby. "Go on, now. And keep your mouth closed."

She watched Lavinia as she stumbled away. Her stomach and the cheese under her arm throwing her off balance, she grabbed her skirt, and looking back a few times, finally began to run. Easter didn't have the courage to do what needed to be done. "God have mercy on me." Maybe someone else would catch Lavinia and finish.

When she could not see Lavinia anymore, Easter walked across the floor and sat on her master's bed. It would most likely be her last time. She sighed and then strained to hear her freedom running down the road.

Nancie/
Nikahywot

chapter 38

Southampton County, Virginia
January 1831

Nancie had been in the New World for more than thirty-one years.

Sometimes, when she looked out the window, she tried to imagine it was Ethiopia. But in this place there were no monasteries carved from stone, no holy men dressed in robes, no olive trees, no drums, and no rushing waters.

It would have been easier to forget, to be who they wanted her to be. It would have been easier to be a slave, to be a nothing, to laugh and smile and play the monkey for her captors.

It would have been easier to surrender. But when she remembered Josef and she remembered the Nile, when she remembered her father and mother, when she remembered her daughter, and her cousin's body sinking into the deep, she could not forget. She had to live to pass the truth. She was the storyteller.

She was not written down here, and she knew most would give up, despairing that they would be forgotten. But someone would remember. "Remember me," she prayed. Someday someone would remember. "Remember my son."

The heavy December snow was almost gone, but the ground was still hard and the trees bare. The Ethiopian highlands could be cold, but the Virginia winter was unforgiving. The sun, cutting through the cold, was stark.

Nancie ran her hands through the cornmeal in the sea-blue bowl before her. The light was still dim before full sunrise, so it was gray, not gold like the sand along the Nile. The meal was cool on her fingers and she felt herself slipping.

There was no teff in America to make the *injera*, the spongy bread her family had eaten in Ethiopia. She would make corn bread today, like every day. There was no papaya. The one thing that gave her comfort was the smell of the *kaffa*, the warm drink her family had shared. Here in America they called it "coffee." The smell of the drink was enough to move her closer to the highlands.

They wanted her to forget who she was and to forget Ethiopia. They wanted her to forget God, to forget Krestos, and to forget the beautiful brown face of the Kidane Mehret. They wanted her to forget her name.

Nancie sometimes wanted to forget. She could not remember the sand and the river without remembering her mother, her father, her husband, her daughter, Ribka, and her cousin Misha. Though the memories caused her pain, it was her son's legacy, it was his lineage—she could count back more than seven generations—and she owed it to him to remember. If she did not remember, how would she teach her son? If he did not know, how would he find his way home?

Her memory was a painful sacrifice. Even the good memories were hurtful because even the memories beside the water brought her back here. *Ribka*. She whispered her daughter's name and wondered if in Africa Ribka still wept for her. Her daughter must be a woman now with children of her own.

Nancie watched the cornmeal trickling down. Egzi'abher Ab was sovereign. Egzi'abher, the Many-Breasted One, the One who cared for strangers and the oppressed, had brought her here to give birth. All she had left of her beloved Ethiopia was memories, the blood that ran through her son's veins, and the tatter.

Nancie turned from the bowl, walked to her pallet in the corner, and stooped to feel underneath it. She searched with her fingertips until she found it—a shred of white cloth, so soft and fragile now. She crouched over it, shielding it and holding it like a delicate feather.

The tatter was all she had left of the clothes and the life the captors had stolen from her. She took it out at night to remind herself. Nancie closed her eyes, whispered her real name, "Nikahywot." She rubbed her finger over the tatter and hummed the song she sang for her mother.

I *am black but comely,*
O *ye daughters of Jerusalem,*
As *the tents of Kedar,*
As *the curtains of Solomon.*
Look *not upon me because I am black,*
Because *the sun hath looked upon me.*

Remember me. Remember my son.

chapter 39

Ethiopian Highlands
Circa 1798

The sun hung in the sky over the highlands of Ethiopia like a gold coin against a curtain of blue silk with yellow and red ribbons. The water that roared off the edge of the Tis Isat falls was deafening to strangers; it roared like lions and smoked like fire. But after many, many generations the Habesha, the people of the highlands, were used to the falls. Nikahywot loved them.

For centuries her family lived at the crest of the waterfall that, like a midwife, guided the waters of Lake Tana to give birth to the Nile—Ethiopia's gift to Sudan and to Egypt. And so it was her grandmother had told Nikahywot that the banks of the Nile parted to give birth to her.

Nikahywot was a daughter of Ethiopia, daughter of her mother, Afework. She was her mother's firstborn child and she was drawn to water. So Afework told her that water would be part of her destiny. Perhaps in service to Egzi'abher Ab, Nikahywot's mother told her she would travel by water to a place far away.

Nikahywot's father, Kelile, was their protector, a broad-shouldered man of the earth—a wise man whose feet were always planted. His answer was always the same: "We have lived at the summit of this great wall of rushing water all our lives. Like our father before us, we have worshiped Iyyesus Krestos, honored his mother, Maryam, our Kidane Mehret, who watches over the dark children of the world, and we have made the pilgrimage to the holy city of Lalibela, the city of the thirteen stone cathedrals. The mist from the falls of Tis Isat washes our faces, the water feeds the land to grow trees for shade from the sun, and fish swim almost to our door. We have what we need. Why must we dream of leaving? Why must you speak the words to send my only child away?"

"We have been safe here, my husband. But who knows what the Great One will require of us? Who knows but that His spirit, Menfes Qeddus, might come with a lamp to find us at the foot of these falls and bid us go?"

"Dream dreams of staying, my wife, not dreams of going away." They had been childhood friends and sweethearts and her parents' arguments were always the same.

Like her daughter, Ribka, and her mother before her, Nikahywot was born with a veil over her face. The old people in the village said that it gave the bearer sight, vision not only to the past but also to what was to be. "It is a gift," the old women told her. But it was a gift Nikahywot did not want because sometimes at night she had dreams, dreams that left her wet with sweat, her heart beating like the holy men's drums. Dreams about losing her family. But by morning the waters of the falls washed the dreams away.

Instead of the dreams and thoughts of veils, Nikahywot loved to sit by the river, her head on her mother's lap. Her mother's legs stuck out straight in front of her, resting on the high grass, and seemed to stretch to the water's edge. The cloth wrapped around her mother's waist was soft from years of river washing, the stiffness beaten out of it by twisting and pounding on rocks. Her mother, a sprinkle of gray hair at her temples, ran her fingers gently over Nikahywot's hair.

The rainy season had ended, the storms were gone, and everything was green now—and red and gold and blue. From where they sat Nikahywot could see Ras Dashen—the head guard, the general who fights in front of the emperor—the highest peak in the Semien Mountains. The rains were gone and now there was a rainbow over the mountains, over the highlands—a promise that the sun would always shine again.

Beyond them, a herd of elephants bathed in the river. Blue hermit thrush and tiny zebra finch with orange bills twittered in the trees. Yellow wildflowers and white ones with pink centers peeked out from between long, shiny, spiky green leaves. Tall green grass stretched as far as she could see. It was *ghe net*, paradise.

Nikahywot stretched out her hand to touch her daughter's head, which lay on Nikahywot's lap. She rubbed the hair along her daughter's temple. "Sing me a song, Ribka."

She heard the pouting in her daughter's voice. "I don't want to sing, Mama."

"Don't frown so," her grandmother warned Ribka. "You will get lines and no man will marry you. He will know from twenty steps away that you are mean. Smile and let him marry you first before he finds out your mother has raised a spoiled child."

Ribka giggled. "Oh, Grandmother. I am not spoiled. It is your daughter who is spoiled, and who is responsible for that?"

Afework chuckled quietly. "You are too smart, just like your mother. It is the way with African women." Nikahywot's eyes were closed but she could feel her mother smiling. Nikahywot turned so that her mother could stroke her forehead. "Watch out, baby," she said to Ribka as she shifted. "Mama is turning."

Ribka lifted her head and then snuggled back into place when Nikahywot had settled. "Sing the song for me, Ribka. Sing one of the old songs."

"Only if you tell me one of the old stories, Mama."

"No, Ribka, Mama is resting." She opened her eyes to look at her daughter.

Afework continued stroking Nikahywot's head. "The child is right, Nikahywot. She is not a slave, she is not *barya*; she will not do your dirty work. She will sing if you will tell one of the old stories. I told the stories to you. That is how you remember. Now you must tell them to her or she will forget, and if she forgets, how will she find her way back home? Tell a story and then she will sing."

The place where they lay was quiet and there was shade from

the African sun. It was cooler in the highlands, but the sun still made its presence known. The trees were full and green, the grass tall, and the stream full of fish. But sometimes at night, when she dreamed, Nikahywot dreamed of a barren Africa. The water was gone, and with it the fish and the trees, even people—and the few who were left stared ahead like ghosts, as though their insides had died.

"Tell me a story, Mama, and I will sing," Ribka insisted.

If she told the story, she wouldn't have to think of the dream. So, Nikahywot began her favorite story. "Long, long ago, there was a wise king named Solomon from Israel." Nikahywot closed her eyes again so that she could see the pictures in her mind more clearly. "Many generations past, he lived in a great house filled with gold." Nikahywot stroked her daughter's hair. Her mother's breathing slowed and deepened. "But greater than his wealth, King Solomon was known throughout the world of civilized men for his wisdom and for his heart. Men from far and near came to meet him and bring him treasure to honor him.

"One day a queen of Ethiopia, our queen of long ago, heard of Solomon. Now this queen, Makeda, was a woman of great power, great wealth, and great wisdom herself."

"Queen of the South," Ribka said.

"Yes, granddaughter, Queen of the South and a great beauty!" Afework interrupted. "Don't forget to tell about the beauty."

"Yes, she was a dark woman of great beauty." Nikahywot could feel her mother nodding.

Her mother interrupted again, telling her favorite part. "Makeda was beyond beautiful, as are *all* women of Ethiopia!" Nikahywot opened her eyes to see her mother shrugging. "What can we do? We cannot help ourselves. Even the Greeks tell stories of our beauty—you have heard the stories of Andromeda and Cassiopeia. We cannot help our beauty. Egzi'abher Ab has blessed us. Black eyes so beautiful we must console Charaqa, the moon, so she won't be jealous." Afework lifted her smooth hand to point at the sky, and then she touched her fingertips to her mouth. "To be sure, we live in a land where the men are brave like lions; they are protectors and providers and quite handsome themselves. They are strong men, not easily conquered." She clapped her hands. "But the women? Our lips are as juicy as pomegranates." Afework wiggled on the grass. "And behind us we carry the perfect soft pillow for a king's head.

"We are blessed with beauty. What can we do? Our beauty is intoxicating to men, so that is why we wear the *netela*, the shawl wrapped around our shoulders that also covers our heads so the poor men will not faint when we walk by."

Nikahywot smiled at her mother. "Perhaps you should tell my daughter the story, my mother."

Afework shook her head and batted her eyelashes like a young girl. "No. No. You tell the story. You are doing a very good job."

Nikahywot closed her eyes again, drifting on her mother's voice. "Afework, your grandmother, tells the truth, my daughter. Queen Makeda was beautiful, and she, too, like Solomon, was wise and very rich and very powerful. And when the merchants who traveled between our country and his told her of Solomon, that his wealth and his wisdom were greater than hers, she asked, 'How can this be?'

"For Ethiopia had an army that fought on land and water. So powerful was the name of Ethiopia that its mention was enough to cause kings of other nations to fall to their knees and give up their treasuries. And the land of Ethiopia, our home, as you can see even now, was fertile and rich. Queen Makeda could not believe the story she heard. How could there be a king wealthier and wiser than she? So she journeyed to see King Solomon for herself."

"By camel?" Ribka asked.

"Yes, and she and the hundreds who traveled with her by caravan also journeyed on the Nile. When she reached Israel, Solomon was captivated by her wisdom, her storytelling, and her great wealth."

Afework clapped her hands sharply. "And her beauty! You must not forget to tell my granddaughter about the queen's beauty! The poor man was overcome! He lost his head! What man can keep his head when he is enraptured by our beauty? She brought him wealth and he sent her back with an unintended gift in her belly—a son!"

Nikahywot opened her eyes. "I think you should tell the story, my mother."

"Don't look at me that way, Nikahywot. I am your mother. That look could wither a fig tree! Do you want to kill me?"

Nikahywot smiled at her mother. "Are you certain that you do not want to tell the story?"

Afework waved her hand. "No, you are doing a good job. Don't forget, though, to say that the son's name was Menelik, son of Solomon, and that he became a great, great leader! A man of two nations born in Ethiopia!"

Nikahywot told her daughter the rest of the story, of Menelik's journey to visit his father, Solomon, about his journey home with Jewish holy men, and how the Ark of the Covenant came to rest in the highlands of Ethiopia. "Now," she told her daughter, "you must sing."

Ribka held her grandmother's hand and began to sing.

I am black but comely,
O ye daughters of Jerusalem . . .

chapter 40

Southampton County
1831

Nancie sighed as she rubbed her fingers over the tatter. She tucked it back underneath her pallet and returned to the bowl. The sun had found its place in the sky and kissed the bowl in front of her. Nancie dragged her fingers through the meal like sand.

This burden from Egzi'abher Ab was so much for her son, Nathan, for her Negasi, her prince. It was too much for someone so quiet and so gentle. He should have been in Ethiopia, with his grandmother and sister, sitting beside the Nile. Now, instead, he waited for a sign.

She hummed the song her daughter, Ribka, had sung and let her mind travel back to Ethiopia.

1798

NIKAHYWOT LOOKED AT the Ethiopian sky. It was almost time for the evening meal. Her husband would be home soon. The smell of eucalyptus wood burning sweetened the aroma of the food bubbling in the pot. It was a fast day, like every Wednesday and Friday, so there would be no meat, but the pot was filled with fish, onions, carrots, and peppers. Misha, the daughter of a distant uncle, gathered wood to keep the fire burning.

Nikahywot's husband had been to the great market at Gondar—a market where merchants from all over the East gathered—

trading cattle, selling goods. She imagined him there among the thousands in the marketplace. She imagined Josef walking past the castles, palaces, baths, and churches built more than a hundred years before by Ethiopian emperors Fasilides and Johannes. She had heard there were artesian wells there, like at the churches in Lalibela. She imagined the smells of the food and exotic spices, the sight of the great fortress there and the army that guarded what had once been Ethiopia's capital city. She imagined Josef stopping to peer into the great libraries there, running his hands over the pages, the leaves written by scholars and clerics. Over sixty thousand people lived in Gondar, numerous as stars in the sky. There were beautiful religious paintings there, music, and dancing. She imagined the din of the marketplace—merchants hawking wares, men like her husband trading cattle, priests reading the holy words aloud to the people, prayers and the drums. Josef would return soon and she wondered what gift he would bring to her—a small piece of silk or a hand-sized picture of one of the saints.

Misha's husband was off tending their sheep, but soon, when his work was finished, the smell of the fire would draw him, too.

While Nikahywot and her mother, Afework, cooked, her father played the game they had played since she was a little girl. They expected her to read the holy words, to memorize them, and to understand them.

"So, what is the greatest commandment?" he called to them.

Her mother called back to him. "Well, even a fool knows the answer to that! 'Love the Lord your Egzi'abher with all your heart and with all your soul and with all your mind.'"

Nikahywot's father and mother, childhood sweethearts, squabbled like brother and sister. They both had been born near the falls, as had been her husband, her daughter, and as, Nikahywot was sure, the rest of her children would be.

Misha, Nikahywot's cousin, bent arranging the wood and tending the evening's fire. Nikahywot's father stepped around Misha to face his wife. "You speak well." Her mother was much shorter than her father and reached up, from where she stirred the pot, to touch his face. He smiled and kissed her palm, and then she resumed stirring the pot as her husband took his seat. She smiled at him, still blushing as though she were a young girl.

"Maybe someone else will know the answer to this next question," Nikahywot's father, Kelile, the protector, said. "So, what is the second greatest commandment?"

"I am not as wise as you two elders," Nikahywot said to her father. "You are wise like Menelik, the son of Solomon and Sheba. You are both wise like the *shimaghilles*. I can only pray that in my old age I will be as wise and as honored as you two."

Her father patted his head. "The girl is not only beautiful like her mother, but she is like her father the fox!"

"But I believe I have the answer, Father."

"Tell me then, daughter."

"The second greatest commandment is like the first, 'Love your neighbor as yourself.'"

They all answered together, as they had done hundreds of times before. "'On these two commandments hang all the law and the prophets.'"

Nikahywot was a dreamer. Her daydream was to always look upon the rushing waters of the Tis Isat, to watch the waters fall, crashing against the rocks until they finally spilled into the Nile, sacrificing themselves so that those who lived along the Nile's shores might survive.

Her mother bent again, stirring the pot, while Misha silently stooped, adding more wood. "I have heard rumors," Nikahywot's mother said.

"Women are always talking." Kelile nodded at Nikahywot's husband, who had come to join them. Sitting next to Kelile, he looked around to take it all in. Josef was a quiet man.

Nikahywot's husband was shy and would not do more than nod to her in front of the others, but she knew secrets the others did not know. She nodded back to him and the wind blew her *ne-*

tela across her face. Josef was also a man of great passion. He was quiet, but his few words carried great weight. And there was a lion in his heart; when his arms were around her Nikahywot knew she was safe. She knew she was loved.

It was planting season and Josef had to oversee the fields, to check on the teff, the wheat, and the barley. He was praying for a good harvest.

Nikahywot smiled at Josef again. She would bear him many children.

"It is a good thing women are always talking," Nikahywot's mother answered her husband, still stirring. "If women did not talk, who would tell the stories?" She motioned to Misha for more wood. "The women are saying that in villages not far from here, daughters and sons have gone missing—the strongest ones, the fairest ones."

Nikahywot's father's face lost its smile. "Daughters? Gone missing?" Just as quickly as it left, his smile returned. He tapped Josef on the shoulder. "Do we have sorcerers among us now? Making children vanish in thin air?"

Nikahywot's husband, a brave man but always a peacekeeper, nodded at her father and then at her mother—he never chose sides unless it mattered.

Afework kept stirring. "No, not in thin air, my husband. Taken. Stolen."

Nikahywot watched their performance while she tossed more fish and vegetables in the stewpot, waiting for the next response.

"Taken? By whom? River goblins?" Her father nodded again at Nikahywot's husband and then at Misha's husband, who had come in from the hills, hoping the men would join the game as his allies.

"No. By men who sell them for money, my husband."

Nikahywot's father laughed. "You women should bathe and not gossip. You frighten yourselves."

"It is not gossip."

"More likely, whoever is missing was careless and eaten by

crocodiles. No one steals men. Maybe a chicken or a fish, but no one steals men. No servant of Egzi'abher steals a man or a woman. It is forbidden."

"When have wicked men ever cared about the law?" Afework lifted the wooden spoon, blew on it, tasted, and then stirred again. "The women say these men serve other gods and they are free to steal."

"Ridiculous," her husband said and stood. *Ridiculous* was always the word Nikahywot's father said when he wanted no further discussion. "Enough of this gossip that frightens you." He pointed at Nikahywot's daughter, Ribka. "The sun will set soon and you will give my granddaughter bad dreams." He patted his belly. "Keep your mind on the pot. My stomach is growling and it is time for us to eat."

Nikahywot sliced a papaya and handed a piece to her father and then a piece to her husband. The meal would be ready soon.

WHEN THEY HAD finished eating, after the fire burned low and there was no sound except an owl complaining and a hyena barking in the distance, they settled into the *tukul*. Her mother and father lived and slept in the innermost ring of their large round house. Nikahywot and her husband, Josef, and their daughter, Ribka, slept in the middle ring, while Misha and her husband slept in the outermost ring. Misha and her husband had to always be ready to serve, to haul water or whatever was needed.

Nikahywot listened to her daughter and husband breathing, deep in untroubled sleep. She rubbed her husband's back and let the faraway falls sing to her. She counted the straw bundles that made up the roof and waited for sleep to catch her.

Nikahywot heard her mother's whispers coming from the inner room. "Perhaps Egzi'abher Ab, who loves us, is allowing the Arabs, the Muslims, to chase us so that we will open our own eyes to see the mote that is there."

Her father grunted. "Open my eyes? My eyes are open though

I have been trying for hours now to shut them. It is late and I am trying to sleep, but someone will not allow my eyes to close. I am kept awake while you, I believe, are dreaming, talking in your sleep again.

"There have been fights between Christians and Muslims in the great cities—Aksum, Jerusalem, Gondar—but this is a quiet place. There is no trouble here. No one steals people here."

Her mother persisted. "Perhaps Egzi'abher is displeased that we keep Misha and her husband as *barya*, as our slaves."

Her father sighed, whining like a small child. "Not tonight. I want to sleep."

"What if Egzi'abher is displeased? Do you think that Egzi'abher will care if we are sleepy when He is displeased?"

"It is not against the law. We do not mistreat them. We keep them in our home, we feed them, and they are warm. They are *barya* and we are *chewa*, we are their masters. But we treat them as family."

"But still. Egzi'abher has given us the moon, this land, and the stars. What if He is displeased that this is not enough for us? Why do we need *barya*?"

"If I freed them, where would they go? Who would take care of them?"

"We take good care of them, my husband. But still."

Nikahywot heard her father yawn dramatically and she imagined him giving her mother the impatiently patient look he reserved for the woman he loved. "They are able to have children and I will lay no claim on their children. Her husband is building a small herd of his own while he tends to mine."

"Yes, but—"

"He will not leave here penniless. It will be a good start for him. It is a benefit to us both."

"Yes, my husband, but I keep thinking."

"You are not thinking. You are dreaming. You are sleepy—the sweet air and your sleepiness, the moon hanging in the sky, all keep you from being practical. If I free them, who will tend our flocks? I cannot do it alone. Who will wash our clothes? Who will carry the wood and haul the water?"

"You are right, my husband. You are the practical one. But I cannot help but think that years from now, people who pass by our home will no longer remember who built this *tukul* and who farmed this land for us. They will forget who gathered the *kaffa* so we could make our hot drinks, who herded our sheep, and who gathered the wood. All this will look like magic to them. Our families will remember our names and they will see pictures painted of us and cloth woven by us, but who will remember them? Who will sing songs about how hard they worked? What will they or their children's children have to show for how hard they worked for us?"

"Afework, you speak words as beautiful as you are, but they are not practical words. You are romantic, my wife. We did not create this world. We did not create this life. Some were meant to rule. Some were meant to serve. Some were meant to do the dirty work. It is the way of the world."

"Of course, Kelile, my husband."

Her father grunted. "Now, let me sleep."

There was silence. The wind rustled the leaves in the trees, night birds sang, and Nikahywot could hear the roar of the waterfall in the distance. Free Misha? Misha had never once said she was unhappy and Nikahywot had known her all her life.

Their great-grandfathers were brothers. Nikahywot's own great-grandfather had married among the *chewa*, as expected. But Misha's great-grandfather had married with his heart, marrying a girl from among *barya*—any man who slept with a slave must marry her—and had cursed his family line. It was not Nikahywot's fault that Misha was a servant; it was her great-grandfather's sin, the sin of the family he married into that cursed Misha's family. It was that family's forefathers who dishonored Noah.

"Still, my husband." Her mother's voice cut through the quiet. "It is the law and the prophets."

Her father groaned. "You are talking in your sleep."

"No, I am awake. I cannot sleep. It is the law and the prophets . . . and love."

Nikahywot could hear exasperation in her father's voice. "What do you mean? *Please* tell me so I can sleep!"

"Love Egzi'abher. Love others as yourself. On this hangs the law and the prophets."

"You have been drinking the *tej*. You are dreaming or you have been drinking the wine. I will check the wine in the morning, you can be certain of that!"

"Love others as myself. 'Therefore all things whatsoever ye would that men should do to you, do ye even so to them: for this is the law and the prophets.' What would I want for myself? What would I want for my daughter, for Nikahywot? Would I want her to be a slave, even a beloved one?"

"Our daughter is not a slave. I am not wealthy, not compared to some of the others. We have no palace, but we have not wanted for anything. She will never be a slave."

"But would we *want* her to be a slave, my husband? Would we think that slavery is the best that life could offer her?"

"Slavery is not against the law. Slavery is written into the law."

"And divorce is written into the law, my husband, but it is not what is best."

"At this moment, I am not so certain."

"My husband, you are silly while I am earnest."

"You are confused and I am sleepy."

"Everything hangs on love. You have taught us that. The law and prophets hang on love. Is that not right?"

"Yes, of course, my wife."

"So, the best thing, the greater thing, is to treat *barya* as I would want to be treated, to dream for them what I dream for myself or for my own daughter. If I am too greedy or too hard-hearted or too weak, then Moshe has provided a lesser path, rules to force us to treat them well if we are not strong enough to love them as

Egzi'abher loves them. These are not rules that say we *must* have slaves or that it is *good* to have slaves. These laws protect them and protect us from our wicked ways."

"Why are we debating this now, my wife? It is night. There are stars in the sky. Feel the wind from the falls blowing over us to cool us? This is the time for sleep." It was quiet again and Nikahywot heard cicadas chirping. Then her father's voice again. His voice sounded husky. "It is the time for sleep . . . or for love."

"Do not play around now, Kelile. I am serious." Nikahywot imagined her mother slapping Kelile's arm.

"You are like a baby; your day and night are all confused, wife!"

"No spooning, husband! I am serious. I have been thinking that maybe Egzi'abher wants us to do the greater thing. We know that Egzi'abher Ab hates divorce. If Our Father hates divorce between a man and wife, how He must have hated those words Noah spoke that day to curse his own son! Words that ripped the family apart! If He hates divorce, how can He not grieve at our turning our backs on one another over such a small thing? How His heart must bleed that we continue, separated—not only divorced, but harming one another, hating one another, in the name of the One who is love!"

"But there have always been slaves, Afework. Do you want to change the world? What would you have me to do? I am one man."

"Maybe Egzi'abher is trying to help us to love better, to see the greater thing. We cannot account for the whole world, but you and I can do better. Each one of us can. He loves us so much."

"Of course, He loves us."

"He has given us grass and eucalyptus trees. Olives and honey."

"Now you are making me hungry, again, wife."

"Perhaps, now, Egzi'abher is trying to give us the greatest gift, to teach us to love. And He, like a parent, is trying to show us that we are wrong."

Nikahywot's father yawned again. "I do not believe that I am wrong, but if I am, then Egzi'abher the Father of love will show me."

"Yes."

"May I sleep now, Afework?"

"Yes," her mother said. "Good night, my husband."

Nikahywot, in the middle circle of their *tukul*, draped an arm around the shoulder of her husband, who snored softly beside her. She touched the small painting of the saint that Josef had brought to her. She had never thought that Misha and her husband might want something different. It had not occurred to her that they might not be happy. She was happy. How could her Misha not be happy? There was food for her and a place to sleep. If she was unhappy, would not Misha have told her?

"Kelile?" She heard her mother, still sounding wide awake, call her father's name. "We have to listen to Krestos. Iyyesus Krestos does not always say what I want to hear. Sometimes I want to take a path that seems easier for me. I want to keep things the way they've always been. I like being *chewa* and not having to do the dirty work. But if it is what Iyyesus Krestos wants me to do, even if it makes me uncomfortable or seems wrong to my mind, I have to do it. When Egzi'abher frees Misha while I am left to do my own dirty work, then I must trust Him and obey. Egzi'abher ways are not our ways. I must not fight against what He's doing, not if I really love Him. If I truly believe that He loves me, then I must surrender and settle in my heart that what He says to me is best, even if it does not seem best at the time. It may frighten me, but it is good. I may lose everything I own, but it is good.

"Krestos loves us right or wrong, slave or free, *barya* and *chewa*. And that is how Krestos wants us to love—and He's willing to fight us to teach us to love.

"We have to stop being disobedient children always wanting our own way. Love is more important than comfort or things. What has Misha done wrong that she should suffer? She is a good girl. I love her like my daughter. I think Krestos wants us to set her free."

"No more, woman! I can take no more. I will let them go when the next harvest is over. Please! Please! Let me sleep!"

"I love you. That is all I want to say."

"Good. Now, let me sleep."

"You are a good man. I knew it when you were a boy. That is why I did not run away when my parents told me that your father had chosen me to marry you."

"Woman, please!"

"You are a good man, Kelile, a good husband, and a good father . . ." Her mother's words were muffled.

Her father whined, pretending that he was crying. "Lord, please send sleep and shut my wife's mouth."

Nikahywot kissed her husband's shoulder and closed her eyes.

chapter 41

Shouting woke Nikahywot from her sleep. Outside the *tukul*, in the distance, she heard the shepherds' voices, saying, "Run! Run!" She heard the sheep bleating and the cows moaning desperately.

Her husband was already on his feet, throwing on his cloak. "I think I hear rifles!" He stepped into the doorway that joined their ring with Misha's. Josef joined Misha's husband and the two of them ran out into the night.

Nikahywot's father ran through her home from the innermost circle. "Stay together!" he yelled behind him.

Nikahywot held her daughter to her. Misha and Afework joined her. They stood in the outer doorway. They heard shouting and saw flashes of light in the darkness and heard sharp cracks, as though the sky were breaking.

"Mama, I'm afraid!" Ribka squeezed Nikahywot tightly around her waist. It was impossible to see. Clouds covered the moon like scarves over their eyes.

THEY FLED—HER MOTHER, her cousin Misha, her daughter, Ribka, and she—from the ones who said they were the followers of Islam, the new religion, from the schemers who twisted the words of the prophet Muhammed for profit. "Make your way to Gondar! We will find you," her father had yelled to them. "If you do not find us there, then Aksum!" He, her husband, Josef, and Misha's husband stayed behind to stall the captors.

Nikahywot heard her husband and father shouting, rousing the other men of the village. The anxiousness in their voices made her heart pound. She did not want to leave them. "No! We must stay together!" She wanted to stay and fight with them.

"We will only be in the way," her mother told her, pulling Nikahywot by the arm. "We must get away! Think of your daughter. We women hold the future in our bellies; we must get away or they will do to us what the Romans did to the Israelites!"

Nikahywot stumbled running through the high grass and her daughter cried out reaching for her.

"Nikahywot, you must not look back!" her mother chided her. She had never seen fear in her mother's eyes before. "You will get us all killed! We must run!"

They ran, panting, falling, crying, until they reached a safe place, a place close to the falls.

chapter 42

It was a miracle that in the darkness they made it from the base to halfway to the crest of the falls. They traveled swiftly. Then they sat huddled together in a clearing in the darkness, afraid a fire would give them away, afraid that the darkness would draw hungry animals to them. "We must pray," her mother said to them. "We must pray for our men and we must pray for peace."

Peace? How could there be peace now? Curse the captors and curse all their descendants! Nikahywot wrapped her arms around her daughter to keep her warm. They had been able to grab only a few gowns and shawls. "Let Egzi'abher Medhin smite them! It is clear that all the followers of Islam are wicked, wicked men!"

"Don't let anger speak for you, my daughter. Don't let it blind you. All Muslims cannot be evil. These are the greedy ones, the connivers who use religion to get what they want."

"But look at the trouble they cause, Mother! Look what they are doing to our family! How can we pray for them? They show us no honor, though Jesus was long before Mohammed, though the story of virgin birth is told in the Quran! They only honor money. It is only Iyyesus Krestos who has the power to resurrect men. They are the filthy infidels!"

"We will pray for them because we are all from the same family!"

"They are not my brothers! How could brothers send us running out into the cold night? Why do my father and husband have to defend me from my brothers?"

"Don't speak anger in front of your daughter, Nikahywot. We are all Abrahm's children. It grieves Abrahm when we harm one another. It saddens Egzi'abher Ab that His children destroy one another. We must pray for understanding and peace. We must pray for love."

They said good-bye to Lake Tana. They scrounged berries and fruit, following the road to Gondar, but were careful to stay out of sight.

When things were quiet, just before dawn, Nikahywot stole away to pray.

chapter 43

She was always drawn to water. Nikahywot turned, though she was far away from the falls, in its direction. Away from her falls, she realized, the falling water screamed and cried for the family it left behind as it rushed to join the Nile.

Her family was like a pattern woven into a prayer shawl or a coat of many colors. Her family was being torn apart, leaving the strings to dangle, unraveling what had been woven together for centuries. Nikahywot imagined the spray from the Nile, the water that had carried kings and queens and pharaohs, wet the *netela* that covered her hair and shoulders.

Gondar? How would they make it to Gondar, three women and a girl traveling alone? If they did not starve, thieves would overtake them. Journey to Aksum? It was impossible, like crossing the Danakil desert without camels. If they survived, they would never be able to find one another lost among the thousands in those great cities. Her husband would never hear her voice calling him, drowned out by the sounds of the marketplace. The cities were huge and the men would not know where to look. Nikahywot imagined what her mother would tell her. *Do not worry; trust God. Each day is a journey of its own.*

Her mother was a dreamer. How could she pray for peace? How could she pray for love?

A sliver of gold on the horizon said the sun was rising. Above that golden band, the sky rapidly went from turquoise to deep dark blue until overhead the sky was still almost black. The moon was covered by clouds, but here and there were stars.

Nikahywot opened her mouth and began softly to sing her

morning song to Egzi'abher. It was the song she had been singing since she could remember.

>Hearken unto the voice of my cry,
>My King, and my Egzi'abher:
>For unto thee will I pray.
>My voice shalt thou hear in the morning, O LORD . . .

A hand touched her shoulder. Nikahywot gasped.

chapter 44

Nikahywot gasped and then turned to see Misha standing behind her. Her cousin had come to attend to her. "Is it safe to be here?"

"You startled me, foolish girl!" Nikahywot forced her heart to stop pounding and calmed her voice. "My mother and Ribka?"

"They are fine, still sleeping."

Her mother was wrong; Nikahywot was certain that Misha did not want to be free.

"There is something I have wanted to tell you, Nikahywot. I have news and I wanted to share it with you first!" Misha smiled at her. Then her face saddened. "But in all the confusion . . . Do you think the men are safe?" Worry furrowed her brow.

"Of course. We will meet soon. They will find us at Gondar." Nikahywot was irritated with her cousin. She did not like being interrupted. She wanted Misha to be quiet, but she knew the foolish girl would not be quiet until she delivered her news. "What is it?" Her cousin was just like her great-grandfather—too foolish to be anything but *barya*.

Misha patted her stomach and then covered her smile with her hand. "A baby."

"Good for you." Nikahywot smiled wanly. "We will talk later," she said.

Misha walked away, dropped to her knees, lowered her head, and began to pray in silence.

A baby? Nikahywot looked at her cousin. A baby would only disturb things. Nikahywot would have to get another servant with Misha with child. The foolish girl would be tired and complaining.

Misha would want to rest instead of doing her chores. But Nikahywot would not think of her cousin now. This was her quiet time, her time for singing.

> Hearken unto the voice of my cry,
> My King, and my Egzi'abher:
> For unto thee will I pray. . . .

It was a miracle to sing, to open her mouth and feel the sound born inside her wrap around her. It was a blessing that Egzi'abher heard her.

She fretted for nothing. All this would be over and they would all be together soon. Nikahywot thanked Egzi'abher for her life, for her family, for her servants, and for her people. She thanked Him for her husband, her provider. Josef was probably already asleep in the *tukul* now—the trouble over. She thanked Egzi'abher Ab for her beautiful mother and her daughter.

In thanks, the Nile sent her a breeze that caressed her face. The wind wrapped her gown around her legs and arms. Nikahywot lifted her arms to pray to Egzi'abher Ab.

A hand grabbed her wrist.

chapter 45

They were captured well before Gondar. They were captured at the falls.

Her captors were wicked men. Cruel hands bound Misha and Nikahywot together and carried them first across desert and then on board a ship. Her hands and feet, like Misha's, were bound with rope. They were not allowed to speak. The captors shook their heads at them, raised their rifles, threatening them.

Aboard the ship, the captors threw the captives below. All were naked, stacked on three levels in the belly of the ship. The men were bound together—hand to hand and foot to foot—in pairs on the lowest level of the ship, lying on their backs, to make it more difficult for them to fight. There was not room to stand and they were squeezed in tight, like sheaves of wheat being taken to market. The men were always growling, fighting to be free, and it was tense each time they were allowed on deck, even in chains. Bile.

Just above them were the boys, chained in twos, foot to foot and hand to hand. They were unable to move and rolled about as the ship tossed. Confined in the middle—like tender fruit, few of them survived. Death.

The girls and women, like Misha, were nearest the deck so that the ship's crew might have easy access. Modest women, the captors paraded them about and made sport of them. Blood. The women screamed while far beneath them men clothed in chains yelled and cried.

When weather was fair, the captors removed them from their quarters, chained them to the deck so they could not escape, and threw buckets of water on them if it could be spared—and maybe a bucket or two of water in the hole. When weather was foul they might stay below weeks at a time. But whenever they were brought from below, there was always death. On a good day, one or two died. By the time they arrived at port, more than a third of the captives were dead.

For Nikahywot there was a special disgrace. The captors took the shawl that covered her head and ripped away most of her gown so that her legs and arms were exposed. She tried to cover her hair, to cover her body, so that they could not see her. The captors laughed, and the more she tried to hide, the more they tore away. No man had seen her this way except Josef. She silently prayed, as she cried, for Josef to rescue her. She prayed to Krestos, she prayed for mercy.

They saved her for one of the ship's officers. He used her, who had been raised humbly, to warm his feet. The shame on her husband, on her family—how could they take her back if she returned?

The captors would not allow Nikahywot to pray. They would not allow her to sing her morning song. "No mumbo jumbo," they told her.

She heard the cries and smelled the foulness of humans bound in chains deep in the belly of the ship beneath her. How could the captors not hear them? Why didn't they retch at the smells? Couldn't they hear the children crying for their mothers?

To the captors the people below seemed to mean nothing. The sounds and the smells of the people merged with those of the cows and the pigs they carried on board.

In the hole for months, only allowed sun occasionally, the captives wore fecal matter, blood, and vomit dried to them like a second skin. Nikahywot saw them and heard the heavy clank of the chains they dragged. Who would do this? Not even oxen were yoked this way. Women and men crying, swearing, threatening, chained together, some trying to throw themselves overboard.

She would not forget. There were mothers and fathers among

them, and sons and daughters. There were teachers, merchants, and farmers. There were new brides and shepherds. There was someone she recognized from the market, a wealthy young woman who sold cloth. There was a young man aboard who she had heard described as the promise of his village. The captors herded them along with animals. She had to remember so that she could tell their families what had become of them.

She had to remember it all—the dead bodies, the sick heaved over the side—men bobbing on the waves. Children she had heard wailing—rotting and thrown overboard so they would not infect others. Mothers who died in childbirth—children conceived in Africa and children conceived at sea—their mortified babies tied to them by strings.

Sometimes, among all the other voices, Nikahywot thought she heard Misha crying, crying out to Egzi'abher Medhin, to Iyyesus Krestos. Nikahywot heard her praying for mercy. She thought she heard Misha screaming her husband's name. Nikahywot tasted the bitter, salty filth as she pressed her lips against a crack in the floor. "Don't die, Misha!" She tasted the brackish spray as she yelled to Misha, to her friend. In the trouble, they were no longer *barya* and *chewa*; trouble had made them sisters. "We will be together again! Somehow, I promise to rescue you!"

chapter 46

Nikahywot could not keep her promise.

They traveled through strange waters and she recognized only the sun and the moon. Nikahywot tried to count the moons, but she cried, she was sick, and she despaired. It was hard to remember. But she would remember. She forced herself to look, to remember the faces in the water.

The bodies floating in the water—the large angry fish that had been trailing the boats swam closer and then began darting at the bodies, tearing away pieces. Arms disappeared, legs, torsos. The corpses hardly resembled anything human at all. The fish devoured bodies, chains, hair, cloth—whatever was there. Then, there was Misha.

It would have been easier to forget. But she could not forget. She would not forget Misha. She would always remember. She would not forget that her cousin was a person, a daughter loved by Egzi'abher. Misha was a wife, a mother, she had a name.

Nikahywot looked away. She would never forget.

chapter 47

They took them off the ship at night bound in chains and crowded them into a land-bound, dark place. Some of the guards with guns repeated a word to each other: "Ha-tee! Ha-tee!" In the place with no light they were crowded together.

In the closeness of the room, she smelled up close the same stench from the belly of the ship—dried vomit, feces, and blood. And sadness. Anger and fear. From the accents she could tell that there were Somali, Sudanese, and some from the west, from nations like Igboland and Hausaland, in the crowded room. But most of them, she thought, were Ethiopian, many Amhara.

Nikahywot heard people crying. "Where are we?" "What has happened to us?" "Will they eat us? Are they cannibals?"

They were all *barya* here.

"A quarter of the captives on my ship died!" Many others said the same. "Half of us died!" The captors had packed them on board like a farmer taking mangoes to market—packing too many knowing some would bruise and spoil. Misha was one of those thrown away.

Nikahywot would never forget. Egzi'abher Medhin would repay the captors.

There was no priest among them. But there was a young *shimaghilles* who had survived. The wise holy man prayed and talked with those who spoke Amharic. He spoke of followers of Krestos captured by Muslims. But strangest, he said he had heard of white men going from the coasts into the heart of Africa to take God's people captive. He had heard that they instigated fights between the African nations so the nations would take captives that the whites then bought. "Isn't their own land, aren't their own people enough?"

The *shimaghilles* whispered to them. "You must not weep or cry out. We must not alarm them or allow them to hear us speak our own languages." She had seen men and women beaten for speaking. The captors called them "ee-vil" and "witch doktor." "No mumbo jumbo," they said when the captives prayed to Egzi'abher for mercy. "We are not forsaken. We are in the hands of Egzi'abher Medhin," said the *shimaghilles*.

"But where are we? Who are these people?"

"Shark people. I think these *ferengi* are shark people." The *shimaghilles* reminded them of the sharks that swam alongside the large boats. "The sharks ate everything!"

If her husband, Josef, were here he would protect her. She wrapped her arms around her legs and leaned her head on her knees.

The *shimaghilles* tried to comfort them. "Many years ago, when I was a boy, my mother told me there were fetish worshippers. I saw none, but I believed her.

"I have been watching these pale men and I think they are the ones my mother spoke of. They worship their own skin."

It made sense to Nikahywot. The captors were only cruel to people with dark skin. She shook her head in the darkness. What kind of person worshipped his own skin? The *shimaghilles* whispered in the darkness, "They treat us like animals while they behave like animals themselves. You have seen for yourselves that they eat bloody meat and even swine."

It was true. No one in Nikahywot's homeland would eat a pig. It dishonored Egzi'abher. It was disrespectful before Iyyesus Krestos. Heathen.

She tried to pay attention to the young *shimaghilles*'s voice. "But it is better that I close my eyes, or that I am blind, than to allow what I see to stop me from offering them Krestos's love."

The captors weren't worthy of Krestos's love. Why would He want them in the kingdom? Close her eyes? She would never forget what she had seen.

The *shimaghilles*'s voice was insistent. "We must try to forget what we see. They are wicked, they are heathens, but we must love them anyhow. We must forgive and pray for our captors."

She thought of Misha floating in the water. Offer them love? If her husband had been there he would have slaughtered them. The *shimaghilles* might be wise, but he had no common sense. The only prayers Nikahywot would pray would be for the captors' destruction.

> Break thou the arm of the wicked and the evil man:
> Seek out his wickedness till thou find none.

She did not have time to pray for heathens. She had her own worries. She did not want mercy for them, she wanted them to suffer!

THERE WAS NO way to keep track of the time in the dark place, Ha-tee, hot days with no sun. Though he was not a priest, the *shimaghilles* led them, whispering daily prayers. He repeated a few prayers in the holy language, Ge'ez. When he judged that a new day had begun he began the prayer cycle—morning, midmorning, noon, afternoon, evening, and night—all over again.

Nikahywot would never forgive them. She would pray the songs of King David against them. She would pray the captives' laments. May Egzi'abher Medhin do to the captors all they had done to the captives and more!

> O daughter of Babylon, who art to be destroyed;
> Happy shall he be
> That rewardeth thee as thou hast served us.
> Happy shall he be,

That taketh and dasheth
Thy little ones against the stones.

May Egzi'abher curse them and their offspring! Nikahywot would never forgive.

chapter 48

At night, once a day, the captors came. Moonlight flooded the space around their silhouettes in the doorway. The captors slid in a tub of water and a tub of gruel for them to share.

Nikahywot settled into the closed, dark space, the stench, and the murmuring. At least there were no hands. At least she was near her people. Then, after several days, the captives opened the doors. When they opened the doors the fresh air outside made her more aware of the putrid smell inside. The daylight hurt her eyes.

In the daylight, looking at the other unclothed captives, Nikahywot remembered that she was almost naked and she was ashamed.

A captor's hand reached for what remained of her clothes. She fought to hold on to them. They were ripped away, leaving only the tiny shred in her hand. She squeezed the tatter, balling her fist around it.

She bowed her head. *Downcast.*

The word came to Nikahywot, as though her mother could see her from far away, as though someone knew her name and would tell her father and her husband that strange men had seen her naked. The hot wind blew over her body and the sun scorched her. She closed her eyes, hoping to fade like a ghost.

The captors forced them into a communal bath—men and women together. The women covered their faces, crying, hoping not to see, hoping not to be seen. At gunpoint, the captives were forced to wash. Dirty water splashed into her mouth and eyes.

Nikahywot slipped the tiny shred, the tatter, into her mouth and closed her lips around all that was left.

Once the captives were out of the bath, the captors used their hands to smear them with foul-smelling grease—not the oil she had known all her life, not the fine oil scented with myrrh. Nikahy-wot cried when the men touched her. Who were these men? Who had raised them? Who were their mothers?

She was chained again. *Forgive me for whatever I have done and send me home, Krestos!* Chained in line with the others. *Send me back to my daughter, to my husband, my family.*

The captors marched them to the center of the village.

By the rivers of Babylon, there we sat down. . . .

It was the same blue sky with white clouds like over Ethiopia. But it was not Ethiopia. Instead of green grass there was gray, hot sand that burned the soles of her feet. Nikahywot saw mountains, but they were not hers. She saw blue water, but it was not her Nile. Far beyond them in the mountains she saw a waterfall, but it was not her waterfall; it was not the great Tis Isat.

Ha-tee was wicked, full of drunk men staggering and leering. The captors led them out one by one, loosing them one at a time from the bunch. White men, tightly clothed men, pointed at them. The white men argued, haggling over prices. *And they have cast lots for my people; and have given a boy for an harlot, and sold a girl for wine, that they might drink.*

A scream!

chapter 49

Nikahywot turned her head toward the sound; a naked captive man. First a roar and then a panicked sound, a whining. He bolted after a naked woman—she might have been his wife or his sister—who was being taken away in chains. He lunged, his hands clawing after her, tears on his face. One of the white men with guns rammed the man's face with his rifle butt. Teeth fell from the captive's mouth, his scream replaced with gushing blood.

One of the captors loosed Nikahywot from the chains that connected her to the others and led her to a wood platform. There was no cover. Eyes roamed her body. She pressed her legs together and covered her breasts with her hands.

Captors pushed her hands away and forced her legs apart, touched her, felt places no man had touched except her husband. They squeezed her breasts and pushed back her lips. Nikahywot moved the tatter with her tongue, hiding it. All she had left to her was the tatter and her name, Nikahywot, the one who brings life.

Her tears covered their hands. Shame took her tongue. They squeezed her as though she were a melon. Men pointed at her, shouting, laughing.

"Black," they kept saying. "Nigger." They treated her as though she were *barya*, as though her forefathers had offended Noah. Couldn't Egzi'abher see? Didn't He care? Nikahywot raised an arm again to cover herself. One of the men swatted it away. The captors gave her to the white man who touched her last.

If her husband had been there . . . *As Gabriel greeted you, Hail Maryam, full of grace* . . . She moaned, longing for her family. Why had Egzi'abher abandoned her? What had she done? Nikahywot prayed the nightmare would end.

chapter 50

They laughed and frowned at her old name, Nikahywot, the source of life. They told Nikahywot that her name was Nancie. Nancie was a better name. They smiled, nodding. It was so much easier for them to say. So, in an instant, all the things that went with her name—being a daughter, a mother, a beautiful wife, being *chewa*, being Ethiopian, her ancestors, being Egzi'abher's daughter—were gone. Her family was gone, her village was gone, and her church. Her language dissolved and there was no Tis Isat, no Nile, and no mountains. When they took her name, there were no stories and no songs, no hopes and dreams or faith. When they took her name they murdered her. They took Ethiopia and Krestos.

They re-created her with the new name that was easier for them to say. She began with them, the name said to her. They gave birth to her with the new name and with the new name they became gods.

Her robes were gone and so was her shawl, her *netela*. They dressed her in a muslin shift. She touched the tip of her tongue to the tatter tucked inside her cheek. She did it so they would not see it and take the last thing she had away.

There was nothing before, the new name told her. But Nikahywot vowed that she would not forget.

By the rivers of Babylon, there we sat down,
yea, we wept, when we remembered Zion.
We hanged our harps upon the willows in the midst thereof.
For there they that carried us away captive required of us a song;

and they that wasted us required of us mirth, saying,
Sing us one of the songs of Zion.

She sang it in Amharic, the language of her birth, the cousin to Iyyesus Krestos's Aramaic.

How shall we sing the LORD'S song in a strange land?

Nikahywot substituted the name of her homeland.

If I forget thee, O Ethiopia, let my right hand forget her cunning.
If I do not remember thee, let my tongue cleave to the roof of my mouth;
if I prefer not Ethiopia above my chief joy.

The captors heard her and she saw fear and anger on their faces. They waved at her to stop. "No mumbo jumbo! No voodoo!" they yelled at her. "English!" One of them shook a whip.

They put her on a wagon. Nancie watched the Ethiopians behind her as the bumpy movement of the wagon jostled her head side to side. Her people grew smaller and smaller as the captors forced her up the road.

In no more than a week's time, the captors put her on board another ship. Nancie did not think anything else could break her heart, but from the deck, where she stood with a manacle around her ankle, Nancie looked back at the shore to see the other Ethiopians and Africans.

The ship began to move, and the distance and the water between them and her increased. The waves rocked the ship and she strained to keep the Africans in sight. Soon they were no more than dots and then Nancie could no longer distinguish them from the sand or the mountains.

The sails caught the wind and moved the ship through the water and Nancie knew she would never see them again. She left the last of her kindred on Ha-tee's shores.

chapter 51

A dusting of snowflakes swirled around her. The hard snowfalls of December and Christmas had passed. Most of the captives had survived. Nancie looked down at her feet, at the fissures; she could never get used to winter and snow with no shoes. She wrapped her arms tight around herself and remembered the heavy wool shawls she had worn in the highlands.

The butcher had arrived, knives on his belt and in his bag, that morning. Nancie had seen him strap on his apron and pull his hammer and cleaver from the bag. The pigs squealed, like babies. Long ago, Benjamin Turner had approved that Nancie stay far away from it all. The others celebrated the butcher's work: the captors, the dogs, and even the captives. It would mean ham, roasts, and bacon for the captors. It might mean pig ears, pig tails, and pig feet—whatever the captors gave to them instead of the dogs.

Dried leaves tumbled along the ground and made a crackling sound as they gathered at the hem of her drawstring muslin skirt. She looked down the road, hoping to see her son.

Each day she worried that she would never see Nathan again.

She wanted him alive. She wanted him with her. But, in a place she held secret even from herself, she prayed that he would go, that he would find a ship and return to Ethiopia. She prayed that he would find her husband and his sister.

Her Nathan had left some years ago after being beaten by Samuel Turner. When he returned she both rejoiced and lamented.

Her son was a man born of two continents, two peoples. Like Moses's mother, who floated her son down the Nile, Nancie at once hoped her son would be a foreign prince in Pharaoh's palace and also a deliverer to his suffering people.

She had lived in Virginia long enough, she had seen the end from the beginning, and she knew what would be his fate. The *ferengi* would hate him. Egzi'abher had placed a burden on her son. Though their blood also flowed in his veins, the *ferengi* would kill him.

If her Negasi had been born lame or feeble, if he were a slobbering simpleton, then he might have a chance or a quicker end. But he had been born perfect. Every day he grew smarter and more capable, and who he was threatened the captors.

He walked into rooms heavy with nigger jokes and his presence made the joke tellers feel foolish, ashamed. He was the one who said prayers, who quoted Scripture, who offered hands and opened doors. He was the Southern gentleman they idolized, and in his presence they saw themselves as niggers. Her son was doomed.

Nancie reached into her pocket and touched the tatter. If he had been born in Ethiopia, her son might have been a *shimaghilles*, a priest, or a great general, a Ras Dashen—the general who fights in front of the emperor. He might have been a great teacher. He was a wise man and he had a great mind for planning and inventing. He might have built cathedrals. But he was born in this America. Curse the *ferengi*. Curse the children of the *ferengi* for all they had done to her and her son.

chapter 52

Nancie remembered few names from on board the ships now. She remembered only a few, like Yusuf and Newton and Mordecai. There were white faces and brown faces and black faces, some with beards while others were beardless, some with turbans while others wore top hats.

What she could not forget was the screams of women being raped, night after night, by the captors on board the ships; so that many arrived in port pregnant, while others died in childbirth on board. Some died of disease. Some were shot, beaten with whips, or tortured to death trying to escape or trying to protect their loved ones. Some died of broken hearts. What she could not forget was the hysterical cries of mothers, their babies thrown overboard, or family members who saw a deceased loved one floating away on the sea.

She would not forget that when they came ashore in Virginia, some of the captives had lost their minds and could no longer speak. Some had become animals. Some had broken legs and arms; some had broken minds. Some of them came ashore monsters, ready to do to others what had been done to them. And what of the captive boys? Who would show them the way?

Full of fear, waiting for the captors to slaughter them, they cried, waiting for the captors to butcher them and eat them as they butchered the cows and the pigs.

She would not forget that their beautiful hair was matted and full of dung. She would not forget that the captors pointed at them and laughed.

She would not forget that those who had devoured them on

board, who had raped them, the captors who had been married to them for months by cruelty, walked away in Virginia as though they did not know them—as though they had not seen them bleeding, had not heard their screams. The captives no longer existed; they were cargo, ghosts.

It was when she came to this place, to this Virginia, that she began to hear and understand the words they spoke to her—calling her Negro, darkie, black, and nigger: the captives were no longer people of different nations, no longer Igbo or Hausa, no longer royal or servant, scholar or priest, no longer *barya* or *chewa*. The Africans were no longer people, but beasts. She was to understand there was something wrong with her and the others like her, something wrong because of their dark skin. Cursed.

She saw it on the captives who had been in America for a generation or more; they did not know they were beautiful. The people who worshipped white skin had taught them to hate their dark skin, their black hair—hair like sheep's wool, like Egzi'abher's hair. They had forgotten the beauty birthed into them by Africa.

They were all afraid—men and women—so love and beauty stood in line behind survival. The men here in America had been taken from the women and turned into cattle. The women did not have men to hold them, to tell them they were beautiful.

But Nancie remembered that she had had a husband. She remembered the sound of his voice, the touch of his hand. She whispered his name, "Josef."

The *ferengi* who worshipped white skin showed the captives here painted pictures of a white *amlak*, a white mother cradling her baby. White was beautiful, the captives said; black was cursed and ugly.

But Nancie would not forget.

I am the rose of Sharon, and the lily of the valleys. As the lily among thorns, so is my love among the daughters.

She knew Egzi'abher Ab, Egzi'abher Bezawi, the Almighty, the Many-Breasted One.

He brought me to the banqueting house, and his banner over me was love.

She knew Egzi'abher, she knew Krestos, and the Menfes Qeddus. She had seen the beautiful brown face of Maryam the Weladite Amlak, the Kidane Mehret. She heard them whispering to her.

O my dove, that art in the clefts of the rock, in the secret places of the stairs, let me see thy countenance, let me hear thy voice; for sweet is thy voice, and thy countenance is comely.

The captors wanted her to forget, but she could not forget. She could not forget that when the captives washed up on the shores of Virginia, one way or another they were all dead.

chapter 53

The squealing of the pigs made her heart pound. She turned away, walked away so that she would not see the blood. She rubbed the tatter to slow her beating heart.

WHEN SHE CAME to Virginia she began to recognize what was wrong with the captors' faces. These *ferengi* were not like the Greeks or the Turks; they had no color—they were pale like dead men, as though the color had been drained from them. It frightened her to see the blue veins showing through their white skin like chickens without feathers. Some of them had straight yellow hair, hair without life that flattened to their faces. But the ones that frightened her most had cold blue eyes that chilled her like the ice in the mountains in winter, and red hair like flames so that when they opened their mouths it looked as though they were screaming with their heads ablaze.

But finally she realized that it was not their skin, or their eyes, or their hair. It was their mouths—mouths with no lips, like the sharks, with teeth ready to devour.

IN VIRGINIA, THEY delivered her to Benjamin Turner. He was a husband and a father. He paid her no attention by day in front of his wife. But when his wife was not present, when darkness came, he forced her—he kept her for himself like the officer on board the ship—and soon she was with child.

The night that Nathan Turner was born, the *qayy charaqa*, the *dam charaqa*, the harvest moon, was so large that Nancie thought it might swallow her and the baby. It was a blood moon, ghostly red.

The midwife called it a hunter's moon. Nancie was certain it was an omen that she would die in childbirth, an omen that the world would end.

> *The sun shall be turned into darkness, and the moon into blood,*
> *before the great and terrible day of the LORD come.*

Her sweat drenched the sheets. Nancie did not want to look at the red moon. She did not want to look at the gray child. She turned her face to the wall. The birth of her second child, her first son, should be a time for celebration. But the people in Virginia were wicked. The white man had raped her. Egzi'abher could never bring good from such a thing. How could she give to birth a *ferengi* child, a child of rape.

This birth in a strange land could bring her no joy. Where were the women who would gather outside to pray while she gave birth? There was no one to pray to Maryam on her behalf for mercy from the pain.

The midwife wrapped Nancie's son in rags and handed him to her. "Look at your baby. Look at his eyes, so wide open and alert, like he's been here before."

It was not the blood moon that drove her mad. She had seen many moons before in Ethiopia, even blood moons. In the short time that now seemed like eternity the captives had shown her what they would do to her, and what they would do to her son. The moon told her they were bloody men, spillers of blood, *dam afsash*. Better to save him now. Better to kill him before the shark people stole his life away.

She wrapped the cord around the baby's neck and pressed rags over his nose and mouth. Better to send him to Egzi'abher.

chapter 54

The midwife fought Nancie for the baby. "You must be out your mind, you crazy African! You mustn't kill this baby! You can't kill your son!" She wrestled the crying baby away.

Nancie turned back toward the wall and prayed for death. His tiny arms and fingers reaching, his squalling mouth and pink skin, he was born in chains.

She was an honorable woman with a husband who adored her. She had a daughter in Ethiopia. Now she bore the child of another man, betrayer of the husband she loved. How could she betray her daughter's love? Why were they trying to save him? They did not care about his life, only his birth and his fetching price.

In Ethiopia she would have given birth at her parents' home, among her people. In Ethiopia, after the birth, the women would care for her for forty days while she rested.

These people knew nothing. There was no one here to announce the birth of her son underneath the moon. Where were the women who would gather to sing his welcome and tell the village that he had arrived? *Born today is the son of eight generations of warriors! Born today is the son of ten generations of prophets! Born today is the son of seven generations of wise women! The son of ancient fathers who walked with Abba Selama! Behold their aspects bloom in him!*

There was no one to make the special food, to oversee the tasting day. Who would make the *genfo* of barley and ghee? No midwife praying prayers. No beautiful clothes for her baby's presentation. No special chair she should sit in for the presentation of the baby to the town. No priest to circumcise and bless her baby. No fragrant oil to massage his little body. No one was there to watch over her and protect her and her son from evil. Would no one play the *begena*, the harp, to put her to sleep?

He was a child of shame. A girl who gave birth to a bastard child would be driven from her home or die of shame. But here was her son and she was still alive. He slipped from the womb in shackles; Nancie could see them. And as surely as he wore them, with every jerk of his arm or kick of his tiny leg Nancie heard their rattle. He would be a dreamer like Nancie's mother and they would kill him for it.

Born dead. How could she give birth to a living baby when she was a dead woman? She had nothing left to give. No dead woman could produce milk, *watat*, to sustain a child.

chapter 55

The squealing pigs had reminded her of her son's birth and of the cries of the children on board the ships. It was quiet now. The butcher had ridden away, little trace left of the bloody work he had done. Now she smelled the grease and the stink in the air; the women were at work rendering the fat. Methodically, they cut the fat away from beneath the butchered pigs' hides, then boiled it in hot water until the fat melted. When the fat cooled again, the lard was scooped from on top of the water. The men did the butchering, but rendering was woman's work.

Nancie let go the tatter in her pocket and then wrapped her arms back around herself. The ground was hard and cold. She stamped her feet to stay warm. She looked up at the sky; the days were still short and darkness would come soon. She looked down the road hoping to see her son.

"Nathan!" She waved when she saw him. He was walking slowly. When he was close enough, she whispered in his ear, "My son, Negasi, my prince." Because no one was listening, they whispered to each other in the old language.

He kissed her cheek. "My mother, you worry too much."

She hugged him as though she would not see him again. "I love you."

He kissed her cheek. "And you, also."

"Say my name. My real name, so that I will not forget who I am."

"You are my mother. Your name is Nikahywot, you are my source of life, a princess of Ethiopia, borne across the seas in the belly of a ship and spit out on dry land, like Jonah at the gates of Nineveh."

"I am no slave." She tried not to cry in front of him, but shame made her eyes water and her lips tremble. "I am no man's concubine."

"You are a beloved daughter of Egzi'abher Ab, and someday, again, you will be free." He kissed her cheek again. "I promise." He stretched out his arm, pointing in the direction of the ocean. "Someday you will see the water again."

"I am drawn to water."

"You will find the water, again, Nikahywot, my mother. Egzi'abher has told me so."

She wiped her tears. "Forgive me; I am an old woman lonely for my home."

He nodded, silent.

"But no mother could have asked for a finer son. You are my joy."

He looked at the dimming sun. "I have to leave now." He reached into his pockets. "I found these pecans for you." It was two hands' full.

"Take them to your wife." She pushed his hand away. "Take them to your son." She smiled. "He must be a big boy now." She had seen her grandson when he was a baby. But after Cherry and Riddick were sold, she was only able to see Negasi.

"He is growing. My son has your eyes." Nathan pressed the pecans toward her. "I have gifts for them, but the bird that dropped these said to deliver them to an Ethiopian princess—a gift of love."

"How can I refuse then?"

He hugged her again and then turned to walk away.

"Next week?" she called after him. He nodded and continued down the road.

chapter 56

Nancie used a board to stir the boiling water she used to clean Elizabeth Turner's white clothes—petticoats, collars, cuffs, nightcaps, and underthings. The steam from the large pot dampened her face and helped ward off the cold.

She had thought no good would come of her son's birth, but good had come. In his eyes, in her son's smile, she found hope that she would live again. She found hope that she would be free again. And to prove that there was hope Egzi'abher Ab gave her *watat*, sweet mother's milk, to nurse her baby. When no one was around, she called him by the Ethiopian name she had given him, Negasi, the prince. He was good, sweetness come from bitter water. Nathan lived and grew and Nancie breathed through him.

Benjamin Turner's wife, Elizabeth, hated Nancie, and when Benjamin was not around, Elizabeth spat at Nancie and kicked at her as though what had happened was Nancie's fault. Elizabeth taught her children, especially her sons, Samuel and John Clarke, to despise Nathan, as though his existence was Nathan's own fault. Even though he was smaller, they punched him and kicked him. He was not their brother, they told him; he was a slave, a nigger. There was always a new bruise, a swollen eye, or a bloody lip.

"Why not me?" she had asked the Breath Giver. But she knew the journey was for her son, for her warrior prince, who would speak as Jonah spoke to Nineveh. Her baby had been so young, so tender. His curly hair was soft to the touch. He should have been in Ethiopia hunting with his grandfather or fishing in the Nile. Nathan held the pages she had given him, the ones written on paper she found lying about, written with sticks dipped in berry juice, written in her mother tongue. A Bible, given to him by his father, rested on the floor in front of him. "You are the truth that stands against the lie." Nathan was so young. How could he understand? "Egzi'abher called me to this place, traveling the length of the Nile—through Ethiopia, the kingdom of Sudan, past the ancient pyramids of Kush, to Egypt, and then across the seas to this place, where we have no friends and no family."

He was hope and truth was in his mouth. He was the deliverer. She was the ship that carried him to Nineveh. She was the basket that carried him through the rushes on the Nile. "Egzi'abher has not abandoned us," she had told Nathan, even as she fought to believe it herself. Her son had looked at her with such large, innocent, believing eyes. "He is friend to the homeless, to the stranger in foreign lands. The Many-Breasted One hears our cries."

Nancie wondered if her mother was still alive and if she was looking for her. She wondered if her mother still called her name. It was hard to believe, after all she had suffered, that Egzi'abher loved her, but Nancie needed to believe for her son.

"You know your father of this land, of America, of Virginia, but you are so much more. You are also a child of Africa, my son. You are a prince called out of Egypt. You are the Ethiopian who stretches forth his hands to Egzi'abher." Little Nathan held the pages she had given to him, the ones written in Amharic, the ones they had to hide. "We are called to Virginia, to this Nineveh, to set them free. We are called to light the way because the people here are lost in darkness and we must bring light."

Negasi was her miracle, her proof of Egzi'abher. "They are lost in darkness. We must tell them of the light that shines on Ethiopia. You are their deliverer!"

"Lost in darkness?" Nathan blinked at her. She wanted to grab him in her arms and run away. But where would she go? This place was not her home.

Nancie grabbed the Bible that lay in front of him and reached for the pages, but he would not let them go. Nathan studied the pages every day—pulling them out of the place where they hid them—learning first the Amharic letters, then words, and then sentences. Nancie had shown him, using berry juice, how in Ethiopia the first words of the passages were always written in red. She had written what she could remember. She should have been a better student.

There was a reason that she had survived and that her son had lived. She was the ship that brought him to the shores of Nineveh. So many women, like Misha, had died on the journey over. *Misha! Misha!* Her cousin's body had rocked gently on the water, the baby still tied to her, rocking, and then the two of them were drawn to the ocean's watery breasts. But she, Nikahywot, had lived and there was no choice.

There had been no choice for Maryam, the mother of Iyyesus Krestos, and so there was no choice for Nancie. Egzi'abher had sent her son to deliver His people. There was no other choice for her son. If Egzi'abher was Father to all, if He was who she knew Him to be, then she and her son had no choice. She had nothing else but Egzi'abher. There was no other choice but to believe.

"Lost in darkness?" her son had repeated.

He was a small child and he should not have to bear such a weight on his shoulders, the weight not only of all those who had been stolen, but also of those who stole Egzi'abher's beloved children and lied in the name of Egzi'abher to justify their crimes.

"Yes, lost in darkness." He should have been a poet or a singer like David the shepherd boy. But this was Nathan's lot. This was the service to which he was called. Even a mother could not stand in the way of Egzi'abher's will. "You were born here, a son of two continents—your inheritance is also America, and Egzi'abher has heard the cries of your people. They have lost their way."

If not her Nathan's shoulders, then whose? Jonah's mother, Jeremiah's mother, Isaiah's mother—they all must have cried the same tears for their sons. Her Nathan, her Negasi, was too young, but was not Moses too young to be set adrift on the Nile, to be raised as a prince of two nations? Wasn't Joseph too young to be sold into slavery by his own brothers only to become a ruler over Egypt—a prince of two nations?

"You are a son of two continents, a son of Africa and of America, the son of the captors and those held in captivity. You are the son Egzi'abher has called to this storm. The captors are lost in darkness because they are young in the way. They do not recognize who is brother, who is wheat or chaff, because they judge without the heart. You must speak to them as Jonah spoke to Nineveh—a city greater than Gondar, maybe greater than Aksum. Who knows but that they will repent." As she spoke to her son, Nancie thought of Misha floating in the water, and in her heart she hoped the captors would not be like Nineveh, but instead would be like Pharaoh and get the judgment they deserved.

She pressed a finger to her son's tiny chest. "The captives who were taken from Africa no longer remember that all flesh is from one family, one Father. They no longer remember how the Father loves them. You must awaken them. You must help them remember. Life's rhythm began in Africa."

chapter 57

Another winter passed and they were still in America, still in Virginia. She prayed for rescue. She prayed silently to Egzi'abher Ab. *Take this cup from my son, Lord and Master.*

She combed her hand through the curls on top of Nathan's head. "The captors teach that Egzi'abher is the Amlak of anger, wrath, and war. They teach that He is the Egzi'abher of vengeance. They teach that He is a respecter of persons—but our Egzi'abher, the only true Amlak, loves all His children."

Her son was so young. He could have been a boy running over the Ethiopian highlands, wading through the grass, chasing butterflies, catching fish, or hunting. "You must speak the truth about Egzi'abher, that He is all-powerful, that He is holy and righteous. But you must also tell them that Egzi'abher is the Father and the Many-Breasted One; Egzi'abher feeds the hungry and welcomes the stranger and defends the oppressed. He is all-powerful and all-knowing, but like a mother He gathers the rejected, the homeless, and those who are least. He is the Breath Giver and Lover of all.

"You must be brave and listen closely for the voice of Egzi'abher. He will speak to you out of the deep." Nancie pressed her son closer into her embrace. She would not have him with her long. Soon they would sell him away, like a calf or a pig. Or worse. She told him the stories her mother had told her. "Let me tell you the story of the Ethiopian Jew who heard the truth of Krestos from the apostle Philip and took the truth of Krestos back to Ethiopia." She told him of the saints and the churches. "Sit with me and listen and then we will pray."

Nancie rocked her son in her arms. She knew she would not

have the joy long. Her son was a man of two peoples, like Paul, who was both Jew and Roman, and his life would be full of storms.

"Lift the heads of your brothers in chains. Remind them that, like Moses, they are children of the Nile. Remind them that they are great warriors, sons of Nimrod, the very first warrior. Remind them that their fate is written by Egzi'abher Ab, not by the ones who have stolen them. Remind them of who they are. Remind them that we Ethiopians stand guard at the tombs, at the holy places in Jerusalem."

She kissed her son's forehead. "You are a holy man and a great warrior, like Saint Moses of Ethiopia. Promise you will remember?" Her son nodded. "What is your real name?"

"Negasi!" He nodded again for emphasis.

"And what is your mother's real name?"

"Nikahywot." He touched her face with his small hand.

"You must remember. You are Egzi'abher's messenger, and you must remember the truth. You will see. The truth will rise and Ethiopia, this new Ethiopia in America, once again will lift her hands toward Egzi'abher!"

chapter 58

Three more winters passed and she watched her Nathan, her Negasi, grow taller, though he was still shorter than the other boys his age. Nancie smiled down at him. "Help them to remember that our roots are long and deep. Tell them of the ancient Bibles in Lalibela."

She taught him the prayers that she could remember. She told him the stories that she could recall—of the Good Samaritan, King David, Apollos of Egypt, Maryam at the tomb, Moses and the Exodus, and others.

"Remind them that their history and their fates are written by Egzi'abher Ab, not by man, not by manstealers—let no oppressor tell you your name, Negasi!"

Nancie could see the highlands, the tall green grass waving before her. "The truth will rise and Ethiopia will, once again, lift her hands toward Egzi'abher!" She could see her village, the *tukul*, the church, and the processional of the priests carrying the draped crosses. She heard the drums and saw the birds, like jewels, flying overhead. She saw the highlands and the rainbow.

How could Egzi'abher ask her to birth a son only to sacrifice him?

Over and over, Nancie told him the stories her mother had told her. "Remember Simon of Cyrene carried the cross for the Anointed One. Remember the ancient monasteries in Ethiopia, the churches and monasteries of Lalibela carved from stone long before this nation was born. Help them to remember the faces of Maryam, the Madonna, the Kidane Mehret, and of Krestos on the walls, and remind them that their skin was just like ours." She told him the story of her capture, of the slave ships, of the dying, moaning captives, the dead and sick thrown overboard to the sharks, and of Misha and her baby floating on the water. She shared the names she could remember.

It was so much weight to put on her son's shoulders. Nathan had wrapped his little fist in her ragged shirt and laid his head on her chest. Nancie felt her heart beating through him.

Nancie had rocked Negasi in her arms. "You are no man's slave. You are a prince of Ethiopia, born of the Nile. You have been chosen, chosen before you were born, to be Egzi'abher's messenger, to bear the truth and call the captives home, to call the captors to repentance." She blew out the candle next to the pallet where they slept on the floor. "We are all captives and you must set us all free." She gathered him closer in her arms. "You must be brave and you must remember."

"I will not forget."

chapter 59

Nancie kissed her son's forehead and his eyes. More summers had passed and now he was ashamed for her to kiss him in front of the other boys. Manhood, from far away, was whispering to her Nathan.

"I did not study well, Nathan. My mother told me, as her mother told her, and her mother before that, that the day would come when I would need to remember. But I could not see the day ahead of me and did not think it would come. You must do better.

"The captives know nothing of the story of the Samaritan and so they judge neighbor and brother by tradition, by language, and by color. You must tell them the truth and let Egzi'abher decide their fates." She taught him knowing that each word, each precept brought her son closer to his destiny and to his death.

She taught her son the passages she had memorized in Amharic. She taught Nathan the law and the prophets. "Remember, my son, it all hangs on love."

She kept to herself; she devoted her time to her son. She was a married woman. She did not take up time with New World men; she could not allow herself to be pacified spending time with a man who did not know who he was. She had to think first of her son. Nancie looked around her and she could see the truth: women who spent time loving fools raised sons who were fools. Women who loved brutes raised sons who were brutes. Sons would always try to become the man their mother loved. So Nancie talked of her Ethiopian father and her husband, and shared the stories of the holy men her mother had taught her.

Nancie taught Nathan about keeping the fast days on

Wednesdays and Fridays. She taught him about her father. "His name was Kelile, the guardian of his family." She taught her son about her husband. "His name was Josef, and he was wise and kind and strong. The last time I saw them both they were defending my family and defending our village."

She looked down at her son, so young, so young. She was alone. Alone, she must help her son become a man. *You must help me, Egzi'abher! You must be father.*

"We have no time for foolishness. It is a sin to squander your life on whiskey and cider at Christmastime." Nancie could see the shame and the anger in the captive men's eyes. She had seen it on board the ships, she saw it now in the fields and in the barns. It was hard not to be able to be a man, to have another, one younger than you—like mean Nathaniel Francis or foolish John Clarke Turner—boss you, whip you simply because of skin color. It was hard to be a man when another man, in front of you, could rape your wife. She kissed her son's cheek and whispered in his ear, "Do you think that Moses could have delivered his people if he was drunk? You must always have your wits about you."

Nancie insisted, "Remember who you are. If they call you dog, you don't have to bark. They give hard liquor to the captives so they will be confused and placated, so the captives will act like fools and believe that they are who the captors say they are. How will you protect your family if you are drunk? You cannot save your village if you are in a stupor. You must be like your grandfather, Kelile, a temperate man." She added, "And you must stay away from strange women."

She taught him to read and then write what she could remember of Ge'ez, the holy language, and Amharic. He learned to write the letters on the leaves like a master. Taking what she had taught him, he studied comparing the Bible and the leaves. Figuring them out was a puzzle for Negasi.

"You cannot afford to be foolish, Nathan. There is no time to waste. Do you think Saint Moses of Ethiopia was a sot? Do you think he spent himself on wild women? Of course, not! Instead, though you are in chains, remember that you are a prince! My son"—she held his face in her hands—"you must believe that you are a prince, a warrior priest sent to redeem the people."

Nathan pulled at his clothes. "How can I be a prince?"

"A prince in rags is still a prince. Royalty bound in chains, made to sleep with the pigs, is still royalty."

"But my brothers . . . the other boys say I am a slave—"

"You are Negasi, my prince. You are Egzi'abher's prophet to America. You are a warrior priest."

Nathan fell asleep without saying a word.

chapter 60

There were many things about Virginia that confused Nancie. Like why fetish worshippers, who did not believe in Egzi'abher, would name a Virginia town Jerusalem—a half day's walk from Cross Keys. What kind of coincidence was it that they would name this awful place after the place where Iyyesus Krestos walked, where he was beaten and betrayed? It unnerved her that nearby there was a town called Bethlehem, named after the place of Jesus's birth. Perhaps it was the hand of Egzi'abher reassuring her that He was with her.

She would never forget Ethiopia. She would never stop praying for Egzi'abher to break the arms of the wicked man. She cursed the *ferengi* and their descendants.

Hiding, Nancie knelt praying, her face to the ground. They sat quietly in their buildings, unmoving, with no instruments, no drums or dancing. Their buildings were square, not round *tukuls*, and they had no great churches carved out of stone like those in Lalibela.

She had held little Nathan's hand tightly while they peeked inside the windows. There were no murals on the wall—no pictures of Krestos and his mother, Maryam, no images of their sweet smiling brown faces. There were no pictures of Saint George on his stallion. There was no ark, no mercy seat. There were no images of the sweet brown saints with smiling faces and beautiful kinky black hair. There was no processional with their cross—it was not glorious; it was naked, uncovered, undressed.

The *ferengi* who worshipped white skin had pictures on the walls of a white man and of a white woman and her child. It frightened Nancie to live among the heathen, to be held captive by them. The man they worshipped must be a monster.

She prayed that Krestos would send her and her son home to Ethiopia, away from this false Jerusalem, this Cross Keys, and back to where people knew the one true Amlak . . . where people were civilized.

Skin color was god to them. Some men she had known in her village used a stubbed toe, a hangnail, or a cloud in the sky as an excuse to drink too much *tej*, too much wine. But it was dark skin that seemed to inflame the whites to do evil. Nancie had not seen such wickedness among her own people—had not imagined that any person, unprovoked, could treat another so viciously.

She had not come to Virginia believing that all black men were related because of the color of their skin—that was foolishness. Most were from the same continent, but not the same nation. She was Ethiopian. The one next to her might be Sudanese or Nigerian. They did not speak the same language, they did not have the same customs or religion. But the *ferengi* treated them all the same.

She and the others no longer had language or land rights to join or divide them. She walked unrecognized past allies and shared water with those who would have been her enemies. The affliction they shared had made them one—all children of Africa, all captives. *Ease us of our adversaries and avenge us of our enemies.* She prayed for Africa's children.

chapter 61

Two more barley harvests passed and Nancie noticed down appearing on her Nathan's upper lip. She saw the longing in his eyes when his father walked by—when Benjamin took his white sons to town or sat near them in church while overlooking his darker son.

Nathan was a good student and he quickly learned all she taught him. Benjamin Turner could not openly call him son, but he sometimes allowed Nathan to sit in the doorway of the room where his other sons were being taught, so Nathan learned Benjamin's English, too. Sitting by candlelight, Nathan began to compare the Amharic words and the American words.

His arms gangling, though he was still smaller than the other boys, young Nathan began to teach her.

He grabbed her hand and pulled her away to a nearby clearing in the woods so they would not be overheard. He was breathing heavily, excited.

"Calm yourself, Nathan."

But he would not be quieted. He pulled the Bible and the Amharic pages from beneath his shirt. He shook them at her. "The One we call Egzi'abher, they call God!"

Nancie smiled remembering how easily she was excited when she was Nathan's age. Everything was important, dramatic. "Nathan, you must quiet yourself." She reached for his curls, but he dodged her hand, insistent that she pay attention.

"Listen to me, Mother. The One we call Egzi'abher, they call God! Almighty!"

Nancie felt lightheaded. "God? Almighty?" she repeated. "What do you mean?"

"I mean our Gods are the same."

It was impossible! "You have misunderstood, Nathan. They don't know Iyyesus Krestos."

"They call Iyyesus Krestos by the name Jesus Christ."

Nancie looked around her for someplace to sit. She looked for something to hold on to. "Are you sure, Nathan?"

"I am sure, Mother. I have been studying, but I did not want to tell you until I was certain."

No follower of Krestos could be a manstealer. No follower of Krestos could treat a stranger so cruelly. "Do they know about Egzi'abher, that He is the One who cares for the oppressed, for the rejected and forsaken, the One who cares for the stranger? Do they know that Egzi'abher Ab is Father to us all?"

Nathan shook his head. "I think they have forgotten. I think it is part of what was lost. It is part of why we are here."

"Like Joseph," she said. How could God send her away for these *ferengi*? How could they be children of Egzi'abher?

"Like Jonah"—he smiled as though he were trying to comfort her—"carried in the belly of a fish and spat out on dry land."

Nancie looked at the trees, at the grass, and at the ground beneath her feet. "Nineveh!" Though she had fought it, she had been carried across the seas to Nineveh!

> Then the word of the LORD came unto Jonah a second time, saying, Arise, go to Nineveh, that great city, and preach unto it the preaching that I bid thee.

She had been the ship that carried her son. Nancie looked at Nathan's face. He was no longer a baby; a boy, but not yet a man. The vision was true: she had seen the end from the beginning. They would kill him.

Nathan pulled a folded piece of paper from his pocket. On it,

there was a painting of a woman wearing a robe, a mother em-
bracing a child—like the picture Nancie had seen on the walls of
their churches. Nancie lightly rubbed her finger over the smooth
paper.

"And this is Mary and her child."

Nancie touched the picture. "They are beautiful."

"She is the Blessed Virgin. She is Maryam. Weladite Amlak,
the Mother of God."

Nancie staggered. She tried to speak but could not find her
tongue. She reached into her pocket to touch the tatter. She must
calm herself. She could not be panicked in front of her son. She
knew who Egzi'abher was. She knew Maryam and Krestos. Her
son was still a boy, he was confused. "This is not the Blessed Virgin.
This is not Maryam. The Blessed Virgin, I've seen her picture on
the temple walls, and she looked like my cousin Misha. You remember the stories of Misha, of the ships, of the people in chains,
of Misha floating in the water."

"I remember," Nathan assured her, his face solemn.

"My cousin was beautiful and her color was brown, darker
than honey. And I imagined that when her baby came and she held
the little one in her arms . . ." Nancie touched the picture again. "I
imagined that Misha and her baby would look like Maryam and
her holy child. Where is her color?"

"It has been lost."

"Lost?" How could a person lose her color? "What about the
hair? Why is it yellow and straight?"

"They only know her this way."

"But the Lord gave us to her as her special people! Maryam
watches over us! She is our Kidane Mehret, we are always protected because of her!" Nancie realized that she was waving her
arms in the air. She was yelling. "Well, we must tell them! We must
make them see! You must remind them, teach them that in Africa,
in Egypt and Ethiopia, in the time before their fathers came to
know Egzi'abher, the arms and face of the Blessed Maryam and her

child were black like ours!" Nancie realized that she was speaking Amharic. "Her hair was like yours and mine. Their holy images are on the temple walls and in the ancient holy books! In the churches at Lalibela!"

Nancie turned away and began to weep.

chapter 62

Nancie had pressed her apron to her face. Again they had stolen from her! How could this be? How could Egzi'abher abandon them in America, in this false Jerusalem, in this Nineveh? How could He allow this to happen? She heard her son's voice, but he sounded far away. "Our Egzi'abher Ab they call God the Father. Egzi'abher Bezawi is God the Redeemer, Egzi'abher Medhin is God the Deliverer, and God the Healer is our Mefewwis. Our Ab, Weld, we-Menfes Qeddus they call Father, Son, and Holy Ghost."

How could Krestos and Maryam turn their backs? Nancie sank to her knees and bowed her face to the ground.

"They say there are no followers of Krestos in Africa. They call our homeland the Dark Continent. They say—"

She jerked upright. "Who says such things? Who tells such lies?"

His voice lowered, he dropped to his knees beside her. "The captors, Mother. They say the Egzi'abher's light does not shine on Africa."

"But we were there in the beginning! You know the stories! You know about Queen Candace, you know about the great man baptized by Philip, even before Peter opened the door to the Gentiles!"

"The whites say we are all cannibals and fetish worshippers swinging like monkeys from tree to tree. And the captives, the slaves, believe it is true."

"No one could believe such foolishness." Nancie felt panic slowly freezing her heart and her stomach inside her twisted into a hard rock. "Fetish worshippers? Cannibals?" Of course the captors believed; they needed to believe to keep the guilt away. Of course the captives believed; they were lost far from home, so many generations from home, and there was no one to tell them the truth, to show them the way.

His brow knit together, he shook his head. "They say all Africans are ignorant heathens who do not love Egzi'abher or each other."

How could they believe such foolishness? "Don't they know us? Don't they know the Great Church?" She turned to Nathan. "Do you? Do you believe them?"

He lowered his eyes, his shoulders drooped. "I know because you have taught me, but they have forgotten. All they know is what they have learned here—they know Baptists, Methodists, Presbyterians, and some Catholics—"

"Baptists? Methodists? But don't they know that before the children of Muhammed, even before the Catholics, there was the Great Church and we have always been part of it? How could they not know?" The *ferengi* had teachers. Many of the *ferengi* read. "What is in their books?" She pulled at her dress.

"They teach that we are the children of Ham and that all Ham's children have been cursed by Egzi'abher Ab to be the slaves of white people—they teach that the whites are the children of Japheth."

The children of Japheth? No children of Japheth were white, with their blue veins showing. No children of Japheth had dead yellow hair. "Nathan, how can they believe this? The Greeks know, why don't they tell them? The Armenians know! Rome knows! Rome knows we were there in the beginning. Why doesn't Rome tell them the sin they are committing against Egzi'abher's children?"

Her mother had told her that long ago there had been an argument between Rome and Ethiopia, a fight about who loved the Father, about whom the Father loved most.

All of them—Ethiopia, Alexandria, Greece, Turkey, Armenia, India, and Rome—had been sisters in one great family, one Great

Church. Her mother had told her that Rome and Ethiopia were the sisters chosen to lead the family. But the two sisters—the empires of Rome and Ethiopia—had had a squabble, neither one willing to forgive the other, and had torn the family apart. There was no love and reasoning between the two, only hot words and argument. Rome was angry, but she would not abandon her sister to death, to perpetual slavery, would she?

"The white people say God does not love us, we are heathen. They say we are cursed."

Nancie thought she saw tears in his eyes. "Cursed!" It was a nightmare! To be called heathen by those who were heathens themselves. To be called cursed!

Nancie looked at the sky, at the ground, and at the trees around her. This was not Ethiopia. It was not paradise. What her son was telling her was true. They had been abandoned here. No one would help them. No one would send an army to rescue them. Rome would not lift a finger. No one would even lift a voice.

Nathan tried to reassure her. "But, now, we will be able to pray together. You in Ge'ez and I will pray in English." He tried to comfort her when he needed comfort himself.

"But how?"

"They are the same prayers, Mother."

"Here they call it the Lord's Prayer. 'Our Father, who art in heaven, hallowed be Thy Name . . .' It is the same prayer you taught me."

"The Lord's Prayer?"

"If we are quiet, no one will hear us, no one will harm us. No one will know."

She touched her hand to her lips as she stared at the page he showed her and the leaf. "Are you certain?"

He beamed at her, thinking he had pleased her. "Yes." Thinking of her when his own heart must be broken.

The *ferengi* had stolen her family, her homeland, and her name. When she thought there was no more they could take, they took something else. But how could they steal Krestos? How could they steal the Kidane Mehret?

Her mother had taught her. And her mother's mother had taught her. They had told her the holy stories. They had shown her the pictures in the churches. Had she imagined it all?

She sat up and looked at the sky. No, it had been real. Nancie remembered the African skies, the Tis Isat falls that roared like a lion. She remembered the highlands, the mountains, the birds painted like jewels, and the rainbows. She remembered the prayers and the songs . . . her father, her mother, her husband, and her daughter, Ribka . . . and Misha floating on the water.

She enfolded her son in her arms. She kissed his forehead. She would be strong for him, she would remember, she would re-assure him.

It was all true. She was a daughter of Ethiopia. She had sat beside the stream and slept in the *tukul*. Her mother had told her the day would come when she would have to remember.

Nancie wiped her face and stood on her feet again. She looked at her son. She was the fish that had carried Nathan, her Negasi, to Nineveh's shores to speak the truth. She was the mother who had birthed Moses, sending him through the rushes to live in Pharaoh's household. "These *ferengi*, they are our brothers?" She could barely spit out the words.

"They are our brothers, but they say we are cursed."

She was *chewa*. It was Misha's family that was cursed, it was Misha's forefathers that sinned against Noah. "Don't they know that we are *chewa*? If they read the book, don't they know the truth?" If the captors read the book, then they must know it was a sin to sell your brother into slavery. The book said it was wrong to treat even *barya* the way they treated the captives in America. It was against the law, it was sin, to murder *barya*. It was sin to rape them. It was sin . . . If the captors had read the book, they must know the greatness of Ethiopia, of Africa.

How could Egzi'abher love the *ferengi*?

She nodded at Nathan. She would have to be brave for her son. She would have to set her face like flint. Nancie touched the picture again. "You will remember? The holy words are on the leaves in Ethiopia. The pictures are on the walls there. Their holy faces, faces like yours and mine, are written on the leaves. And their faces are brown like ours."

Nancie calmed herself for her son's sake. "How much does it matter? It is good that men see themselves in Egzi'abher and Egzi'abher in them. He is the God of all nations, all tongues, and kindred."

God? The *ferengi* word felt funny in her mouth. "You must tell them the truth. They will follow Krestos no matter His color. We all would, wouldn't we? No matter what color we paint Him, He is Creator and King of Kings." She nodded, mostly to reassure herself. She cleared her throat. "No matter. They will still love Him when they find out He looks like us."

"King of Kings," Nathan repeated.

"You must tell the people," she whispered to him. "You must tell the captives that in Ethiopia Iyyesus Krestos looks like us." She had rubbed the tatter in her pocket. It was real. "You must help them awaken!"

This strange Jerusalem . . . She smelled the stink, the foulness of the ships that brought her to the New World. She heard the cries of the people. She felt dizzy, as though she would faint. Then Nancie looked into her son's eyes. God was like Father Abrahm, who loved all his children. Egzi'abher was like Jacob, Father Israel, who loved all his sons—even those who would sell their brother into slavery.

But if the pale ones knew, if they had read the book, how could they repeat the sins of Joseph's brothers? If they knew . . .

If Benjamin Turner knew, how could he?

Nancie grabbed the book and the pages from Nathan and she began to run.

Nancie yelled in Amharic as soon as she saw him.

"What kind of man are you to force yourself on a woman? What kind of man are you to leave a son with no inheritance? What kind of man are you to leave a son with no name?" She was forbidden to speak the language of her people, but she didn't care! They had taken everything from her. Let him kill her. Let her blood be on Benjamin Turner's hands!

chapter 63

Nancie had found Benjamin Turner in the fields and shook the Bible at him. "You are no man of God! You are no holy man!" The English words, the American words, were still hard for her to say. They twisted her tongue and stank in her mouth, but she forced herself to say them. The old man had to understand. "You have shamed me and shamed your wife! You have stolen me from my husband, my family, and my country! You lie and say you are not an adulterer, not a thief, not a rapist!"

She did not care if Benjamin Turner beat her or even if he killed her. "You are no man! Even David provided for all his children. The Lord even gave inheritance to Abrahm's son by the handmaid Hagar. Are you one of these people who would keep your own child for a slave? Are you one of these who would abandon your child, who would sell him for profit?"

Nancie did not care what he thought and she did not fear him. "You have violated me before the eyes of Egzi'abher, before God! Don't you know the holy words?"

These men called themselves masters, who slept with slaves as well as wife, decided who would be their children by skin color. They counted their children as possessions, as money in their purses. How could fathers put their sons and daughters in chains and sell them away? No father would deny and sell his own son. No man would sleep with a slave without making her his wife! Love always broke the curse!

They pretended it did not happen and they demanded that everyone else participate in the lie, that the children never name the father, that his white wife and children deny the existence of the child. That the women who were violated never speak a word.

What were the captors teaching the sons and daughters they denied? To be like Cain, to hate and slay their brethren?

"You know the words?" She shook the book at him, yelling. "What have you done?"

BENJAMIN DID NOT force himself on her again after that. He built her a tiny cabin of her own but still kept her and Nathan near him, so that she was still a splinter in his wife's eye. He promised to free her and Nathan and began calling him not his son, but Nat Turner.

His wife, Elizabeth, spat at Nancie when Benjamin was not around. She kicked Negasi and taught her sons to despise him even more.

In October of 1810, Benjamin donated a piece of land. "We will build a church there, a church where all of us—master and slave—may worship together." He put Nathan's name on the deed for Turner's Meeting Place. "I cannot give him land outright. It is the best I can do," he told Nancie. "Nathan is bright. He studies the Bible. He listens to the Methodist preachers. He will not own the land, but Nathan will be a trustee. No one will ever be able to put him out. It is the best inheritance I can give to him.

"He is free now. I cannot give him manumission papers—Virginia will not allow it. But I promise you Nathan will never be sold. He will be known as Nathan Turner. I will not deny him—at least best as I can. I have a wife and daughters . . . I have other children. It is the best inheritance I can give him."

chapter 64

Virginia
Mid-February 1831

It was cold and it did not feel like spring would ever come again. The water froze in the buckets, the birds were gone, and the trees were bare. Nancie looked down and lifted her skirt. Winter in Virginia—the time of bleeding feet.

Her son had passed by to visit her yesterday. She looked up, smiled, and waved when he came into sight. He was a man now, a man with hair on his chin. Still young—thirty summers had passed since his birth—though his hair was already beginning to thin, like his father's. Nancie hugged him when he was close enough.

They no longer lived on the same farm—Elizabeth Turner's cruelty had sold him to the Moores and his wife to Giles Reese. Nancie was grateful now when she saw him—on Sundays and occasionally during the week, just moments. The joy she had felt at the birth of her grandson was now an ache; she rarely saw him.

Yesterday, Nathan had shared news with her about his son, Riddick, and about his wife, Cherry. He seemed sad, though, as though the weight was heavier on his shoulders. It had been several years since his return from the Great Dismal Swamp, and Nathan seemed to grow more pensive each day. They were waiting for a sign.

After Benjamin Turner had died, not many years after building Turner's Meeting Place, everything changed. The family he left behind had stolen her son's birthright. With Benjamin gone, they would not allow Nathan to become trustee. Benjamin's oldest son, Samuel, had forced Nathan to work as a slave.

Still smaller than many of the other men, he had worked in the fields. He would not quit. Her son had persevered. Nathan had married.

His wife, Cherry, bore him a child. Nancie had felt as much contentment as she'd felt since they tore her away from Ethiopia. She had a little Ethiopia on the Turner farm in Virginia—every day she was able to hold her little grandson and tell him the stories. Every day she was able to look on her son and his wife. They were captives, but they were together. So many other families were torn apart.

Then Samuel had died and his wife, Elizabeth, had sold Nathan and Cherry away from the Turner farm, away from each other. Cruel New World.

Nathan and Cherry were not hers to sell, but Elizabeth Turner was corseted in ice. She pretended that she needed to sell those she did not own to pay debts. She was not paying a debt, she was settling a score. The promises were broken.

Elizabeth Turner had broken Nathan when she sold his family. He had run away and Nancie had thought, had hoped, that she would never see him again; had hoped that he would come back again. When a month passed, she imagined that he had made it to Norfolk and boarded a ship that would take him back to Ethiopia.

Then, as suddenly as he was gone, he was back. He came back with heaviness on his shoulders. And she knew. He had come back waiting for the sign.

It had been ten years or so since her son's flight to the Great Dismal. He and other captives described it as a dark place, a hiding place, a jungle that was two or three days' walk from Cross Keys. Despair had driven him there—he had given up any hope of legal freedom. A month later, he had returned. He spoke little of his time there, but he had come back a changed man. He had left an angry young man, but had returned a prophet. He spoke little of his mission, but he was waiting for the sign, a sign in the heavens. She did not know the details, but she knew it would take her son away. She knew vengeance would come.

Her son had looked up at the sky and then down the road. "Do you think it will be soon, my son?" He didn't answer. The weariness seemed bone deep. He would not be with her much longer. "When you go, I will go with you, Nathan."

"No, Mother. You cannot go where I go. You must tell what you have seen and what you have heard."

"How will I live without you?"

"You must remain." When did things change? When did her little boy begin to speak to her with the firmness of a man? He was her Ethiopia and she did not want to lose him.

The wind blew his shirt, not much more than rags. "You will remember that you are no man's slave, my son."

"I am no man's slave."

"You are an African prince, a prince of Ethiopia, a man of two continents—of this America and our mother, Africa."

"I am a prince of Ethiopia."

She had watched him walking away.

Nancie turned toward the kitchen to bake the evening's bread, enough for tomorrow's Sunday meal. She knew what was weighing Nathan down. He was exhausted; they were all exhausted, waiting for their captivity to turn, all worn out waiting for the sign.

Each day she thought it was the last that she could bear. Even the captive children were sad . . . and hungry, fighting with the dogs for scraps. They might smile and play, but hopelessness was in their eyes.

She looked up at the heavens. Though it was cold, the afternoon sun warmed her forehead. *How long, Egzi'abher?* She looked at the tree branches waving and then back at the sky. *How much more can we give?*

The sin was so deep and old. Would the people in this new Nineveh turn?

Years ago, when Nathan was very young, she had walked to Jerusalem and stood along the Petersburg Road when President Jefferson's carriages came near to Southampton County. Southampton men had worn their best clothes, women had worn their best patched gowns.

When the Jefferson carriages stopped, sandy-haired slaves, dressed in finery, had disembarked, wiping dust off their shoes. The crowd had waved and twittered over Jefferson's youngest daughter, a sandy-haired woman, who remained in the carriage fanning herself against the heat.

Nancie removed a large bowl from the pantry and sifted flour into it.

That day her eyes had been drawn to a woman, one of Jefferson's slaves. When she had stepped from the carriage, for a brief moment, her eyes had connected with Nancie's. The woman, the color of cream, favored Jefferson's daughter, but did not have the sandy-colored hair. A young man, one of the sandy-haired slaves, took the woman's arm. He fussed over her as a son would his mother. Nancie had nodded at the woman as, in return, she had nodded at Nancie. Both their sons—Nathan and the sandy-haired footman—told the story. Without opening their mouths, their sons spoke the truth.

The sin was so deep and so old—so open and so hidden by lies. They had the power to do wrong in plain sight and call it right. If they did not turn, Nancie knew there would be blood, names and families removed from the face of the earth, just as in the time of Pharaoh.

Nancie sighed. Nathan had looked so weary walking away yesterday. *We are dying, Egzi'abher. We are brokenhearted. We are angry. Our brothers mistreat us, rob us, kill us. How long?*

She was tired of waiting and praying. She was tired of believing for someday, for a new Ethiopia. It had been over thirty years. She had seen too much and heard too much. Alone with Nathan in this New World, she had continued to pray and believe. She had continued, with no choice about what was offered to her to eat, to keep the fasts. She was more than thirty years weary of the evildoers who only seemed to prosper.

Her son had returned from the Great Dismal Swamp—so close to freedom, so close to a boat to Ethiopia—to deliver his people. For years Nathan had been waiting on the sign. He did not tell her much—he had not been released yet to speak the prophecy to others—but she knew the sign would be the beginning, change would come or the time of mercy for the *ferengi* would soon end.

> *Hear this, O ye that swallow up the needy, even to make the poor of the land to fail,*
>
> *Saying, When will the new moon be gone, that we may sell corn? and the sabbath, that we may set forth wheat, making the ephah small, and the shekel great, and falsifying the balances by deceit?*
>
> *That we may buy the poor for silver, and the needy for a pair of shoes; yea, and sell the refuse of the wheat?*
>
> *The LORD hath sworn by the excellency of Jacob, Surely I will never forget any of their works. . . .*
>
> *And it shall come to pass in that day, saith the Lord [EGZI'ABHER], that I will cause the sun to go down at noon, and I will darken the earth in the clear day. . . .*
>
> *And I will turn your feasts into mourning, and all your songs into lamentation. . . .*

When would the dark day come? On that day the captors' songs of glory would turn to lamentations, a day when mercy would no longer shine on the evildoers. A day would come when the Kidane Mehret would no longer shine her merciful face on the captors.

How long until the captivity was turned? Nancie looked out of the kitchen window. She could not bear much more.

Then, suddenly . . .

. . . as though a cloud were drifting by . . .

the sky darkened.

EARLY IN THE day, the sky turned black.

The time had come. The sign they had been waiting for. The Kidane Mehret, the Covenant of Mercy, finally turned her head.

chapter 65

Hot days, stiff green cornstalks in the field, no wind. Sweat trickled down her neck. The short days of winter had passed, now there was still daylight when Nathan came to visit her. Her son stood before her, tired from the week's work. He was anxious, with little time to spare.

The dark day, the day of the lamentations, had finally come. It had been a cold day in February, but inside Nancie had rejoiced that day. She had been obedient to Egzi'abher. Over thirty years, she had suffered—the boats, the hands on her, the shame—and her son had suffered. Over thirty years away from her home and her family. But it was time now. Egzi'abher would repay the captors. He would speak to them through the sword!

Her son had changed since the sky had darkened. Each time she saw him, she saw more warrior than priest. Each time she saw him, she was worried that it would be the last. Nancie prayed for her son and the other captives. *Strengthen their arms, Lord. Prepare them for battle.*

Nathan whispered only the slightest things to her when he came to visit now. He did not want to put her at risk. She did not know the day, but she knew it was coming soon. There were so few of them to fight and no weapons.

By faith the walls of Jericho fell down, after they were compassed about seven days. . . .

And what shall I more say? for the time would fail me to tell of
Gedeon, and of Barak, and of Samson, and of Jephthae; of David
also, and Samuel, and of the prophets:

Who through faith subdued kingdoms, wrought righteousness,
obtained promises, stopped the mouths of lions.

By faith, Nancie had prayed for more than thirty years,
through winter, into spring, and into the summer heat. She had
prayed through the frozen ground, into the thaw, the planting, and
through the plants rising tall from the ground. Finally, the Kidane
Mehret had turned her head. She must have faith.

"They force our hands, Mother! What choice do we have?
Though we are brothers, they force us to be enemies, to be at war.
They are merciless—they refuse to offer mercy and they refuse to
accept God's offer of mercy."

"They are hard-hearted, like Pharaoh," she agreed. There was
no other choice. The day had come that she had been praying for.
God's day of judgment was at hand.

Nancie continued nodding. Then stopped. Though the day
was hot, cold slowly crept up her spine.

It was not Saint Moses or King David speaking of going to
war; it was her son, her only son. She knew what war meant: death
and blood. Nancie shivered. Then, as suddenly, she was hot again.
Nancie smelled heat in the air and felt the smoothness of the silk
on her arms, the silk of the flowing robes she wore in Ethiopia.
The dark day had come, but Nancie wondered if she would ever
see paradise again.

chapter 66

Nathan had tried to tell them, but they would not listen—he bore the scars of proof. She wanted vengeance, but Nancie did not want to sacrifice her son.

"It is finished, Mother. My course is set."

She had lost enough. "We could pray more. We could study. Maybe there is a way to peace that we have not reckoned." She had been praying for war, and now, because she did not want to risk losing Nathan, she heard the words of peace come from her mouth, on her tongue like bitter molasses.

"I have prayed for peace. I have spoken the truth. They are not like Nineveh; they will not hear.

"We have selected a date—their July Fourth, their Independence Day." The gentleness was gone from his eyes. "Instead of their celebration, it will be the day of our independence in Cross Keys. Instead of glory songs . . ."

There would be lamentations. "Maybe it is too soon?" It was only two days. She heard her voice whining even though she was whispering. "You need more time to gather weapons. Who knows? Maybe tomorrow they will listen."

"It is too late, Mother. You saw the sun—just like the prophecy. You told me as a boy that this day would come. 'I will cause the sun to go down at noon, and I will darken the earth in the clear day. . . .'"

"But not so soon." She could not stop wringing her hands. She was willing to take up arms herself, but not to lose her son. "What about your family—your wife and child?"

"I do this for my family. I do this for you, Mother."

His words made her feel ashamed. She did not want him to die for her . . . or for anyone else. He was a man—she looked up at him—but he was her son. He was all she had left, except for the tatter, of Ethiopia. "Don't do it for me!"

"Then for the family debt we owe."

Nancie felt her shoulders drop. Debt? She felt her heart sinking, sinking like Misha's body beneath the waves.

"Mother, I don't want to fight. I have been studying peace, hoping they would listen to God and there would be no blood."

"But you are only one man. Can you do it all? Virginia is too big for you." How little shame she had; she would do anything to keep her son.

He laid his hand on her shoulder. "Mother. You taught me all my life not to fear the man who can kill me but cannot take my soul."

She turned her head away. She did not want to hear it. She did not want to hear her own teaching tearing her son from her arms.

He touched her chin, turning her head toward him. "Lift up your head, Mother."

Tears burned her eyes. She was his mother, she gave birth to him; she could not let him go. In his eyes she saw the baby she nursed, the little boy who sat on her lap.

"You taught me to prepare for battle. You taught me about warrior priests, warrior saints. You must not make this harder for me, Mother. You must help me to be brave."

She tried to turn her head but he would not allow it. When had he gotten so tall, so wise? When had he gotten so strong? Who had taught him so well?

"You taught me to be obedient to God, to be obedient unto death. Did you mean it?"

A stinging tear slid down her face.

"I cannot do it all, but I must take a step, Mother. If I die in defeat, I still must try. How can I refuse to do what Egzi'abher has commanded me to do? How can I be obedient when He tells me to make peace and not be obedient when He tells me to make war? I cannot be a man and see my mother live this way. I cannot say I am a man and stand by while my wife and son are stolen.

"You told me my grandfather and your husband took up arms to defend your family. What would they think of me if I do nothing?"

She looked at Negasi and saw his grandfather. She saw her father and her husband on that last day when they sent her cousin Misha, her mother, Afework, her daughter, Ribka, and her ahead. She saw all his forefathers standing up in her son.

"If I die and I have not secured the promise, I still know freedom will come. Krestos has promised me. Maybe I am only the first thaw, the first bird of spring. Still I know freedom will come. If I die for freedom, for the freedom of those I love, I could not die for a better cause. I would rather die fighting for freedom, and obedient to Egzi'abher, than live a slave." He kissed her forehead. "Lift up your head, Mother. Ethiopia will arise and stretch her hands toward Egzi'abher."

He hugged her to him. But she would not respond. He whispered in her ear, "I am a prince out of Egypt, a prince of Ethiopia, a prince of Africa. I am a prince of two continents.

"I know I am a prince, a son of God, because God's word promises it. I know it because God Almighty, Egzi'abher Ab, cares for the oppressed." He kissed her forehead again. "I know it because my mother told me."

Nancie threw her arms around him—her baby, her son, her prince. She buried her face in his chest so that she would not scream.

"It may be a long battle. The spirits of hate and greed are strong and they will not give ground easily. The people have been lied to; they don't want to believe that we are brothers, children of the same Father. They don't want to give up the wealth and power. I don't rejoice to take my brothers' lives, but they give us no choice. I may be lost in the battle, but they will be defeated. I may not live to see it, Mother, but you will see paradise again."

Nancie squeezed Nathan as tightly as she could. She tasted her own salty tears. "Why don't we just leave this place, Negasi? We could get away. We could go to the Great Dismal Swamp just as you went before. We could go to Newtown, the place you told me of. We could go to the Norfolk you spoke of and board a ship back to Ethiopia!"

The weariness was on his face again. Nathan sighed and his shoulders drooped. "Egzi'abher will not let me go, Mother. You know the story. You told me the story of how Jonah ran. I cannot run and put others in danger because of my disobedience.

"Who will I be if I give up, if I am afraid to give my life for my family, for my people? Perhaps being a peacemaker means sometimes you must sacrifice your own peace, your own life.

"This is my home. My family is here." He sighed. "And I must pay the family debt."

"What family debt?" She pleaded with him one last time. "If there is a family debt, it is not yours to repay."

"Children inherit the work left undone by their parents."

There was no point. The hot sun was drying the tears on her face. "I will pray, my son. I will pray that the captors will hear you. I will call to your grandmother across the ocean—she is a brave and wise woman—and who knows but that she will hear, join our prayers, and the hearts of these manstealers may turn." She whispered to Nathan, her Negasi, "'From beyond the rivers of Ethiopia my suppliants, even the daughter of my dispersed, shall bring mine offering.' Maybe your grandmother's prayers will be enough."

There were so few of them to fight, so few that her son could trust to tell the secret; David against Goliath. Though her knees knocked and she thought her heart would melt into her bowels, by faith, Nancie continued to pray, counting the days. By faith, she prayed that Egzi'abher would stay His hand and allow July 4 to pass, that the day would come and go and her son would still be alive.

* * *

THE NIGHT OF the Fourth there were stars and fireworks in the sky. *Lord, spare my son. Lord, stop the battle. Lord . . .* Nancie wanted to pray brave prayers, but it was her son, the only child who could hold her and whisper her real name. Nancie was not ready to lose him. *Lord, spare my son.*

The Fourth came and went without a peep—screams, no sharp reports from rifles in the darkness—and Nancie thought she must be dreaming. She wanted to be brave, but she could not help rejoicing. Maybe it was over. Maybe the captors had repented and turned.

When daybreak came again, she smiled.

chapter 67

Almost two weeks passed with no visit from her son. He had been ill; his friend Hark had sent word to her from the farm where they were both captives.

It was a hot Sunday morning and Nancie wrapped a white rag around her head to stop the sweat from dripping in her eyes as she walked to church.

She stood with the other captives outside Turner's Meeting Place. Nancie looked at the whitewashed building. It was not that long ago that Benjamin Turner had promised that Nathan would be a trustee. It was not that long ago that all of them had been able to worship inside.

Nancie looked at his wife, Cherry, and nodded. She was not the girl that his father would have chosen for him if they had lived in Ethiopia—too much like *barya*. She was not Ethiopian. Still, Cherry was a fine woman worth a great bride price. She was a fine wife for America; Cherry gave Nathan peace. Cherry helped him be strong. She made fire burn in his eyes. What more could a mother ask?

It was a day to be grateful. All the worry about the sign and the day of lamentations was over. July 4 had passed and her son was alive. He was still a captive, but he was alive. This was a good day, a beautiful day—not a perfect day, but a good enough day.

Nancie tilted her head to see the birds flying overhead and smiled, listening to their calls. The birds' chirping blended with the singing voices around her. Then she heard Nathan's voice. He never sang, but today the words rang from him, shaking the air around them.

Are there no foes for me to face?
Must I not stem the flood?

As usual, they stood near the church building, the place that had been their home. Some of the older ones and children sat on the church steps listening to Nathan. Nancie looked at her son, listening to him. He was not singing, but it was close enough. She smiled at him. In Ethiopia he might have been a singer, a priest, or a great farmer. But this was enough—he was still alive, still with her.

She would speak with him when they were finished. She would ask him if the white men had turned. Maybe Egzi'abher had repented of the vengeance He had promised.

Is this vile world a friend to grace,
To help me on to God?

Whatever the case, she would enjoy this day. The grass was warm underneath her bare feet. A gentle breeze blew the hair that escaped her head rag. She had never known her son to speak this way, dizzying, as though he were calling the words down to them from on top a hill.

It was a good enough day.

chapter 68

The white men inside charged out of the church door-way—knocking into one another, tripping over their rage. They screamed at Nathan. They pinned him to the church wall.

"No! No! No!" Nancie heard herself screaming. July 4 had passed, now they were going to kill her baby right in front of her eyes. She tried to run to him but something, someone, held her. They would not let her go because they knew the captors would kill her. They knew she would kill the captors.

They had spilled out of the church and now blood was pouring from Nathan. They yelled at him, but Nancie could not remember what the American words meant. Her mind was screaming Amharic. *Not my baby! Not my son!*

As Gabriel greeted you, Hail Maryam, full of grace, the Lord is with you . . . blessed is the fruit of your womb . . .

Where was Krestos? Where was Egzi'abher Ab? How could the Kidane Mehret stand by and watch them killing her son? She struggled against the arms holding her.

Nathan's warm blood splashed on her face and Nancie tasted the salty wine of his life in her mouth. They ripped the flesh from his back. Blood-soaked pieces of him on the ground. They were killing him. Everyone shouting. They were killing him! Killing her son, the apple of her eye, her hope. "Negasi! Negasi!"

chapter 69

Two days passed and Elizabeth Turner, Samuel's widow, came to her smiling. "You may go say good-bye to your son. Mistress Sallie Francis Moore Travis has agreed that you can see him, though I don't know why." How could a woman smile over the death of another woman's child? She had known Nathan all his life. How could she smile over the death of her husband's brother?

Nancie carried a pail of water with her and went first to Turner's Meeting Place. She knelt on the ground, took the rag she had tied around her head, and dipped it in the water. When it was soaked, she used the rag to scrub the ground, to scrub the place where her son had been. Back and forth, grass tore from the ground.

How much, Egzi'abher? How long?

She repented. It had been she who had not wanted to lose her son on July 4. She had prayed and snatched him back from Egzi'abher's arms, from the mission Egzi'abher had for him. She had tried to snatch Negasi from the road to Nineveh.

Nancie scrubbed and the rag turned red with blood, black with earth, and green with torn grass. She dipped the rag in the pail and the water turned the color of *tej*, of wine. The broken grass floated to the top.

"I give him back to you!" Nancie yelled to Krestos. "He is yours! But I beg you, think of your mother, Maryam, and do not let my boy suffer!" Nancie sat back on her heels and pounded her chest with the wet rag.

From beyond the rivers of Ethiopia my suppliants, even the daughter of my dispersed, shall bring mine offering.

Negasi was her Ethiopia, he was her hope. "From beyond the rivers of Ethiopia . . . I give you my best offering . . . my only son!" She did not want to let him go. "Do not let my boy suffer! Do not let him suffer because of me!"

Nancie emptied the bucket and rose to see her son for the last time.

chapter 70

Nancie walked the road to the Travis place. There had been no rain and the road was dusty.

In her country, she would have been *chewa*. In her country, women like Cherry would have been *barya*. In Ethiopia, she would never have treated Cherry so cruelly. She would have treated her as she treated Misha.

Poor Misha.

Now they were all mixed up together—Igbo and Ethiopian, *chewa* and *barya*. It was like wheat and tares. Now the *ferengi* lorded it over them all. *Lord, break the arms of the wicked man!*

Virginia dust on her feet, Nancie looked toward the heavens. "Behold my son, Negasi, Krestos. I am a daughter of Ethiopia and I surrender to you my only son, my best offering. Forgive my family; forgive my people our sin." She saw her son's back as they beat him, but she heard her parents' voices from the night the captors first came, the night her family was forced to flee their *tukul*.

Her mother's voice was especially clear to her. *"Perhaps Egzi'abher is displeased that we keep Misha and her husband as* barya, *as our slaves. . . . Egzi'abher has given us the moon, this land, and the stars. What if he is displeased that this is not enough for us? Why do we need* barya? *. . . Love others as myself. . . . What would I want for myself? What would I want for my daughter, for Nikahywot? Would I want her to be a slave, even a beloved one? . . . Perhaps, now, Egzi'abher is trying to give us the greatest gift, to teach us to love . . . and He's willing to fight us to teach us to love."*

Nancie had lost her family. She had lost everything. She was *barya* now and lived among heathens. What had she done? Why had all this happened?

On the hot, dry day, an unexpected wind blew. It startled her and briefly lifted her skirt. Nancie stopped and looked around her. It was quiet, no birds were singing, but something whispered to her heart.

The *ferengi* worshipped their skin. Perhaps her people worshipped their lineage.

Solomon begat Menelik and Menelik begat Menelik the Second . . . Saint Moses, the warrior priest begat . . . It made them proud so that they exalted themselves above others, so that Misha wasn't good enough—so that one was *chewa* and the other *barya*.

Nancie looked around her—up at the blue sky, at the white clouds, back at the grass, at the trees now waving in the wind. She had created none of it. Who was she to say who was better and who was worse? Who was she to say who was blessed or cursed? In Ethiopia she was *chewa*, here she was *barya*, but what did it matter? It must all look like foolishness to Egzi'abher.

The *ferengi* worshipped their white skin, but maybe her people worshipped their nationality and their paradise, so they put being Ethiopian before caring for their other African brothers, before offering them Krestos's love. Maybe they had buried Krestos's love, like the man with one talent, and now it was being taken away.

There was blood on Nancie's hands from where she had scrubbed the ground.

There was blood on her hands.

There is a family debt we owe.

Forgive me, Father.

Long ago her mother had told her that all new life was preceded by blood. "Let this be enough! I pray that this is enough!"

chapter 71

Nathan was delirious and Nancie was not sure what he heard or if he understood at all. He burned with fever, but sometimes he spoke to her—though his voice was weak and raspy—as though his head was clear. Other times he tossed and turned; crazy came from his mouth.

She saw her son lying on the straw—stomach down, his face toward her—the son she had birthed beneath a blood moon so large it looked as though it would swallow her. His breathing was ragged, the breath of a man slipping into death. She wanted him to go. Nancie lightly touched a finger to his forehead. He had suffered enough. He had given enough. He had paid enough.

Nancie heard a cow with a newborn calf in the next stall. She heard the calf sucking and heard the cow making contented sounds. Beside Nancie, Nathan moaned. She wanted him to go . . . she wanted him to stay, her Nathan, her Negasi. He was her hope. He was her Ethiopia. "Bring him back to me," she whispered to Krestos. Her Nathan was the only one in this New World who remembered her name.

She smiled down at him and a tear rolled down her nose and dropped onto his cheek. She whispered, "You knew all along, didn't you, Negasi? You knew.

"I would have never left on my own. I didn't care about those who were near me suffering." Nancie looked at her son and beneath him was the water, the waves, carrying him away, and beyond him were Misha and her baby and the sharks. "I never gave thought to those far away who were suffering. I didn't know that they were my brothers and sisters. I didn't care that they were in need. But you knew, didn't you, Negasi?" Another tear dropped next to the first one. "You knew all along."

Nancie leaned to kiss him on a safe spot, careful not to touch him anywhere else. She did not want to cause him more pain. "You knew all along, didn't you? Such a wise son. Forgive me for all the trouble I have caused you." She knew it now. Like Jonah, she had caused the shipwreck. She had caused their lives to crash on Virginia's shores.

"In Ethiopia, I would be the slave owner." She looked away from her son. "I was the slave owner." She looked back at him, looked into his eyes to see what he thought of her, to see if he still loved her, to see if he understood her, to see if she had changed how he felt about her, to see if he was still alive.

"I didn't want to do the dirty work." She looked at her hands, scarred and ugly now. "I did not want to dirty my hands. I was so proud of my hands, how soft they were, how beautiful. I am not guilty, I told myself. I have done nothing wrong. I did not create this world."

She reached for her son's hand, to hold him. She did not want him to leave her. She did not want death to take him. "I did not want to give it up, you see? I was too proud to tell Misha I was sorry. I was too selfish to imagine her life. I was a good person, I told myself. I obeyed my mother and father. I said my prayers. How could I be wrong? How could I be a sinner?

"We were first; we were the masters, *chewa*. They were *barya*, servants. Egzi'abher chose us. He preferred us. How can I fight Egzi'abher? I asked myself. Because of Misha, I did not have to lift heavy things. I had time to dream. Her forefathers brought the curse on her, it was not my fault."

Nancie sighed remembering Misha. "She was so beautiful, so like Maryam. Sometimes I was angry with her and I called her ugly. There were times when I made fun of her round face and her kinky hair. But she was so beautiful.

"I could have freed her. If I had asked my father . . ." She felt her hand squeezing Negasi's. "I could have freed her and maybe . . ." She wanted to stop squeezing, but she could not. "I did not ask her if she wanted to be free—I did not want to hear her answer. Maybe if I had, she would still be alive." Nancie could see them, mother and child, floating in the water. "Maybe Misha and the baby would be alive, happy somewhere on a small farm with her husband, a family." Her other hand clutched his bloodstained shirt now. "You knew all along. There is a family debt I owe. What if I have cursed you, my son? What if you go through all of this because of me?"

Nancie leaned down to look more closely into her son's eyes. "When I think of my Misha floating away, I am angry for what the *ferengi* have done to us. When I remember Ethiopia and the Nile, when I think of what you could have been—how the people there would have loved you . . . But I played a part. What I did to Misha . . . my hands are stained.

"I thank Egzi'abher for you and that you are here with me. Left to me, I would have no one, no son." She smiled at him through her tears. She had tried to take his life, but Egzi'abher was wiser. Egzi'abher was great. "Then I think—despite all that we have been through, despite the evil plan that was laid for us—of what you have become. You are a great man. No mother has a greater son. Who am I that Egzi'abher should give me such a precious gift?" Nathan stirred as though he wanted to speak to her, but no words came from his mouth.

"And then I remember that even though I did not love Misha as I loved myself, still Iyyesus Krestos loved me—He proved His love through you. Krestos has proven that Egzi'abher Ab loves all His children, the just as well as the unjust, *chewa* and *barya*.

"My pride, my greed brought this on all of us, my son. It is the family debt *I* owe." Her tears burned her face and in the barn it was hard to breathe. A dove cooed overhead.

Nathan weakly patted her hand, as though trying to quiet her, as though he was aware, but Nancie could not be quiet. There might not be another chance to ask his forgiveness. She had lost the opportunity to beg Misha's pardon. "This family debt you owe is because of me! I could have freed her. I was selfish; I only thought of myself. I am sorry I did not beg Misha's forgiveness. I knew all along that I was wrong; there was always a sinking feeling in my heart."

Nancy cried, screaming silently as she spoke to her son. He must listen. He must not pay for her sins. "She was always the beautiful one. Her face was round like the faces of the beautiful saints; her face was round like the face of the Blessed Mother. Her hair made a crown, a halo, like that of the saints and the Kidane Mehret." She grabbed the collar of Nathan's tunic in her hands, then let it go; she did not want to hurt him. He had been hurt enough. He had borne enough. "I am sorry that I did not free her. She was beautiful and I did not tell her." Nancie looked toward heaven. "Lord, I repent. Take me! If it is Your will, spare my son." She looked back at her son. Nancie gripped the fabric of his shirt so tight she thought she might tear it. "We were the same but I treated her as a stranger, as though she was *ferengi*. Why did I force Egzi'abher Ab to make me naked before I could see there was no difference between her and me?

"I heard my mother speaking, telling the truth, speaking of love. But I pretended I did not know Misha wanted to live her own life. My heart was hard. My heart was dead.

"And then I saw them, her and her baby still tied to her, floating in the water. The sharks were all around them. Why didn't I repent? When she was floating away, it was too late."

It was harder and harder to breathe in the barn. How would she live if Egzi'abher took her Negasi away? "I am one of the wicked ones, like these people of Virginia! All along, when I was praying for Egzi'abher to punish others, I didn't know I was praying for Egzi'abher to punish me. When I prayed for God to break the arms of the wicked ones, I was praying against them and against myself. When I prayed that the captors' children would be killed, why couldn't I see that I was praying a curse on you? Why did I have to suffer before I was willing to understand?" She raised her shoulder to swipe tears from her face.

"But you knew all along, didn't you? So wise, such a good man, a sweet son.

"Why didn't I love her enough to free her?" Why hadn't she loved her enough to break the curse?

"The truth is there was never any difference—we are all *barya*; we are all servants; we are all black. We are all Ethiopians, no matter our lineage, no matter our shade or our hair. We are all Egzi'abher's children no matter what nation. We are all lilies in Egzi'abher's field. It is not what we look like that makes us the same; it is in the heart that we are brothers.

"The family debt is mine, Nathan." She leaned closer to his ear. "The family debt is mine, Negasi!" She looked toward heaven. "The family debt is mine!"

Nancie stopped crying then. She let go of her son's shirt and gently touched his face as though she would rub the tearstains away. "I will pray that all will repent and be forgiven. I will pray that there will be no bloodshed. I will pray that Egzi'abher will raise you up again."

Nancie heard the death rattle in her son's chest. Blood bubbled at the side of his mouth, her sweet baby's mouth. She touched his hand again, gently. "Wake up, my son." She prayed for his peace, rose, and staggered away.

chapter 72

Virginia
August 1831

Nancie waited by the gate, craning her neck, hoping to see her son. Before the beating, before they almost killed her son, she had seen him most Sundays. But now . . . She fingered the tatter in her pocket.

She had once had a life in Ethiopia. She had lived on the highlands and she had had a wonderful husband, a beautiful daughter—more than she deserved, more than one woman could ask for in a lifetime.

Though she had gotten word that he still lingered, Nancie had accepted that she would never see her son again. But she still prayed for him to come up the road. She still stole moments and waited by the gate.

The sun was hot and it burned her neck. It was too hot for her to be waiting there with no shade. She was a foolish old woman. A dreamer.

Then she heard his voice.

It was her Negasi! Her son! He was walking slowly, but he was not dead.

Alive!

She waved her hands at him. She jumped up and down like a young girl. "My son! My son!" She ran to him and threw her arms around him. He flinched, but he did not pull away. "Oh, my Negasi!" Nancie laid her head on his chest. It was really him. His heart was beating. She threw her head back and silently thanked Egzi'abher Ab.

Nathan bent and whispered in her ear, "Is it all true? We are people of Ethiopia? There is a God who loves us? There is another place besides here?"

Nancie looked up at her son and placed one of her hands on each side of his face. She reminded him of all she had taught him, of Solomon and Sheba, of the saints and the paintings on the church walls. "We know that Egzi'abher sent His Son to walk among us. Iyyesus Krestos healed the sick, raised the dead, and championed the cause of the poor and the brokenhearted. He stood up to the powerful, greedy, wicked ones. And in exchange for his love and mercy and courage, they tore the flesh from his body and hung him from a cross." Nancie could not take her son back. He was her best sacrifice, her best gift. She had given him as Maryam gave her son, as Moses's mother had given her son, as Jonah's mother had given. "Krestos did not despair because He knew there was a better place. He died for us all and left us peace, and love, and hope, and His mother, Kidane Mehret, our Covenant of Mercy, to plead our cause.

"It is all true, my son. It is all true, my Negasi." She whispered his Ethiopian name, his Amharic name, to him.

"I am your mother. I would not lie. The Nile is Ethiopia's gift to Egypt. It begins at Lake Tana and is fed by the Tis Isat falls. We know that the grass in the Ethiopian highlands, where we come from, is green like emeralds, and birds of paradise, birds colored like jewels, fly over fields of tall grass. Even now the holy men are there beating their drums and worshipping before Krestos. Even now they pray for us."

She smiled up at him. He was the best of her. "I am your mother and I saw it all, the paintings of Maryam, her face brown like ours." Maybe it was enough that she had offered him, as Abraham offered Isaac. Maybe it was enough that so much of his blood had been shed and that his heart had been broken—so many times broken. Maybe her repentance was enough. Maybe nothing else would be required of him. Nothing except that she and he continue to live their lives as captives.

Nancie's eyes filled with tears. She removed her right hand, searched in her apron pocket, and pulled out the tatter. "I had many dresses and many shawls in Ethiopia. This is all that is left. It is not much, but it is ours and it is our proof. And we have greater proof of God's promise; there are rainbows over Africa!

"You are Negasi!"

Though his eyes were sad, he smiled at her. "And you are Nikah-ywot, my source of life."

She gently pressed the tatter to his face. "Holy men must have courage and speak the truth. We were sent here, I in the belly of a ship and you in mine, to bring hope to Egzi'abher's forgotten people." Captive or not, she knew this life was not the end. Captive or not, she knew a better life awaited them.

chapter 73

August 12, 1831

She would never have thought, sitting by the stream in Ethiopia, that she would end up in a place called Virginia. She never would have thought that she would be a captive, *barya*, a slave, and that she would give birth to a son—that she would walk the streets of a place called Jerusalem.

Nancie looked around her. Things had been quiet. The fields were full and ripe. It was harvesttime. She had seen the men going to the fields with sickles in their hands. She prayed the prayers she had been praying all her life.

As Gabriel greeted you, Hail Maryam, full of grace, the Lord is with you . . .

Egzi'abher is great! Let His will be done!

Nancie looked to the sky and saw that the noon sun, the *tzahay*, suddenly . . . turned . . . blue . . . the *samayawi tzahay*.

August 22, 1831

AFTER THE NIGHT of the sickle moon, there were flashes in the darkness and screams, men screaming, and shots, and squeals—she could not tell if they were women, children, or pigs—that jolted her awake. For weeks, when she bolted upright in the dark, the room moving about her, it was hard for Nancie to remember where she was. In the darkness wolves howled, wild dogs barked, in daylight buzzards circled overhead. The screaming, the shooting, the fire continued many nights. Until General Eppes, the American general, the white *ras dashen*, made the white men lay down their arms.

Harriet

chapter 74

I t was blood money!" In the dim light, the face of the man near her crumpled.

Harriet looked at him. They were alone. She had not committed to write, Harriet reminded herself, only to listen. She looked around her at the concrete block walls of Mother Bethel Church. With threats against her life because of *Uncle Tom's Cabin*, Philadelphia was as far south as she dared travel.

The City of Brotherly Love, William Penn's vision along the Delaware, was a city of arms and letters. Birthplace of the Declaration of Independence and home of the First Continental Congress, it was also home to the Continental Army and Navy. The nation's financial heart, it was the home of the First United States Bank. The Liberty Bell rang there while merchants and patrons bustled on Market Street.

Theaters, railroads, shipping, manufacturing. Caribbean refugees: Cuba, Trinidad, Haiti, Tobago, Puerto Rico, Santo Domingo, Jamaica, Barbados—African and native refugees from thousands of islands. Islands infected with the catastrophe of colonial slavery—Francophone, Anglophone, German, Portuguese, Dutch. Among them all walked William Penn's Quakers.

The sons and grandsons of Revolutionary warriors—including thousands of Negro veterans of the war—had become fishermen, bakers, butchers, lawyers, and bankers. Freedom still burned in their hearts and many of them were drawn to complete the business their forefathers had left undone. It was Pennsylvania, led by Benjamin Franklin and the Pennsylvania Abolition Society, which in 1790 presented the first petition to President Washington— who himself owned hundreds of slaves—calling for the gradual abolition of slavery in the nation. The same society's members, incensed by Southern slavers' aggressions into Pennsylvania to capture runaway slaves, sent lawyers south to fight for the slaves' return to freedom. Where else but Philadelphia might have given birth to Bethel?

Born a slave in 1760, after converting to Methodism, Bethel's founder, Richard Allen, gained his freedom during the revolutionary period. He was ordained by Bishop Asbury, the first Negro deacon in the Methodist Church. He went on to become founding bishop of the African Methodist Episcopal Church and the first pastor of Bethel.

The church was not as elaborate as she had imagined, having heard of it long ago from William Lloyd Garrison. Mother Bethel was the site of the first National Negro Convention in 1830. At the 1831 Convention, also in Philadelphia, Garrison spoke, calling for immediate emancipation. Harriet looked around the room and tried to imagine the delegates seated in the pews with Bishop Richard Allen, his arms raised, speaking before them.

Since then the conventions had been held around the country, like the 1852 Convention that Frederick Douglass presided over in Rochester, New York. But Mother Bethel was the convention's birthplace and was—like her brother Henry's Plymouth Congregational Church in Brooklyn—a stop on the Underground Railroad. She had thought Bethel would be grander—but perhaps it did not need columns, stone cherubs, or stained-glass windows, perhaps its beauty lay within.

Harriet shifted her gaze to the man. He might have been a scarecrow. He seemed intimidated by the surroundings, frightened by even the plain wooden benches. "What does it feel like to own people?"

The man, Benjamin Phipps, his face lit by scant light from the plain glass windows, stammered. "They are not people like we are."

"Oh. Tell me how they are different."

Bishop Allen's wife, Sarah, had been born near Southampton County. Through her family there, her brother Henry and Frederick Douglass had arranged for Phipps to meet with Harriet. Phipps, they said, had information to which even William, the runaway slave, might not be privy. Phipps had never been north of Southampton County, they said.

"It's as Mr. Jefferson has said, they are lower than we are." Phipps shifted in his seat. "They don't have high thoughts, no morals. Not capable of learning. They are animals and not our equals."

They had told her to take care with Phipps. They said he was gentle, a poor farmer, but she saw no reason to be civil with him. Southerners had done enough to ruin thousands, maybe millions of lives, including her own. "You mean 'Thou shalt not steal' does not apply to men? Thou shalt not steal my cow or my mule, but feel free to steal my soul, my freedom, and my labor? Please explain it to me."

He turned toward her and even in the dim light she saw Phipps's face reddening. "We are not all the same! Are there no men in the North who hold mean thoughts? Southerners do not all believe the same! I am trying to explain to you what slavery men believe, but I am not a slavery man."

Harriet listened but did not respond.

"There are others in the South who believe like me." His blue eyes were watery. "But what could we do? Beating, killing, they were even tar-and-feathering white men who spoke against them. Who knows how long the killing would have gone on—Virginia, North Carolina—if General Eppes had not come?"

She felt no sympathy for him. Harriet was not convinced that Nat Turner was not a fiend, or that she should use her pen to resurrect his name. But there were no innocents in the matter.

Benjamin Phipps had received the bounty reward for Nat Turner. "What of your part?"

"They have tried to make me some kind of hero." Phipps dropped his head. "We all, whether we wanted to or not, played our parts. But we weren't all monsters. We knew it was wrong, but what could we do? His attorney, William Parker, tried. John French tried."

"William Parker? You misspeak, you mean Thomas Gray. Thomas Gray was Nat Turner's attorney."

Phipps's slight smile was sarcastic. "I see you have read *The Confessions*." He shook his head. "William Parker was Nat's attorney. I know. I was there. Thomas Gray was part of the conspiracy, the plot to bury the truth."

"Why isn't this known?"

"Who was in the courtroom to repeat the truth? No Negroes were allowed, at least none who lived. So much hate . . . and fear." Phipps turned. "None of them were strangers. They all knew . . . we all knew each other . . . raised together." He held his hat in one hand. "The lie has been repeated so long. I did not want to be involved." He swiped with the other hand through his thin gray hair. "Do you think silence is a sin?"

Harriet thought she heard a mouse in the rafters. She had not agreed to write. She still wasn't convinced the Turner matter was her business.

Phipps cleared his throat. "I saw it all. The villains—Francis, Trezvant, Waller—their names have escaped any disgrace. And those who would be heroes, like French and Williams—their names have faded away. I want to talk now. Need to talk."

Curious, Harriet removed her bonnet and turned toward Phipps to listen.

Nathaniel Francis

For there is nothing covered, that shall not be revealed; neither hid, that shall not be known.

Therefore whatsoever ye have spoken in darkness shall be heard in the light; and that which ye have spoken in the ear in closets shall be proclaimed upon the housetops.

—Luke 12:2–3

chapter 75

Jerusalem, Virginia
Spring 1831

Wild spring brought leaves and planting; he must finish the work before summer. He had to watch the slaves—his overseer wasn't worth his pay—they would steal the kernels off the cob and leave the husk. His mind was on his fields.

Nathaniel Francis stood next to his brother, Salathiel, at Mahone's Tavern in Jerusalem. In this place eight miles from Cross Keys, he normally had no time for lollygagging, or money to spend on apple brandy at a bar among townsfolk—not when there was work to be done and whiskey for free. It was planting season, and if he was going to get ahead, there was work to do.

But this day was special. He leaned against the bar and looked over the shoulder of the man standing next to him. The man held the poll book where names would be written and votes recorded.

To his right, two men down, James Rochelle, Southampton County Clerk, read the newspaper aloud since six or seven out of ten men could not read beyond recognizing and writing their own names. The Richmond paper was only three weeks old—having been passed from hand to hand. There was news from Richmond, Washington, and beyond. There was even a short piece about goings-on in Petersburg.

Nathaniel Francis sucked in the aroma of Mahone's. The women sometimes came after church to socialize, but Mahone's smelled of men—stale sweat and earth dragged in from outdoors. The dark, sweet musk of tobacco mingled with the smell of fermentation. Underneath it all, wafting from the carved wood of the hand-carved, Boston-made bar was the sharp bite of turpentine; the keeper, Fielding Mahone, was a tidy man and kept his hand-carved, Boston-made showpiece polished.

Two years over twenty-one, he was about to vote. This was America, Andrew Jackson's America, and the common man now stood shoulder to shoulder with the uptown men of Jerusalem—wealthy men—like Samuel Hines, the Edwardses, the Porters, and the elder Thomas Gray. Wealthy men with many slaves, old aristocrats, could no longer look down on those like him and his brother, who only dreamed of owning more. Their votes, rich or not, counted just the same.

The Virginians from the west, poor men who didn't own even a single slave, were clamoring to vote. Nathaniel Francis was a common man himself, but if the westerners wanted to vote, let them work to earn it. He would not be one of the ones to give the vote away. He and his brother had not been born with silver spoons in their mouths, like Jefferson, like Thomas Gray and his family. Like Andrew Jackson, they worked and scratched for everything they owned. A white man had to earn his way: no work, no vote; no property, no vote.

The silver spooners, the aristocrats, had come overseas to America with papers, influence, and lines of credit. His great-grandfather, like the forefathers of most of the men in the bar, had come to America as an indentured servant. His people were men and women who sold their labor, most often for seven years, to get a footing.

Gray and the other silver spooners had come to America toting elitist manners, pompous vocabularies, and titles. Gray—with his jackets and ties, his sirs and ma'ams, and his fancy ways—never let him and Salathiel forget that their father had come only with papers of indenture. The Jeffersons, the Parkers, the Grays were the spoiled grandchildren of royals lording it over everyone else. But property, and the vote, the vote of the common man, exalted the valleys and lowered the mountains.

The common man had to fight for every inch. Nathaniel's grandfather had been beaten and cheated out of what was due him by rich skinflints who cared more for pocketbooks than for men. People just like Gray, though they were no better or smarter, had held his father in bondage. The law was on the side of the wealthy and powerful, who used it to steal other men's dreams and labor.

But his grandfather would be no man's slave; he had run away, slogging his way through the rocky, treacherous land of the Eastern Shore. Had run away with three others, one of them a darkie. They'd been caught, but vindicated in the courts, given what was due.

His grandfather had come to Southampton County to buy land with what he had earned from selling his labor. Gray and his kind hadn't expected people like Nathaniel's grandfather to survive. The wealthy ones had expected that, starving, they would crawl back on their hands and knees and sign themselves into servitude again. But he had worked to own—green grass, cornfields, apple trees, niggers, and a house.

That was long ago, and now, no matter how rich he was, no silver spooner could own a white man. People had come to their senses. It was against God's law, against natural law to hold white men and women in bondage. Mr. Jefferson had made it clear—all men were endowed by the Creator. Never again, if he had to work day and night, if he had to beat his slaves until meat fell off their bones, would he give up his property or his freedom. No white man worth his salt would.

But then there were lazy men like his sister's husband, Travis. There were others, white trash, peckerwoods, white men who stole to eat, who begged by the road, who barely scraped by hunting possums or whatever they could find to fill a pot. And there were men like Benjamin Phipps, too good, too holy, without backbone enough to take their God-given place as owners, masters. All morals, all dreams, and no ambition.

James Trezvant, the congressman, the postmaster's brother,

knocked on the end of the bar. "Good gentlemen, give me your attention." When things quieted, Trezvant continued. "You know this vote is important, a vote on our new Virginia constitution. Think carefully on your vote. Most likely, this constitution will extend suffrage to more of our western brothers." He paused, looking around the room. "There's no need to remind you of their position—like that of our governor, a mountain man himself—on slavery. Look to your property rights as you vote." If there was a way to tell a story that would get him a vote, Trezvant dogged it, always at the center of things and seeking his own glory. He found a way to wrap every discussion around himself. But Trezvant was right about the westerners and slave property.

The westerners, who were too poor to own slaves, would try to work together to overthrow Nathaniel Francis and those like him so they would lose all they had worked hard to gain. The western Virginians, just like the abolitionists, wanted to take his property and his right to freely make his own decisions.

The Tidewater region, the eastern portion of Virginia, was not a place where abolitionists, Quakers and other religious fanatics, or even westerners could tell a man how to live his life. It was not an aristocracy where a few wealthy men, or even poor men who did not own slaves, could force their will on another. He was free and this was a land that belonged to the common man—a land where every free landowner or property owner had a vote. A land where he could exercise his God-given right to own slaves and to do with his property as he desired.

When gray-haired Jeremiah Cobb called his name to vote, Nathaniel Francis felt a chill. It was a powerful thing to have a vote, a say. He lifted his voice so that all could hear him, "Nay!" As men answered the roll call, Nathaniel felt a hand on his shoulder. "How goes it, young Nathaniel Francis?" He turned. It was Samuel Hines, one of the old aristocrats.

He shook the elderly man's hand. "Hello, sir."

Samuel Hines clapped him on the back. "You're an up-and-comer and I have my eye on you, Nathaniel Francis. Any day, I'm expecting you'll leave Cross Keys and purchase property in town."

Nathaniel flushed. "Yes, sir."

"How many head do you own now?"

"Eight or so, sir."

The older man smiled. "Well, you are making a good start, a good start." He tapped Nathaniel's shoulder. "You've got a good head there." Hines ignored Nathaniel's older brother, Salathiel, as though he weren't there. "Remember, babies and breeders. If you want to profit, remember my rule, babies and breeders. You only need one grandmother to watch over the little ones." Hines did not offer his wisdom to John Clarke Turner, to William Williams, or to the other men of Cross Keys.

"Babies and breeders, sir."

"And watch out for the free ones. They'll ruin everything. Like bad apples. You know that God never intended the races to live together—not with them as freemen. If we do, it will be like Babel falling down around us." Hines took a drink of sherry. "You have some freemen living on your place. Keep them far away from your Negroes so they don't get any ideas. In fact, I recommend you use the law and rid yourself of them. Send them out of state and claim their land." He laughed. "More land for you."

"Yes, Mr. Hines."

"Call me Samuel."

The balding old man slapped him on the back again and Nathaniel felt his face warming. "Yes, Samuel." He cleared his throat and spoke louder so the older man could hear him over the noise. He wanted the older man to respect him, to know that despite his youth, he was no fool. "They are free in name, but not otherwise." He exacted hefty rent from the freemen who lived on his place, so hefty that in time he would own everything the freemen had—maybe even come to own them. "They live on my property and by my rules. They pay goodly rent and the greater share of their crops. They pay for seed. None of them have been able to pay free of the debt. If they cross me . . ." He smiled. "They do not cross me."

"Good enough then. Turning a profit. Smart young man. Keep them in line." Hines glanced over Nathaniel's shoulder at Red Nelson. "Keep them in their place. They get confused and cause trouble otherwise."

"I heartily agree with you, sir." Nathaniel was younger and none of his brothers or sisters wanted to listen to him. Nathaniel had told his older brother not to bring Red Nelson, but Salathiel said the boy was amusing, the other men enjoyed him. No one bothered about Red Nelson drinking with them, Salathiel said. Red Nelson never talked back. But allowing him to drink with white men could only put bad ideas in the slave's head. He would have to speak to Salathiel about Red just like he needed to speak to Sallie about her Nat Turner.

Hines had turned his attention back to Nathaniel. "Are you keeping your nose clean?"

"Yes, sir."

"I am with Thomas Jefferson in saying that whiskey is ruining some of our finest young men. Doing them in. Fields are going unplanted. We who work hard are being drained to pay for the families of drunkards living on the dole." Hines frowned at the backs of some of the men of Cross Keys, then he looked back at Nathaniel Francis. "Of course, don't drink the water—that and milk will kill you quick as a snakebite. Niggers can tolerate it. Redskins can stomach it, but water is death to the white man.

"But we have to be more modern. Whiskey is the old way for a gentleman to refresh himself when he works. Wine, Jefferson has taught us, is the new way—the way for the modern man. You aren't drowning in corn liquor, are you?"

Glasses clanked together as men toasted one another and smoke curled in the air. Nathaniel laughed. With a slight movement he pushed his whiskey glass away. "Of course not, sir." He was not a drunk. He was not a man who could not control himself.

"Stick to the apple brandy and try the wine when you need refreshing. Don't be tripped by the whiskey. Stick to the brandy and the wine; both good for whatever ails you." Old Hines lifted his glass. "And be sure to get a good overseer. Important as you acquire more property, and a good, big buck to drive them."

"Henry Doyle's my overseer."

Hines gave a noncommittal nod. "If you ever need another, contact me. I know a fellow who can beat them to submission, but leave enough life for them to recover and work again. It's a balance—too many don't have the stomach to do enough or else they go too far." They shook hands again and then Samuel Hines left to join some of the others.

It felt good to be slapped on the back, to have others see him slapped on the back by the wealthy older man.

But he had work to do, crops to plant. Salathiel tapped him on the shoulder and pointed at the window. "Look who it is, Phipps! He's got a nerve showing his face in town when free men are voting." Salathiel smiled and nudged Nathaniel. "Come on," he said and headed for the door.

chapter 76

Salathiel was right. Phipps was an embarrassment. He looked more like a scarecrow—a poor one at that—than a man. Couldn't Phipps see how men like Hines and Gray and Trezvant looked at him? It was men like Phipps who made some of the silver spooners say that poor whites would be better off as slaves.

Nathaniel Francis fell in walking behind Phipps. Nathaniel got closer, his toes catching the back of Phipps's worn-out shoes, causing Phipps to stumble. "Has thee lost thy way?" He mocked Phipps, hoping the man would lose his temper, hoping he would give Nathaniel a chance to thrash him. He danced around to stand in front of Phipps and tugged at his jacket collar. Phipps looked frightened, just like he did when he was a sniveling child.

Nathaniel heard Salathiel behind him laughing. He turned to see his brother pointing at him, leaning against a hitching post. Salathiel's slave, Red Nelson, was laughing also and standing by his side. "Let him have it." Salathiel laughed.

Beyond Salathiel, farther down the street, Nathaniel Francis saw Nat Turner. There he was, the bothersome nigger, with some white men standing near him. Showing off, reading to them; one of the white men patted him on the back. That was the problem; they were always fawning over him. The nigger could do no wrong. He could read and no one questioned it. He had a Bible and no one questioned it—all because he was Old Ben's favorite. Nathaniel would take care of the slave later; he was dealing with the white trash now.

Nathaniel turned back to the scrawny man before him. "Why

would you wear field hand clothes to town?" He jerked at Phipps's collar. "No respectable white man would wear these kinds of rags." The man brought shame to every white man. Mud clung to the man's shoes and dragged the torn hem of his pants. He would have been better off, better fed, as a slave.

Nathaniel was not like Phipps. Nathaniel was a man now and he would take his rightful place. He would put his feet on the neck of his slaves and step up to the place that God had appointed him. He would work until he was ahead of men like Gray, until he built a mansion like Mr. Jefferson.

Nathaniel Francis knocked the croker sack Phipps carried from his arms. Potatoes rolled at the coward's feet. "Is thou deaf and dumb?" The whelp was a weakling who hid behind religion or anything else that would protect him. Phipps looked down briefly at the potatoes, then back at Nathaniel, but said nothing. "You're a frightened puppy, that's what you are. You're a cracker, aren't you? Thou is a coward!"

Phipps took a step backward, his skinny face contorted as though rage were getting the better of him. "I am not a Quaker, I'm a Methodist just like you; I just want to live in peace. Why can't you, you and your brother, leave me alone?"

Nathaniel hissed at him. "Come on. Hit me!"

"Why can't you leave me alone, Nathaniel? We're not children anymore. Let me go in peace."

"Are you getting angry, Phipps? Dost thou want to take a swing at me? Hit me and let me put you out of your misery!" He stepped closer, his gaze drilling into Phipps. Nathaniel heard the sound of horses and wagons as they passed by. He knew no one would try to stop him. No one would have the nerve to try to stop him. Phipps deserved what he got and anyone who meddled would get the same.

"Why don't you mind your own business? Why don't you and your brother go back into the bar and do what you do best?"

"Why don't you be a man and take care of your family?" He

jerked at Phipps's torn jacket again. "Why don't you be a man, instead of trying to be holier-than-thou, and get some slaves so you can do your duty and vote? You're a disgrace to the Tidewater, to the county, and to the state. Work your land and show some self-respect!" Nathaniel pushed Phipps.

"Why does how I live my life bother you? What interest is my family to you? I choose to live, I and my family, on what I can grow myself and earn. Why does that trouble you? I don't ask anything from you. I choose to believe that every man—not just a white man—has the right to be free. That is my choice to believe. What does it have to do with you?"

"And look what you have to show for it. Look at you. You make all white men and God ashamed!" But Nathaniel would not be ashamed for long. The shame would go away when his fist pounded Phipps's face. "Are you some abolitionist?"

"Are these yours?" Out of nowhere, Nat Turner appeared and stooped over, picking up the potatoes. Nat Turner stood, staring at Phipps as though he were an equal, as though he had the right to look into the man's eyes, and dropped the potatoes in Phipps's bag.

Nathaniel glared. Nat Turner was always everywhere except where he should have been: in the fields. Sallie trotted him about like a show pony. He was always there and lording it over everyone, as if he had some privilege, as if he knew more than everyone else. He was always there like he was smarter and as though he were superior. Nat Turner was always looking down his nose at Nathaniel as though he were a little kid. Well, Sallie could put up with it, but he wasn't taking anything off a nigger. Her fondness for the slave was a dishonor and an embarrassment.

Nathaniel Francis balled his fist and struck Turner in the temple. He felt pleasure at the sound his fist made, like the thud of raw meat when it hits the butcher's table. There was pleasure from the sting in Nathaniel's hand; though he felt the feeling he always felt when he hit someone as though he had not been able to hit them hard enough. The slave stumbled, slipped in the thick brown mud, but did not fall. "What has this got to do with you, boy?"

Phipps stooped to help Nat Turner, placing himself between Nathaniel Francis and Turner's boy. "Stop!" Phipps yelled at Nathaniel Francis.

Nathaniel felt air rushing in his nose, felt his muscles hardening. "I will kill you! My sister won't do it, I'll save her the trouble!" Nathaniel Francis swung again, but missed; Phipps was blocking him. Nat Turner regained his footing and stared straight up at Nathaniel, as though he were his equal. The slave was crazy and insolent. He fought his way around Phipps, raising his fist in the air. "Nat Turner, I will see you sold up the river! I'll see you sold to the Deep South where they'll teach you who you are!"

Phipps stepped in the way again. "It's me you're quarreling with, Francis."

Nathaniel pushed the scarecrow out of the way. It was Turner's boy, always Turner's boy, taunting him. Turner's boy stared at him, not saying a word, but staring as though he were the master, as though he were smarter. He would goad Nat Turner into hitting him. Nathaniel didn't care who Nat Turner's father was, Nat Turner was a slave and no slave could hit a white man and live. Let him try! "Who do you think you are? When will you get it through your head that you are not free? Never will be." He wanted to make Turner angry. Let the slave raise his hand. He'd be swinging from a tree before nightfall. Nathaniel swung again and this time Phipps could not block it; blood gushed from Turner's nose. Turner slid in the mud but did not lose his footing.

Nathaniel was so angry he felt his sides heaving, felt a rushing in his head. Old Benjamin Turner had ruined Nat Turner, telling him he was too smart to be a slave, and Sallie was only making it worse. Like Hines said, it didn't do to pamper them.

Nathaniel Francis felt someone brush his shoulder. Now Salathiel was beside him. The two of them were going to tear Nat

Turner apart, gut him like a pig. Who would stop them? They would be doing Southampton County a favor.

Phipps stepped in the way again and grabbed Nathaniel's arm. "You must not do this! There is no need for this."

Nathaniel jerked his arm away. "Off of me!"

Salathiel yelled at Phipps, "I would advise you to keep your hands off my brother, you trash!" The two brothers stepped closer, one on either side of Nat Turner. Though there was fire in his eyes, Nat Turner's hands remained at his side. Nathaniel would take pleasure in beating him.

"Nat? Nat Turner? Nat Turner, come over here right now!" It was his sister Sallie's voice.

chapter 77

Nathaniel turned to see his sister standing outside the dry goods store. "Nat Turner, come over here. I need you to carry these things."

His hands still lowered, Turner's boy turned toward her.

Nathaniel grabbed for Turner's collar, but Phipps stepped in the way again. Turner's boy turned to look again, still that look on his face as though he were a prince—but with a coolness, as though he were not concerned. As though nothing could happen to him that he did not expect. But Sallie called to him again, ordering him, and Nat Turner turned to respond.

Nathaniel called after him. "Running away, coward?"

The slave turned as if he were about to speak. His eyes blazed white hot and then, just as suddenly, cooled. He crossed the muddy street, avoiding a man riding a mule with a mangy dog that trotted beside him. Nat Turner took the package and the baskets from Sallie's arms. Nathaniel could hear his sister speaking from where he stood. "What have you been up to, Nat? Just like a little boy. I have to keep you by my side to keep you out of mischief."

Nat Turner shouldn't think this was over. He shouldn't think he had gotten away. Nathaniel Francis called across the street to him, "She won't always be here to protect you, you can count on that. I'll see you sold down the river, or I'll see you dead, Nat Turner!"

Nathaniel straightened his shirtsleeves. Salathiel patted him on the back. Nathaniel watched Nat Turner crossing the street to take the packages to the wagon. "Did you see his eyes blaze, like he would fight us?"

Salathiel nodded. "He is getting worse every day."

"He thinks he can hide behind our sister's apron strings, but this is not over." Before Nathaniel could go to her, Sallie had crossed the street and headed toward him. Sallie watched Nat Turner walking to the wagon. Benjamin Phipps shuffled in the other direction.

Sallie smiled her simpering smile. "Nathaniel, Salathiel, I see that you two are voting. I have just come from the store. I saw some lovely fabric there."

"Boys"? It enraged him even more that she would think he was too stupid, too young to know that she was trying to mollify him. "I have told you, Sallie, that you must get rid of him. He is impudent. Do you see him standing there looking at me, looking at us like he's a man?" He raked his hand through his hair. "Look at Salathiel's Red Nelson, there. You never see him out of place."

Sallie smiled her pacifying smile at Red Nelson. Red Nelson bowed. Sallie kept the placating smile on her face. "Nat Turner is my property. I will handle him."

It was infuriating. She was always protecting him, treating Nat Turner like she was his nursemaid. You would think that the slave, and not he or Salathiel, was her brother. She was smiling, but Nathaniel saw through it; she thought she was smarter than him. She still thought he was her little brother; she did not respect him as a man.

Nathaniel put one hand on his hip, and bent over to look into her eyes. He was no longer little brother to her older sister. "I believe Nat Turner is actually your Putnam's property. At least he was last time I observed."

Nathaniel Francis saw that he had shaken his sister. She was still smiling, but could not hold his gaze.

"Nat Turner is Putnam's property, brother, but he is my responsibility until Putnam comes of age."

She was a sassy one, his sister; but not sassy enough to make her husband earn a decent living or keep her slave in line. "Well, if you intend for your son to have him, then I suggest you keep your mutt on a shorter rope." Nathaniel stood upright. "If he tramples in my garden, I promise I will shoot him."

He sent his sister scampering away, her skirts dragging on the muddy ground. "I will tell Mother you asked after her," he called to her retreat. Sallie nodded and hurried to her wagon.

chapter 78

Spring and voting were behind them and soon, he hoped, so would be his trouble with Nat Turner. Nathaniel swiped his forehead with his shirtsleeve. The blackness did nothing to diminish the heat of the Sunday night. The moon was full. Nathaniel Francis sat on a stool with his sweating back to the corner watching people as they entered the door. John Clarke Turner, the Williams brothers, and all the regulars, the usual Cross Keys gang, were at Levi Waller's still.

A few women sat at a small table near a window refreshing themselves. His wife, though this would likely be her last Sunday—she was getting to be too far along with child—and his mother were among them.

Mary Barrow was present, unaccompanied and unconcerned. Mary had married well, wore pretty gowns and lace, but there was still a bit of the sport in her. She had been a jealous girl—she was not satisfied unless she was the prettiest girl in the room, pretty like his slavegirl Charlotte, Wicked Charlotte—and she had grown into an even more jealous woman.

The women giggled to themselves and shared a jar among them. Clear corn liquor; a passerby might have thought it was water.

The still was on the other side of the room against the wall. Nathaniel looked down at his hand of cards; there was nothing in it. He kept his face set, took three coins from his pile, and threw them on the rough, grog-stained table. The place smelled of liquor, smoke, and sweat. He rested his back against the wall.

Jacob Williams looked at him, trying to read him, Nathaniel knew. Jacob downed his whiskey and folded his hand. "It is hot. I need more." He wiped his face and raised his glass. John Clarke Turner folded as well.

Waller had already played too long, more at drinking than at cards, and was sprawled out on the dirt floor. One by one the men folded and Nathaniel Francis raked in the pile of coins.

When young Thomas Gray walked through the door Nathaniel Francis smiled. "Come sit down, friend Gray." It was always good to see a Jerusalem man with silver spoon money. There wasn't much that pleased Nathaniel more than separating a thirsty Jerusalemite from his coins. Nathaniel Francis pointed to Waller's empty chair. Gray looked out of place at Waller's still, wearing his starched collar and tie in the midst of the others in the dirt-floor cabin. Nathaniel smirked, thinking how disappointed the elder Gray and the others—like the Edwardses, the Hineses, and the Parkers—would be to see young Thomas Gray at Waller's still.

When Gray settled and had his cards, Nathaniel Francis stared at him. "I suppose, by now, you have heard the news of your friend?"

"What news do you mean, sir?" Gray tried to look calm, tried a bit too hard. "What friend?"

"Your friend Nat Turner. By now you've heard of the comeuppance he got at Turner's Meeting Place. He's lucky he hasn't died." Nathaniel laughed. "Yet." The other men, except for Gray, laughed with him.

"No, I hadn't heard." Gray swallowed and Nathaniel Francis was certain he had.

"A month or so ago, I spied him in the woods." He paused to watch Gray react. "Alone, praying out loud like a madman. I demanded of my sister that she do something, but she coddled him. Been coddled all his life."

He looked at John Clarke Turner. "You would think, with his reading and the way he has been treated—preaching and going where he pleases—that he was Old Benjamin Turner's son." Nathaniel enjoyed watching John Clarke Turner's face redden. "The way he's celebrated around here, you'd think Nat Turner was Old Ben's favorite son." He laughed, the others laughed, but John Clarke frowned at the whiskey in his glass.

Nathaniel shifted his sight back to Thomas Gray. "Your friend got taken down a peg at Turner's Meeting Place. Reminded that he is a slave." Nathaniel laughed and slapped his knee. "Preaching to us, white men, as though we would listen to a nigger! Spouting off like the Fourth of July!" The others laughed with him. "But when Richard Whitehead took the whip to him, Nat Turner was not so high and mighty then."

Gray stared at the cards in front of him. Nathaniel Francis nudged John Clarke Turner sitting next to him. "You should have seen our little preacher wielding that snake! I didn't know old Dickie had it in him. You should have been there!" Gray's shoulders were frozen, his eyes still focused on his cards.

"Whitehead took that nigger to church. He whipped your friend Nat Turner until he got tired. Then a few of us helped out." Nathaniel Francis pointed at John Clarke Turner. "You should have been there. Even Sallie took a turn." Nathaniel Francis nodded at Jacob Williams. "Wasn't that something?"

Williams slammed his cards on the table. "Nat Turner will never forget that day!"

John Clarke Turner adjusted his seat and then leaned forward against the table. "It serves the rascal right. He has always been uppity. Much of the blame has to be laid, God rest his soul, at my father's feet."

"How do you bear the shame he caused you, your family, especially your dear mother?"

John Clarke's face reddened, but he did not answer. Nathaniel looked away from the poker table. He yelled to Waller. Perhaps the man would hear him through his whiskey fog. "Waller, get up and get some whiskey for your customers." Waller, his mouth open and slack, never moved. Nathaniel Francis spoke to one of the other men, drunk but still on his feet. "Get Mr. Gray here some whiskey. He didn't come slumming to sit here dry." He smiled at Gray. "And he looks a little peaked."

Thomas Gray nodded. "Thank you."

Nathaniel Francis yelled again to the man. "While you're at it, I'm sure Gray would be happy to pay for a round for all of us Cross Keys men."

Gray looked up from his cards then.

Nathaniel Francis leaned forward. "Why, Mr. Gray, do you object?"

Gray shook his head, then looked back at his cards.

"You should have been there last Sunday. Your friend squealed like a pig under Pettigrew's slaughter." Nathaniel enjoyed watching Gray squirm.

Gray downed his whiskey and held up his glass for another.

"Or maybe Nat Turner screamed more like a little girl."

Gray gulped down the next glass and motioned to the man to fill it again.

Nathaniel Francis laughed. "Be careful or you're going to look like Waller over there lying on the floor."

"What if I do?" The whiskey was speaking to Gray's tongue, giving him courage to talk back, lending him courage he really didn't have.

"Well, I know the senior Mr. Gray would be very disappointed in you. In fact, I'm sure he would be just as disappointed to know that you are spending your Sunday nights here in Cross Keys instead of in town in Jerusalem with your wife and daughter."

Gray sucked the liquid from his glass. "I'm my own man."

"Is that whiskey putting hair on your chest? Too bad you and the bottle weren't there to rescue your friend."

Gray got his glass refilled again. "You seem to be making a point of calling Nat Turner my friend."

"He's not?"

"I am a white Southern gentleman." Gray added, "As you are." He took a gulp. "Nat Turner is not a white man, he is a slave." He finished his glass and for the fifth time had it refilled.

Nathaniel Francis chuckled. "For a gentleman, in this hot weather you don't seem too concerned about refreshing your friends. How about another round?"

Thomas Gray waved his hand at the man serving them.

Nathaniel Francis let the air settle. He looked down then at the cards he'd been dealt. Nothing again. He looked up, threw out five coins, closed his hand, and leaned back against the wall.

The men folded one by one except for Gray.

"So, Mr. Gray the younger, you say Nat Turner is not your friend?"

"He is a slave." Gray threw out enough coins to cover Nathaniel Francis's bet and then raised him three. He leaned forward and then leaned back as though he were calm, but Nathaniel Francis noticed his hands shaking. "He likes to hear himself philosophize, but Nat Turner is simply another slave. I find him amusing, that's all."

Nathaniel Francis raised the bet again. "Is that so? Just a slave? That why you meet him alone in the woods?"

The color drained from Gray's face and the other men quieted. Gray stammered, "I-I-I don't know what you mean."

"You remember. This past spring, near Cabin Pond. I saw the two of you. Had him in the site of my rifle. You handed him a package. You were speaking to each other earnestly. Not like slave and master, but like friends."

Gray looked at Nathaniel Francis and at the others as if the walls of the small cabin were closing in on him. He shifted in his chair and looked toward the door. He breathed rapidly. He turned back, smiling, and shrugged. "Oh, now I remember what you mean. He had done some work for me and I paid him with some goods."

"Why not pay my sister? When a slave is hired out, it's the master that gets paid."

"I'm sure he had her permission. At least, that's what he said." Gray could not hold Nathaniel's gaze.

Nathaniel Francis stared him down. "I'll check with her," he said. He called Gray's bet. "You think you are better than us, Mr. Gray, better than us Cross Keys men?"

"I don't know what you mean."

Nathaniel Francis looked at Gray's face, at the color draining. He had struck the truth. "You, Mr. Gray, have a few niggers you handpick, like your mammy and your Nat Turner, that you think are worthy of your special treatment. It makes you feel like you're better than the rest of us. You don't call any of your niggers names—not even the ones you think deserve it. You give them more food and more whiskey at Christmas. You hire someone else to beat them, but you are no different than me.

"You think I am a poor ignorant farmer, a cracker, white trash—I know what you call me. We know what you call us. You think men like me, the slave dealers with their chains and their seedy auctions, and the overseers with their whips, are all less than you. You—Jefferson, Cobb, Hines, and Trezvant, Edwards, Porter—think you're better and that God will excuse you. You think your hands aren't dirty.

"Well, guess what, Mr. Gray? If there is a wrong in this, you also bear your share. Men like you make it possible for there to be men like me." Nathaniel Francis pointed around the room. "You make it possible for the patrollers, the overseers, the slave merchants—for all of us to do what we do. So you can get what you want, you turn your head and we can get our share. You hold your niggers and you live off of them just like I do.

"Maybe you're worse. You're a slavery man but you like the pleasure of thinking you're better—but you're just like the rest of us. You fawn over your chosen niggers to make yourself feel better. You are the ones—you rich and powerful men, you readers and writers with your fancy words—you're the ones who make the laws. If we do evil, it's because your class has written it in stone— not for us poor men, but so you can ride on flowery beds of ease. You take advantage of the niggers and men like me. Don't fool yourself. You're a peckerwood just like we are."

Thomas Gray folded his hand then and Nathaniel Francis raked the coins from the table as Waller, slobbering now, curled into the fetal position on the floor.

Nathaniel Francis lifted his cup of whiskey and nodded at Thomas Gray. "Thanks to you, Gray." He stared at the Jerusalem lawyer. "If we are guilty, then you and yours, my friend, lead the way."

chapter 79

August 22, 1831

It was late August, more than a month since Nat Turner's beating—harvesttime. Nathaniel Francis's bladder told the time for him. He had been at Waller's all night, but he could not spend the day there. There was work to do.

It was hot already, though there was still no glimmer of sun. Nathaniel Francis wiped his mouth with the back of his hand. Not far away, he heard Waller snoring. Nathaniel grunted, laughing to himself. He had been laughing for weeks now. *Did you see the niggers take off running when the sun turned blue? Ran like cannibals were chasing them in the jungle. Would have shot them dead if it hadn't been so funny. They ran like someone had already lit the fire to boil the pot.*

Nathaniel's overseer, Henry Doyle, said Sam, Dred, and Will had taken off like jackrabbits, had almost mowed down the corn. "Too bad the jigs didn't pick while they were running. Harvesting would have been done!" Doyle had bent over laughing.

Nathaniel Francis had been on his way to Waller's and he had seen some of the darkies running, superstitious niggers running from the sun. It had been almost two weeks, but even now he laughed thinking of their running like rabbits. They were ignorant cowards, all of them. All he could see, they were moving so fast, was the bottoms of their dirty black feet.

Last night he was still laughing. "It is ironic, ain't it," he said to Waller and Jacob Williams, "that darkies are afraid of their own shadows!" Early morning now, his eyes still closed, Nathaniel Francis reached to wipe the dew off his face, then drifted back toward sleep.

When Nathaniel Francis was a boy, he was afraid of the dark. He jumped at every shadow and his father teased him. His mother kept a candle lit for him, the youngest of her children, to chase the hobgoblins away. His father, standing beside his older sons, shook his head and asked Nathaniel what kind of man he would become. "She indulges you," his father had spat at Nathaniel's feet. "I will leave you to your mother. You seem to be more timid, like her kind."

His mother doted on him, but Nathaniel Francis knew it was not really him she loved. It was his father for whom she yearned. No matter how disagreeable, no matter how much, after church, he drank and cursed, no matter what he didn't provide, it was his father she held her breath for until he walked back in the door. Even now, after he was long dead, she still missed him.

Nathaniel Francis had heard that in Europe there were castles where music played night and day. There was so much oil and so many candles that men and women had been blinded by the reflection of the light off crystal chandeliers. There was so much wealth they never worried about not having enough.

He had been told that Mr. Jefferson had lived on a five-thousand-acre plantation and that he had almost two hundred loyal servants who sang spirituals just to comfort and delight their master. Why, he had even heard that the shacks in which Mr. Jefferson's slaves lived were bigger than the house he and his wife, Lavinia, lived in . . . and the slave shacks were made of bricks.

He had been told that in the Deep South all the farmers were plantation owners living in sprawling mansions surrounded by grass that was always lush and green. They were wealthy men—wealthier than the Grays, the Trezvants, and the Hineses, the rich and powerful men of Jerusalem, Virginia, wealthier even than Thomas Jefferson. They drank the finest whiskey and ate the finest food. The plantation owners stayed young and their wives beautiful because they did not work. They did not have to; loyal slave men did the laborious work, the dirty work, while loyal slave women did the washing, the cooking, the ironing. The slave women even pressed white babies to their black breasts so that their beautiful mistresses did not have to sacrifice their figures to child nurture. The darkies in the Deep South wanted to be slaves and wanted to please their masters. They wanted no more than what they were given; they wanted to stay in their place.

Those scenes were far away and sometimes he thought the stories must be lies. In Petersburg, in Richmond, there were lamps that burned all night. But the nights in his house were dark.

Nathaniel Francis forced himself up from sleep. He could not be lazy. Besides, sleep only meant worry. He worried that in the darkness his horse would leave, his pigs would wander, and his slaves would betray him and leave. Everything could be lost in one dark night.

His slaves were children and they could be wooed away by some Pied Piper—like that Gabriel from Henrico County or that Denmark Vesey from South Carolina—who promised them freedom, land of their own, and beds of their own. They were never satisfied. He gave them everything they had, but every night's sleep was still a risk. He might awaken to nothing. A freethinking nigger was trouble.

He tried to stay awake each night to listen, but he could not win and each night he surrendered to sleep. His sister, Sallie, said she loved the night, the moon, the stars. She was a romantic like his wife, and talked of the stars as diamonds and the moon as a giant pearl. The two of them could afford to be romantic: they were not men.

They were not responsible to hold on and build up. They did not know, and he did not want them to know, the dread of night or how close they were to no food, no clothes, to nothing.

He could not stay abed. He could not spend the night at Waller's. Nathaniel Francis opened his eyes in the darkness and used his hands to push himself upright. There was wet grass under his hands, not Waller's dirt floor.

Slowly, like tree sap draining into a pail, it came back to him.

Like every other Sunday night, they refreshed themselves, him with his back to the wall. All the regulars were there, except John Clarke Turner, who hadn't arrived yet, and Thomas Gray, who had been rarely seen at the still since late July, and Lavinia—she was too far along now. Otherwise, it was the usual group. Laughing, "Did you ever see a blue sun?" He laughed at the darkies, but he had been frightened too, too frightened to move.

Then a nigger voice from outside the window, "Get up, masters! You better run!" A strange nigger. "You better get up now, and get away from here. British coming!"

Nathaniel Francis had mocked the voice. "You better get away from here. Booga! Booga!" he shouted, waving his hands like a nigger at church meeting. He dropped his hands. "Show yourself, boy!" If the boy thought they were so drunk that they could be fooled by such a simple, bald-faced lie, then he was mistaken— some nigger trick to get the liquor. "You think we're going to run and leave all this moonshine to you?"

Jacob Williams and Waller laughed.

"No, sir!" the darkie hollered. "Not lying, sir! They are killing white folks! British coming!"

Frighten them? Talk about an 1812 war long over. No British would come to Virginia's shores again. Not if they wanted to live.

The darkie voice again. "Already started." The disembodied voice was farther from the window. "Already beginning! Starting with the ones at home." Farther away. Nathaniel Francis stumbled to the window but saw no one. "Starting with the house of God. Then your house the meeting place."

"Who are you?" Nathaniel Francis stumbled, caught himself on the window ledge. "Show yourself!"

The voice was almost impossible to hear. "Your house the meeting place."

"Show yourself!" Men had gone blind, gone crazy on moonshine. An apparition.

"British coming for you. Easy target—drunk at Mr. Waller's still—just before dawn, all of you drunk asleep."

It was a vision, like the blue sun. "Hide in the woods so they don't kill you."

The rascal could not fool him. "No British are coming here, boy!"

"Not the British. Niggers coming for you! The Lord crying out for your blood!" Then the ghost was gone.

He laughed, at first, with Jacob Williams and Waller. "Crazy nigger!"

Then they counted the regulars missing. John Clarke Turner had not stumbled through the door. Thomas Gray had not come slumming. Waller scratched his head. "Do you suppose it's true?" Maybe the two of them were already dead.

But it couldn't be true. No slave would dare raise a hand to his master, especially in Cross Keys.

Jacob Williams panicked first. "They are going to kill us!" Then Waller began to yell and the two men ran back and forth, shaking as they looked out the windows into the night. Nathaniel Francis heard his mother across the room, crying. "We've got to get out of here! They'll rape us, those niggers!" She ran out the door, Mary Barrow followed, Jacob Williams ran after her.

They grabbed the jugs, abandoned their horses at the still, and left the lanterns burning. All of them tumbled out and then in among the trees, each one running his own way. Nathaniel Francis heard women sobbing in the dark, heard others panting. They crashed, stumbling, falling, as they felt their way in the darkness, the blackness, like blind men. "Keep quiet!" he hissed at them. He hated cowards, drunken cowards.

It was probably nothing. They were allowing a nigger, and whiskey, to make them act like fools. It was probably a lie. He was sure it was a lie. But he ran into the woods. He and the others waded in deep so that they would be out of sight. "Shut up!" He hated the sound of them. If the darkies didn't kill them, he would.

Finally, they were quiet except for sporadic moaning. Every croak, every crack, every chirp was the niggers coming. It couldn't be true. No slave had the nerve to kill a white man.

Will. Nathaniel Francis pressed his back against a tree. Will.

He had seen something, some craziness in Will's eyes. A rogue slave. Will was showing signs that he might be turning—an angry glance here or a frown there. Maybe Will, or perhaps runaways from the Great Dismal Swamp.

Every breeze that touched him was a snake or some midnight-colored hand. The sound of whimpering, from one or two of the men, unnerved him. He had lost his shoes.

Nathaniel Francis tried to remind himself not to be afraid. But all was blackness. The grass beneath his feet was cool and damp, the mossy ground was spongy, and water from it seeped up between his toes. He remembered the games. *Red Rover, Red Rover.*

His team always won. His brother Salathiel was always the tallest boy, the biggest boy, the strongest boy, and everyone feared him. No matter who they called over—*Red Rover, Red Rover, send Thomas right over!*—each child was already defeated before he struck the line. Nathaniel Francis saw it in their eyes; their hearts fainted, they were like grasshoppers before Salathiel; they never really tried. His team always won.

Nathaniel Francis recognized the panic in them, he felt it because he had been afraid for so long—afraid of his brothers, afraid of the dark. Salathiel was his only protector. Nathaniel was the frightened baby and the rest of his family mocked him. But he watched Salathiel. He used his size, his eyes to intimidate others; Nathaniel Francis had stopped being afraid. Salathiel had taught Nathaniel Francis to get the other man first. Soon the other boys, even the older ones, were afraid of him.

All of them were afraid, except for Nat Turner. But this was not the time to think of the coward Nat Turner. Runaways from the Great Dismal were hunting them.

Nathaniel Francis made out Waller's shape not far away.

Waller got to his feet laughing, stumbling between the trees. Someone called, "Quiet!" Waller tripped, hit the ground, and then began to weep.

Nathaniel recognized his mother's voice from time to time, but she was far away, too far away for him to reach her. Every crawling thing was a threat. Each shaking leaf stirred by fiendish breath.

In the darkness, Nathaniel saw Will. He saw the axe Will carried lifted over his head, ready to strike, the axe he whispered to. What if slaves from the Great Dismal Swamp had crept on the farm and seduced Will to insurrection?

Nathaniel tried to run, but the trees stretched out their limbs and joined hands against him. *Red Rover.*

It was probably nothing. They were all on edge. Nathaniel Francis wished for his brother Salathiel. He heard the darkie voice. "Your house the meeting place."

The meeting place? If it was true . . . Oh, Lavinia! He should go to her, but he was frozen. His heart pounded so loudly Nathaniel was certain the others heard it. He could not force his legs to move.

He had passed out then. He dreamed he heard his father's voice questioning what kind of man he would become.

NOW HE WAS awake. He felt daylight coming. Nathaniel Francis crawled on his belly, making his way back to Waller's still. They were all probably afraid for nothing, all afraid of a nigger lie. He crawled through the darkness; the earth's filth smeared him. He headed for the dim light coming from the cabin that housed the still.

When he was close, he waited, listening. He watched, looking for any movement. When he felt assured that no one was there, no one hidden, he ran to his waiting horse.

Nathaniel Francis galloped into the darkness hoping no one would catch him, hoping that what the nigger had told them at Waller's still wasn't true.

chapter 80

Nathaniel Francis hoped he would find his brother alive. Salathiel would rise up from his bed and mock him for being afraid. "Must I light a candle for you, baby brother?" He would find it was all a hoax. Salathiel would know what to do. Salathiel would ride with him to check on Lavinia, their mother, and their sister, Sallie.

He rode through the darkness, thankful that the moon was just a sliver. He stayed away from open roads, hoping that he wouldn't see anything, that nothing would see him.

When he reached Salathiel's, his big brother was already gone. There was only a bleeding corpse that resembled him. Oh, Salathiel! Salathiel! The giant who had protected him was cold and still on the hard ground.

Red Nelson was missing. The darkies had most likely killed Red Nelson and left his body amid the corn. Fear staggered Nathaniel Francis. His body shook, betraying him, his legs weakened and he fell to his knees outside his brother's bloody door.

If Salathiel was dead . . . Then Lavinia, sweet Lavinia, was already dead. It was too late to rescue her now. Will and the niggers from the Great Dismal Swamp were drunk already on his brandy and whiskey. He knew it. Nathaniel Francis imagined their evil blackened faces. Poor Lavinia, his sweet Lavinia! What must she have suffered in their filthy hands? He knew what they wanted. All white men knew what they wanted. He prayed that she had died quickly. Everything was stolen, his house ransacked; he knew it. Will was with them. Ungrateful. Nathaniel had been good to him. He had given Will more than he deserved. And now?

He crawled to his snorting horse, threw himself into his saddle. He made his way, his shoulders slumping, to his sister Sallie's place.

chapter 81

In the darkness, Nathaniel Francis stumbled on the front steps, recovered, and then opened the front door of his sister's home and called her name. It was close to morning, but still dark, so he was not surprised that Sallie did not answer.

The moon gave him no light to see. He called her name again and again, a little louder. "Sallie!" She did not respond. No one stirred.

He felt for the lamp Sallie kept by the front door. His sister was not smart but she was reliable. Nathaniel Francis lit it and gave himself light to see. He held the lamp high and looked around. There was nothing disturbed, nothing broken, and nothing appeared to be stolen. Everything was in place, including the quiet, too much quiet. He could not even hear her husband snoring; Joseph Travis always snored to shake the house.

Nathaniel Francis tiptoed up the stairs—every creak made him uneasy—and walked down the hallway to his sister and her husband's bedroom. At the entrance to the room, he looked in to see their feet making tents of the sheet at the foot of their bed. He inhaled with relief—relief that his elder sister was alive.

On that relief rode the comfort to criticize her living. As usual, she and her husband overslept. That's why Sallie and Joseph had nothing. They were dreamers, sloths; sleeping when they should be rising from the bed.

Still, he was relieved to find them and to know that all his worry was for nothing.

Nathaniel Francis stepped inside the room, the lamplight leading, and found his sister and her husband, unrecognizable; their heads severed where they lay.

chapter 82

Where would he go? There was nothing and no place left to him. And poor, poor Lavinia. Nathaniel Francis mounted his panting horse. Guilt and shame road with him. And what of his loyal slaves? Easter? Wicked Charlotte? Sam? They were niggers but loyal, and had probably met the same end.

Nathaniel Frances rode until he came to a thick patch of woods. He pulled his horse in and hid himself away. He shivered. His teeth chattered. He cried. But he did not even have the freedom to cry out loud; if they heard him, if the niggers heard him, they would find him and kill him. Darkness was his only cover.

His poor sister and his brother! He closed his eyes hoping to forget the last time he saw them—Sallie and Salathiel, their lifeless bodies, the emptiness in their eyes. He would never see them again. How would he tell his mother? There was no way he could explain. He sat on the ground, crumpled in a ball, his arms around his head.

WHEN DAYLIGHT CAME Nathaniel Francis moved even deeper into the woods. He imagined his mother hiding in the woods. He must find her, but at least for now she was not alone—if the others from the still had survived.

He imagined his wife, his beautiful wife with his child inside her. He remembered courting her. He moaned for his wife and his murdered son. Nathaniel Francis imagined soot-colored hands molesting her and his stomach ached. He rolled on the ground, there in the woods, afraid to scream.

Then he saw her.

chapter 83

Lavinia! The flicker of her dress through the trees. Nathaniel Francis thought he saw the flash of a satin ribbon. Closer, he heard her. She was crying and holding her stomach. Alive! His sweet Lavinia!

Nathaniel Francis ran to her. He scooped up his wife. Clinging to a wheel of cheese, she pounded on him with her elbows. "You left me! You left me behind and the niggers tried to kill me. Your Charlotte! Your precious little Charlotte! She was the one who tried to kill me. If it had not been for Easter, I would be dead!"

Nathaniel Francis felt his face flush. His Charlotte? Lavinia was frightened. She was confused.

"You think I didn't see you, Nathaniel? All that time you were running after that nigger girl, you think I didn't know? Well, she tried to kill me! She tried to kill our baby! And she made a fool of you!"

Nathaniel Francis said nothing. He had no choice. There were no good words. After all she had been through. "Did they hurt you? The niggers, did they harm you?"

"I told you, your girl Charlotte tried to kill me!"

"But the men?"

"No one touched me. I . . . I fainted when it all started."

"Who was it? Who did you see?"

"I told you I fainted!"

It was the niggers from the Great Dismal Swamp, the runaways. They should have burned it down years ago along with all the niggers hiding there. The Dismal Swamp runaways had probably turned Will and they had turned Charlotte, poor confused

Wicked Charlotte—turned by her jealousy and her envy of his wife, of his love.

"But Easter helped me get away. She's the reason I am alive!" She hit him again. "You left me! You left me and almost got me killed! That wench of yours—if it hadn't been for Easter . . ." Lavinia, her face tearstained and smudged with dirt, began to cry. "Charlotte stole my clothes, the two of them fighting over my clothes! Somebody ought to kill that nigger baby inside her!" Scorn edged her sobs.

They mounted his horse and under cover of daylight they rode away. Lavinia cried all the way to the North Carolina border. "You left my Easter there! Now my poor Easter is probably dead! I fainted when they came. You weren't there! She's the one who saved my life!"

He headed south to her father's house. He had no choice; there was no other safe place to go.

chapter 84

Lavinia's family tended to her; fed her, bathed her, and got her quickly to bed. When she was settled, Nathaniel Francis told his father-in-law more about the slave insurrection. Later that evening, when Lavinia was asleep in a bed with cool sheets and many pillows, with a lamp lit to give her comfort, his father-in-law took him outside.

"Where were you? Late at night and her with child, why did you leave her alone? Where were you? It's not as if you live in Richmond or Raleigh, or like you are a wealthy man tending to business that keeps you away. Where were you?"

His father-in-law stomped the ground. "I told Lavinia all along that you were just a boy playing at being a man."

There was nothing good Nathaniel Francis could say.

"She won't be traveling back to Southampton until all of this mess is over. When I get word all this is over and you're ready to be a man, then maybe, just maybe, you'll get her back!" His father-in-law spat. "I lent Easter to you to care for Lavinia. You get down there and you get my nigger Easter back! You secure my property!" His father-in-law turned and walked back toward the house, a candle lighting every window.

HE NEEDED TO search for his mother, he needed to secure his property, but first he must care for his wife. Nathaniel Francis rode with the North Carolina men long enough to see their good works. They made certain no darkie would consider an insurrection in Northampton County.

They hamstrung them, cutting their tendons, leaving them

disabled and easy prey for those who followed. All over North Carolina—from Charlotte to Raleigh—white men had been polling darkies, bringing them in for serious questioning, questioning that gave them incentive to talk, to make certain there were no more insurgents among them. They put them to the rack and put them to the fire—beat them and cut them until they confessed the truth, or even owned up to lies if that was all they had. When they confessed, as most of them did, the militia finished them off. Every scream, every drop of blood, every plea for mercy made Nathaniel Francis feel better—revenge for his brother and sister and for his fear. Every nigger they hung, shot, or set afire brought renewed life.

Three days later, when Nathaniel Francis returned to Southampton, he rode with a militia group from North Carolina. Most of the work of setting things back to right, back to God's order, had already been done. There wasn't much left to do to show the niggers—to show everyone—he was not afraid.

He found his mother among a group of survivors huddled at the Jerusalem armory. She was in despair, having already heard the news of Salathiel and Sallie. She had feared that he, too, was dead. Relieved to learn of his survival, she was frightened and hungry, but still alive.

The men of Jerusalem and Cross Keys weren't sure who was involved, the men told him, so they'd asked the overseers to tell them which darkies were hard to control, which ones were angry. Men about town had rounded up those most likely involved, those most likely to be persuaded by the runaways from the Great Dismal Swamp, and dispatched them. "We taught them a lesson!" Then troops from Petersburg and Norfolk, led by General Eppes, began to arrive.

When the government's army came, they forced the militias to put some of the darkies in jail. "We must have order," Eppes insisted. Good property was being destroyed, innocent people were being killed. It was to be expected, in light of what had happened, but enough was enough. Things were out of hand. Mangled bodies everywhere; who would bury them? To protect the people and to protect the slaves, he had rounded most of the Cross Keys jigs into jail. There would be no more slaughter, Eppes said. He would order the troops to fire on anyone—white or black—who did not obey his orders. But much of the work was already done.

Nathaniel Francis rode back to Cross Keys, stopping at the Jerusalem jail. Backed by the armed militia, he pushed his way inside. There he found Easter and hugged her to him. "She saved my wife and child," he told the others. Behind her, in a corner, Nathaniel Francis saw Charlotte in the crowded cell—a cell full of moaning, stinking darkies all crying innocent. He grabbed Wicked Charlotte by the arm. "Who made you do this? Was it the Dismal Swamp niggers?" He shook her and twisted her arm.

She stared at him but she did not plead. "I should have killed her!"

He balled his fist and hit her. "Who made you do this?"

"You!"

He hit her again. "Tell me and I'll let you live."

"The only regret I have is that you lived!"

She wasn't much more than a dumb animal, a fool to let the runaways deceive her. Because of her he might have lost Lavinia forever.

Nathaniel Francis dragged her outside and tied her to a tree. Easter stood by watching with her hand clamped to her mouth, tears on her face. Nathaniel Francis nodded at poor old Easter, relieved and grateful to be out of prison. Wicked Charlotte was his property, his to do with as he pleased. He pointed to her. "This nigger tried to kill my wife and unborn child!" If Eppes and his troops thought to make good on Eppes's promise, let them draw their weapons and face the militia. Nathaniel doubted they would risk their lives for one nigger gal.

Nathaniel pulled his pistol, the pearl-handled one, and shot Charlotte. He unloaded his weapon. Then he reloaded. Other men joined in. They fired until the tree smoked. All that was left of

Wicked Charlotte was tattered rope and a bloody, torn sagging ragdoll of a corpse.

Nathaniel Francis wiped his face and turned to hug Easter again. He gave her a paper pass so she could travel the roads safely and ordered her to gather his mother—he had left her with some of the others at Mahone's Tavern—and to make their way straight home. He would get word to Lavinia's father that his property was secure.

When Eppes and his troops withdrew and Nathaniel Francis completed his business in Jerusalem, he continued traveling with the militia. The others in the Northampton County militia were not familiar with Southampton. With Eppes out of the way, Nathaniel Francis led them to farms, showed them where they might find belligerent slaves—but the truth was it didn't matter. The only good nigger was a dead one.

chapter 85

The Dismal Swamp niggers hadn't acted alone; they had gotten fools like Charlotte to join them. But there was a ringleader somewhere. Nathaniel had lived among niggers all his life; he knew their capabilities. Abolitionists had probably infiltrated. Maybe the British. Or local sympathizers. He led the militia to the regulars who had not been at the still.

He led the North Carolina militia the way Congressman Trezvant led the militia from Southampton. Each time he was relied on to lead, he felt more stable, more assured Lavinia would come home. He didn't care if he had to kill every slave in Southampton County, he would do whatever it took to bring Lavinia back.

He could not ride far without seeing a black body dangling from a tree. Trezvant's militia and the others had swooped through Southampton County. Many of the niggers were dead, but he and the boys hunted and found a few, here or there, out in the fields or traveling along the roads. They made the darkies pay. One white man said they had killed over a hundred niggers, but another said it had been over two hundred.

Nathaniel Francis found Levi Waller staggering down the road, a jug in one hand and a rifle in the other. "Where you been, Nathaniel?" Waller slurred and smiled, toasting the air with the jug. His clothes sagged on his body and he was unshaven. "Where you been?" Waller sidestepped, looked as though he might fall, but caught himself, stood aright, and bowed. "Looked all over for you. Thought the niggers had you." Waller was staggering again. "All your niggers gone. We took them to jail days ago."

Nathaniel tried to humor his drunken friend. "Well, you did a nice job with that, Levi. I found them right there in the Jerusalem jail."

"That damn Charlotte! She was trouble." Levi wobbled, lifting the bottle to toast again. "All of Jerusalem is talking about how you took care of her!" Waller took a long pull from the jug. "Yes, sir! Vengeance is mine!" Waller staggered again.

Nathaniel reached out and caught him so that he would not fall. "Whoa, friend."

"Made sausage of her!"

Nathaniel nodded.

"But not me, Nathaniel." Waller lurched, almost pulling both of them down. "Not me. All my people are gone. My wife, my children. My son. Even the schoolteacher. And I don't know who did it." Waller drank from the jug again. He grabbed Nathaniel's collar. He sounded close to tears. "All of them at the house gone! Blood everywhere."

Waller sat down in the road, shaking his head. "Richard Whitehead's gone, his whole family. The widows, Elizabeth Turner and Widow Newsom. Whole William Williams family gone, except Jacob. Your overseer gone." Waller dropped his rifle so he could count off on his fingers. "Sallie and Salathiel gone. Joseph Travis gone. Putnam gone. All gone. Blood everywhere."

Nathaniel Francis's jaw muscles tightened.

"No blood at your house, but blood at mine!" Waller thumped his chest. "Blood everywhere, but no vengeance for Levi." He lifted the jug again. "We been burying people. Niggers been burying our people. But still don't know who done it." Waller began to cry. "All gone and no vengeance."

Nathaniel Francis helped his weeping friend to his feet.

"But you got yours, Nathaniel! Vengeance is yours!" Waller threw his arms around Nathaniel's neck. "Where you been, Nathaniel? Where you been?" Waller was weeping openly now. "Those Dismal Swamp runaways! Over two hundred of them! That's what

Colonel Trezvant says." The congressman called himself "colonel" now, leading the Southampton militia in search of the swamp runaways and any other nigger who might have information.

"You come on with me now, Levi." Nathaniel pried the jug out of Waller's hand. "We're going to get them all if we have to burn down the whole damn swamp, if we have to kill every nigger in Southampton County. Don't you worry, you will get your vengeance. I promise you. We all will!"

Nathaniel Francis led the militia to John Clarke Turner and cornered him. Every white man who survived had to account for himself. "Where were you? Why weren't you at Waller's that night? Why did the niggers pass by your house and leave you and your family alive?" It was just blind luck, John Clarke insisted.

Nathaniel Francis led the militia to Thomas Gray. Nathaniel pulled a gun on the lawyer and promised him he would kill him if Gray didn't tell what he knew. "Why did the niggers pass by you? Did you know it was coming?" Gray was a nigger-lover and all nigger-lovers were suspect. "Did you know they planned to kill us at the still?" Nathaniel shot questions at Thomas Gray, looking for tells that would give Gray's hand away. "I saw you with him. You mean to tell me you didn't know? The niggers killed my family, but they passed by your door. Am I supposed to believe it was coincidence? And that night neither you nor John Clarke Turner was at Waller's!"

In truth, Nathaniel was not much surprised. Thomas Gray had tempered his drinking for the last few months and become a rarity at the still. But he didn't care. It was Thomas Gray and people like him, people who were too easy on their slaves, people who didn't keep control, who were responsible for all this.

"I am a white man, sir," Thomas Gray said. "How can you accuse me?" Nathaniel Francis read the lawyer. Gray didn't know anything. Instead, Gray was worried that he would be called a traitor or a coward. Nathaniel and the militia surrounded Gray. Levi Waller joined them in their interrogations, shoving

Gray. Nathaniel Francis sniffed the air. "Smells like a nigger-lover to me."

Thomas Gray's face reddened, sweat smeared his forehead. "We share a common interest in books. He knows I once had a secret desire, as a boy, to be a writer. That is all! Nothing more!" Gray cleared his throat and raised his hands, pleading. "He is a nigger! I would never take his side against my own people!"

Fools like Thomas Gray made niggers believe they were just as good as any white man, convinced them they could read, let them believe they could be preachers. People like Gray, like Phipps and the Quakers, were to blame.

All the Quaker homes were passed by, so their inhabitants were also suspect. The Dismal Swamp runaways and the few local slaves who joined them had passed by the Parkers, the Edwardses, and the Harrises. Each white family spared was questioned.

They walked around untouched, walked around as though this were a Cross Keys problem, another problem with the ne'er-do-wells. But people like Nathaniel and Colonel Trezvant led the militias right up to their doors. It wasn't just his problem, or Waller's—all white people were at risk. They would stand together or die together. The slaves had planned to kill them all!

As days passed, it seemed to Nathaniel Francis that some white people who had missed being attacked felt guilty to be alive. Some fabricated stories of how the insurgents had tried to molest them and how they had successfully run them away.

The niggers attacked them but they didn't ride to Jerusalem to alarm the others and alert the militia? Let them have their stories. Everyone knew they were passed by because they were cowards who coddled the niggers. Let the lies be their badges of courage. But Nathaniel Francis knew better. Let them keep their lies. The truth was that he had lost his brother and his sister, friends and families because of white men without backbone. They were as guilty as the Dismal Swamp niggers. They had blood on their hands.

* * *

HE RODE WITH the militia down the road that had no name. As he traveled, Nathaniel Francis came upon poles stuck deep into the ground. Atop each pole was a battered orb barely recognizable as a man's head. Nigger heads. Beaten, hacked, and shot. Heads without eyes, missing ears and noses. Some cleanly severed, others looking torn away. Some bore the marks of dragging. Some had been torched. The skulls were serenaded by cawing birds and buzzing flies. Nathaniel Francis smiled. The road now had a name: Black Head Sign Post Road.

It was a nice touch, the sign, the work of true patriots! And they would keep at the work until they found out who led the Dismal Swamp runaways, until they ferreted out each local nigger involved.

Levi Waller pointed at him, laughing. "Look, a redskin!" Nathaniel Francis looked at his hands, his clothes. "So I am!" Waller's face was red with blood, his sopping clothes maroon. "You too, my friend!"

The niggers were learning their lessons. In the dark, by firelight, they roasted one alive. He screamed and kicked at first, then he was silent, smoke rising in the air.

They dragged one of Giles Reese's little nigger boys out before the fire where the nigger was cooking. The yellow glow highlighted the boy's face. Nathaniel Francis stooped down and looked into the boy's eyes. "You remember now. You remember or one day this could be you." He stood up and pointed at the boy. "Go ahead now, you dance and sing."

The boy looked at Nathaniel Francis and then at the burning man hanging in the tree.

"You go ahead there, boy, and make us laugh." He breathed deeply; he could smell the boy's fear. The boy was shaking.

"Boy, I told you twice already. Don't let me tell you again." The boy's trembling made Nathaniel burn on the inside like Waller's corn whiskey. It was a sweet burn like apple brandy.

The boy, his skin almost blue in the darkness, began to sing.

O ole Zip Coon he is a larned skoler,
Sings possum up a gum tree an coony in a holler,
Den over dubble trubble, Zip Coon will jump.

Nathaniel Francis laughed at the boy and felt his troubles lifting. His shoulders rose and his back straightened. The trouble with Wicked Charlotte and the trouble with Lavinia had begun to stoop him like an old man.

What they did was not just for revenge or entertainment. They did what they did to protect white people everywhere, to protect white women, to put the niggers back in their place—to return things to normal. Nathaniel Francis did it so that Lavinia could return home. He did it for life. Nathaniel Francis was twenty-four again! Alive at his birthday party!

The little fellow's arms and legs flapped like a chicken. There was something natural about the slaves, the way they sang and danced, about the way they could shine a man's cares away.

Nathaniel Francis clapped his hands in time as the boy danced. Some of the white men began to sing and dance along, like dancing scarecrows against the background of fire. Listening to the boy and the foolishness helped Nathaniel Francis believe that this would all be over. Lavinia would be home soon. He threw back his head and laughed.

I tell you what will happin den, now bery soon,
De Nited States Bank will be blone to de moon;
Dare General Jackson, will him lampoon,
An de bery nex President, will be Zip Coon.

Nathaniel Francis took a drink from the jug and allowed himself to dance with the others. He looped arms with Levi Waller and they swung each other around.

Soon it would all be over and his sweet Lavinia would be back with him. It would be over, all the foolishness, and the darkies would be back in the fields.

And wen Zip Coon our President shall be,
He make all de little Coons sing possum up a tree;
O how de little Coons, will dance an sing,
Wen he tie dare tails togedder, cross de lim dey swing.

Nathaniel Francis laughed with the other men at the boy as they passed the jug. Soon all their troubles would be over.

Now mind wat you arter, you tarnel kritter Crocket,
You shant go head widout ole Zip, he is de boy to block it;
Zip shall be President, Crocket shall be vice,
An den dey two togedder, will hab de tings nice.

When the fire had burned out, Nathaniel Francis made his way home—back to his mother and back to Easter. It was quiet. All of his slaves, except for Easter, except for Charlotte, were in jail.

He had seen them all there . . . except Will. He was probably lying dead somewhere. Maybe his was one of the heads atop one of the posts on the road with no name. Every day he hoped to see Nat Turner's head—but Turner was too much of a coward to be involved in all this. Hid away. Still, he could hope; Nat Turner might as well die.

It was quiet at his house now. But at night when he slept now, Nathaniel kept a lamp burning.

chapter 86

Nathaniel's crops had gone to seed and there was nothing to tend. By day, he traveled with the other men to Jerusalem. It was a game now, and sometimes they taunted the guards—the troops left behind by General Eppes to watch over the jailed niggers. He and the other Cross Keys men fought with the guards to grab the niggers from the courthouse cells. Despite their weapons and uniforms, Nathaniel Francis saw in their eyes the fear he needed. Beyond them, he saw the fear in the eyes of the darkies in the cells. Somebody would talk. Someone would tell them what happened.

The people from town joined with them to patrol. There was even an occasional out-of-towner. But Nathaniel and the other men kept their eyes open for impostors. One man Nathaniel was now sure had been an abolitionist pretended to be with them. He carried guns and rode with the patriots. But then, while refreshing himself at Mahone's, the impostor lost his tongue to liquor. "One day, most certainly, the blacks will be free."

Nathaniel Francis had grabbed the man and the others joined him. They dragged the coward down the street in Jerusalem, bathed him in tar, powdered him with feathers, and sent him on his way.

He spent time at the still with Waller—the lamps burning and his back against the wall. Or else he rode night patrol with some of the other Cross Keys men. Any darkie caught got what he deserved. Any wench out at night got what she was asking for.

It was a game. Nathaniel played Red Rover—only he did not wait for them to try to break through the line, he brought the line to the niggers. Rack them, dunk them, smoke them like Virginia hams.

chapter 87

Left to Nathaniel Francis, there would have been no trials. The darkies needed to be put down. What man would take a rabid animal to court? Besides, the niggers were property. What right did Virginia have to interfere with what he chose to do with his property? He had the right to burn down his barn; he had the right to kill his slaves. Whose business was it but his?

But Nathaniel Francis knew the uptowners, the silver spooners, needed trials to make themselves feel better. They needed trials to reassure themselves that they were civilized.

Before the uprising, the Jerusalemites didn't truck with Cross Keys folk. They looked down their noses at them. Now, though none of them had died in the insurrection, the spooners stood with Cross Keys men yelling outside the jail. Now they were all one family against the niggers. They were all one clan—except for the Quakers, and the ones like Benjamin Phipps who wouldn't go out riding to find darkies. But John Clarke Turner rode with them; in fact, he was one of the most aggressive. Even Thomas Gray stood with the Cross Keys men.

The spooners, the starched shirts, the hooped skirts and parasols, assured him there was no reason to worry. The trials were for the sake of law and order. "We have it all in hand. In a short time you'll get what you want. Darkies will swing from the Jerusalem hanging tree."

The trials weren't really trials at all, but hearings—slaves weren't entitled to trials. The judges, the prosecutors, and the defending attorneys were all slavery men. The judges would be men like Nathaniel who wanted to see justice done: Sam Hines, James

Trezvant, Jeremiah Cobb, Thomas Gray, and others—men who knew him, who would look out for him. They assured him the court would be full of local men. "They have a stake in this, too. Some of them have relatives who died." Nathaniel was still not convinced; none of the darkies deserved to live. He was not sure what the niggers knew, but he knew they were cunning and sneaky.

The spooners seemed eager for the hearings. They needed the pretense of the trials. "Just hearings. You won't have to hear the voices. None of them will speak in court in their own defense. Only their attorneys." It pleased him not to hear their gibberish, white men's words chewed in their mouths.

Then the spooners threw in the kicker.

"The state will pay you a generous price for your property— for every nigger we hang. Leave the hanging to us and the great Commonwealth of Virginia will pay you for the privilege. She will pay you to let her be the hero."

So Nathaniel Francis went along and he told his compatri- ots—Waller, Mary Barrow, Jacob Williams, John Clarke Turner, and the others—about the money and about the other things they could claim. They could file claims for stolen property—guns, whiskey, horses, money.

They turned in slaves, the ones they no longer wanted. They turned in the weak ones, the loudmouthed ones, the feeble and the lame. They only had to tolerate the hearings for them to be hanged; the state paid promptly. The price for the slaves was the conscience money the spooners, the Jerusalem men, were willing to pay. Be- sides, when darkies began to hang, Nathaniel Francis was certain, the other niggers would tell whatever they knew to avoid death.

In the courtroom, no matter how they might be dressed, Na- thaniel knew the townspeople would not be so civilized. For all their proper ways, Nathaniel Francis knew that the silver spooners were just like him—same desires were in them. He needed noth- ing; he was honest. But they needed to prove to the abolitionists, to the governor, and to the nation that they were righteous; all they really wanted was blood.

The hearings would not satisfy them, only hangings. The hangings would take away their guilt over being alive. The hangings would kill their shame that they were, in part, to blame for what had happened at Cross Keys. The hangings would help them feel safe again. The hangings, and the carvings by the town doctor of the dead bodies for souvenir pieces, would help their faces relax again. They would be joyful and content then, like children playing in the field. *Red Rover.* The hangings would return order. Law and order would reign.

chapter 88

Some slave owners were reluctant to testify. Most slaves refused to comply. Even Red Nelson begged off, though around town he told several stories—all of them where he was the hero. He had tried to rescue Salathiel. He had run to Nathaniel's home to rouse him, but found him gone. It was he who had rescued Lavinia, hiding her away in the jump. He was a hero, but he was too shy and modest a man to testify, Red Nelson said.

The prosecuting attorney for the commonwealth, Meriwether Broadnax, told Nathaniel Francis and the others who *would* testify that winning the cases and getting the niggers hung was all strategy. "We have to have people willing to testify, even if they are slaves." Hubbard and Venus, two old grayheads who belonged to the Whiteheads, proved to be loyal slaves.

Broadnax was pleased. "If we can connect Negroes with the attack at the Whiteheads' and use Hubbard and Venus to testify against them, then we'll have them. If only we had more. You would think more of them would be willing to stand up for their masters." A few others straggled forward, sniveling and pleading for their lives. But no matter how they were beaten, threatened, and some even killed to frighten others, most of them stayed close-lipped.

Broadnax said going to court was not about truth, it was about winning the war. Nathaniel Francis admired Broadnax's lack of sentimentality. "We will use whatever ammunition we have available: fear and anger." Broadnax nodded at Nathaniel Francis. "Sympathy." He looked at Waller and Mary Barrow— Waller had lost his whole family and Mary had lost her doctor husband. "Rest assured," Broadnax said. "We will see the niggers hanged."

Nathaniel Francis insisted that he testify. He would not sit by and do nothing.

"But you weren't at home, were you?"

"No." But Nathaniel continued to insist. He owed it to Salathiel and Sallie. He owed it to his friends. He owed it to Levi Waller. In the end Broadnax decided that Nathaniel Francis would be the witness to give the background, to speak generally about what happened. "You will be a compelling witness. For a young man, you have great respect among the businessmen in Jerusalem, like Samuel Hines. People will believe you."

Broadnax turned to Jacob Williams then. "Your testimony could be very helpful, but you weren't at home either."

Jacob folded his arms. "I was away from the house . . . on business."

"Business? In the middle of the night?"

"I was away on business," Jacob repeated, stone-faced.

The prosecutor drummed his fingers. "Then you will testify only about the murder of your family. The defense won't dare to question you about that, they won't want to alienate the judges."

Broadnax then called on Mary Barrow. "Do you think, with all you've been through, that you are up to this?"

Mary Barrow said she was happy to take the stand; it was her patriotic duty. Nathaniel Francis admired her; she was always ready to steal the scene and show off her beauty. She was always ready to be the centerpiece. "I will say what must be said."

The prosecutor questioned her. "So, tell me again, how was it that you escaped and not your husband?"

She fanned herself with an expensive lace handkerchief. "My husband told me to get ready, that a band of Negroes was coming." Nathaniel turned his head away. Mary should have been an actress.

Broadnax interrupted her. "How did your husband know the Negroes were coming?"

Mary's handkerchief paused. "Right now, I don't recall."

Broadnax pursed his lips. "Go on with your story."

"He was awaiting them and had gathered his arms to fend them off while I was dressing. You know I've always been careful about my appearance. My husband knew that. He wanted to give me time to dress."

Nathaniel had to force himself not to laugh.

Mary lifted her lace handkerchief to her forehead as though she were about to swoon. "He was patient and waited for me, poor darling. He was such a dear man." She dabbed her cheeks. "The wretched insurgents got there just as I finished my hair. My dear husband stayed behind while I ran out the back to escape."

"You're certain?"

Mary's face turned to stone. "Of course I am. I am a Southern lady. Are you challenging my word?"

"No, ma'am." Neither would the defending attorneys.

Broadnax said the key to all the hearings would be Levi Waller's testimony. Levi would be the star—the linchpin. Everything rested on Waller's story. "The Negroes—forty or fifty of them—came thundering up to my house, most of them on horseback. We were all there and caught unawares. We all—my wife, my children, the teacher—tried to escape, but I was the only one who got away." Waller's eyes filled with tears.

"You are the only eyewitness we have, the only white eyewitness. Jacob Williams and Nathaniel Francis were away from home. Mrs. Barrow was running for her life and didn't see, couldn't see the insurgents who killed her husband. But the scoundrels can't lie their way out of what Levi Waller saw! We'll find out sooner or later what happened—they'll tell us what locals were involved and where the ringleader is hidden in the swamp."

Broadnax told Waller he would use him over and over again. "With the severity of your loss, no one will dare question you. The town is with us!" Broadnax had looked around the room at them.

"Even the little old ladies are ready for blood! The defense attorneys won't dare challenge you if they want to live."

Most of the cases, then, would connect the insurgents with the Whiteheads, the Barrows, and Waller's farm, Broadnax said. He would rely on Hubbard's and Venus's testimony to connect local insurgents to the murders at the Whiteheads, Mrs. Barrow would testify against those she might have seen as she ran out the back of her home, but Waller would be the key. He was the father and husband who had suffered to actually seen the insurgents attack his home. Broadnax laid his hand on Waller's shoulder. "The safety and life of Southampton County rest with you."

chapter 89

Nathaniel Francis had had to coach his friends on their stories, on what testimony would bring them the most profit. He had to work especially hard with Waller. When the first trial began on August 31, they were ready. He helped dress his friend and combed his hair. "Remember, this is for your family, Levi. This is the day of vengeance."

Waller nodded.

"I promised you we would get 'em, didn't I?"

Waller nodded again.

"And don't forget about the claims."

I SWEAR TO tell the truth, the whole truth . . . The courtroom was full of angry white people—men in suits and women in their best lacy gowns and Cross Keys folks in bare threads, like the Fourth of July. So much noise—ladies and gentlemen screaming threats, shaking their fists, and throwing things at the prisoners. One woman screamed so long and so loud that she fainted and other women had to revive her. The people shouted obscenities.

Lawyer/Congressman James Trezvant, the brave militia colonel, sat as chief justice—if not by official title, then by sheer hubris and gumption. Cobb don't have the nerve to stand up to Trezvant. Jeremiah Cobb, also a lawyer, joined him. The other judges were men of good name, all excellent slavery men—James Massenburg, Meriwether Peete, Ores Browne.

The first trial was the *Commonwealth of Virginia v. Daniel*, a slave who belonged to Richard Porter. Daniel's defense attorney, William Parker, said the slave pleaded not guilty.

Porter, Daniel's owner, was a fool, like Sallie. Porter, a sorry excuse for a white man, took the stand in Daniel's defense, claiming
Daniel's innocence. What self-respecting white man would give
testimony to defend a slave against a white man?

When Levi Waller came forward to testify against Daniel,
some of the women began to weep. They reached out their hands
to comfort him as he went by. They pressed perfumed handkerchiefs into Waller's hand. Nervous, Waller shook and kept looking
up to the ceiling. "I swear to tell the truth, the whole truth . . ." But
he remembered most of the story he and Nathaniel had rehearsed.

"I was at home with my family on Monday when forty or fifty
Negroes on horseback with guns came to my home. My family and
I ran but only I was able to escape." Waller wrung his hands. "But I
didn't run far away. From where I was I could see almost everything that transpired at the house.

"I saw Daniel and two other Negroes—Aaron and Sam—go
into the log cabin where my wife was with our little girl." Waller
began to shake. "My poor sweet wife and my poor little girl, they
tried to hide themselves away." Waller wept. "Daniel came back
outside with a gun in one hand and my sweet wife's golden chain in
the other." Waller sniffled. "I ran for the swamp then and two of the
Negroes ran after me but did not overtake me. After the Negroes
left I went back to the house and found my wife, the little girl, and
other members of my family, including an infant who was mortally
wounded and died the next day." He described the blood and gore.
"Blood everywhere!" Waller was inconsolable and had to be carried
from the courtroom.

Nathaniel Francis saw that despite Porter's testimony claiming
Daniel was not one of the insurgents, Levi had the sympathy of the
crowd and the judges.

When the bailiff called Nathaniel Francis's name, he made his
way to the front and the people cheered as though he were a hero,
like ice cream on the Fourth of July.

He told the story the spooners needed to hear. "A number of

free white people"—he paused for dramatic effect—"say between fifty and sixty were murdered on Sunday night the twenty-first and Monday morning the twenty-second of August, 1831, by a number of Negroes, and it was generally believed that there was an insurrection among the Negroes of the Southampton County."

The people gasped and shook their heads. When he stepped down and walked back through the courtroom, they shook his hand. "Patriot!" they said.

When Sampson Reese took the stand he said that he was in the company of some other gentlemen and in pursuit of the Negroes involved in the insurrection. Reese and his group were the ones who had turned Daniel in. "We came upon them at Parker's Field." The Reeses were good old Cross Keys boys and Sampson, as he spoke, threw a snarling look across the room at the Parker family. The uppity Parker family—weaklings—had been bypassed in the attack. "Daniel was on Dr. Musgrave's horse." Reese said he shot at Daniel. "The prisoner had no arms that I saw."

They found Daniel guilty and valued him—Daniel was old and feeble-minded—for claims purposes against the commonwealth at one hundred dollars. The judges sentenced him to hang September 5 at the usual place of execution.

The *Commonwealth of Virginia v. Tom*. Tom, who had belonged to poor Caty Whitehead, was defended by Thomas French and discharged, not guilty. No one, not even Hubbard or Venus, would give testimony against him. Nathaniel Francis hissed at French, the defense attorney. "Mind whose side you stand on!"

Broadnax, disappointed by the acquittal, asked for time to get his witnesses in order. The other hearings were held over for the next day.

Next day, September 1, the courtroom was packed again as it was each day of trial. The fans, handkerchiefs, and hats only stirred the stifling September air. Collars melted, curls drooped, and the women's fans hummed and blew the curses they yelled around the blistering room.

Baiting was Nathaniel Francis's day work now—that and attending the hearings. He smiled to himself. The truth was whatever they needed it to be.

None of the insurgents pleaded guilty; but a few of them, giving testimony to defend other niggers, confessed some involvement. The crazy niggers said it was their duty as patriots. Nigger patriots! Nigger patriots!

Then two of the darkies—loyal slaves, Caty Whitehead's old Hubbard and Venus—shaking like leaves, came forward to tell what they knew.

The *Commonwealth of Virginia v. Jack and Andrew.* When the slave Jack was put to the bar, it was faithful Hubbard who put him under. Hubbard didn't see the murders. "But when the insurgents came, Jack and Andrew left. The insurgents murdered my poor mistress." Hubbard twisted his hands. "When the insurgents left, Jack and Andrew came back. They looked upset. They got on a horse and rode away. I think they went to join the insurgents." Venus said when Jack and Andrew came by they told her "they were going to ride after the insurgents."

As Venus and Hubbard left the courtroom, Nathaniel Francis stood to pat them on the back. They were faithful slaves. If they had not been too old and of little worth, Nathaniel would have taken them for his own.

Andrew and Jack were convicted. Jack was valued at four hundred fifty dollars, Andrew at four hundred, and both were sentenced to be hanged on September 12.

COMMONWEALTH OF VIRGINIA *v. Curtis and Stephen.* John Clarke Turner had shown himself faithful. When they couldn't find Cross Keys niggers to grab, John Clarke spurred his horse and rode to the other side of the county. He brought back two slaves—Curtis and Stephen, slaves whom John Clarke caught riding together on a mule—the property of Thomas Ridley. John Clarke brought the two slaves back to Cross Keys for convincing.

Nathaniel Francis snickered. The slaves got what they deserved. There were no innocent niggers—no matter how far they lived from Cross Keys.

In court, looking at the prisoners' battered faces, William Parker, attorney for Curtis and Stephen, asked if the men had been tortured. John Clarke sneered at the lawyer's question.

John Clarke Turner reared back in his seat. "No, indeed!" He said the slaves hadn't been beaten, though his party was pretty well mounted, armed, and willing to do what they had to to protect Southampton County. "The niggers didn't come with us willingly." John Clarke Turner laughed and mugged for the crowd. "We did whatever we had to to get to the truth."

Nathaniel Francis had never seen John Clarke so self-assured. The prisoners hadn't been promised anything, John Clarke said. "In the end, they were happy to give confessions." He laughed again and the courtroom crowd laughed with him. John Clarke looked around the courtroom as though he wanted to be certain all eyes were on him.

The Negroes appeared to be drunk, he said. He paused dramatically, looking over the crowd. When he was sure everyone was listening, John Clarke Turner snarled, "The niggers Curtis and Stephen said they were with the insurgents." He nodded. When the courtroom was completely silent, except for the fans, he leaned forward. John Clarke Turner smiled, then leaned back in his seat. "Said old Nat Turner was the ringleader!"

chapter 90

The fans halted.

The courtroom was quiet. It inhaled, a vacuum. The men and women stared at John Clarke Turner, whose face was painted with a smug smile.

Nat Turner? Nat Turner the ringleader?

The spooners all knew him as the pious one. He fancied himself a preacher and he was a dreamer. He was the slave who could quote Scripture.

But leading an insurrection? No one would have pictured the small Negro as a firebrand. How could he even be involved? No one had thought of him; no one had mentioned his name in connection with the insurrection!

But as soon as he heard it, Nathaniel Francis knew that John Clarke was right. Nat Turner had been missing since the night of the murders; Nathaniel had assumed the slave had been killed in the chaos. But this was the truth. Nathaniel Francis felt it in his gut. He had told them all along that Nat Turner was trouble!

He looked around the courtroom. The silver spooners all looked as though the wind had been knocked out of them. They had all—like Ethelred Brantley—been hoodwinked by Nat Turner. If there was a Negro they trusted, it was Nat Turner. They knew Nat Turner as the one who didn't drink, steal, or curse. He was a novelty to them, a circus act, the Cross Keys slave who could write and read when most of the white men there could not.

Frozen in place—fans in the air, handkerchiefs pressed to mouths, pens poised. Then Nathaniel saw it all begin to crack.

They had been fooled! The nigger was a thief, an insurrectionist, an outlaw!

Nathaniel Francis had always known. He had never been fooled by Nat Turner's sanctimonious ways. He had known Nat Turner as a boy, always thinking he was better—thinking himself free and a man of property. Uppity, he didn't know his place.

Reading and writing were dangerous to a slave's mind.

John Clarke Turner's father had ruined Nat Turner. Old Benjamin was to blame. John Clarke Turner had been stumbling around with the image of Nat Turner chained to him, dragging him down, long enough. John Clarke knew niggers were meant for the fields. He knew it was a danger to let a nigger pray to God and to think that God cared for him.

Nathaniel Francis knew better. He knew Nat Turner.

Suddenly, the courtroom was alive, roaring. John Clarke Turner's testimony had lit a blaze. John Clarke had set the record straight, had put the finger on Nat Turner.

People nodded, buzzing to one another. All along, they knew it! They had tried to tell others not to trust him. Worse than being a murderer, he had betrayed them and made fools of them.

Nat Turner.

Congressman Trezvant, the chief justice, his face flush, rose quickly and excused himself from the courtroom.

If Nat Turner had been in the courtroom, they would have crucified him. But he was not, so Curtis and Stephen took his place. Curtis and Stephen were sentenced to hang on September 12. Curtis was valued at four hundred dollars and Stephen at four hundred fifty.

chapter 91

While Trezvant was absent, the lawyers and some of the judges pulled a fast one—the Parker family slaves were quickly brought to the bar and all of them were acquitted.

But John Clarke Turner was the prince, the hero of the day. The men hoisted John Clarke on their shoulders and carried him to Mahone's for a toast. Nathaniel Francis stood back smiling. Now was John Clarke Turner's moment. He was the hero. He was the smart one, not Nat Turner. It was John Clarke now who was the talk of all Jerusalem. Likely, John Clarke was going to take care of Nathaniel's Nat Turner problem after all.

The next day, newspapers across the country ran the news—Nat Turner was the culprit, Nat Turner was the Pied Piper who had led all the other nigger insurgents astray.

The Great Dismal Swamp runaways were forgotten. Thanks to John Clarke Turner—and an anonymous telegram from an individual who said he had to rush back to court, most likely Trezvant—the nation had the villain they desired, the murderer of innocent whites! The nation had a black preacher on whom to focus their outrage! Now Virginia had her culprit.

Southampton County had a homegrown wolf in sheep's clothing. Jerusalem had a scoundrel to hate, one nursed at its bosom that it could tell stories about. But the rogue belonged to Cross Keys—John Clarke Turner, Salathiel Francis, Richard Whitehead, and Levi Waller had grown up with him. Nathaniel Francis had always known Nat Turner was no good. He had tried to tell them all along.

chapter 92

Commonwealth of Virginia v. Sam. As the fourth day of the hearings began, tales of Nat Turner spinning in the air, Levi Waller was back on the stand to testify against Nathaniel's slave Sam. Nathaniel could rely on Levi to say what needed to be said and he could rely on Thomas to say nothing. Thomas Gray showed himself faithful to the Cross Keys cause. Sam pleaded innocent, as Sam insisted, but Thomas Gray offered no other defense on behalf of the slave.

As Waller, now an available widower, walked down the aisle, women pressed more handkerchiefs into his hand. Waller was still nervous. "I am positive I saw Sam at my home. He was one of the insurgents. I know it was him because I've known him for several years. From where I was hiding, I saw him go into the house where my family was murdered."

Sam was sentenced to hang September 9 and the commonwealth promised to pay Nathaniel Francis four hundred dollars for him. He would be able to buy more seed and pretty curtains for Lavinia's windows—and more slave babies.

COMMONWEALTH OF VIRGINIA v. Hark. Sallie's Hark was tried next. Like all the other insurgents, Hark insisted that he was innocent. Nathaniel shook his head. It was a waste of money, a waste of a good bull; all because of Nat Turner.

Waller said he saw Hark in the yard with a gun in his hands. "I heard some of the other insurgents call him Captain Moore." Thomas Ridley said that when Hark was arrested at Blunt's he had powder and shot and some silver in his pockets. Mary Barrow, weeping, said Hark was with the insurgents that came to her home. "I saw him out in front. I was standing there, near him, out front. And I saw it. It was Hark. He had a gun in his hand. He fired it in the air and then threw the gun to the ground. Maybe that's why others didn't see Hark with the gun in his hand." Mary was an actress; tears wet her collar.

Hark was sentenced to hang September 9; Nathaniel Francis received four hundred fifty dollars for him—wood to build an add-on to his home. Maybe Nathaniel would build a private room for himself and Lavinia or a nursery for the baby.

COMMONWEALTH OF VIRGINIA v. Nelson. Jacob Williams took the stand against his slave Yellow Nelson. Benjamin Drewry, a relative of Edward Drewry, had joined the group of judges to hear the case of his relative's death.

Jacob settled onto the witness stand. When the questioning began he said he had been out all night on business. "I had not heard of the insurrection, but when I came home, just before noon, I was suspicious from his looks that Nelson might want to attack me."

None of the locals questioned where Jacob was; they knew he had been at Waller's still. As he sat in the courtroom, the darkness closed in around Nathaniel. He remembered that night—crawling on the damp ground, trying to reach the woods, trying to reach safety. Nathaniel heard himself moaning. Farther away, he heard Jacob Williams and Levi Waller yelping, frightened. He heard the women sobbing, his mother and Mary Barrow, as they all crawled through the blackness trying to save their lives, trying to get away from the still.

Jacob's voice brought Nathaniel Francis back into the courtroom. Jacob described how he had left his family at home, after Nelson had given him threatening looks, and went to the woods to measure some timber. "I returned in the evening to find my family dead."

Jacob Williams's overseer, Caswell Worrell, testified that he recollected that the Thursday preceding the uprising, Nelson had warned him to look out and take care of himself—that something would happen before long. He was a preacher, Yellow Nelson said, and he could see it coming. "Monday of the uprising I came by Jacob Williams's and Yellow Nelson was still home. The rest of the Negroes were already at work at the new ground. Nelson came out to the fields dressed in his best clothes and said he was too sick to work. He asked me to go back to the house with him." Caswell said he did go back to the house with Nelson, but left soon. He left before the insurgents came. "I think he meant to trap me so I might be killed."

Cynthia, one of Jacob Williams's slaves, said Nelson was home when the insurgents came. "He went to his house and dressed himself very clean. He stepped over the dead bodies without any grief and took some meat out of my mistress's pot." Cynthia lifted her hands to illustrate Nelson's movements. "Then Nelson looked at me. 'Cynthia, you do not know me. I do not know when you will see me again.' Then he left with the others." She did not explain why she didn't, after the murders, alert the militia.

Nathaniel Francis smiled. Cynthia was smart enough to repeat what Jacob had directed her to say. She was smarter than Wicked Charlotte; Cynthia didn't want to die.

Stephen, a slave who belonged to Edward Drewry, said he and his master went to Jacob Williams's to see about some corn. "Mr. Drewry looked up and said, 'Lord, who is that coming?' Immediately the Negroes rose up and killed Mr. Drewry, Mr. Williams's wife and children, and told Nelson to go with them." Stephen shook his head. "He was forced to go with them. Nelson went with them to Mrs. Vaughan's but didn't participate in the murders. Nelson did drink brandy with the insurgents and asked for more."

"Did you go with the insurgents?" James French, the defense attorney asked Stephen.

"Oh, no, sir!"

"If they made Nelson go, why didn't they force you?"

Stephen dropped his head. "I don't know, sir."

"If you didn't go with them, how do you know Nelson was at the Vaughans'?"

Stephen looked at Jacob Williams and then shook his head. "I don't know, sir."

"If you weren't with the insurgents, how do you know Nelson was drinking?"

Stephen fingered a lump on his forehead. He looked at Jacob Williams again. "All I can tell you, Mr. French, is what I know."

When it was over, Benjamin and the other judges found Nelson guilty and paid four hundred dollars for the pleasure of hanging him.

COMMONWEALTH OF VIRGINIA v. Davy. Waller, who had given witness at least four times now, had gained confidence. He testified at the trial of his own slave, Davy. "Davy wasn't home on the twenty-second of August when the band of Negroes came to my house and killed all my family. But he came up while the Negroes were there." Waller looked around the courtroom. "He dressed himself clean. They all dressed up clean." Waller stood up, illustrating with his hands. "Oh, and they were drinking and Davy drank with them." Waller sat back in his seat.

Nathaniel Francis nodded at his friend. Waller didn't need any more coaching.

"Davy rode off on my horse in good spirits and I heard one of the insurgents call him Brother Clements, as though he was a preacher or something." Waller turned to the judges. "He left in great glee." Waller had memorized all his lines.

Jacob, a slave, said he saw Davy at William Williams's.

Jarrell Judkins said Davy gave him his confession. Davy shook his bowed head.

William Boyle, Davy's counsel, did not object to the confession, despite the fact that Davy pleaded innocent.

"Davy went with the Negroes to the homes of Jacob Williams and William Williams and murdered their families. He was also at Mrs. Vaughan's and got drunk there," Jacob said.

William Boyle quoted the slave, "Davy said Captain Nat, passing a house where some poor white people lived, said he would not kill them because they thought no better of themselves than they did of the Negroes."

Nathaniel Francis looked around the courtroom at the angry scarlet faces. Any who had felt comfort in being passed over now felt insulted that Nat Turner and his rogues had overlooked them. What might have been given as a compliment by the slave was received as offense.

Davy was sentenced to hang and Levi Waller was promised three hundred dollars. Not a fortune, but he would be able to purchase lots of seed and maybe more land for planting corn.

Nathaniel Francis nodded at Waller. Well done.

COMMONWEALTH OF VIRGINIA v. Moses. When Moses, his sister Sallie's boy slave, was brought into the courtroom dragging chains behind him down the aisle, Nathaniel Francis almost could not breathe. In all the confusion, he had forgotten about the sniveling boy! Nathaniel stood to his feet and demanded the boy, demanded his property. He grabbed the boy around his neck and dragged him from the room.

chapter 93

Outside in the heat, Nathaniel Francis slammed Moses's body against the wall of the building. "Shut up! You shut up! Stop blubbering!" He punched the boy several times, the punches never feeling hard enough. Moses doubled over and fell to the ground; Nathaniel Francis kicked him. He dragged the boy back to his feet. A few well-placed blows and twistings convinced Moses to cooperate, to become a witness for the state. "Say the right things and you may not hang." Moses was there when Nathaniel's sister, Sallie, was killed. He would say what Nathaniel Francis told him to say.

"Here he is." Nathaniel Francis dragged little Moses back to the sheriff. "Take him. Use him as you like. He wants to please his masters." Nathaniel Francis laughed and whispered to Broadnax as he passed by, "Another witness for you."

Commonwealth of Virginia v. Jack, Nathan, Tom, and Davy. Boy Moses's trial was adjourned until September 8. But that day he returned to court as a prosecution witness. The commonwealth used little Moses to testify against the slave Jack. They used him again to testify against Nathaniel Francis's boy slaves, Nathan, Tom, and Davy (Two Feet). All were sentenced to be hanged.

ON SEPTEMBER 5, Nathaniel Francis was there with the others to watch the first slaves hang.

chapter 94

It was a celebration. Men drank and passed the jug along. The hanging tree was about a quarter mile from Mahone's and drunken men spilled out of the tavern. All the grown-ups and the children grinned and cheered. The mothers brought sweet treats for their little ones. They all pointed at the dangling slaves and laughed; once he was captured, there would be worse for Nat Turner.

Daniel and Mary Barrow's Moses were hanged the first day of hanging, September 5, 1831.

Nathaniel Francis joked to himself. The hangman was a "fisher of men." It was a pleasure to watch the niggers flopping. Fish on a pole—their sides heaving, fighting for air, while their legs, ankles tied together, flipped like a fish's tail. It was a beautiful sight to see, and every fish that had been his or Sallie's brought him more money from the commonwealth.

When the hangings were over, still excited, all the people went back to court.

COMMONWEALTH OF VIRGINIA v. Dred. Waller took the stand again, this time against Nathaniel Francis's slave Dred. More relaxed, Waller was almost a celebrity now—almost as famous as Andrew Jackson or Thomas Jefferson. "I saw the prisoner," Waller said. "He was one of the insurgents that came to my home on Monday, August twenty-second, and killed my family! There was so much blood." Levi was getting his vengeance—over and over again.

French, Dred's attorney, questioned Waller. He pointed at Dred. "Considering you have testified that you were hiding, among all the other slaves you claim to have seen, are you certain that it was Dred you saw?"

Nathaniel Francis dreamed of crushing French. French had no business questioning a white man's story. Levi deserved his revenge.

But Waller was self-assured. "Oh, Dred was right beside me and I knew him well. He belonged to my good friend Nathaniel Francis."

"Right beside you? Why didn't Dred reach out and kill you then? If you saw him, certainly Dred saw you. Why didn't you kill him?"

Waller paused, looked around like a drowning pup. But just as suddenly, Levi sat up. He straightened his shoulders. "All I know is Dred was there. He was mounted on a horse and armed with a gun or a rifle! I saw it clear as day and I remember!"

"Clear as day? So, which was it?"

"Which was what?"

"You saw it clear as day, Mr. Waller. Was Dred standing next to you or seated on a horse? Did the defendant have a gun or a rifle?"

Nathaniel Francis ground his teeth. French was overstepping his bounds. Others in the courtroom booed the lawyer. Waller seemed encouraged by the protest. He sat back in his seat. He mocked French and mugged for the judges and court. His lips pursed with smugness, Levi said, "I don't know, Mr. French. It might have been a gun. It might have been a rifle."

"If you are confused about the weapon, how can you be certain of the man?"

Waller was indignant. Nathaniel Francis looked around to see others, including the judges, wearing masks of displeasure. How dare French defend the nigger. It didn't matter which one of them did it; all were guilty. None of them could be trusted: Nat Turner proved that.

"I don't know what kind of weapon, but I am not mistaken about the nigger. He rode up on one side of the fence looking for me. If I'd have had a gun I would have blasted him. He would have killed me if he'd seen me! But I was on one side of the fence and he was on t'other."

French turned away from Waller, ready to dismiss him. But Waller had more to say. "After that, I crept within sixty yards of the house and I saw him"—Waller pointed at Dred—"drinking with the others!"

Dred was sentenced to hang on September 12 and Nathaniel Francis was paid four hundred dollars. Another fireplace. More land and, perhaps, more slaves—the market was depressed and he could get a good price.

COMMONWEALTH OF VIRGINIA v. Jack. The commonwealth used Sallie's boy Moses again, against William Reese's Jack. They used Moses where they needed him.

There were so many slaves sentenced to hang on the next usual hanging day, Monday, September 12, that the judges added a special day for the overflow. The judges joked that they did not want to overwork the hangman and kill him as he went about his duty.

Most of the hearings were over by September 12. Twenty-nine slaves had been brought to the bar by then, most of them guilty. Nathaniel Francis smiled. All of them should be hanged. Clean the slate. None could be trusted, like Nat Turner.

chapter 95

After the twelfth, there was a spurt of copycat hearings—twelve between September 19 and 22. When others learned of Nathaniel Francis and his friends' good fortune, they brought their unwanted slaves to court: quick, easy money. Why bother providing upkeep for an old uncle or aunt when the commonwealth would hang and pay? Why keep a slave not worth his salt? Why be bothered? Farmers had fallen on hard times—sacrifices had to be made. In most of the copycat cases, though, slaves were discharged.

But not Mary Barrow's.

Commonwealth of Virginia v. Lucy. Nathaniel Francis smiled as he watched Mary in court on September 19. She brought in a pretty young slave girl of hers, about twenty, named Lucy. Lucy's husband had been hanged on September 5 as an insurrectionist and Mary Barrow no longer trusted her. So, almost a month later, Mary brought Lucy to court—Lucy had tried to kill her, Mary said.

Mary fanned herself with a new lace fan. "On Monday, August twenty-second, when I was running away . . . my poor husband didn't survive." She paused to weep. "He waited while I was getting dressed. You all know how careful I am about my appearance." Mary waved her fan and nodded to the judges. "Mr. Barrow was such a gallant man and provided so well for me and all our slaves. He gave his life so I could escape." She lifted an expensive lace handkerchief to her eyes, then rested it on her heart. "My husband was a hero!"

Nathaniel Francis smiled to himself. There was no one like Mary.

"When I was running away, out back, as my husband directed, why, Lucy grabbed my arm and held me. I think she was trying to delay me so that I would be killed."

Nathaniel snickered behind his hand. Previously, Mary had said nothing of Lucy holding her. Instead, Mary had insisted that she was steps away from an insurrectionist who fired a shot in the air and then threw his gun to the ground. Nathaniel looked at the judges, entranced by her beauty and tears. They did not question her earlier testimony, did not ask her why the slave did not shoot her instead of firing into the air. They did not question her then and they would not question her now.

Mary played to the audience, demonstrating for the crowd. "She held me hoping to kill me." She turned to the judges. "But I could not say for certain." Mary lifted her handkerchief to her eyes again.

Mary had one of her slaves, Bird, testify against Lucy. "Several weeks or so after the August twenty-second insurrection, Mistress Barrow had me go through Lucy's room. I found a bag of feathers, and just like Mrs. Barrow suspected, there were several silver coins in it."

That was the case then. Nathaniel chuckled to himself. How convenient that the bag of feathers and coins should appear in Lucy's room a month later. Nathaniel looked at the slave girl. Too pretty to live. Mary could never abide anyone prettier than her. Lucy hung from the rope on September 26 and put two hundred seventy-five dollars in pretty Mary Barrow's pocket. Hats, scarves, umbrellas.

Commonwealth of Virginia v. Joe. John Clarke Turner's slave Joe was also convicted that day based on faithful old Hubbard's testimony. Joe was sentenced to hang on September 26, and the commonwealth paid John Clarke four hundred fifty dollars, something to pacify him until he saw Nat Turner hanged.

chapter 96

Life in Southampton County was quieting again. The hearings had dwindled to those of just a few freemen the spooners thought it would be best to be rid of; freemen would only cause trouble in Southampton County, poison the minds of weak-minded slaves. Thomas Hathcock, Berry Newsom (whiteness was wasted on him), and Exum Artis were set for hearings.

The court was smart with Exum. The judges made a deal with William Dick, who owed the commonwealth three hundred dollars. If William would bring two of his slaves, Burwell and Ben, to court to testify against Exum, Virginia would forgive William Dick's debt. Following their hearings, the freemen were held over for trials in the regular Superior Court.

There was also an attempt, while things were quiet, to get rid of the Ridley, Porter, and Bell slaves. They were all acquitted. It was still hard, even with Cross Keys questioning—fire, whips, and knives—to find witnesses. Most slaves refused to cooperate; they weren't loyal like Hubbard and Venus. Some died rather than give testimony like little Moses. If they wouldn't testify, they deserved to be hanged or mounted on a pole. Clean the slate, Nathaniel thought. Start all over again with slaves untainted by Nat Turner.

But there were a few exceptions. Like the most unusual slave girl, Beck.

Commonwealth of Virginia v. Jim, Isaac, and Frank. Beck's mistress came home to Southampton County in late September from Sussex, where she had hidden out for fear of the insurgents. Her mistress said Beck had a pretty story.

While in Sussex, after receiving news of the hearings and the hangings, and of how the Parker slaves had gotten off, Beck said she had known about the insurrection all along. She had overhead slave discussions at Solomon Parker's slave quarters.

Nathaniel Francis smiled. The Parker family members had attempted to protect all their slaves from the noose. Beck wasn't pointing the finger at one of attorney William Parker's slaves, but Solomon was a relative—close enough that it stung.

Beck was outside one of the slave houses and overhead the slaves talking, she said. "I didn't come forward because they told me it was a secret and that they would kill me if I told. I didn't understand it all."

Beck pointed her fingers at three slaves in Southampton—Jim and Isaac, who belonged to Samuel Champion, and Frank, a blacksmith, who belonged to Solomon Parker, and accused them of being involved in the August 15 insurrection. "They said if the black people came they would join and help kill the white people."

Jim and Isaac were sentenced to hang on September 30. Jim was valued at three hundred and Isaac at four hundred dollars. Frank was also convicted, but James French, the attorney, was able to get the Parker slave's sentence commuted so that he was sold farther south. A very skilled blacksmith, he was valued at six hundred dollars.

Nathaniel Francis saw the girl in town after the September 22 hearings wearing pretty dresses. The white people on the street stopped her and called her by name. They filled her arms with sweet tea cakes and patted her on the head.

They pointed Beck out as an example to the other slaves. "You should be more like her." Nathaniel Francis heard that her master took Beck to several other counties to testify against slaves. Of course, the insurgents tried to wiggle out of it, saying they didn't know her. Beck answered that she was a house slave and didn't know the field niggers by name.

Some of the courts, in counties where she had never been before, called her a liar and would not hear her testimony. But in

Southampton, based on Beck's good and loyal testimony, two slaves hanged and one was sold into the Deep South away from his family.

Beck's witness and the new round of hearings stirred the people and they became rowdy again. The judges called for twenty-five more able guards to protect the prisoners and the court.

chapter 97

Parker and French. Turncoats! Traitors! The few slaves who escaped hanging from August through November were aided by the attorneys William Parker and John French. Nathaniel Francis imagined ways to torture them. For their service, they deserved to join those dangling from the tree.

French and Parker had worked to get all the Parker family slaves discharged, saying this uprising had nothing to do with them, it was a Cross Keys matter. White-shirted and stiff-collared, they used fancy words to keep eleven niggers from the hangman's rope, the fishing hook for insurgents—six by French and five by Parker. They used the same finagling to get many of the Edwards family slaves dismissed.

Nathaniel Francis sat close enough in the courtroom to overhear snatches of the attorneys' arguments at the bench: . . . *the Negroes were offended at the church . . . torture . . . false confessions . . . dubious witnesses . . . isn't even Negro life precious . . . will we not one day be judged ourselves by what we do here?* And though Nathaniel Francis and the crowd booed the two lawyers, shoved them, and threatened them, the two attorneys would not be dissuaded.

Nathaniel Francis would have thrashed the two turncoat lawyers on the spot, but he did not want the Jerusalemites to turn against him. Not before he got what he wanted—not before more of the niggers died. Not before they got Nat Turner.

Only Thomas Gray was a sure thing, money in the pocket. He offered no defense for any of the slaves he represented. He sat silent, joking with the Cross Keys men as the cases against the insurgents he represented went forth. Gray made certain the fish were hooked and fried. He was an even more welcome guest now at Waller's still.

chapter 98

September passed and, in the Virginia way, it was still warm. Benjamin Blunt bragged about town that none of his slaves revolted. "I keep mine with an iron hand—not like the Cross Keys drunkards. My darkies stand with me or die." According to him, they all stood by him, even if it was at gunpoint. Nathaniel Francis laughed at the good doctor when three of his slaves were brought to court. The judges could find no cause against one, but the other two were convicted. Either Blunt was padding his ego with stories or padding his pockets with the seven hundred seventy-five dollars he received.

Most everything was quiet now that the September hearings were finished. Still, for Nathaniel Francis, night was the most difficult time. He was afraid of the dark again. Night terrors, hobgoblins, fear crept back on him. He jumped at every sound and kept a lamp full of oil and a rifle in his hand. When Easter wasn't cooking, he posted her as lookout.

She never saw anything. But there were many nights when he thought he saw Nat Turner and fired into the darkness.

chapter 99

October came and coolness lifted its head. Nathaniel Francis sat up early in the morning, before sunrise, as he always had. There were no crops to tend and no slaves to call to the field. And there was still no Lavinia. Nathaniel Francis rubbed his hand over the empty spot next to him in bed. Her father refused to allow her to come home; he would not send his daughter and grandchild to Southampton to be murdered.

His life was ruined, but the people of Southampton, the spooners of Jerusalem, had turned back to business as usual. Back to their fields, back to church, and back to Sunday at Mahone's Tavern.

For the people of Jerusalem, it was all over. What about his life and the lives of the other Cross Keys folk? The sheriff pestered Nathaniel to come and collect Sallie's boy Moses, who was still in jail. "Mr. Broadnax says we have no need for him now."

The people of Cross Keys had been forgotten, but they were still gathering at Waller's still and mourning—Mary Barrow, Levi Waller, Jacob Williams, and the others. They were mourning while people like Peter Edwards, who had gotten away free, no family members lost and no property lost, smiled like Christmas. Edwards's life was whole.

Peter Edwards's life went on and Nathaniel Francis hated him. Edwards acted as though he did not know the Cross Keys men, as though he had decided he was not like them—he was a starched shirt, a family man, a Jerusalem man. He walked among his crops laughing with his overseer, laughing with his slaves. Sanctimonious, he cuddled wife and children.

Nathaniel Francis needed to remind Peter Edwards and those like him. Nathaniel had lost his sister and his brother. He had lost his wife and child, his property. Waller had lost his whole family. John Clarke Turner had lost his sister-in-law . . . while the main culprit, the ringleader, Nat Turner, was still at large. People said he was gone now. There had been reports that he had gone to the Dismal Swamp. Others said he was in Baltimore. No one cared.

But for Nathaniel Francis, none of it was finished. None of it would be over until Lavinia was home and Nat Turner was in his grave. He needed to remind Jerusalem.

He needed to bring Edwards down a peg.

IN MID-OCTOBER, NATHANIEL took Waller and the boys out hunting—they caught Peter Edwards's beloved slave Sam.

In all, Levi Waller testified at seven hearings, and Nathaniel Francis was at each one of them. He testified on October 17—almost two months after the first hearing—at the hearing of Peter Edwards's slave Sam.

Commonwealth of Virginia v. Sam. Nathaniel testified first that they had caught Sam under his mother's house. Nathaniel had gone there with the others to examine the slave. Sam was part of the insurrection and on the Tuesday after the insurrection had gone to his mother's house.

Mr. French, the defense attorney, could not keep the frustration off his face. "You live in Cross Keys, Mr. Francis. How far away is that from Peter Edwards's farm?"

Nathaniel Francis didn't see the point. "Eight or nine miles."

"A long way by foot." French looked at the judges and then back at Nathaniel. "It's been over a month. Why were you looking for insurgents there?"

"No rest for the weary." Nathaniel Francis laughed. The people in the courtroom, obviously eager for comic relief, laughed with him.

"Did you question the prisoner's mother?"

"Don't remember. But we found him hiding underneath her house."

"Could he have hidden himself there since you and your friends were after him?"

"He was under the house, and that nigger was part of the insurrection."

Peter Edwards, acting like a spooner instead of a good slave-owning white man, gave testimony on Sam's behalf. A slave of good character, Sam returned home Monday morning on time, according to his overseer, and took no part in any insurrection.

Nathaniel Francis was disgusted. Edwards thought he was better than the rest, but if he thought he was going to get away without paying a price, he was mistaken.

Levi Waller came through. "I was hidden in the bushes part of the time the insurgents were at my house. I saw two of the insurgents murdering my family. Sam wasn't one of them. He was some distance away wiping his eyes."

French was short with him. "So, this time you actually saw *inside*, witnessed two people murdering your family? You were close enough to see into the house?"

"Yes. And that's when I heard Nat Turner tell Sam to get on his horse."

"Nat Turner? Nat Turner? Heretofore you have not mentioned him."

"That's right, I said Nat Turner. He was there! He killed my family! I heard him and saw him with my own two eyes! Sam didn't look as though he was disposed to go, but he did go with them."

"Do you know whether Sam was forced to go?"

"No. But I saw Sam talking to Nat Turner, and I saw Sam go with the insurgents."

Sam was scheduled to hang November 4 and Peter Edwards was paid four hundred twenty-five dollars for Sam's life.

* * *

TWO OTHER SLAVES, Jack and Shadrach, not part of the insurrection but in agreement with it, were charged with treason. Because they were property and not citizens, their cases were dismissed. Archer, Arthur Reese's slave, because of French escaped the fate he deserved.

But Nathaniel Francis and others managed to get the freeman Isham Turner sent forward to Superior Court, where he was ultimately sentenced to hang.

In court, the sheriff hounded Nathaniel Francis again about taking the boy Moses. "He did what you required and testified at the hearings." But Nathaniel Francis did not want the tainted boy. Let him hang.

Commonwealth of Virginia v. Moses. They brought Moses to the hearing bar with Thomas Gray as his attorney. Nathaniel knew that he could count on Thomas Gray not to offer any defense for the boy. Gray assured the court that nothing had been promised the boy, he had not been threatened, and he gave his testimony freely. The judges found Moses guilty, but the judges unanimously agreed the boy's sentence should be commuted. So Nathaniel Francis received three hundred dollars for the boy, and Moses, the commonwealth's witness, was turned over to a state-sanctioned slave dealer and auctioned into the Deep South.

There should have been more hearings and more convictions, Nathaniel Francis thought. But most of the slaves were not like Hubbard and Venus and Beck. They were not like Isham, Stephen, or Jack, who confessed—the defense lawyers calling it torture—though they pleaded innocent in court. But the hangings they did get were satisfying. Each one was hanged for Sallie and Salathiel. Each one gave Levi Waller the vengeance he deserved. Each one who was hanged brought Lavinia a little closer to home.

chapter 100

Edwards and the other spooners had been taken down a peg, but the matter of Nat Turner remained. Nathaniel Francis and the other men continued to ride to keep the peace, patrolling the roads at night. Before it was all over, before Lavinia could return home, they had to put an end to Nat Turner.

Congressman Trezvant and Nathaniel Francis led a group, Thomas Gray included, determined to question Nat Turner's wife, Cherry. She knew something; she would talk. They would make her. It was in her interest and that of her child to tell.

Gray had cheered at the appropriate times and Trezvant had used his fists to persuade her. When it did not work, they took the whip to her. "If you want to live, tell us where he is!"

Cherry was like her husband, a raving lunatic. "All of you, try to act like you own him, even if he's dead you think you own him; but you know you don't. You want to kill him because there's too much truth in him! Too much truth!" She spat blood from her mouth when they hit her.

"Tell us where that nigger is!" They struck her again, and she fell down but then got back to her feet.

"You gonna kill him! I know it! But you can't kill what we have! He's mine, not yours! He's mine! You can't take that from me."

"You want to die for him? What did he do for you?"

She coughed and sputtered after they choked her.

"You can't stop it. That nigger is going to die," they promised her. "Sooner or later, he is going to die!"

Her words were strangled. "If you're going to kill him, you better kill him quick! You slice him open and truth is going to jump out and grab you." Cherry was a crying, ranting madwoman. "Nathan is a man of truth! That's why you hate him!"

"Tell us where that yellow monster is!" They ripped the clothes from her.

Cherry was naked and bleeding, but still talking. "Nathan is a freeman in this world. Too smart to bow down to you. You been knocking him all along. Nathan tried to tell you God's judgment is coming. Every time he tried, you knocked him."

She was panting now. "Someday you might get his body, but he still free . . . still mine! If you kill him he'll just keep shouting truth from the grave." They kicked her then, to shut her up.

John Clarke Turner pounded her head against the ground, but she still grunted, saying, "A man of God, and you know it, John Clarke. He loves you!" John Clarke pounded harder. Cherry gasped, "Stole what was his. Looking for a monster? It's you!"

Giles Reese inserted himself then. He pulled a gun and held it to Thomas Gray's head and ordered them off his property. They came away with nothing more than some of Nat Turner's papers and his Bible. Nathaniel Francis shook his head looking at the book. The crazy loon had written in the book, some fanciful script that looked like hieroglyphics.

They would get Nat Turner sooner or later, and he would hang.

chapter 101

Nat Turner!

Nathaniel Francis bolted to his feet when he heard that they had caught him. Of all people, it was Benjamin Phipps who brought Nat Turner in, claiming the eleven-hundred-dollar reward. Nat had been in Cross Keys all the while, hidden near Giles Reese's farm. They said Benjamin Phipps had taken Nat to Peter Edwards's farm. Two of the judges had questioned him there.

A crowd surrounded Edwards's house. Their faces lit by torches, they demanded Nat Turner. When Nathaniel Francis caught up to the crowd, Nat Turner was already bloodied, plucked, and mauled. Nathaniel Francis added his whacks until the sheriff and an armed guard surrounded the slave and took what was left of Nat Turner away. "If you kill him, Mr. Francis," the sheriff yelled, "he won't get to trial and you won't get paid!"

Nathaniel Francis followed the crowd, followed Nat Turner to Jerusalem. Stumbling, bleeding, his eyes swollen shut. People yelled, "Kill him! Hang the nigger!"

That night, people kept vigil with torches. They shouted. They charged the building and threatened the jailors. They drank and danced in the Jerusalem streets. Nat Turner was going to hang!

Nathaniel Francis was relieved Nat Turner was in jail, but he did not think it was enough. He would not be satisfied until he saw the murderer hanged. He would not be satisfied until Lavinia was home.

Nat Turner awakened on November 1, 1831, in the Jerusalem courthouse jail.

chapter 102

Jerusalem was frenzy. Day and night, outside the court building, men shot off their guns so the metallic smell of gunpowder filled the air. The guards at the doors were no longer boys, but old-timers who could not be frightened by death threats. Women screamed, others threw themselves down on the court-house steps, moaning like sacrifices. Others rammed the walls with their bodies.

Nathaniel Francis did not join them. Dred, Sam, Hark were all dead. Will's body hadn't been found, but he was probably a shriveling head on Black Head Sign Post Road. And now Nat Turner was behind bars. Nathaniel slept the most peaceful sleep he had had in months, even without Lavinia beside him.

On Friday, November 4, 1831, Peter Edwards's Sam, the slave Edwards protested was innocent, was hanged at the usual place. Nathaniel Francis dozed, on and off, through the event. On Saturday, November 5, 1831, Nat, alias Nat Turner, was scheduled for a hearing.

chapter 103

As was his custom, Nathaniel awoke in the dark of the morning. Winter had begun to announce herself. Days were shortening. Cold had begun to creep through the windows again. By lamplight, he saw Easter lying on the floor.

He relieved himself and called her to take away the steaming pot by his bed. When she did not rouse, he walked to the old woman and nudged her with his foot. "Get the pot, Easter. I will not tell you the same thing every day. If Lavinia's father would not make me pay him recompense, I would drag your old carcass with me to court today and let them hang you."

Easter stumbled to her feet, but slowly, and he kicked her. "Get the fire started. Make something to eat. I'm going to see to the hanging of your prophet today."

When Nathaniel Francis arrived at the courthouse in Jerusalem, the perpetual crowd was there—men, women, and children—shouting, cursing, wailing. They gave way when they recognized him. "Don't worry, young Mr. Francis, one way or another there'll be justice today!"

Though there was a crowd outside, he was the first to be seated in the courtroom. Close enough to hear and see it all. He felt for the pistol inside his jacket—just in case the judges came to the wrong conclusion. John Clarke Turner arrived soon and sat on his left. He felt the hardness of the gun strapped to John Clarke's side. When Levi Waller arrived, he sat on his right, closest to the aisle. Other men made a show of their firearms when they came through the door.

The judges, afraid of the crowd, called for an additional

twenty-five guards, strong guards, to march Nat Turner from the jailhouse to the courtroom. The guards remained in the courtroom to ensure Nat Turner would survive to be hanged. His eyes swollen, one of them shut, he dragged chains. His clothes hung in bloody tatters.

The morning was gray. Nat Turner pleaded innocent, like all the others, to charges of conspiring to rebel and make insurrection. Prosecutor Broadnax patted Levi Waller on the back. "This will be an easy one. Relax. Your work will soon be over. It will be an easy morning. His lawyer won't dare challenge your testimony today. In a short time you'll put that yellow nigger away."

Ten judges—James Trezvant, presiding, Jeremiah Cobb, Samuel Hines, James Massenburg, James Parker, Robert Goodwin, Ores Browne, Carr Bowers, Thomas Pretlow, and Richard Urquardt—heard Nat Turner's case. Three of them were attorneys by practice—James Trezvant was a congressman as well—the rest were gentlemen of good standing, all good slavery men.

There was no standing room available; outside, people jostled to press their faces to the windows. Glass muffled their catcalls; still, the judges called for additional guards.

Meriwether Broadnax brought the commonwealth's case against Nat Turner and called Levi Waller as his first and only witness against the prisoner. Hubbard and Venus would not testify against "Prophet Nat"; neither would any of the other slaves. But there was no need for other witnesses—Levi had seen and heard it all, Broadnax said. The case was open-and-shut.

chapter 104

Commonwealth of Virginia v. Nat, alias Nat Turner. The air was cooler now and Nathaniel Francis realized he missed the perpetual humming of the fans. People slapped Waller on the back as he approached the stand.

"Hurry up, Levi, the hangman is getting lonely!"

"Get it finished—last pig to the slaughter!"

"We've got celebrating to do!"

Levi sauntered to the stand in fine form.

He slumped in the chair like it belonged to him, like a stuffed chair at home. "On the morning of the twenty-second August last, in the morning between nine and ten, I heard that Negroes had risen and were murdering the whites and were coming in the direction of my home."

Nathaniel Francis flinched. At the first hearing, Levi had said that the insurgents had come unexpectedly upon his family. Nathaniel looked around. No one seemed to notice. No one seemed to care. What difference did it make? Nat Turner was going to hang. Nathaniel took a breath, relaxed, and continued listening.

"I sent my son Thomas to the schoolhouse, which was about a quarter of a mile off, to tell them about the uprising and to tell his brothers and sisters to come home."

A man in the courtroom offered Waller a drink from his flask to refresh himself. Waller took a drink, wiped his mouth, and continued with his story. "Mr. Crocker, the schoolmaster, came back with my children. I told him to go to the house and load the guns. But before the guns were loaded, Mr. Crocker came to the still where I was and said the insurgent Negroes were in sight."

Waller took another drink. "I ran from the still and hid myself in the corner of the fence there in the weeds, behind the garden, on the opposite side of the house. Several Negroes pursued me but I escaped by falling among the weeds over the fence—one Negro rode up and looked over, but he didn't see me." Levi took another gulp. "I think the nigger got distracted by some of his number going off after someone else they thought was me, but it was my blacksmith. I ran to the swamp then."

Waller stammered then, as though realizing the twist in his tale. "The swamp was not far off." Levi cleared his throat. "I remained in the swamp for a while, then I approached the house. Before I retreated again, I saw several of my family members murdered by the niggers. I crept right up by the house so I could see what they were doing and concealed myself in the plum orchard behind the garden." He swallowed hard. "The Negroes were drinking. I saw them. Especially that one!" Waller pointed at Nat Turner. "I know that rascal well. He had all you all fooled but I never trusted him myself. Just like Nathaniel Francis always said. Just like John Clarke Turner said. It was Nat Turner, all right, leading everything, and he was mounted on Dr. Musgrave's horse. Nat commanded the party and made Peter Edwards's Negro man Sam—who seemed disposed to remain—to go with him and the rest of the insurgents."

Satisfied with Levi Waller's testimony, prosecutor Broadnax took his seat.

William Parker, Nat Turner's defense attorney, who had probably received almost as many threats as Nat Turner, approached the bench. "Are you certain, Mr. Waller, that you saw this man, the prisoner?" Parker pointed at Nat Turner.

"Yes, sir, it was him. I have no doubt. Known him all my life."

Parker rubbed his chin. "You didn't mention Nat Turner being with the insurgents the first five times you testified."

Nathaniel Francis ran his hand over the butt of his gun. Parker had no right to question Levi, especially not for the likes of Nat

Turner. He was a murderer; he was property; the only thing he deserved was death.

Levi wasn't rattled. "Well, I'm saying it now. I told you, it was him."

Parker was persistent. "Something troubles me, Mr. Waller. You say, today, you saw Nat Turner on Dr. Musgrave's horse."

"I did."

"In the first hearing at which you testified, it was reported that it was Richard Porter's slave Daniel who rode Dr. Musgrave's horse. In fact, Sampson Reese testified that Daniel was riding Dr. Musgrave's horse. Was Reese confused?"

"It might have been Daniel, too. Maybe both of them were on the horse. But I know the leader was him, that nigger right there!" Waller jabbed his finger at Nat.

William Parker turned to walk away. Nathaniel Francis relaxed again. It was over. Nat Turner was the next fish for the pole.

Then William Parker turned back to Levi Waller, as though he had an afterthought. "Mr. Waller, I am sorry for your grief." He motioned to the court and judges. "We all are." Parker stepped closer to the witness stand. "But there is still something that troubles me." He paused. "At a previous trial you testified that you were in the house with your family when the insurgents surprised you, and you all ran for your lives. Do you remember that? You were the only one to escape. You hid. You remember?"

"Sure I do." Levi flushed.

"I don't mean to offend you, Mr. Waller. It just seems strange to me that a man would leave his family, would run ahead and leave his family behind. You said there was a baby there, am I correct?"

Waller looked confused at first, but then he recovered. "Yes."

"I've never experienced the horror you have, but it seems strange to me." Parker turned to look at the judges and then back at Waller. "Later you testified that you hid yourself away but you could still see what was going on at your house. You testified that you were unsure whether one of the prisoners had a rifle or a gun. You seem unsure about many things, Mr. Waller."

Waller shook. His face reddened. "I'm sure I saw Nat Turner and you're not going to make me say any different!"

"All right then, Mr. Waller. I don't mean to offend you."

Nathaniel Francis glared at Parker's back.

William Parker walked toward Waller as though he were his friend, then as though he were tired, weighed down. He sighed. "My question is this: Where were you, Mr. Waller?" Parker sighed again. "You testified you were in your home, and then you testified you were hidden in the weeds. Now, today, you tell us you were hidden in the plum grove and then in the swamp. Is there a swamp close to your house?"

Levi Waller was silent.

Parker cleared his throat. "Where were you? Where were you, Mr. Waller?" Levi looked at the judges but did not answer.

"You mentioned some other place I've never heard you mention before, Mr. Waller. You said the teacher came to meet you there. Where was it you said you were?"

Waller looked at Nathaniel Francis. He nodded at Levi to reassure him, but Levi's mouth began to tremble. He hung his head. "My still."

Parker seemed to have new life. "That just seems peculiar to me. Insurgents are coming, your family is threatened—you have them loading guns—but you're at your still? Your wife and children must have been out of their minds with fear! Your family must have been terrified! But you chose to remain at the still? You left your wife and your children to fend for themselves? Explain that to me, Levi."

Parker stepped closer. "Where were you, Mr. Waller? And please say it loud enough so that all the people can hear the truth." Parker stepped even closer. "Where were you?"

Parker lost his smile, his sympathetic tone. "Tell us the truth, Mr. Waller. Men and women have lost their lives based on your testimony. You didn't see anyone, did you? You have no idea who was or wasn't there. The British? Nat Turner? Sam? Daniel? Runaways from the Great Dismal Swamp? When your family was insane with fear, when your family was killed, where were you, Mr. Waller?"

Waller whispered his confession.

"My still."

chapter 105

Waller confessed—he had been at his still. "Then I ran to the house, like I said."

Parker had twisted Levi Waller's words hoping to get Nat Turner discharged, but Nathaniel Francis knew human nature. The good people of Jerusalem stood without apology. They could not turn back now. They would rather hang one more than be guilty, party to the murder of innocents, even if they were Negroes. One more nigger wasn't worth sleepless nights.

The spooners had ridden the trail with Waller. This was the end to the journey. They had clamored for Nat Turner's blood. Those who had celebrated Nat Turner's reading had been shamed into despising him. Those who had once patted him on the back had allowed their guilt and anger to call for his hanging. They could not turn back now. No one was going to raise a word against the voice of the group. They could not admit that they might have been wrong, that they might have murdered slaves for money.

Too much they had relied on all their lives had already changed. They were just beginning to feel normal again. To acquit Nat Turner, they would have to admit that Levi Waller was wrong, that he had lied—a white man had lied. They needed to feel normal—niggers lied, not white men. Not Levi Waller. Not them. With Nat Turner dead, bad times would be behind them. When Nat Turner hanged, life would be as before.

The judges could not acquit Nat Turner unless they wanted to join him in death. The judges could not acquit Nat Turner unless they wanted crimson streets in Jerusalem. The judges were afraid, like Thomas Gray; they did not want to be called nigger-lovers. They wouldn't stand for that, not even for Jesus Christ Himself. They were afraid of being shunned, of poverty, of death. No white man—not even the Parkers or the Edwardses—was going to die for a slave, especially not Nat Turner. They had already invested too much energy, too many words, and too many prayers on hating him.

No one could stand in the face of the wind that was blowing. No one wanted to be Ethelred Brantley, no one wanted to be the fool.

Amused, Nathaniel Francis relaxed. Somehow, Nat Turner would hang.

chapter 106

The commonwealth's star witness, its only eyewitness, had perjured himself. Whispering at an off-the-record sidebar, the judges, the attorneys, and the court clerk, James Rochelle, argued how to proceed. When it was over, the court's chief justice, Congressman Trezvant, colonel in the Southampton militia, was sworn in as the commonwealth's new witness. He would give Nat Turner's confession.

The spectators quieted to hear every word. Nathaniel knew the judges' lives, Jerusalem's life, depended on Trezvant's words. He needed to make them all forget what they'd heard, forget that Levi had lied. Trezvant needed to make Jerusalem feel good about hanging Nat Turner.

The judge told the court that he and fellow judge James Parker had questioned Nat—no doubt Trezvant was glad now that young Parker, related to the defense attorney, was with him when the prisoner was examined before being taken into custody. "Nat was in confinement"—Trezvant looked over the top of his spectacles—"but no threats or promises were held out to him to make any disclosures." The judge did not use Nat Turner's surname.

"He admitted to us that he was one of the insurgents—chief among them—from the first moment to the moment of their dispersion on Tuesday morning after the insurrection took place." Congressman Justice Trezvant cleared his throat. "Nat confessed that he gave to his master and mistress"—Congressman Trezvant looked at Nathaniel Francis and nodded—"Mr. Travis and his wife, Sallie Francis Travis, the first blow before they were dispatched and that he alone killed Miss Peggy Whitehead."

The courtroom crowd exploded. "Kill that nigger!" It was all they had dreamed of and all they'd expected, what they needed to hear. It dissolved the hint of Levi Waller's failure, of any cowardice. Almost fifteen minutes passed before there was enough calm to proceed. Nathaniel Francis sat quietly. He knew a bluff when he saw one.

When the courtroom settled, Congressman Trezvant continued. "Nat gave a long account of the motives which led him finally to commence the bloody scenes which took place. He pretended to have had intimated by signed omens from God that he should embark in the desperate attempt."

It was cool in the room, but Trezvant was sweating. "Nat and his comrades seemed to believe he was a prophet and had mystical powers, that by laying on hands he could cure disease." The judge, the militia colonel, looked at the people in the courtroom. His expression said he was one of them, a great slavery man. He was no believer in emancipation. He was their congressman, one of the people.

Trezvant spoke to them in a down-home way. "Nat related a particular instance in which it was believed that he had in that manner affected a cure upon one of his comrades." He nodded. "And you all remember the story of Ethelred Brantley." The courtroom spectators murmured to themselves. The judged chuckled, as though to intimate how insane Nat was.

Nathaniel Francis watched the judge's expression. When he was certain the people were with him, Trezvant continued his testimony. "He is a madman. As you would expect, he went on to detail a medley of incoherent and confused opinions about his communications with God, his command over the clouds. He had been entertaining these thoughts, if you would call them that, as far back as 1826."

Unanimous, the judges swiftly rendered their decision. They found the prisoner guilty in manner and form. No longer a witness, but now a judge, Congressman Trezvant asked William

Parker, Nat Turner's attorney, if there were any final words on behalf of the prisoner. "No more than what has already been said," Parker said, shaking his lowered head, motioning toward Levi Waller.

Justice Jeremiah Cobb rendered the verdict. "The court values the said slave at the sum of three hundred and fifty—"

Nathaniel Francis stood to his feet and objected. "He is trouble, but he is worth more than that!"

Jeremiah Cobb continued. "Three hundred and *seventy-five* dollars. It is ordered that the sum of ten dollars be rendered as a fee for defending Nat, alias Nat Turner, late the property of Putnam Moore, an infant."

Cobb continued. "Therefore, it is considered by the court that he be taken hence to the jail from whence he was taken therein to remain until Friday, the eleventh day of November instant, on which day between the hours of ten o'clock in the forenoon and four o'clock in the afternoon he is to be taken by the sheriff to the usual place of execution and there be hanged by the neck until he be dead."

chapter 107

"That nigger is going to hang!" Waller lay on the floor near his still, kicking his feet.

Nathaniel Francis's thoughts were of Lavinia. She would be home soon. He would bring her and the new baby back from North Carolina. He watched the sun receding. Everything would be as good as or better than before.

Levi Waller giggled. "It will be better than watching all the rest of them swing together! Gonna do worse to him than any of the rest put together!" He staggered to his feet and clapped his hands.

Nathaniel Francis sat in his usual place in the cabin still with his back against the wall. Thomas Gray sat hunched in his seat, a glass of whiskey in his hand. He had been quiet since the trial's end.

"It felt good getting to the truth," Waller said. He did not mention his own testimony and Nathaniel Francis did not mention it either, no one did. Waller rose, staggering, with a jug in his hand. "I can't wait to see that nigger flopping."

Nathaniel Francis laughed. "Like a goldfish on a pole."

John Clarke Turner refused to laugh; he repeated that it was his father's fault. "You all knew my father. Too kindhearted." John Clarke Turner looked around. He drank. "Why would he choose a nigger over his own flesh and blood? Why would he trust him more than his own son?" He gulped again. "Why a darkie? Why not me?"

Nathaniel looked at John Clarke, then at the shadow that blocked the door.

* * *

GOVERNOR JOHN FLOYD stood in front of his ornately framed bedroom mirror and smiled, pretending to greet a constituent. Congressman James Trezvant waited nearby.

Since September 26, 1831, the county courts of Southampton, Isle of Wight, Nansemond, Sussex, and Prince George had been under executive order of the governor to provide accurate, certified, verbatim records of the slave hearings. The certified transcripts were provided via overnight express. The trial record of November 5 had excited the governor. He ordered that a note be sent back to the congressman requesting an immediate audience. Congressman Trezvant had been up all night.

Governor Floyd continued scrutinizing his appearance in the mirror. "We have a problem, don't we?"

"Things are settled now, I think. At least in Southampton County. I . . . we've gotten things well in hand." Trezvant smiled, satisfied with himself.

The governor sighed and turned to face him. "I wish slavery was never among us. Slavery and these troublesome Negro preachers may be Virginia's undoing. I intend to make it my business to rid us of this burden—the slaves, the freemen, the preachers, the whole caboodle—send them all to Africa. But for now we are stuck, you and I, with the hand we've been dealt."

Congressman Trezvant watched the man, wondering where this was all going—like most of the men from western Virginia, where he'd been raised, Governor Floyd was opposed to slavery.

"Parker's Field—I understand that's where your militia overtook the Negroes?"

"Yes, Governor, the Southampton men fought valiantly."

"I understand there is some question as to whether the Negroes were armed."

Representative Trezvant shifted on his seat. "I myself led part of the militia. No doubt there were some axes, some clubs, perhaps a sword or two. But you are correct; there have been conflicting reports about whether any of the Negroes had guns. We have had courtroom testimony that there were weapons, but no guns were found among the corpses at Parker's Field. None of my men were wounded."

"Not a battle worthy of a ballad, is it? Using guns and rifles to fight men armed with axes and sticks." Governor Floyd sighed again and took a seat. "As you know, I've read the transcript and other documents I've received." The governor lifted up newspaper clippings. Trezvant recognized them as stories he had submitted about the insurrection to local newspapers—the *Petersburg Intelligencer,* the *Richmond Constitutional Whig,* and the *Richmond Enquirer.* The stories had put him and Southampton on the map.

"Congressman," the governor said, "you and your brothers have been very busy in Jerusalem." Among the articles, Trezvant noticed a clipping of the article about Cherry's beating.

Congressman Trezvant felt the governor sizing him up.

The governor looked toward the window. "I have tried to save as many of the wretches as I could from the noose and turned them over to state-approved slave dealers for sale farther south." He shrugged. "Hanging, death now; slower death, Deep South."

Floyd cleared his throat and leaned forward so that the early morning sun from the window touched his face. "I have a vision for our great state, Congressman. I see train tracks laid right through the Dismal Swamp, and on those tracks are trains that carry Virginia goods to distant markets. Our economy has gone through a difficult time, but I see us recovering. I see good things ahead of us.

"I know you are a slavery man, but I am against it. A working railroad would allow for gradual emancipation and deportation of all our Negroes to Liberia in Africa—slave and free. A problem transferred is a problem solved. A working railroad would allow our citizens to gradually prosper in a system not dependent on slaves."

The governor looked back from the window. Trezvant did not

like the man's hawk-shaped nose or his receding hairline. "Have you heard of the Negro Gabriel Prosser, Congressman?"

Trezvant nodded.

"Of course you have. He was from right here in Richmond, Henrico County. Gabriel planned to overthrow the whites. He was a smart one, a preacher like your Nat Turner, and he almost pulled it off. But the sitting governor of Virginia got wind of the conspiracy, the insurrection was thwarted, and Gabriel was hanged. That was 1800, the year your Nat Turner was born.

"Swift action by the governor made the people of the commonwealth feel calm and secure. The grateful people helped make that governor our fifth president."

"President James Monroe."

"Of course you know all this. I don't mean to bore you with my little history lesson. But yes, James Monroe.

"Now, Mr. Trezvant, I'm not saying that I'm going to be president or that you are going to be, let's say, a senator. But I will say our chances of any kind of advancement will be dimmed if the situation with this preaching slave isn't delicately handled. Not only our constituents but our investors will be rattled, and the railroad I dream of will remain a dream."

The governor stretched out his legs and folded his hands. "I have read the transcript of the trial and I think we have ourselves a mess. You know the state of things as well as I do."

"We have things well under control."

"Perhaps, Congressman, you don't realize how dire things are. There are conspirators from the North plotting our demise. I have received anonymous letters that talk of men like the Negro preacher Allen from Philadelphia, that fiendish William Lloyd Garrison, and conspirators from Boston, New York, and Philadelphia, who plan to aid the slaves in insurrection.

"You and I know that our slaves are no more than laborers; they know nothing of true slavery. But these outside agitators seek to rile them up against us. Can you imagine, Congressman, if the conspirators heard of this? If they heard that innocent slaves were put to the gallows because of the false witness of a drunkard? Can you imagine how Garrison and the others would trumpet it in their newspapers? They might gain the sympathy of poor ignorant widows and bleeding-heart liberals. If the conspirators got someone like Lyman Beecher on their side, he could turn the whole country against us. All the abolitionists need is *one* Negro martyr. Ten might be our undoing. A hundred? If the abolitionists get news of this, that at a liar's word we have hung innocent Negroes..."

"The slaves were not innocent!"

"So you say, Trezvant, but this matter is greater than Southampton. There are arguments in the Capitol about slavery and whether it will survive, you know that. Hard-fought arguments. If we lose our slaves immediately our economy will collapse. Our way of life is at stake and you gentlemen in Southampton may be the linchpin."

Trezvant felt his lips pursing. He was not a little boy. He would not be lectured, not even by the governor.

"Every time we have challenged our Union brothers on slavery they have eventually caved; but news of what has happened in Jerusalem might give them the moral footing to stand resolute." The governor tented his fingers and shook his head. "They don't care what happens with the Negro as long as it does not trouble them. The wrong kind of news or story"—the governor laid his hand on the newspaper accounts again—"could send things tilting the other way. Our investors will take their business elsewhere."

"Governor, with all due respect, I don't believe it's as serious as all that. I don't think the nation cares what happens to a few slaves in Southampton."

"You don't believe that, Congressman. Not after all the effort you've gone through. I have word that you've left court to post stories with the newspapers. It was your accounts that first said the insurrectionists—hundreds of runaways from the Great Dismal

Swamp—were invading Cross Keys." The governor nodded. "You have quite an imagination. Do you know how much money your imagination has cost Virginia? Do you know how much it cost to mobilize Eppes and his troops?" He picked up one of the articles and scanned it briefly. "You have worked people into a frenzy, Congressman. If that's what you wanted—along with some personal notoriety—then I would say you have done your job."

He didn't have to defend himself to the governor or anyone else. "The American people have a right to know. It's for their safety."

"It is your article, Congressman, in the *Richmond Enquirer* on September 1 that points the nation's finger at Nat Turner. It was hundreds of goblins from the Dismal Swamp you first accused, but then the afternoon John Clarke Turner testified against Nat Turner you rushed to make certain the news of the new monster quickly reached the nation. The transcript records show you absented yourself from court."

Who had been spying on him? He didn't have to justify his actions to any man. "As I said before, I don't think the American people care about such details."

The governor did not pause. "The American people do care, Congressman, and you would be surprised the extent they would go to to make something like this right."

"Governor, I think you are blowing this out of proportion."

Governor Floyd waved his hand. "This story has been covered in newspapers all over the country. Even President Jackson has inquired about it." The governor leaned forward in his chair. "We want to project an image to our voters, to our investors, to the nation that things in Virginia run smoothly and quietly.

"This cannot be a story about freemen of color being enslaved or robbed of their property. This cannot be a story of pitiful Negroes without arms rising up against despotic oppressors." The governor pointed at a painting of Valley Forge on the wall. "This cannot be a story about a man's madness and revenge because his family is stolen from him. The American people don't want to hear stories with a bunch of lawless peckerwoods for heroes. They don't want to hear that Negroes are being hanged on the word of a drunken perjurer."

Congressman Trezvant felt himself bristling. "The people of Southampton are my people, good people, sir." The governor hadn't sat in the room with Nat Turner. He hadn't listened to Nat Turner's crazy ranting, to his lies. He hadn't listened while Nat Turner talked about killing people he knew and loved, good people.

"That may be." Governor Floyd tapped his chin with his two index fingers. "But the American people don't want to hear stories about the abuse of power—not even by good people. The Commonwealth of Virginia, the state I govern, has built its case on liars, taking their word against even the words of the slaves' owners. We have destroyed property based on the words of perjurers and we are liable.

"To make matters worse, we have a congressman standing in two branches—as judge and congressman—and now, as judge and witness. Oh, don't let me neglect to also say as militia leader and newspaperman. It is hard to believe that none of this has raised eyebrows at home."

It was easy for the governor to sit in his well-appointed room and judge, safe from the hands of angry men. It was easy for him to look down on other men. Congressman Trezvant felt his face reddening. "As you have said, sir, we are peasants and peckerwoods, white trash, not sophisticated people. How would we know any better?" He cleared his throat. "If you feel there is a problem, Governor Floyd, what is your prescription?"

"I don't think 'if there is a problem' covers this. You still don't grasp the gravity of this situation. Until now Virginia has been the premier state in this nation. It won't be on my watch that that reputation changes." Governor Floyd tapped the sheath of papers beside him. "The American people are good people. It soothes national conscience to believe that slavery is good, Christian, and

fair. They like hearing of happy slaves. They don't want to hear
about torture and false confessions.

"This is America, Congressman Trezvant. We are good gentlemen! The American citizens don't want to think of themselves as
tyrants or oppressors keeping others from freedom. Americans
don't want some homegrown Toussaint-Louverture rallying the
slaves.

"And what if the Negroes hear that we murdered hundreds of
their number with no cause? There are places in Virginia and in
the other Southern states where the blacks clearly outnumber
whites. Haiti is close enough. We don't need an uprising here."

"Sir, I think you are exaggerating."

"Not long ago, no one would care what happened in Southampton. But through your own Herculean efforts and those of
your brother the postmaster, this is now a national story. And
you've got a defense attorney in Southampton County nosing
about, inquiring about appeals and making noise that the trial was
not only unfair but that the proceedings were illegal. Railing that
the state is sanctioning Negro genocide!"

What defense attorney? What illegal proceedings?

"The abolitionists are breathing fire. Garrison is using this
story to make himself a name." The governor raised an eyebrow.
"There is enough here for him to ride to national fame. There are
enough martyrs here to pave his way to the White House! Can you
see him spinning a story about the crucifixion of a young prophet
from Jerusalem?"

Congressman Trezvant thought he recognized the other papers. Besides the newspaper clippings there were handwritten cop-
ies of trial transcripts and a copy of the Turner's Meeting Place
deed and a will.

Governor Floyd continued railing. "There are Negro abolitionists, preachers like David Walker, calling for revolt—we have to
discourage them."

Congressman Trezvant leaned forward in his chair. He wasn't

going to sit still and allow himself or his people to be maligned. "The slave is a religious zealot, Governor. A maniac. He talks about deeds and imagines he is a freeman. It is his opinion that God told him, a darkie, that judgment begins with the house of God." The governor's face was serious, but Trezvant could not help but laugh. "As though America were some Egypt and we should be visited by plagues. He said he saw visions." Trezvant laughed again. He shook his head. "I don't think there is any need to worry."

"Well, I am worried, sir. Your letters to the newspapers have people thirsting for blood. I am not naïve—this preacher will hang—the people demand it. His guilt or innocence means nothing."

Trezvant's face burned. "Innocent! The murderer savaged more than fifty innocent people!"

The governor looked nonplussed. "Do you have any evidence? Any real witnesses to connect him with the crime?"

"Governor, I demand—"

The governor raised his hand. "Calm yourself, Congressman."

The room was quiet. The sun was rising, more sunlight painted the room. Congressman Trezvant saw dust particles riding the stream of light.

The governor sighed. "There's no need for us to argue, Congressman Trezvant. We must assure the nation that we have our slaves in hand and that they are loyal and grateful for slavery. The nation doesn't want to hear stories of smiling slaves rising up to kill their masters at night. They don't want to hear about gallant Christian revolutionaries called by God." The governor lost his composure. Governor Floyd's face darkened and he began to pound with his fist on a nearby table. "The great Commonwealth of Virginia will not be undone by a few drunken, ignorant crackers! I will not have my name or this state's reputation associated with this debacle. You handle this, Trezvant! You handle it or I'll see you all hanged!"

The governor calmed himself. "You are a congressman . . . an ambitious one . . . and I won't presume to tell you how to handle this situation." The governor leveled his gaze. "But I will say that what we need from Southampton is a good American story, a Southern story that will tug at the heartstrings of even the abolitionists. We need a story that will make everyone glad, even slaves, that the villain has been put away from us.

"We need a story that will reassure the people! We need a story that will leave our voters grateful." The governor stood and extended his hand. He gave Trezvant a small, tight smile. "There was no meeting between us, Congressman." He tapped the papers on the table next to him. "For the good of our state and our nation you will dispose of this matter." He tapped the papers again. "I will dispose of these." He nodded. "Thank Providence there were no Negroes in the courtroom to hear the truth. None that will live." He nodded. "A year from now no one will remember."

Trezvant understood that he was being dismissed.

chapter 108

Nathaniel Francis looked up to see the shadow that blocked the doorway. Congressman Trezvant nodded at all present.

Waller tottered and giggled. Trezvant gazed at him with disdain, then looked back at Nathaniel Francis. "Governor Floyd is concerned about Nat Turner's trial. He is afraid that if news gets out about the testimony . . ." Congressman Trezvant briefly glanced at Waller. "He is concerned about my acting as judge and witness. We need a new story that will . . . clarify the events and the characters, that will reassure people we have gotten all the scoundrels. We need a quick answer and you are an enterprising young man." The congressman smiled.

Nathaniel Francis looked at John Clarke Turner, at Thomas Gray, and then back at the congressman. He had an answer. "Did you know Mr. Gray, here, is an aspiring writer?" He motioned to Waller to pour the congressman a drink. "Have a seat. I believe I have a solution."

Thomas Gray had been Nat Turner's friend; he knew secrets. John Clarke Turner had practically been raised with Nat Turner; he would supply stories from Nat's childhood. Trezvant had written the news accounts. Nat Turner had been Nathaniel's sister's slave and he knew firsthand all the trouble he had caused her.

Each one of them knew something about Nat Turner and together they would tell the story the way it needed to be told. Thomas Gray would be the writer and they would work with him. They would fashion an official document, a confession, an official transcript that re-created the trial. Thomas R. Gray, not William

Parker, would be the attorney of record. In the reconstructed record of the trial there would be no congressman acting as judge and witness, there would be no record of Levi Waller or his perjury, and they would take Nat Turner down a peg—Nathaniel Francis would see to it.

Congressman Trezvant smiled. "Then we will have Nat Turner's head."

Nathaniel Francis nodded his agreement. "We'll have his head."

John Clarke Turner sat up; the possibilities began to dawn on him. "We'll tell the truth about his daddy, a slave right out of Africa."

Nathaniel Francis began to dictate to Thomas Gray. "They were all drunk, I'm sure of it. They probably drank all the apple brandy in Southampton County. That's the only way the cowards had the nerve to do what they did."

Thomas Gray winced. "Not Nat Turner. Everyone knows he never drank."

"Well, the others sure were drunk! And they were thieves, stealing everything along the way. All this trouble because the niggers were stupid enough to follow a nigger preacher."

"Monsters!" John Clarke Turner pounded the table. "Killing innocent women and children! Killing babies! The ringleaders probably forced the others to go with them at gunpoint." Then he crowed, "We will have his head! We will have that nigger's head!"

Congressman Trezvant pulled newspaper clippings from his pocket—his stories about Nat Turner, the insurrection, and Cherry's beating. "Use these as you please." He handed them to Thomas Gray.

Gray was silent.

Nathaniel Francis looked around the table. They would write Nat Turner's confession. He would be there to keep the effort on track and embellish the story. He would wring Gray's secrets from him. Congressman Trezvant would convince the other judges to sign off on the confession. He would order the county clerk to sign. In the end the wretched insurrectionist would not only die but be undone.

WHAT WAS MEANT to be a quiet cover-up Thomas Gray saw as an opportunity. He rushed to have the new record, the confession, copyrighted and published, saying it was only fair that he should profit like the others.

THE

CONFESSIONS

OF

NAT TURNER,

THE LEADER OF THE LATE

INSURRECTION IN SOUTHAMPTON, VA.

As fully and voluntarily made to

THOMAS R. GRAY,

In the prison where he was confined, and acknowledged by

him to be such when read before the Court of Southampton;

with the certificate, under seal of

the Court convened at Jerusalem,

Nov. 5, 1831, for his trial.

ALSO, AN AUTHENTIC

ACCOUNT OF THE WHOLE INSURRECTION,

WITH LISTS OF THE WHITES WHO WERE MURDERED,

AND OF THE NEGROES BROUGHT BEFORE THE COURT

OF SOUTHAMPTON, AND THERE SENTENCED, ETC.

AUTHORED BY THOMAS R. GRAY, WAS DELIVERED

TO EDMUND LEE, THE CLERK OF THE DISTRICT

OF COLUMBIA, ON NOVEMBER 10, 1831, TO CERTIFY

PROOF OF THOMAS GRAY'S COPYRIGHT.

The confessions bore the November 5, 1831, dated seal of the Southampton clerk of the court, James Rochelle, and the sealed signatures of six judges of the ten judges who sat for Nat Turner's hearing: Jeremiah Cobb, Thomas Pretlow, James W. Parker, Carr Bowers, Samuel B. Hines, and Ores Browne.

The signatures and seals of four judges—James D. Massenburg, Robert Goodwin, Richard Urquardt, and Congressman Justice Trezvant—were missing.

Thomas Gray was back in time to see his friend Nat Turner hanged.

chapter 109

November 11, 1831, was a dark gray morning, but Nathaniel Francis was jubilant. Everywhere people laughed and children darted in and out of the crowd. He stood near the leafless hanging tree with Levi Waller beside him. Most of Southampton was crowded there, though there were a few missing—like Benjamin Phipps, Peter Edwards, Congressman Trezvant, and all the dearly departed. Nat Turner would soon be joining them.

He did not have to turn his head to see when Nat Turner approached. He heard the crowd shouting. A small man to have caused so much trouble.

Nat Turner, flanked by burly guards, bound in chains, hobbled to the tree. They slipped the noose around his neck. The hangman allowed him last words. Nathaniel Francis saw the nigger's lips move but could not hear him.

When the chair was kicked from underneath his feet, Nat Turner's body hitched a few times, his face reddened, his eyes bulged, his neck stretched, and then tilted. The whole thing, the moment Nathaniel Francis had waited for for months, was over too soon.

People shot off guns, drank, and celebrated. It was Pettigrew the traveling butcher's idea to render him. Some of the Cross Keys women, even persnickety Mary Barrow, got involved, set themselves to work. They built a fire to heat the large kettle of boiling water.

Pettigrew cut the throat to bleed him, the way you would any pig. The neck bone was already broken, so Pettigrew's work was easy. Nat Turner's body was practically hairless, so there was no need to scald him. The butcher gently skinned Nat Turner, he gutted him, and delivered his head, skin, and body to the town doctor.

The town doctor dissected Nat Turner, kept the skin, the head, and very choice pieces of the body. What was left was turned back to the butcher.

Pettigrew gave the intestines, the chitterlings, to the women to scrape the fat, and they threw it into their pot. What was left over they tossed to the waiting dogs.

Pettigrew swung the carcass, thudding and splattering, onto a table they had set in plain sight. He used an axe to cut the backbone away. With every cut, the people cheered.

He used his hand and pulled away the leaf lard, the layer of fat against the ribs, and gave it to the women. There was not much fat on the body, but what there was, he gave to them. Pettigrew severed the limbs. People came and took pieces of meat and bones away.

The women stirred the fatty pieces in the boiling pot. When the fire was out, and the kettle cooled, they skimmed off the fat and sold it.

To honor them, the doctor gave away souvenirs of Nat Turner to people whose families had suffered. The rest of the skin and other parts were sold, some of it turned into wallets, belts, and lampshades.

Nathaniel Francis mounted his horse and rode back to Cross Keys with Waller, who said, "Did you see his face? It was red at first and then purple! Did you see his head, the way it tilted?" Waller mocked Nat Turner.

"Did you see his feet kicking? He flopped like a fish on dry land!" Nathaniel Francis laughed.

Later he headed for North Carolina to bring his sweet Lavinia home.

Even many years after, he remembered the fragrant aroma of

the day. He planned the belts he would make for himself and his sweet wife.

Mary Barrow earned six hundred seventy-five dollars as a result of the slave trials—Lucy and Moses—more than four times what a farmer in Southampton County could expect to earn in a year. John Clarke Turner was awarded nine hundred dollars—Joe and Davy. Jacob Williams was given four hundred dollars for Yellow Nelson.

Nathaniel Francis smiled to himself. No one person received more than he: almost three thousand dollars, more than he could have earned in twenty years—Nat Turner; the boys Moses, Nathan, Tom, and Davy; Dred; Hark; and Sam. He had Levi Waller to thank for many of the slaves' hangings—Waller as well as Thomas Gray, who offered no defense. Levi Waller earned only three hundred dollars for himself, still more than he could earn in two years—thanks to the death of his Davy.

William Parker, Esquire

chapter 110

Its mane and Parker's cape flying, his legs clamped tight to its sides and the reins bunched in his hands, the horse beneath William Parker thundered down the road to Richmond. He might lose his life. But he had to try.

He had left Jerusalem shortly after the overnight messenger. He had thought to ask John French to ride with him to Richmond, but he did not want to attract attention and it was his cross to bear, not French's.

The Cross Keys bunch were always rowdy troublemakers. William Parker did not want to be one of them.

He did not make the system, he had told himself for years. He had not made himself white; he could just as easily have been born black. One man, he could not change the world. He was as much a victim of fate as anyone. He had no choice but to live out the life he had inherited.

The moon was with him, there was cool light from overhead, but the night was black and breathing. November cold beat against his face and hands and ears. William Parker's horse's hooves pounded the dirt road, his heart pounded in his chest. Every tree was a looming threat. Every bush was one of Nathaniel Francis's minions.

William Parker rarely slept through the night since the hearings had begun. When he did sleep he saw their faces—women and children killed, families tortured, so many innocent men hanged—and he felt powerless to do anything about it.

Slavery was wrong, but he was a peaceful man and did not like to quarrel. He did not create the system of slavery in America or, for that matter, in the world. He had a family, after all, and he had responsibilities. He did not take part in arguments about slavery and he wrote no pamphlets. He imagined himself a peacemaker.

Now, everything was in shambles. He dreamed over and over again that there was a decomposing corpse in his cellar and he did not have the courage to bring it out. William Parker prayed since Nat Turner's capture about what he was supposed to do. He prayed that God would make it all go away.

Since the hearings had begun, ill treatment had become a way of life. It was an everyday thing to be spat upon. Neither he nor his fellow defense attorney, John French, had gone a day without threats to their lives.

Parker's horse charged and his mind ran over all that had happened since the hearings began.

The courtroom was a circus—there were drunken clowns and carny vendors. Thugs like Nathaniel Francis and John Clarke Turner sat in the courtroom openly drinking and brandishing guns.

William Parker had been a practicing attorney for some time and had given up any notions about the nobility and honesty of mankind. Many attorneys found the revelation heartbreaking. Some soothed themselves with strong drink and others with raging cynicism. He comforted himself with faith—there was nothing for one man to do; life was too big; it was all in God's hands—and the ability to feed his family.

But the hearings had shaken him. There wasn't even any pretense at truth. William Parker's mind was like a ledger, turning pages to review the testimony. Mary Barrow had sworn in early September that she had run out the front door of her home and seen Hark with a gun in his hand, a gun he fired into the air instead of firing at her. Later in September she swore she ran out the back door and was grabbed by Lucy, who meant harm against her. John Clarke Turner, like others, had given false "confessions" for slaves. Laughing as he sent innocent men to the gallows.

Nathaniel Francis, Levi Waller, Williams, and Mary Barrow had all offered shifty stories about where each one of them was during the events of August 22 and 23. Yet their testimonies were accepted by the judges without question. The greatest liar was Levi Waller. Each time he testified, he told a different story about where he was or what he did.

As a litigator, it had been hard not to pounce on Waller, ripping his testimonies to shreds. But what was the point in challenging Waller? Nat Turner was already hanged. He was a dead man. How would it serve anyone's peace to stir up more confusion? But today was the worst.

He didn't have to put in the blade, everyone knew Waller was lying. William Parker had told himself he could back away now and leave his world intact. Who would know ten years from now? Who would even care?

William Parker leaned farther forward in the saddle. He felt the horse's muscles contract and expand beneath him. Over the steady pounding was the breathing like an engine, the ears laid back as though the horse understood their mission. In his mind's ledger were the words on the page.

Tell us the truth, Mr. Waller. . . . You didn't see anyone, did you? You have no idea who was or wasn't there. The British? Nat Turner? Sam? Daniel? . . . When your family was insane with fear, when your family was killed, where were you, Mr. Waller?

Waller whispered . . . My still.

Waller had finally let slip the truth about where he was, where they probably all were on August 22—at his still.

Nat Turner was on trial for wretched sins against more than fifty white people, for threatening the law, the community, and the church. Nat Turner was on trial for threatening those in power. He was on trial for refusing to be what they wanted him to be. Words that Thomas Gray had spoken to him before he took Nat Turner's case came back to William Parker.

"People are saying he is ignorant and cowardly, and that his object was to murder and rob for the purpose of obtaining money to make his escape. But it is notorious, that he was never known to have a dollar in his life, to swear an oath, or drink a drop of spirits." Gray had downed his glass of brandy and wiped his mouth. "As to his ignorance, he certainly never had the full advantages of education, but he can read and write. And for natural intelligence and quickness of apprehension, is surpassed by few men I have ever seen. As to his being a coward"—Gray had looked Parker in the eye—"I have not met a braver man."

William Parker had lived in Southampton County all his life and he had seen and heard horrible things. He had heard men laugh about hangings and rapes. He knew of white men who had murdered their slaves in drunken fits of rage the way they would destroy a chair or a lamp. No one was held accountable.

White men, women, and children were dead in Southampton. But in his lifetime, William Parker could not count the number of blacks—men, women, children, babies—he had seen murdered. No one was on trial for those crimes. No one would die for them, or for the heads mounted on poles on Black Head Sign Post Road.

His family had not wanted him to go. He had already done enough and it was foolish to ride at night. His wife, usually shy and obedient, was insistent. "Only a fool would fly on horseback to Richmond by night. The man is going to die; do I have to lose my husband?

"You'll lame the horse! You'll break your neck!"

But he had no choice; he had to go.

Dust and rocks from the horse's hooves pelted him. William Parker heard owls hooting in the darkness. He saw bats fly in front of the moonlight and heard wolves howling.

Until today he had comforted himself knowing he had been able to save most of the Parker family slaves from conviction. But he couldn't live with the lies, the deaths.

It was narcissistic blasphemy, all the teaching about white men being superior. But he had not said a word against it, though he was certain there were others who felt as he did. He was a singular man of peace. He did not want to make war and he had no power.

But in the courtroom as he faced Nat Turner, William Parker had had to face himself. He did not want to risk his life or his family. He did not want to give up his income or his property. But lately he remembered Scripture he had begrudgingly and mindlessly memorized as a boy for his mother.

He that loveth father or mother more than me is not worthy of me: and he that loveth son or daughter more than me is not worthy of me.

And he that taketh not his cross, and followeth after me, is not worthy of me.

For what is a man profited, if he shall gain the whole world, and lose his own soul? . . . He might lose his practice. He might lose everything.

He that loveth his life shall lose it; and he that hateth his life in this world shall keep it unto life eternal.

If any man serve me, let him follow me. . . .

William Parker did not create the system. He could not change the world. It was impossible being the Negro's defense attorney. Nat Turner was so mangled it was almost impossible to recognize him. "I don't think there's much I can do," William Parker had said to the slave through the bars of his cell. He realized after he spoke the words that he had come to Nat Turner seeking absolution.

"You owe me nothing," Nat Turner said. "What you do, do for God."

William Parker spurred his horse and prayed for safe passage.

chapter III

Governor Floyd's study was dark except for one lamp. "General Eppes reports to me that Southampton is very poor, that even the white people are starving." The light of day had not yet appeared and the mansion was quiet—the governor still in his robe and gown. William Parker heard the sound of a clock ticking atop the governor's secretary.

There wasn't a moment to waste. "If all men are created equal—"

The governor made a steeple with his fingers and touched the tips to his chin. "I am not going to argue slavery with you, Mr. Parker. If that is the reason you have come and awakened me—"

William Parker handed Governor Floyd a copy of Samuel Turner's will, which documented the property Samuel bequeathed to his wife, Elizabeth. "Nat Turner's name is not there, nor is the name of his wife, Cherry. They are free people. They are the ones that have been wronged; Elizabeth Turner had no right to sell them." He handed the governor a copy of the deed to Turner's Meeting Place. "He had every right to defend himself, his family, and his property."

"Do you have manumission papers for Nat Turner?"

"There are no papers; it was simply a master who, after acknowledging paternity, freed his slave son. Nat Turner's name is listed as trustee on the deed of Turner's Meeting Place."

"No manumission papers? I'm not sure what I can do, Mr. Parker. We have a separation of powers in this nation. I cannot interfere with the courts. Why come to me? The slave is not a voting citizen of this state. Why not petition your congressman?" The governor was toying with him, trying to find a mouse hole. He knew that Congressman Trezvant was implicated in the matter.

"Nat Turner and his people had every right to take up arms to defend themselves and their interests. If they did not, who else would? I am asking you to grant clemency."

The governor dropped his hands and leaned forward so that the lamplight caught his chin. "I don't take kindly to your inference that we don't protect our property. Do you know how much trouble this one slave has caused us? People are terrified; they see insurrectionists everywhere. They are grabbing Negroes all over North Carolina, in Virginia, and beyond, and torturing confessions out of them with little regard for truth. Just last week I was sent the head of a fellow who, unfortunately for him, turned out not to be Nat—fellows are hungry for the reward. The state will have to empty her coffers to pay the owners for each one hanged. Hundreds more have been maimed or summarily executed— thank goodness we don't have to pay for them. All of this because of your little preacher . . . and you want me to have mercy on him? The whole state of Virginia is inflamed and bloodletting seems the only cure."

William Parker tried to keep his voice to a whisper, but he heard urgency rising in it. "We have already wrongfully convicted enough men! Those testifying in court are liars and drunkards, sir! I give you my word as a gentleman: innocent people have been hanged because of them!" He stretched his hands before him. "But the blood is on all our hands. I am begging you, sir, to intervene!"

The governor sat back in his chair.

"We are a nation that lives by the rule of law, Governor Floyd. No one can prove that Nat Turner did anything. There are no witnesses against him . . . no credible ones. I am his attorney and he has made no confession to me.

"The truth is no one knows what happened that night—no one knows if Nat Turner lifted a finger—though goodness knows if he did it was not without provocation! If all men are created equal and entitled to freedom, why not them? Why not him? Why don't they have the right, before God, to make war to ensure their liberty?"

The governor's tone was measured but cross. "I told you, Mr. Parker, I will not debate slavery."

"Then simply stay the execution! Give me an opportunity to appeal. If the state wants to convict him, let her make a proper case! He is a freeman; allow his case to be heard in Superior Court! I beg you, let me make his case to proper judges and let the state do her best to take his life rightfully!"

The governor tilted the lamp to shine more light on William Parker's face. "You argue like a child unfamiliar with the ways of the court and the state." He raised an eyebrow. The governor righted the lamp and then spoke again. "Excuse my curtness. I have not had much sleep."

William Parker sank to his knees. "In Southampton the mob is ruling. We have a congressman acting as judge, witness, and jury, too. I beg you, Governor, for a chance." It was a small thing to humble himself in hopes of saving another man's life. To do nothing was to be part of the mob.

The governor looked embarrassed. "Please rise!" He came around his desk and extended William Parker his hand. "I see you are sincere." The governor's assistant entered then. "Governor Floyd, I must remind you that you have an early morning appointment."

The governor escorted William Parker to the study door. "I cannot promise anything." The governor shook his hand. "But I promise you I will review the matter."

chapter 112

November 11, 1831, was a gray day. William Parker watched the crowd from inside Mahone's Tavern. Though he and his family had prayed through the nights, with candles burning around them, six days had passed and he had heard nothing from the governor.

But he had heard a rumor from the friend of a friend of the court clerk, James Rochelle. There was an evil plot. Congressman Trezvant had made a visit to the governor and there were plans to remove William Parker's name as Nat Turner's attorney of record—along with Levi Waller's lies. William Parker did not want to believe it, but in his heart he knew it was true. The judges and the prosecutor, Broadnax, would not look him in the eye. Thomas Gray avoided him. Trezvant, Nathaniel Francis, and John Clarke Turner were somehow involved in the conspiracy.

They had the power to make it happen. All the authority was in their hands. He had ridden to Richmond for nothing. They would bury Nat Turner, bury the truth. William Parker looked out the window of Mahone's Tavern and silently prayed a child's prayer. "What is done in the dark, let it come to the light." He watched the crowd, the cheering and the jubilation.

When Nat Turner was hanged, he could not see, but he heard the shout of joy. He could not help but feel that they, the court and the people of Jerusalem and Southampton County, were bringing God's curse and wrath upon themselves. He could not escape the torment that he had not done enough.

When he stepped outside the tavern he smelled the air. Burning. Rendering. The air was heavy. William Parker smelled the smoke of war.

Harriet

chapter 113

Harriet sat at her writing desk scanning her notes by candlelight. Next to the notes was an anonymous letter delivered to her in the afternoon post—most likely a fan or foe letter.

Before her were the witnesses of Sallie, Nancie, and Easter, provided by Will. Phipps had provided her the witnesses of Nathaniel Francis and William Parker.

The notes and the names swirled in her mind—Francis, Trezvant, Waller, Turner, Gray. The published confession, penned by Thomas Gray, had been in existence for twenty-five years and had been accepted as the gospel by abolitionists, refugee slaves, slavery men, politicians, and even historians. Francis, Trezvant, Waller, Turner, Gray. If Phipps and Will were to be believed then *The Confessions of Nat Turner* was a lie. If they were to be believed, then Waller had lied—and he had lied for Nathaniel Francis.

If Phipps and Will were to be believed, then Thomas Gray had assisted Trezvant in lying. If they were to be believed, Gray was a liar to help Trezvant and Waller cover up their roles in the slave trials—particularly in hiding Waller and Trezvant's roles in Nat Turner's trial and death.

If Gray, Waller, Trezvant, Francis, and Barrow had lied, then nothing they had said could be accepted as truth. If they had lied, then what had really happened—who was Nat Turner and what were his motives? It was Will's and Phipps's word against a signed historical document—a document signed by six judges and sealed by Southampton County Clerk James Rochelle.

Only the actual trial records could corroborate or contradict Will and Phipps's stories. But the trial records would be housed in Southampton County, Virginia—if they existed at all—and she was not welcome in the South, particularly not to investigate the life and death of Nat Turner.

Harriet looked again at the papers on her desk. Will, Phipps, Trezvant, Francis, Turner, Waller, Gray. Each most likely had a motive for how he preferred the tale told. The stories were shifting and unsteady, like snowdrifts beneath her boots.

Harriet gazed out the window at late-spring snowflakes that swirled and drifted to the ground against the darkening blue of the evening sky. She would have to find at least one objective source before she could decide. She sighed and then reached for the anonymous letter.

> *Dear Mrs. Stowe,*
> *It has come to my attention that you are at work on a novel recounting the life of Nat Turner. In my position, I have gained access to the following entries—excerpts from Governor James Floyd's diary. It is unsafe for me to provide my name or my position—even twenty-five years later there are those who would kill to keep the truth secret—but I thought these might prove helpful. I trust that you will be able to decipher them, copied in my own hand.*

Harriet scanned down to the bottom of the letter and read the closing:

> *Sincerely, G.T.*

She returned to the top of the letter and read the first diary entry.

August 1831

On Saturday the 12th and the Monday following and also on Wednesday, the sun shown [*sic*] quite blue, fully as blue as indigo.

The indigo sun—it was the same blue sun that Harriet and her brother Henry had witnessed. She read the next copied entry.

Twenty-third day—This will be a very noted day in Virginia. At daylight this morning the Mayor of the City put into my hands a notice to the public, written by James Trezvant of Southampton County, stating that an insurrection of the slaves in that county had taken place, that several families had been massacred, and that it would take a considerable military force to put them down.

Harriet's stomach knotted. She refolded the letter and stuffed it in the envelope. Tomorrow she would begin again.

author letter

When I was a little girl, I read every book in my parents' library that I could reach. While in elementary school, I had read *Gone With the Wind*, *The Prophet*, *The Grapes of Wrath*, and *The Red Pony*. I had read the works of authors like Hemingway, Steinbeck, and Baldwin—though there was much I did not understand.

There were two of my parents' books I did not read: *Valley of the Dolls*, because my mother showed it to me and showed me where she hid it, while warning me that nice girls didn't read such books. The other book was William Styron's *The Confessions of Nat Turner*. I remember the red book cover. I stared at it, resting on my mother's nightstand, but I did not read it until 2007, as part of my preparation for writing *The Resurrection of Nat Turner*.

This is a story about paradigms and puzzle pieces that don't fit together. It is about how we often believe what we are told to believe—even when it doesn't make sense. About how lies repeated often enough are accepted as facts. It is a story about the endurance of truth.

On January 23, 2008, after almost two year's preliminary research, I made my way to Southampton County, Virginia, in hopes of seeing the actual record of Nat Turner's trial. Accompanied by a lawyer acquaintance, who also holds a master's degree in history, I shared with him two thoughts I had written in my journal: I would accept *The Confessions of Nat Turner* as given to his attorney Thomas Gray as true and I would follow the truth wherever it led me. I did not know the two assumptions would be mutually exclusive.

An activist and experienced trial attorney, Richard Manson responded that most confessions weren't worth the paper they were written on. After years of practice, he was a cynic, I told myself—trying to comfort myself. The truth was that I was uncomfortable with *The Confessions* penned by Gray.

During two stints at the Pentagon, working as an analyst and a writer/editor, I had become familiar with reading and analyzing studies and transcripts. Gray's *Confessions* read like a poorly written staff study. It was disjointed.

A staff study is just that: it is a written document on some topic or position that is staffed—that is, it is sent for review and comment to other divisions, directorates, or even services. When the document is returned with comments, it is the writer's job to seamlessly incorporate those comments and develop a document that seems to be authored by one individual or agency.

Gray's document seemed choppy. In it, Nat Turner admits to being a thief and a vandal, as well as a cowardly murderer—a fool who took time during his night of revenge to show off by marching his men through ridiculous, drunken maneuvers. But later in that same document it states:

> It has been said he [Nat Turner] was ignorant and cowardly, and that his object was to murder and rob for the purpose of obtaining money to make his escape. It is notorious, that he was never known to have a dollar in his life; to swear an oath, or drink a drop of spirits. As to his ignorance, he certainly never had the advantages of education, but he can read and write, (it was taught him by his parents,) and for natural intelligence and quickness of apprehension, is surpassed by few men I have ever seen. As to his being a coward, his reason as given for not resisting Mr. Phipps, shews the decision of his character.

I was uncomfortable with *The Confessions*, but it is the primary historical source document for people writing about or researching

Nat Turner. Despite my own misgivings and Mr. Manson's doubts, I determined to accept the confession. I had no intentions to re-write history. Instead, I wanted to explore how different groups, still polarized today, see Turner as folk hero or cowardly fiend. I would write a story where he, despite any faults he might have, would be treated more humanely—I would make his wife and mother more substantial characters in the story. Nat Turner's story would be told through the eyes of those who knew him—both friend and foe, slave and master.

I was on my way to Southampton County to read the actual trial records, handwritten, certified transcripts that would document Thomas Gray, Turner's defense attorney, reading Nat Turner's confession into the record. For some reason I still cannot logically explain, I would not rest until I read the actual record.

In fact, when I began researching Nat Turner I had decided I would try to locate the actual trial records—even though I did not believe that transcripts of slave trials from the year 1831 would still exist, even though part of me thought it would be pointless, just reading in longhand what was printed in Gray's *The Confessions*. Still, I faithfully watched news stories that mentioned Nat Turner hoping that some mention of the trial records would appear.

After more than six months, I was about to give up when I came across a newspaper story that mentioned Rick Francis, the present-day Southampton County, Virginia, court clerk, and his association with Nat Turner. I contacted the reporter and obtained contact information for Mr. Francis. When I called him and inquired about the trial records he assured me that they existed.

They reside in the Southampton County Courthouse in a town called Courtland—once called Jerusalem, Virginia. He assured me that I could see them and touch them. He would be happy to speak with me. He was a descendant of the Francis family—he would not be alive now if Lavinia Francis had not survived—and he would introduce me to descendants of Nat Turner.

On January 23, 2008, I made my way to Courtland/Jerusalem and touched my hands to the Minute Book that holds the records of Nat Turner's trial and those of Hark, Sam, and many others. I began with Nat Turner's trial.

My eyes, adjusting to the script, scanned the page and rested on the following words:

> *For reasons appearing to the Court it is ordered that the Sheriff summon a sufficient additional guard to repel any attempt that may be made to remove Nat alias Nat Turner from the custody of the Sheriff—*
>
> *The prisoner Nat alias Nat Turner was set to the bar in custody of the Jailor of the County, and William C. Parker is by the Court assigned Counsel for the prisoner in his defense, and Meriwether B. Broadnax Attorney for the Commonwealth filed an Information against the prison who upon his arraignment pleaded not guilty and Levi Waller being summoned as a Witness states . . .*

William Parker? There is no mention of Thomas Gray in the official record of Nat Turner's trial. Instead, William Parker was Nat Turner's attorney. Nat Turner pled innocent and offered no confession.

My stomach knotted and I began to have an uneasy feeling that I stood at a crossroads that would lead me to a place I had not anticipated. But I had promised to follow the truth.

It was a long, difficult journey. There were times when I hacked my way through dark, overgrown forests where it was difficult to find the path. When I wanted to turn back, when I was lost, I prayed.

The truth has been buried 180 years. I doubt that we will ever know the whole truth, but I know this much is true: some of what we accept as history is no more than fiction. It was a long journey, but it was worth it to bring to light even a bit of truth. I felt that I owed what I was able to decipher—both good and bad—to the descendants of those who died, to those who have previously read the story, to Nat Turner, to his mother.

I am not the first to put forward issues with the veracity of Thomas Gray's *Confessions*. Historian Henry Irving Tragle—author of *The Southampton Slave Revolt of 1831*, the most in-depth review of documents related to Nat Turner—whose work I learned of after my first visit to Southampton County, writes:

> The fascinating thing about the "Original Confessions" is that, while those who wrote about the revolt, or about Nat Turner, used the pamphlet as a primary source, all, without exception, seem to have done so without applying to it the normal tests which any historian might be expected to apply to a purported contemporary source. How did it square with other information from recognized sources? Was it consistent with the official records which were available?

This book grew out of what I found in the official trial records—of Nat Turner, of slaves, and of freemen—associated with Nat Turner's uprising. It is based on the surviving lore provided by people such as Bruce Turner, Rick Francis, and James McGee. I am indebted to them.

The Resurrection of Nat Turner is based on nonfictional accounts, as well as fictional accounts provided by people such as Harriet Beecher Stowe and Frederick Douglass. It is based on stories my college professor of Southern African literature and African American history, Dr. Evie Adams Welch, told me when I was a second-semester freshman at Western Illinois University in Macomb, Illinois.

In her classroom, in 1975 (I attended Western only one quarter), she told me stories about ancient cathedrals in Ethiopia with paintings of the Madonna and child on the walls, iconic paintings of people with faces and skin like mine. This book grew out of the history she shared and out of her belief in me. "There are so many of our stories still left to be told. You write well enough to tell them, Sharon."

This morning, like so many other mornings since I began this journey, I reread Thomas Gray's *The Confessions of Nat Turner*. After reading it so many times, I reread the sworn statement of the Clerk of the County Court of Southampton in the State of Virginia affixed to Gray's document. James Rochelle was known for being an honest man. How could Thomas Gray's account be a lie if an honest man swore that it was true? How could it be a lie if Rochelle swore that Gray read the confession in front of the court?

This morning I reread and realized that Rochelle's carefully worded statement neither verifies the confession nor indicates that it was read in court. Instead, Rochelle names six of the ten judges who sat for Nat Turner's trial and says they were:

> . . . *members of the Court which convened at Jerusalem, on Saturday the 5th day of November, 1831, for the trial of Nat alias Nat Turner, a negro slave, late the property of Putnam Moore, deceased, who was tried and convicted, as an insurgent in the late insurrection in the county of Southampton aforesaid, and that full faith and credit are due, and ought to be given to their acts as Justices of the peace aforesaid.*
>
> [Seal.]
>
> *In testimony whereof, I have hereunto set my hand and caused the seal of the Court aforesaid, to be affixed this 5th day of November, 1831.*
> *James Rochelle,*
> *C.S.C.C.*

Not a word about Gray or the confession. We see what we expect to see.

There is a Negro spiritual that says, *I been lied on, cheated, talked about, mistreated.* . . . I pray that this book will encourage those who have found themselves imprisoned or buried in lies. I pray that our eyes and our hearts will be opened. I pray that hope, truth, and brotherly love will take a reviving gasp and live again.

Sharon Ewell Foster
April 7, 2011

reader resources

A brief list of resources for further study and entertainment.

For more information and resources concerning Nat Turner, visit www.theresurrectionofnatturner.com.

Books

Applegate, Debby. *The Most Famous Man in America: The Biography of Henry Ward Beecher*. New York: Doubleday, 2006.

Dostoyevsky, Fyodor. *The Brothers Karamazov*. Mineola, NY: Dover, 2005.

Gray, Thomas. *The Confessions of Nat Turner*. Available online.

Haile, Rebecca. *Held at a Distance: A Rediscovery of Ethiopia*. Chicago: Academy Chicago Publishers, 2007.

Hedrick, Joan D. *Harriet Beecher Stowe: A Life*. New York: Oxford University Press, 1995.

The Kebra Nagast. Translated by E. A. Wallis Budge. Charleston, SC: Forgotten Books, 2007.

Newton, John. *Thoughts Upon the African Slave Trade*. Ithaca, NY: Cornell University Library, 1788.

Tolstoy, Leo. *Anna Karenina*. Mineola, NY: Dover, 2004.

Vikan, Gary. *Ethiopian Art: The Walters Art Museum*. Tempe, AZ: Third Millennium Publishers, 2006.

Museums

Harriet Beecher Stowe Center, Hartford, CT
National Underground Railroad Freedom Center, Cincinnati, OH

Harriet Beecher Stowe House, Cincinnati, OH

The Walters Art Museum, Baltimore, MD (largest collection of Ethiopian religious art in United States): http://art.thewalters.org/

Online resources

Colonial Williamsburg: http://www.history.org/

Ethiopian Orthodox Church: http://ethiopianorthodox.org/

Gondar, Ethiopia—Travel Photos by Galen R. Frysinger: http://www.galenfrysinger.com/gondar_ethiopia.htm

Harriet Beecher Stowe Letter to Frederick Douglass: http://www.harrietbeecherstowecenter.org/stowedocuments/Letter_from_Harriet_Beecher_Stowe_to_Frederick_Douglass.pdf

Thomas Jefferson's Monticello: http://www.monticello.org/

Uncle Tom's Cabin & American Culture: http://utc.iath.virginia.edu/index2f.html

"Unearthed, The Ancient Texts That Tell Story of Christianity," *Independent*, July 6, 2000: http://www.independent.co.uk/arts-entertainment/books/features/unearthed-the-ancient-texts-that-tell-story-of-christianity-2019188.html

For information on Ethiopian icons:

Angels of Light (Ethiopian art from the Walters Art Museum, Baltimore, MD, on loan to the Museum of Biblical Art, New York, NY): http://mobia.org/exhibitions/angels-of-light-ethiopian-art-from-the-walters-art-museum#slideshow1

Ethiopian Icons Through the Centuries: http://www29.homepage.villanova.edu/christopher.haas/ethiopian-icons.htm

Vikan, Gary, Ph.D. Interview by Leonard Lopate, *The Leonard Lopate Show: Ethiopian Objects of Worship*, WNYC (radio), March 23, 2007: http://www.wnyc.org/shows/lopate/2007/mar/23/

discussion questions for *The Resurrection of Nat Turner, Part I: The Witnesses*

1. Relationships between captors and captives, slaves and masters were complex—despite slave codes and laws. Discuss examples from the book (for example, Easter and Lavinia, Nat Turner and his father, Nathaniel Francis and Charlotte). Share examples from your own family history.

2. Mosaic Law lays down laws that ameliorate slavery, for example: Exodus 21:20, Exodus 21:26, Deuteronomy 5:14–15, Deuteronomy 21:10–14, Deuteronomy 23:15–16, Deuteronomy 24:14–15, 1 Timothy 1:9–11. Was slavery in America based on biblical law? Why or why not?

3. Many slaves suffered but did not fight back. What in Nat Turner's background might have predisposed him to take up arms?

4. In *The Resurrection of Nat Turner, Part 1: The Witnesses,* names are important, particularly slave names. What is the significance of a slave having one or two names? The author refers to Easter as "auntie Easter" rather than "Auntie Easter" and to Charlotte as "Wicked Charlotte" rather than "wicked Charlotte." What do you think the author is attempting to convey through use of this literary device?

5. Is violence acceptable in efforts to spread the Christian message? To protect one's country? To protect one's property? To protect one's family? Did the slaves have the right to protect themselves?

6. Some of the witnesses at the slave hearings/trials perjured themselves to ensure convictions. Does the end justify the means? If a witness perjures himself, can any of his testimony be trusted?

7. Some Ethiopian Christians had slaves just as white people did in America. Were there differences between the two systems? Explain your answer.

8. It is almost, if not entirely, impossible to find a slave master who describes him- or herself as hating slaves. How would you describe Nathaniel Francis's actions toward his slaves? Give examples. How do you think he would describe himself?

9. How do you feel about Easter's final act? Why do you think she chose it? Why do you think that Charlotte complied?

10. Nat Turner's mother described Ethiopian images of a black Madonna and child. (Visit www.theresurrectionofnatturner .com for more information.) Were you surprised to learn of these images, some of which date back to the fourth and

fifth centuries—predating the images we commonly see by a thousand years? Were you surprised to learn that there were palaces and castles in medieval Ethiopia? What benefits might greater exposure to these historical treasures provide?

a conversation
with Sharon
Ewell Foster

1. What inspired you to use Nat Turner and the slave rebellion he led in August 1831 as the basis for a novel?

In and of itself, the story has wonderful elements for creating a story: conflict, betrayal, vengeance, and even some possible elements of romance. But there is more. Though I don't remember the exact date I acknowledged to myself that I wanted to write a book about Nat Turner, I have been involved with and researching elements of this story for more than thirty years.

I first saw the novel resting on my mother's nightstand when I was a child. It was my habit to read every book my parents had (in elementary school, I had already read *Gone With the Wind* and was familiar with the works of Steinbeck, Khalil Gibran, Hemingway, and James Baldwin). I was fascinated with the book, the cover, but for some reason I did not pick it up to read it.

While attending Western Illinois University in Macomb, Illinois, as a freshman, I met the first instructor who suggested to me that I should be a writer. Dr. Evie Adams Welch actually gave me a charge, telling me that there were so many historical stories to be told and that I wrote well enough to tell them. She also shared stories about Ethiopia, about the ancient Christianity there and about the black Madonnas on the cathedral walls.

I actually began writing the proposal for *The Resurrection of*

Nat Turner more than five years ago. The Ethiopian images, Styron's book cover, those images have stayed with me. The Ethiopian images are part of the book. Finally, there were dreams that troubled me. In *The Resurrection of Nat Turner,* I describe Harriet Beecher Stowe having resurrection dreams, dreams where she resurrected men. Those were actually my dreams, reoccurring dreams that went on for years until I neared completing the book and adopted the title.

2. Why did you choose to tell the story of Jonah and the whale in the novel's prologue? What personal significance does this particular biblical tale have for you?

I am a more organic kind of writer—I write what is whispered in my ear and what flows from my pen, then I attempt to analyze it later. That's how the prologue came to be.

I was away on a speaking engagement several years ago at a location that has been pivotal in my writing, Sandy Cove in North East, Maryland. It's a lovely, quiet place, and I always feel God's Spirit speak to me there. Sandy Cove is also the place where I was "discovered" as a writer. Over lunch, I shared the beginnings of the Nat Turner story with an acquaintance, also sharing with her my reluctance to write a story that I thought should have been written by a man and my discomfort with my resurrection dreams. She looked at me and said, "It's a Jonah story." She was speaking not only of the book but also of my own story and my reluctance to write.

Something clicked inside me, and I began to see Nat Turner as this reluctant prophet. But I think the Jonah prologue does other things for readers. It begins, at the outset, to throw cold water on one of the vestiges of American slavery—the notion that God cursed Africans, and now African Americans. It seems a ridiculous notion, but many people still believe it. The Jonah prologue says that slavery is not a white over black issue—Xerxes was a man of color who enslaved many. Instead, the prologue says, it is a matter of pride, greed, and cruelty, and that even the most powerful are held accountable for how they treat their fellow man. Someone, like Nat Turner, like Jonah, has to be willing to risk his life in order to offer deliverance to both the oppressed and the oppressor.

3. What research did you do for *The Witnesses?* What facts did you uncover that surprised you?

Oh my goodness! I love to research, but this journey has been unbelievable. I have traveled from Hartford, Connecticut, to Cincinnati, to Richmond, Virginia, to Jerusalem, Virginia (now called Courtland), in search of Nat Turner. I've read novels, like William Styron's *The Confessions of Nat Turner*, Harriet Beecher Stowe's *Dred: A Tale of the Great Dismal Swamp* and *Uncle Tom's Cabin*, as well as Dostoyevsky's *The Brothers Karamazov* and Tolstoy's *Anna Karenina*. I've interviewed descendants of people involved in Turner's revolt. I've transcribed handwritten primary source documents. I've studied nonfiction works like Herbert Aptheker's *Nat Turner's Slave Rebellion* and Henry Irving Tragle's *The Southampton Slave Revolt of 1831* and Governor John Floyd's handwritten diary. I've spent years studying the slave trial transcripts and Thomas Gray's *The Confessions of Nat Turner*.

The first day, when I stood in the Southampton County Courthouse reading the trial records—January 23, 2008—I knew immediately that something was wrong. The primary historical source document, Gray's original *Confessions*, indicates that Gray was Nat Turner's defense attorney and that Gray read Nat Turner's confession aloud in court that day. Standing there, bent over the record, my hand touching the pages, I felt this sinking feeling.

According to the official trial record, Gray was *not* Nat Turner's attorney. There is no notation of a confession being read aloud in court. In fact, Nat Turner pled innocent and called out in the courtroom—neither the slaves nor the freemen were allowed to speak in their own defense—that he had done nothing for money. There is no mention in the official record of Thomas Gray even being in the courtroom that day. Since then, I have worked non-stop trying to determine who the real players were, to put the puzzle pieces together, and to answer the unanswered questions. Who was Nat Turner really? Why would powerful men devote time and effort to creating such a confession—after all, Nat Turner was a powerless slave? What motivated Nat Turner? What in his life made him different from his peers? So many unanswered questions.

4. Some authors choose to write either historical or contemporary fiction and yet you do both. What is it about the challenge of writing both contemporary and historical novels that you enjoy? Is one easier for you to write than the other?
I love all kinds of stories—I read fiction and nonfiction, I read contemporary and historical novels, and I read works written by people of different races and ethnicities. Words, sentences, paragraphs, stories—they enrich my life. I don't see a huge barrier between historical and contemporary novels. History feeds my contemporary work; my present-day experiences fuel my historical writing.

As I said before, I'm an organic writer and I write the story that's speaking to me. So I've written nonfiction—plans, reports, and even a repair manual for the Pershing 1a Missile System Blast Deflector—as well as fiction. Both contemporary and historical novels challenge me. They both cause me to be a better writer, a better person.

5. What process do you have for blending fact and fiction? Is it difficult to tell an entertaining story, while also adhering to a historical record? What is it like to create a character based on a historical figure, where there are predetermined facts and perceptions, versus one that comes solely from your imagination?
I think history and research are immensely interesting. When I read history, I'm picturing the story. When I read the Constitution,

it translates in my mind as story. History is who we are, it is the story of our lives—the real story with all the ugly parts and scars left in.

As people, we love stories. We want to know what really happened. We want to see the warts. That, I think, is why reality TV is so popular. That's what I try to give—there are beautiful, soft, pretty parts. But people don't believe the story unless they see the warts. Without the ugliness, people know the story isn't real. People want real.

I promise, when I write, that I will follow the truth where it leads me. I open my heart and my mind to it, even if it hurts. In fact, it should hurt. I know that I am not telling an honest, relevant story if it does not hurt me. I don't try to control the story or the characters. I try to open myself and listen. I pray to hear the story. If I work to tell the story, if I work to be honest, if I let the story tell itself, if I pray, I have been blessed with good results.

Nat Turner's story was especially challenging. He is buried beneath 180 years of history, at least some of which is not true. There were so many facts, and in some ways, I felt allegiance to the history as written and to the historians who've worked so diligently. But the truth led me in a different direction and I had to follow. It was exciting, but in some ways, it was frightening. Then I found people like Tragle, whose questioning of Gray's work bolstered and informed my own.

Finding the discrepancies was a challenge and a great benefit. I had to research, even though this is a work of fiction, to try to support the direction I was taking. What I found swelled the book. But finding the discrepancies also gave me the freedom to try to imagine a new Nat Turner—a Nat Turner who was remembered by many of his contemporaries like Booker T. Washington and William Wells Brown as a folk hero.

Sitting on a mound of research, I found artistic clues in extraordinary places, like Governor Floyd's contemporary diary which referred to the "indigo sun." Those clues helped give me the courage not to try to draw an accurate portrait, but to liberate my-self to paint an impression of this man. I felt it was important to try to show the trials more clearly because they are the key to un-derstanding what happened. But because of the lies in Gray's *Con-fessions*, I felt free to imagine a new Nat Turner. My hope is that real historians will be able to make some use of the interpretation to paint a more accurate picture.

6. Religion seems to be an important part of your life. In what ways is writing a means for you to share your faith with readers? How about with this book in particular?

My faith and God's love are very important to me. They are not an afterthought—I don't think, "I'm going to teach people a lesson about brotherly love." That's kind of condescending, I think. In-stead, my faith weaves itself, like a living thing, through how I live my life and what I write. Love is in me and it spills out onto the pages. I have experienced a God who loves all mankind, so that is woven into my work.

Most times, I'm writing about what I'm wrestling to under-stand. The story, the love, and the truth lead me. It is my incredible good fortune to be able to share my journey with others. I think these stories are like gifts, sweet treats, or good bread—sometimes even bitter medicine—that I've been given to share. It is my joy to meet people along the road and share with them what I've been given. In return, they often share wonderful things with me.

7. You say on your website (www.sharonewellfoster.com) that your daughter and son are your "first editors." What were their reactions to *The Witnesses*? What feedback did they offer you on the storyline and the characters?

My son and daughter are amazing—amazing people and amazing editors. This book evolved differently from my previous books. (I guess they all do.) First, as I was writing, it was like carving a huge block of stone from a mountain. They helped me to see. As the book became more refined, their comments and criticisms were invaluable. They both have great senses of story. They helped me to write boldly and courageously. They helped me to be true to the story and to the characters.

They never try to direct the story—they never try to get me to make the story theirs. Instead, they help me to tell the story within me. They offer suggestions to strengthen the story—technically and creatively. This book, in particular, I would never have made it through without them. They believed in me when I doubted myself.

8. In *The Witnesses*, you write that Harriet Beecher Stowe "was just a woman, a tiny woman at that; who was she to stir in the affairs of men?" (page 13). How unusual was Stowe for her time? Are Sallie and Nancie, two other female characters in the novel, based on real people?

Harriet Beecher Stowe had other contemporaries, like the Grimke sisters, who were outspoken abolitionists. But she was an extraordinary woman. Her writing was courageous. Even now, there are many who would be challenged by what she wrote in the mid-1800s.

There were not many women, or men, willing to say what she said. I did not expect to like her writing given the "Uncle Tom" legacy. She was not without flaws. But she was a brave writer and she was willing to learn. The growth in her understanding of racial issues, her increased sensitivity, is readily apparent when one compares *Uncle Tom* to *Dred*.

She was unusual, but so was the entire Stowe family. It is said that both Robert E. Lee and President Abraham Lincoln said the North would not have won the Civil War had it not been for Harriet and her famous brother Henry Ward Beecher. They fought with words—written and spoken.

She was outspoken, loyal, and willing to risk her own reputation and comfort to stand up for those who were voiceless. She was fierce; she challenged the church, the government, and individual consciences. I admire that. My daughter teases me that Harriet and I have become friends.

Sallie Francis Moore Travis was one of the actual victims in the revolt. Though her son owned Nat Turner, she appears to have been the actual "caretaker." Local lore says that she and Nat Turner were friends. I tried to imagine what that might mean in 1831. When I questioned, one individual said that she cooked for him. I built her story around that.

Easter actually belonged to Lavinia Francis. Charlotte and Easter were dividing the clothes when Lavinia, who was pregnant, came upon the two slave women. The surviving lore says that Easter saved Lavinia from Charlotte.

The whole book circles around facts that I found and the local lore.

9. The Nat Turner Historical Driving Tour is being established in Southampton County, Virginia, where an official remarked that the rebellion is "a segment of our history that we have closed our eyes to. It really needs to be drawn out and given the proper interpretation." Why do you suppose Turner's rebellion isn't a more widely known aspect of American history? Do you hope the novel will help rectify this?

Yes, I do hope that our nation will openly discuss the Nat Turner story, the event, and the cover-up. I think guilt, fear, and shame have kept our mouths closed. I think we are ashamed of our nation's complicity in slavery. His story challenges our accepted hero images. He challenges our complacent slave theories. Maybe we were too immature as a nation to have this discussion.

As we commemorate the 150th anniversary of the start of the Civil War, I hope that we will also commemorate Nat Turner's contribution, as well as that of the many others who died—many of them innocently.

Nat Turner's story is about the human desire for life, liberty, and the pursuit of happiness. It is a desire that transcends race or gender. I think we are mature enough now as a nation to begin the discussion.

10. What would you most like people to know about *The Witnesses*?

This is not a story about plantations or mint juleps, or even about slaves speaking a certain dialect. (In fact, I chose to avoid playing the politics of language.)

Instead, it is a story about freedom. Nat Turner's story is an everyman story. It is 2011, but still all over the world there are people walking in Nat Turner's shoes—victims of trafficking. How would we react if faced with the extraordinary circumstances that confronted him?

Nat Turner is a slave, perhaps a tragic hero, but this is not a story about bondage. Instead it is a story about liberty, about our human struggles to be brothers, and about our individual struggles against all odds to be shining lights in this world.

11. What can you tell us about *The Testimony*, the follow-up novel to *The Witnesses*?

In this second book, after 180 years of silence, Nat Turner speaks and shares with us answers to the mystery that only he can know. "We were all heroes," he first whispered to me.

from *The Resurrection of Nat Turner, Part 2: The Testimony*

Nat Turner felt in his pocket to be certain the gunpowder mixture was still dry. He knew exactly the time and place he would use it. He had been planning for months.

It had been a cruel winter. Snow in Virginia was most often one or two fingers deep; but this winter it had been heavy and so cold that the top of it was frozen. When he stepped, for an instant he stood above it, then, shoeless, he was calf deep again in the icy powder. At first cold pain shot up his knee and through his body with each step he took. Soon his feet were frozen, and he numbly made his way past isolated farms and houses, where he smelled the aroma of meat roasting outside. But he could not breathe deeply; the frozen air stung his lips, the membranes of his nose, ached his teeth.

The snow had snapped the brittle backs of withered corn plants. It covered the roads like a thick blanket so he barely recognized the fences and places he knew. The trees were his guide.

The trees were in the beginning and they had witnessed it all. They had seen husbands and sons dragged from their homes. They had seen women torn from the breasts of their families and raped underneath the moon and stars. They had seen them beaten, burned, starved, and mutilated. The trees had witnessed it all. Their arms had borne the weight of the tortured.

He followed the trees. Every one a signpost and a threat. He passed sleeping apple trees—their feet and hair covered by the snow blanket. In warmer times, their hands and arms gave fruit and all the while told stories of death.

If the trees held the land's memories, then his mother held his. "You are a man of two continents," she told him. "Your father is a man of America. They are the people of justice. An eye for an eye. At least that is what they say. But I am African. Ethiopians are children of mercy. It does not yet appear which will be strongest in you."

Ethiopian memories were rich, ancient, and deep. The images go back, his mother told him, before the *ferengi* began to count time.

His mother told him that her mother's mother had told her that the Ethiopian highlands were waves, disobedient waves that had come crashing too far inland from the sea. The wayward waves had been abandoned by the others, which returned to their watery home. Those left behind dried out and hardened, green grass covering them. But if you looked closely you could see that the mountains were really only waves that had gone too far and lost their way, his mother said.

Most of what he knew about life his mother had taught him. He had a grandmother who had helped raise him, but she was not really his grandmother. She was the old woman who tended all the slave children too old to nurse but too young to work, while their parents slaved in the fields or kitchens. But it was his mother who had taught him most about life, teaching him to honor his elders. "They carry the wisdom and history of a people," she told him. "In Ethiopia they teach us the elders have learned to live a long time and if we honor them they will teach us the way."

Ethiopia was a great nation and at her name other nations quaked.

He was born of a nation of great warriors; the world's first warriors, men who possessed the bravery of lions. A nation of warriors who were also holy men, leaders at the world's great councils of holy men. She told him of the warrior priests and saints, like Saint Moses of Ethiopia.

From the beginning, she told him, Ethiopia had God's favor. They were not rich in currency, but they were wealthy in greater things. There were great cities like Lalibela, Gondar, and Aksum. The spirit of God hovered over Ethiopia and God had given Ethiopia's people to Maryam, the Mother of God, as a precious gift. The proof was in the emerald hills and the ruby valleys; the golden lions and leopards dotted with onyx; exotic birds of topaz, amethyst, and sapphire. The proof was in God's choice of Ethiopia as birthplace of the majestic Nile. God had crowned her with rainbows like jewels.

She told him the Nile's names—Blue and White—and as a child he had tried to imagine how the water divided into two colors, separated one from another. When he had told her, she had laughed and told him that in the old language the word for blue was the same as that for black. The color was not important. What was important was generosity: it was Ethiopia's gift to Egypt, the gift that gave Egypt her flowers.

From the beginning Ethiopia had been part of God's Great Church. She told him of the paintings, Bibles, and crosses that dated from the earliest centuries. She told him of Masqal-Kebra, the beautiful and merciful Ethiopian saint and wife of good king Lalibela and advisor to her husband.

She told him about Moses and his Ethiopian wife and of the Ethiopian who rescued the Prophet Jeremiah. She shared the story of the Ethiopian Jew who, while reading Isaiah, had met Phillip and carried the gospel back to Ethiopia. His mother told him of the ancient bond between Egypt and Ethiopia—holy men had traveled the Nile and the deserts for eons between the great nations. She told him of the great churches of Antioch, Alexandria, Ethiopia, Armenia, and India. She told him about the Ethiopian priests and their families. She told him about the wise men, *shimaghilles*, who lived their lives to serve the people—about people whose prayers awoke thunder and storms thousands of miles away. She told him how Ababa Salaam, Father Peace, had brought Ethiopia the sacraments and helped spread the glory. She taught him of castles, palaces, and Ethiopian cathedrals carved from stone.

She told him that God heard prayers and always answered; He was not bound by space or time. God spoke to people now as He had spoken to their forefathers. "If you open your eyes and your heart, you can hear Him. If your heart is honest and humble you will understand. God always answers, but He does not always say what we desire."

She told him the stories over and over and she always sighed. "I did not want to leave." But other people had prayed and their groans and cries had reached God's ears. "They were captive Africans, like us, taken from their families." God had heard and sent her in the belly of a ship on a journey, like Jonah, to plead with the captors to repent. His mother had been stolen from Ethiopia. She told him of the rapes, the humiliation and bondage, and of Misha and her baby floating to their graves.

She could not bear to speak of her daughter, the little girl she had left behind, could not speak his sister's name. "Sometimes the things we must do for others are more important than our own lives." Her eyes seemed focused on a place far away that he could not see. Then she shrugged and came back to him. "Egzi'abher needed you born here—he needed me to be the ship that carried you here." He was born to be a deliverer, a prophet, a man of mercy. "God is lover of us all, the oppressed and the oppressor."

She told Nat Turner, the son she secretly called Negasi, her prince, that he was a living answer to the captives' prayers. It was a heavy burden for a little boy to bear. He was born to it. It was a family debt he owed.

He was a descendant of a nation of people who were readers and writers, thinkers and builders, lovers of God. The Americans believed no Africans read, wrote, or had language. So, it was Nancie and Nathan Turner's secret that before he could read English, she taught him to write and read Amharic—printing out the words on precious pieces of trashed paper. Or, she used a stick, when there was no paper, drawing the letters on the ground. She had taught him what she could remember of Ge'ez, the holy language. He had taught himself English.

She taught him the prayers. She told him about the great church at Gondar with the brown-faced angels in the ceiling.

Nat Turner was a child of rape. He was his mother's shame and his mother's glory, and the weight of it sometimes weighed him down. When he looked at her, he saw the affection she had for him, the hope that was so much more than love. He was the hope of her triumphant return to Africa. He was the hope of his mother's village. He was the hope and dream of all the slaves. She told him she saw her father and her grandfather in him.

Nathan Turner was born in Southampton County; without her it was all he knew. His mother was his memory of Ethiopia—the shepherds, the lambs, and the tall lion-colored grass. His mother was his Ethiopia. He saw it in her eyes. After more than thirty years, her tongue still lived in Ethiopia, her English still broken—it was her revenge on her captors. But her Amharic, when they were alone, flowed like the Nile he imagined.

When he was a boy he had dreamed a dream. He had dreamed of a family, of a simple farm, and preaching God's word. He dreamed a dream of Africa, of returning to his homeland, the highlands of Ethiopia. But the One God had spoken to him and now he knew in this lifetime he would never journey there.

His mother had taught him the story of his African forefathers and taught him to number the generations. "So King Solomon loved the Queen of Sheba and she bore him a child, Menelik. So Solomon begat Menelik, Menelik begat Menelik the Second. . . ." She counted on her fingers. "And so then Meshech begat your grandfather . . ." He numbered them until she was certain he remembered.

"We are the people of the spirit, the people of God," she told him. "It is our inheritance." The roots of the faith, she told him, were buried in love. "If you have and your brother has not, you must share. To do otherwise is a sin, my Negasi." Sometimes, when they were alone, she asked him to whisper her Ethiopian name—Nikahywot—so that she would not forget. "A man of two continents," she repeated. "One foot firmly planted in mercy and the other in judgment."

Nat Turner followed the trees—the oaks, the pines, the cypresses, and the fruit trees—to a small cabin on a far patch of Nathaniel Francis's land. Smoke curled from the chimney, and he heard people talking and laughing. He felt in his pocket again for the gunpowder. He knocked and then stepped inside.

He had heard the word of God. This would be his last Christmas.